The
Lady
Flees Her
Lord

The Lady Flees Her Lord

Michèle Ann Young

SOURCEBOOKS CASABLANCA™
AN IMPRINT OF SOURCEBOOKS, INC.®
NAPERVILLE, ILLINOIS

Published by Sourcebooks Casablanca, an imprint of
Sourcebooks, Inc.
P.O. Box 4410, Naperville, Illinois 60567-4410
(630) 961-3900
Fax: (630) 961-2168
www.sourcebooks.com

Library of Congress Cataloging-in-Publication Data

Young, Michèle (Michèle Ann)
   The lady flees her lord / Michèle Ann Young.
      p. cm.
   ISBN-13: 978-1-4022-1399-1
   ISBN-10: 1-4022-1399-9
   1. Overweight women—Fiction. I. Title.
   PR9199.4.Y69L33 2008
   813'.6—dc22
                              2008029370

   Printed and bound in the United States of America.
      DR 10 9 8 7 6 5 4 3 2 1

*This book is dedicated to women who love to read,
who like chocolate, and who live life to the fullest,
no matter their shape or size.*

One

London, April 1811

BLISSFUL SILENCE.

Lucinda Palgrave, Countess of Denbigh, lifted her ear from the cool wood of her husband's adjoining chamber door. She wanted to laugh out loud. To twirl. To yell, 'No Denbigh!' A delightful evening free of his presence stretched ahead. It was a giddy sensation, like drinking too much champagne. And utterly inappropriate. Fingers pressed to her lips, she glided out of her bedroom and into the hallway.

A figure in black loomed in front of her.

She gasped, a hand at her throat, her heart pounding wildly. Dash it all. Why did the butler always creep up on her? The supercilious beast ought to care more for life and limb, since according to Denbigh, a mere bump from her hip would knock a man flat. Oh, for the courage to try.

"Yes, Galloway?" To her chagrin, her voice sounded more like a frightened scullery maid than the mistress of her own establishment.

The butler smirked. "Tea awaits you in the drawing room, my lady. As does his lordship."

The lightness dissipated in a sickening rush. She swallowed the sour taste of disappointment tinged with the acid of fear. "Thank you, Galloway. Please have two places set for dinner."

The butler's smirk broadened. "His lordship does not intend to dine at home, my lady."

Relief dulled her irritation at the man's triumphant expression. "Very well. That will be all, thank you." She skirted around him.

He gave as much ground as he might for a scullery maid.

Anger spread out from her chest in hot slow waves. She damped it down. One of these days, she really would speak to Galloway about his insolence. She rubbed her collarbone through the fabric of her gown. But not now. Not while Denbigh waited.

She pattered along the hall, the jewel-toned runner seeming to taunt her with its brightness. With one hot, damp palm on the smooth balustrade, she sped down the curving oak staircase to the first floor of their Mayfair townhouse. Hurry, her heartbeat goaded. He hated when she was late. Not too fast, she reminded herself. He despised her when she appeared all hot and flustered. Dammit. He hated whatever she did.

In the hallway, she confronted the white drawing-room door. Smoothing her ivory skirts, she stole a moment to hide her rapid heartbeat behind a calm demeanor and to suck in her stomach. Slowly, she eased open the door. The tall windows at the west end of the room cast bars of light across the cream-colored carpet, yet the blue walls and white paint gave the room a chilly feel.

Brandy in hand and not a blond hair out of place, her husband, the Earl of Denbigh, slouched on the royal-blue velvet sofa beside the marble hearth. Slender legs crossed at the ankles, he acknowledged her entrance with a sulky grimace that ruined his Apollo-like handsomeness. Had she really once thought his brooding expression romantic? She lowered her lashes to hide the disloyal thought.

"Good afternoon, Denbigh," she murmured.

"For God's sake, stop hovering and sit down."

She scurried to the chair behind the tea tray and perched on its edge.

He stared at her over the rim of his glass. "Where the hell were you?"

Despite the mild tone, her pulse jumped. She eyed the brandy in his half-full glass. The worst of his rants happened after the third refill. At the moment his eyes seemed clear, his words crisp. She offered a smile. "I was dressing for dinner."

The disparaging glance he ran over her person chilled her to the bone. "I can't think why you bother."

A flare of something hot ignited inside her and burnt its way up to her tongue. Only by clenching her jaw did she prevent its eruption in angry words. She inhaled slowly. "I didn't expect you this afternoon." She gestured to the tray. "Can I offer you a dish of bohea?"

As his gaze shifted to the tray, she winced. The chef had outdone himself today. Not only did the tiered cake dish contain her favorite lemon tarts, but he'd included several slices of iced fruitcake and a selection of marchpane fancies. She swallowed.

Denbigh must have caught the involuntary motion, because his lip curled in distaste. "Dear God, are you planning to gobble down the whole lot?"

"No, I—"

"There is no one else here to eat it."

"But I—"

"What happened to the regimen of water biscuits and vinegar the doctor suggested? How can it help your figure, if you are too greedy to try it for less than a week?" He gave a derisive snort. "A cow like you would need months to see any improvement."

"I felt unwell." The diet made her feel weak and, worst of all, seemed to make her crave sweet things more than usual. "If you dislike the way I look so much, why did you marry me?"

His eyes narrowed, the pout becoming more pronounced. "You were supposed to be the answer to my money problems, not eat me out of house and home."

A rush of heat scorched her cheeks. Shame mixed with fury in a volcanic blend and words spilled forth like lava. "The settlement my father provides is more than enough for a comfortable life." From the way his nostrils flared, she'd gone too far, but with financial ruin staring them in the face, she had to make him see sense. "If we invested some of it—"

"Enough. I am a gentleman not some money grubbing cit."

Her stomach plummeted at the note of finality in his voice. Blindly, she reached for a delicate lemon-filled pastry.

Denbigh reached across the table and grabbed her wrist. "Put it down, Lucinda."

Like a dog ordered to put down a bone, she dropped the tart. Shriveling to insignificance on the inside, she attempted to meet his hard gaze through a pain-induced mist. He released her, and blinking to clear her vision, she reached for the teapot. Anything to fill the dreadful silence. The spout chinked miserably on the cup's rim, but she managed to pour without spilling a drop.

The earthy aroma filled her nostrils. She sipped at the comforting brew. "Are you sure you wouldn't like a cup of tea?"

He drained his glass in one gulp and rose. She shrank back as he loomed over her. "No. If you really wanted to help me, you would hand over your allowance. I don't see why your father settled money on you in the first place."

Another bone of contention in their disastrous marriage. She hadn't dared tell him of the last-minute nerves that had prompted her request to her father for some funds of her own.

When she didn't answer, he rang the bell and then strode to the console and the brandy decanter. With his back to her, he poured yet another glass.

A fashionable man, her husband, with his clothes cut to perfection and his air of sophistication. No wonder her family had been overjoyed when their less-than-handsome daughter had attracted his attention. The charming young nobleman had seemed so…perfect, so smitten, the moment she made her debut in London. Smitten by the news of her fortune, she had later discovered.

What a fool not to see behind the charm of manner, she who thought herself so astute. Clearly the business world was far easier to understand than jaded, cynical members of the *ton*. She should never have left Yorkshire. As her husband was so fond of saying, she just wasn't cut out for fashionable life.

Galloway scratched and entered. "You rang, my lord."

"Yes. Her ladyship is finished."

Lucinda's stomach gurgled a protest. She had eaten nothing but dry biscuits with water since dinner yesterday.

Denbigh glared at her.

She licked her lips and resisted the urge to snatch a piece of fruitcake before Galloway picked up the tray. How many hours until dinner? Too many. But soon Denbigh would go to his club, and then she'd wander down to the kitchen and check on the progress of the evening meal. Nothing more natural than the lady of the house making sure the food was edible. She had her own way of dealing with Denbigh's commands.

The front doorbell jangled.

Galloway looked at his master. "James will answer it, my lord. I will return this to the kitchen."

Denbigh returned to his seat and crossed one slender thigh over the other, a pose designed to display the swell of a finely muscled calf. As usual, he made her feel large and ungainly.

Voices in the downstairs hall broke the silence. "Who can that be?" she said with forced brightness.

"It's Vale." He pushed to his feet.

The Duke of Vale. A shudder of distaste shook her frame. "Then I will leave you to greet him."

"You will stay. And you will make him welcome."

She bowed her head in acquiescence. What else could she do?

"Damnation," Denbigh said. "With all your arguing, I almost forgot. The whole reason for my wanting to see you this afternoon was to tell you that we go to Sussex the day after tomorrow. The carriage is ordered for noon. Be ready."

For a moment, she didn't process the words. "Denbigh Hall, you mean?"

"Where else?"

They had not been to her husband's country estate since their honeymoon. He hated the country as much as she loved it. She clasped her cold hands together. Perhaps in the peace of the countryside she could find a way to please him and finally give him his heir.

He glowered. "For God's sake, stop making cow's eyes at me. I swear you get larger by the day, instead of smaller."

She winced and shrank into her chair, hunching her shoulders, folding her hands in her lap. "How long shall we be away?"

"A week or two. I have invited a party of friends to join us."

The faint whisper of hope for a new beginning evaporated. "Friends?" A sense of foreboding formed in her mind, making it hard to breathe. "Surely you do not want me there."

"I need you to play hostess."

"I prefer to remain here. My parents are coming to Town this week. They invited us for dinner. You cannot have forgotten?"

He shuddered. "Another excused to gorge yourself. Nor could I possibly forget the invasion of a pack of country yokels about to inflict another fat sow on society."

Enough was enough. Aware that any moment Vale would be upon them, she kept her voice low. "How dare you? My sister is beautiful and sweet-natured. You know perfectly well I promised to ease her way into society this Season." The longing to bask in the warmth of her family's love brought a sudden lump to her throat. Hot prickles burned at the back of her nose. She swallowed hard. No crying. Not in front of him. "And our family name is just as old as yours, Denbigh. And equally good, if not better."

"Oh, indeed. Your family had nothing but a pile of stones and a few acres of sheep until the war. Face it, Lucinda, your family stinks of the shop. For God's sake, do you think I want that to rub off on me?"

"My father's business is nothing of which to be ashamed. You certainly don't balk at accepting his money."

"He pays me to put up with you." His gaze mocked her.

A knock silenced whatever she might have said next in her own defense. The duke would probably like nothing better than to find them in the midst of a dispute, and she would not give him that pleasure.

The door opened to reveal the tall, spare figure of the Duke of Vale. He sauntered in. Apart from his impeccably starched white cravat, he wore only black. The ladies of the *ton* swooned over his exquisite style and admired his ebony hair and noble features. They gossiped behind their fans about his conquests. To Lucinda, his cynical mouth and straight black brows looked satanic. His chill grey eyes seemed to observe the world from a pinnacle of his own making, while his implacable silences interspersed with cutting remarks jarred her nerves. More than all of that, she hated the way he'd led her husband down the road to ruin.

A sneer curled Vale's thin lips as he perused the room through a quizzing glass held in an elegant white hand. "Lady Denbigh, your servant."

She rose and curtseyed. "Your grace."

He let the quizzing glass fall to dangle from its ribbon around her neck. "Please, don't get up on my account."

Happy to be ignored, she sank into her seat.

"Denbigh, aren't you ready?" Vale sounded impatient, despite his languid posture.

"Care for a brandy, Vale?" Denbigh gestured to the decanter. "Had it shipped up from Rye yesterday."

She dug her fingers into the fabric on the chair arms. Say no.

"Pettigrew expects us for dinner at White's," Vale said.

"Let him wait." Denbigh sauntered over to pour a glass for the duke. "The countess and I were discussing our removal to Denbigh Hall."

Vale's hooded glance moved swiftly from Denbigh to her. "I had no idea Lady Denbigh intended to go along. Perhaps I will cry off from Otford's party and join you after all."

"She'll ensure things run smoothly," Denbigh said. He handed Vale a goblet. "It's about all she can do."

Swirling the amber liquid, his long slender fingers curled around the stem, the duke's gaze returned to her face. This time she gave him stare for stare and felt a little rush of pride when he shifted his attention back to his brandy. His lips curved in a cold smile. "I am sure you will enjoy our company, Lady Denbigh. Your husband has all manner of interesting pursuits in store for the ladies of the party."

Denbigh's sneer, a pale imitation of the duke's, grew more pronounced. "My wife ain't into our kind of pleasures, Vale. But she can organize a damnably fine dinner. Food is her special talent. Isn't it, my dear?"

Lucinda repressed a wince at his sugary tone.

Vale studied her for a moment. His cold gaze seemed to see right inside to the tears and the misery. "Oh, but meat satisfies only one of the appetites. I am sure Lady Denbigh would like to sample sweeter delights." His voice had the purr of a satisfied cat.

A hot flush seared her neck and burned all the way to her hairline. Hateful man. She clenched her fists in the folds of her skirts. "I am more than satisfied with simple English fare, your grace."

The duke toyed with his quizzing glass. "Dear lady, if we are to be in each other's company for the next few days, you must call me Julian. I certainly look forward to getting to know *you* better." His soft voice scraped her nerves like metal grating on stone. She shivered, fighting the urge to run for the door.

To her relief, he kept his chilly gaze fixed on Denbigh. "You have told Lady Denbigh about the er…female company, of course?" he drawled. "She will outrank them all. The little darlings will gnash their teeth."

"In that case, perhaps it will be better if I stayed in London," Lucinda said. She bit her lip as Denbigh swung around to face her, his color high.

Inside, deep inside, she cringed. Once more, she'd let her tongue run ahead of her thoughts.

In long impatient strides Denbigh crossed to her chair, his brow lowered, his mouth hard. "No, it won't be better. I certainly do not want Lady Elizabeth bothered with the ordering of the house while I am entertaining."

A chill flashed through her, like a cold plunge on a hot day. Lady Elizabeth Trubshaw, a widow as slender as a willow and her husband's longtime mistress, was to make one of the party. How could he be so cruel as to humiliate her with his other woman in front of Vale and the rest of his rakish friends? Knowing the least sign of annoyance would further incite his temper, she kept her voice reasonable. "The housekeeper at Denbigh Hall is quite capable of seeing to your guests' needs."

Anger radiated from the rigid set of her husband's shoulders. Had he had more to drink that she'd suspected? Her heart beat a nervous tattoo. Do not shrink. Do not press back into the safety of the cushions. A show of fear only intensified the cruelty of his tongue. She intertwined her fingers, resisting the urge to protect her throat.

"I gave the housekeeper leave to visit her family. I need you at Denbigh Hall," Denbigh said.

If only he truly did need her, things might be different. She caught her bottom lip in her teeth to stem another flow of words.

Vale strolled to the window. One hand on the shutter, he gazed down into the street. The golden light cast his face into the burnished angles and shadowed hollows of some unearthly creature of nightmares. "You see, Lady Denbigh," he murmured, "when we have our special parties, we prefer not to…disturb old family retainers with our festivities."

He swung around to face her, a question mark of dark hair curling on his high forehead, and the sardonic curl to his lips more pronounced. "We prefer to keep our activities within the family, so to speak." He bowed. "I shall be only too pleased to introduce you to the full range of diversions we offer the women who join us. I am sure once you have savored the array of delicacies, you will find your appetite returning again and again."

Her mouth dried. The tightness in her chest increased. She could scarcely credit the unabashed lascivious meaning in every word. Her skin crawled as if steeped in filth.

Denbigh grinned at his friend like some besotted schoolboy. Did he not realize what Vale was saying? Or did he really not care?

"I doubt even your famous charm can stir my wife's blood, Vale," Denbigh said.

In Lucinda's opinion, the duke had as much charm as an adder.

Denbigh glanced down at her. "All she cares about is her next meal, but you are welcome to try."

"I shall look forward to making the attempt," Vale whispered, his suddenly limpid gaze scanning her from head to heel.

Over her dead body.

The desperate thought sent a shiver down her spine. Recently, she'd begun to believe Denbigh might welcome any form of release from his marriage. Damn him. And damn the duke. She would not be intimidated by a pair of shiftless wretches. She rose to her feet.

When Denbigh stepped back to avoid coming into contact with her body, she squashed a smile of triumph. It was all bravado, a saving of face, to little purpose, unless she did something about this new predicament.

"Please excuse me, gentlemen," she said, surprised at the steadiness in her voice, "but if I am to prepare for a journey to Sussex, I have a great deal to do."

Denbigh narrowed his eyes on her face, and she tried not to squirm. "I'll meet you outside, Vale. I need a word with my wife."

The duke hesitated. An expression flickered across his impassive face. It might have been regret or simply impatience. She didn't know; nor did she care as with languid grace, he bowed. "Farewell, Lady Denbigh. Don't be long, Denbigh. My groom hates to keep my cattle idle in the street for too long." He sauntered from the room.

Why did Denbigh need to speak to her? She'd agreed to what he wanted, but from the suspicious glint in his eye, she'd given in too easily. Her knees quivered with the strain of remaining upright before his intent stare. The tremble vibrated deep in her bones. For all his foppishness, Denbigh was no fool. Look how easily he had tricked her into this parody of a marriage and her father out of a fortune.

She clenched her fists at her sides, lifted her chin, and held his gaze.

The sound of the front door closing brought Denbigh to life. He placed a hand on her shoulder.

She tried not to flinch but knew she had failed when his fingers ground against her bones. "I don't trust you." His controlled undertone frightened her more than his shouting.

"I have never given you the kind of reason for the mistrust you have given me." Inwardly, she groaned. Would she never learn the trick of silence?

His gaze dropped to his hand on her shoulder. "If you had done as you were told, that would never have happened."

One of life's little lessons, as Father used to say. She pressed her lips together. Her tongue might be swifter than Denbigh's, her brain quicker, but even though she equaled him in weight and height, he reminded her with increased pressure on her collarbone that his greater strength always won out.

"You will make the arrangements for tomorrow," he said.

"Yes, Denbigh."

He gave her a shake. "Don't think about running off to your precious family, Lucinda. You must obey me. If Vale is pleased, he will drop all kinds of blunt at the faro table. He always does. And since I will be banker, it will help repair some of my losses. You will do everything you can to please him. Do you understand? Everything."

The finality in his tone confirmed what she had suspected for months. Denbigh cared nothing for her or their marriage. Defeat weighted her shoulders. Hopelessness dragged at her spine.

"Well?" he rapped out.

"Yes," she whispered. "I understand."

His gaze searched her face. Once she had thought his eyes the most wonderful shade of blue. Now, she saw only shattered hopes. Emptiness filled her chest, and she welcomed the numbness.

His expression turned sweet, cajoling. "Unless you can help me out with a loan from your allowance this month?"

She wasn't fool enough to fall for that ploy. Not again. Not unless she wanted the bailiffs at the door. Even if she gave him every penny to be rid of him, he would send for her the moment he lost at the tables. She glanced away, fearful he would see the lie on her face. "I spent it on the bills, your tailor, the servants." She brought her gaze back to his handsome face. "I bought this gown."

"What possessed you to choose such a hideous color?" Like talons, his fingers dug deeper into the sensitive hollow at her shoulder. "For God's sake, do not pay any more bills without asking me first."

"We will be ruined."

"Will we?" He gave a hard laugh. "Do you think your father will allow his precious daughter to starve?"

Dizzy from lack of air, she felt nauseated. His scorn buffeted her, weakening her fragile hold on what little remained of herself. She clasped her hands at her breast. "Denbigh, if you have money troubles, there are other ways than gambling to solve them. Even small amounts invested carefully will reap good profits. I could help you, the way I helped my father."

"You, my dear, are of no use at all unless you can produce the next Earl of Denbigh."

Barren. The word hung between them, cold and hard and empty. All fight went out of her, leaving her limp and completely exhausted. The one thing she wanted most in the world, she had been unable to deliver. She'd tried every remedy—herbals, lying in bed for days—but nothing the doctors suggested had worked. As a woman, she was a failure.

He released her shoulder, and she rubbed her aching flesh.

A look of remorse crossed his face. "Did I hurt you?" He brushed his knuckles across her collarbone. "I didn't mean it. You make me so angry sometimes that I don't know what I'm doing."

"It doesn't matter," she said dully.

Now certain of her cooperation, his face resumed its boyishly handsome good looks. "Buck up, Lucinda. Spend tomorrow preparing to leave. I'm relying on you." He strode for the door. Hand on the knob, he turned and flashed his wonderful smile. "I'll tell the chef you are back on your diet. Have a pleasant evening, wife. I will see you in the morning." With a cheery wave he whisked out of the door.

Blast him. She longed to wring his neck. If she thought it would bring him to his senses, she'd give it a try. She stared at the gleaming white door. It might just as well be the bars of a cage. She had no choice but to go to Denbigh Hall. The thought of entertaining his rakish friends drove bile into her throat. She pressed a hand to her lips, afraid she might be sick on the carpet. She sank into the chair she had vacated with all the pride of a countess and buried her face in her hands.

Was the disastrous state of her marriage really her fault? She had tried to please her husband, longed to make him happy, and sought his affection. Yet he despised her, and not only because she could not give him an heir. He didn't like her. Perhaps if she had borne a child in the first year of their marriage, things would have turned out better. Her arms ached for a child. She loved them and had hoped for a large family like that of her parents. Instead, her body was an empty shell, without value. The hot tears she'd fought each month when her courses appeared welled over.

How could she go to Denbigh Hall and be subjected to the kind of shame Vale had described in loving detail? She swallowed a sob. How could she not? No one, not even her family, could interfere in her marriage. If they tried, the scandal might well ruin her younger sisters' chances of making good matches. Truly, it seemed as if her wings were clipped like those of the caged linnets she had seen at the fair as a child. Even if she slipped through the bars, she could not fly.

Or could she? Did she really have no choice? In a blur, she fumbled in her reticule for her handkerchief. She stared at the little scrap of cloth edged in lace, one of a set of six hemmed by a child full of hopes. The carefully embroidered L entwined with tiny heart's ease still waited for her husband's initial. Her parents had been so dazzled when the handsome Denbigh proposed that Lucinda had accepted his offer without a second's hesitation. But for some strange reason, she had never felt inclined to finish the embroidery. An omen perhaps?

Pull yourself together, woman. Moping never helped anyone. She dabbed at her eyes, then blew her nose. The little snort sounded ridiculously pathetic in her elegant Mayfair drawing room. She hauled in a deep breath as she realized she had come to a decision. No matter what, she would not go to Denbigh Hall.

Branded by Denbigh's touch, her collarbone ached anew. She rubbed at it, tossing over alternatives from illness to outright refusal. Only one seemed to hold any hope. Flight. And if that was the case, she had all of one day to plan her escape.

Hugo, Captain Lord Wanstead, glared at the back of the greying head of the army doctor poking at the wound in his left thigh. "What do you mean, you have to operate? I had an operation."

"There's a shell fragment in there, I'm afraid, my lord. It has to come out, unless you want to lose the leg."

A cold sensation slid down his spine. "Hell no. I don't want to lose my leg." Nor did he want to hang around in Lisbon in this makeshift hospital in the corner of a convent. Doing nothing only left him time to think.

He shifted further up the cot. Either his head cocked up at an awkward angle against the wall or his feet hung over the end. "Can't this wait until I get back to England?" England. The last place he thought he'd be headed, but as the last of his line he had no choice. The newly minted Viscount Wellesley had insisted, and Hugo had unwillingly concurred.

The florid-faced surgeon raised a pair of bushy brows. "You are talking about a sea journey, sir. If the object moves, it could nick an artery. Then you won't lose a leg, you will lose your life."

"Very well. Do your worst." Sounding suddenly hoarse, he swallowed.

"I shall do my best, my lord," the surgeon said in clipped tones. He laid his implements out on the battered card table beside the bed.

"How long before I can travel?" Hugo asked.

"Two weeks. Perhaps three. It will all depend on whether you obey my instructions and heal quickly or ignore them and go to an early death."

An unwilling grin pulled at Hugo's mouth. The man had a reputation for being one of the army's finest surgeons and for having a most foul temper. "I promise to behave."

"Then I promise to have you back on your feet in two weeks."

The doctor handed over a bottle of brandy. "Drink this; it will help with the pain and the shock." He stepped back and gave Hugo a measuring glance. "All of it. With your size, you will need it." He stomped to the door and stuck his head out. "Orderly," he shouted. "Send me three men to hold this patient down."

Hugo knew the drill from when the last quack had dug around in his thigh. It had taken three weeks to recover from that little affair. But there had been more wrong with him than his leg. Far worse than the pain from his wound, the guilt of what he'd done gave him horrific nightmares. They left him sweating and shivering, until he dreaded sleep. Only brandy kept them at bay, kept him numb. Who would have guessed courage lurked in the bottom of a bottle? Perhaps that was the real reason Wellesley wanted to be rid of him.

He gulped down a hearty swig. It burned his gullet and landed in his belly in a rush of fire. Oblivion welcomed him like a siren's call.

Two infantry privates and a corporal clumped into the cell of a room.

"'Tis no wonder ye be needing the t'ree of us, doctor, so it is," the skinny leader, an Irishman, declared. "Sure, an' I haven't seen an ox bigger than the Captain here in all my years in Portugal." He winked lewdly. "I hope for the sake of the poor little colleens, your Thomas don't match the rest of you, sir."

The other men laughed.

There wasn't a man alive who didn't wonder the same thing. Stupid bastards. They'd been doing it since he was twelve. "Eat your heart out, soldier," he quipped, glancing down to where the sheet covered his groin. "An ox would be jealous."

He shifted his gaze to the surgeon. "Can we get on with this?"

The surgeon handed him a mangled strip of leather. "Bite down on this."

The thought of what was to come halted his breath. Being large didn't make a man any less afraid. Hugo placed the strip between his teeth, clenched his jaw, and closed his eyes. Rough hands seized his shoulders, arms, and legs. He smelled musky sweat and the sour stink of fear. Theirs? His? Probably both.

"Ready?" the surgeon asked.

He nodded and cursed his ill fortune. The final shot of the day had killed the wrong man. Now he had no choice, if he survived the damn surgeon's ministrations, but to do his duty with the life he'd been granted.

He'd learned a lot about duty in his years in the army, but there was one obligation he would not undertake, not for any price.

Two

THE CASE CLOCK AT THE BOTTOM OF THE STAIRS STRUCK two. Tucked up in bed in the dark, Lucinda listened to its lonely chime. Still no Denbigh. Perhaps he would stay with his mistress tonight? Unlikely, when they were due to leave first thing in the morning. Her heart thudded as she thought about the damning valise hidden under her bed. She'd packed it supposedly to accompany her inside the carriage, while the maid filled the trunks that would follow.

Each careful breath filled her ears as she strained to hear his arrival. A pulse throbbed in her temple, beating out seconds one at a time. The clock chimed the quarter hour. A carriage rumbled over cobbles in the still night air and drew up outside. The front door slammed. Her stomach plummeted. Denbigh had indeed come home.

She resisted the urge to dive beneath the blankets or to throw up. Rigid, she lay listening to her husband's progress up the stairs and into his room, heard his valet's mumble as he helped him to bed.

Absently, she rubbed the raised skin on her collarbone. Would he want his husbandly rights tonight? She shuddered. He often did when he'd been drinking. It didn't matter. He would never look under the bed. He might, if his foot struck the valise or tangled with her hidden clothing.

Heart in her throat, she leaped out of bed, checked all three sides. Nothing stuck out. Breathing hard, she scurried back beneath the covers, smoothed them flat, and lay utterly still. Taking shallow sips of air, she listened.

Slowly, the noises in the chamber next door quieted. The valet's footsteps retreated down the hallway outside. Stiff as a board, Lucinda waited. Please, don't come in here tonight.

The house returned to its nighttime silence of ticking clocks and creaking timbers. The odd gust of wind rattled the windows. Nothing out of the ordinary, then…his gentle snore. She unclenched her grip on the sheets and slid out of bed, pausing to listen, her toes curling into the rug's thick pile. No untoward sound came from his room, and she raked beneath the bed for her traveling gown and cloak.

Shivers racing across her skin, she peeled off her nightgown and slipped into her chemise and stays. She drew on the plain grey gown, tying the tapes and fastening the pins as speedily as shaking fingers would allow, then retrieved her bag containing the few personal items she could carry.

To the sound of her husband's breathing, she glanced around the room. It meant nothing. Beautifully decorated in cream and white before she moved in, it remained the same. She hadn't changed a thing. No pictures, no treasures. Denbigh hated clutter.

And since he came in here whenever he wanted, she had never felt comfortable enough to make it her own.

Squaring her shoulders, she threw on the brown wool cloak and pulled the hood over her head. Slowly, quietly, she turned the door handle. Darkness greeted her in the passage outside. Firmly gripping the balustrade, she crept down the servants' staircase and past the footman slumped on a chair beside the side door. On silent feet, she tiptoed into the kitchen where the scent of rosemary mingled with fresh baked bread for the morning. The banked hearth cast enough light for her to see her way to the kitchen door.

What had the upstairs maid said about the key? Ah, here it was, in the pocket of chef's apron, hanging beside the door. He left it there so the parlor maid could sneak out and visit her beau. A wry smile twisted her lips. Denbigh would be furious if he knew.

The heavy iron key chilled Lucinda's palm as her fingertips fumbled for the keyhole. Breath held, she guided the key into the slot and turned. The well-oiled lock tumbled over. The door opened without a sound. Mr. Galloway was a tartar for a creaking door, the maid had giggled early one morning while making up the bedroom fire. For once, Lucinda offered sincere thanks to the insolent butler.

Outside, cool air brushed her face. She pulled the door closed behind her and scurried down the garden path to the high wooden gate. The iron bolt slid back easily. She peered into the stinking alley behind the mews. No one. She picked up her skirts and ran. With every step, her heart hammered one word into her brain. Freedom.

At the corner, she pulled her cloak tight and glanced back at Denbigh's home. It had never been more than a roof over her head these past few years. Good riddance. If leaving didn't mean she had to lose her mother and father, her real home and family, too, she'd be perfectly happy. The rush of moisture behind her eyes turned the street lamps into a string of haloed moons. No crying. She'd made her decision. She dashed the tears away and set her steps on the path to her future with her small store of coins in the pocket inside her skirts banging against her knee. It wasn't much. A few guineas she'd kept back from her monthly allowance. They would get her to her destination.

She trotted into Charles Street. She allowed a small smile to curve her lips. By underestimating her ability to turn pennies into pounds through investments and by assuming she had used all of her tiny portion to pay the household accounts each month, Denbigh had left her cage door ajar. The knowledge of her success gave her a smidgeon of confidence. Her stride steadied.

The hardest parts had been creating a false identity and locating a man in the City who didn't mind doing business with a woman he thought was a widow. At first, she'd thought to use her profits to help Denbigh with his debts, to surprise him into acknowledging she could make a contribution to their marriage. Then she began to understand. Men, particularly Denbigh, didn't want wives who could think or reason or figure. He wanted a porcelain doll to show off to his friends or a brood mare to produce his children. Since she had failed on both counts, she would use her money to start a new life. Perhaps once she got settled, she could risk a message to her family.

She shivered in the early morning chill. The dim light of the occasional street lamp made the buildings look threatening. Her footsteps echoed as she turned onto Berkeley Street and made her way to Piccadilly. A hackney rattled past. The jarvey perched on his box gave her a hopeful glance. She couldn't afford to ride. And besides, if questioned, a hackney driver might remember her destination. Each step took her farther away from the townhouse, and with each passing moment, she expected to hear a shout, to learn of her flight's discovery, to be dragged home in ignominy.

Footsteps sounded behind her. She stopped, shrinking against the wall and melting into deeper shadows. A gentleman in a beaver hat, his cane twirling, strolled down on the other side of the street without so much as a glance her way.

Breathe. Walk firmly, head high. People will see nothing but a woman on an errand or a servant on her way home. The sounds of the City wafted around her. The all's well call of a Charley, laughter from an inn's glimmering windows, and a couple's raucous singing carried on a breeze heavy with the familiar smell of coal fires and offal.

By the time she reached the stagecoach stop at the Angel Inn, her nerves were pulled so tight her shoulders ached. A light beckoned from the parlor window inside the courtyard. Oh, for a hot cup of coffee. Or chocolate with warm sweet rolls. She would never eat another water biscuit as long as she lived.

Fool. No matter how hungry she felt, she must resist the temptation. A widow buying a ticket and boarding the stage would not likely warrant attention, whereas a woman sitting in a public inn for hours in the middle of the night might well be remarked upon.

The shadows of a nearby building provided a clear view of the approach to the inn. If her husband came looking for her, she would see him first.

Oh, God, she hoped so. Panic weakened her knees and made her stomach churn. She pushed thoughts of Denbigh aside, refusing to think about the kind of punishment he would inflict if he caught her. Anticipation of that sort only led to paralyzing fear. A lesson well learned under Denbigh's harsh tutelage.

Time passed at a crawl. From time to time, she shifted her aching feet. At first she thought the faint trace of grey in the sky was wishful thinking, but then an oxcart squeaked and groaned its way along the cobbled road in the direction of Covent Garden. Morning could not be far away if the farmers were bringing their produce to market. She pressed back against the wall to give the vehicle room to pass. The man at the reins gave her a friendly nod. A few moments later, a ragged street sweeper, a boy of about ten, established himself at the corner.

London was stirring.

A stable lad yawned his way across the inn courtyard opposite, plying his shovel to the dollops of dung. He paused to chat with a chambermaid laden with buckets of coal. Simple folk going about their business as if all was well in the world. How strange it seemed. How uplifting. Soon enough, the stage would draw up in front of the inn and carry her off to a new life.

"Psst. Missus," hissed a voice in her ear.

Lucinda's heart lurched into an awkward gallop. She whirled around, a cry of alarm lodged in her throat and stared at the slatternly woman balancing a child of about two on her hip. Thank God. No one she knew.

How on earth had she missed the woman's approach? It might have been one of her husband's men, or Denbigh himself. She pressed a hand against her breastbone in an attempt to still her heart's flutter.

"Will ye?" the nasal voice repeated.

"Will I what?" she asked gently.

"Will you hold the child while I goes over there? 'E won't let me through the door with the nipper. I wants to ask for work as a chambermaid."

Lucinda shook her head. "I'm so sorry. I'm waiting for a stage."

The woman coughed, a horrid hacking sound that shook her body. The paroxysm subsided, and she dragged her filthy sleeve across her mouth and nose. "I won't be but a moment, miss," she gasped and thrust the sleepy child into Lucinda's arms with so much force that Lucinda staggered. If she had not caught the child, the woman would surely have let it fall to the flagstones.

With a curse at the street sweeper when he tried to clear her a path through the muck, the woman stumbled across the street and ducked into the inn.

The child chose that moment to open a pair of blue orbs and gaze up at Lucinda in solemn contemplation. Lucinda regarded the dirt-smudged cheeks and rosebud lips. Poor little thing, and so thin. She peered anxiously across the street. Just a moment or two, the women had said.

The street urchin sauntered over, his brush over his shoulder, a thumb in his waistband, and a glint of knowing in his eyes. He tipped his hat back at a rakish angle. "Loped off, has she? Properly bubbled you."

"I beg your pardon?"

"Blue Ruin Bonny." He jerked a thumb in the direction of the inn. "She bamboozled you."

The ragamuffin seemed to be speaking a foreign language, although Lucinda recognized some of the words as English. It must be cant. Geoffrey, her brother, had favored it at one time, though his version had been far more comprehensible. "She asked me to hold her child while she applied for work."

He threw his head back and laughed, then pulled a dirty handkerchief from somewhere about his person and wiped his eyes. "You won't see 'er ag'in. Not no how."

"Do you mean she's not coming back?" Lucinda looked down at the child, who stuck a finger in its mouth.

"Naw, not 'er. You'll 'ave to take that there to the work'ouse. They'll take care of it."

"Why didn't she take it?" It? She had just called a child it?

"It ain't 'ers. 'Er sister ran off and left it. The old man wants to chuck it in the river."

"Drown a child?" Her mouth dried.

The boy nodded. "Yerst. Best fing if you asks me. Better than bein' throw'd on the parish and put to a trade."

She flinched at his brutal words. "You seem to be quite all right," she shot back.

"I got me own business," the boy said, scratching at a grimy ear. "This 'ere's my corner. An' I got a place to rest me 'ead. That there's a mort. Only fit for a drab and not for a long while." He shook his head. "Take it to the work'ouse."

Lucinda deduced from this speech that "mort" meant a female, and she didn't want to know what he meant by "a drab." "Impossible. I will miss my coach."

"Catch it tomorrer." He cocked his head on one side. "'Course they might fink you're its ma and keep you, too."

The sense of a trap slamming shut closed off her supply of air. She forced in a deep breath. "Nonsense. Mrs. Bonny er…the aunt went into the inn to seek work. She must come back."

The boy sniggered. "Mrs. Bonny. That's a laugh."

Hefting the child higher on her hip, Lucinda glared down her nose. "I will find this Mrs. Bonny myself." The lad's laughter followed her across the road.

She marched into the Angel. In a room just off the entrance, a bootblack looked up from a row of boots and shoes, his brush poised in midair. "Can I help you, miss?"

"Yes. I'm looking for a woman who came in here a few minutes ago seeking work."

"Saw a baggage come in," he agreed. "She ran out the back door."

"The back door?"

"That's right." He jerked his head. "That way."

Lucinda tried to ignore the apprehension rising in her chest. "She would not have left without this child."

"If you say so, miss." He shook his head. "We gets some bad'uns 'round here we does, no mistake.

Imposing on respectable folks, too. Best take it to the Asylum for Deserted Children. They'll know what to do with it."

"An asylum?" A step up from the workhouse?

"Yes, in Lambeth. You has to explain it h'aint yours, or they won't let you leave it." It again. The little girl rested her head against Lucinda's shoulder.

Outside in the yard, the clatter of horses and the shouts of oslers and customers heralded the arrival of the stage. Her life depended on not missing that coach. "Can you take her to Lambeth? I'll give you some money."

The man shook his head. "See all them boots. Got to be ready by six that lot 'as." He picked up a brown boot large enough to fit a heifer and gave it a swipe. "You best be on your way, miss, before the master finds you in here and calls the constable."

A constable would want to know her name. He might even insist on escorting her home. A sense of disaster left her numb.

The little girl gave a thin sort of wail.

"Sounds hungry," the boots offered helpfully. "They'll give you a pennyworth of bread and milk in the parlor."

Surely, the child's aunt would arrive at any moment with a profusion of apologies about the misunderstanding. She must. Lost for any further idea and wanting the child to stop crying, Lucinda followed the delicious aroma of coffee into the public parlor where a plump-cheeked woman greeted her from behind the counter.

"May I have some warm milk and a roll for the child?" Lucinda asked, miserably aware that she barely had enough funds for her own purposes without spending money on food for another woman's offspring.

Smiling, the woman leaned forward to the child, then reeled back with a gasp. "It's filthy. A lass like you ought to know better."

A lass like her? Lucinda opened her mouth to give the woman a set-down, then pressed her lips together. Any sort of altercation would be sure to attract attention.

"We've been traveling," she said weakly.

"Hmm," the woman said. "All right. Sit over there. I'll bring you some bread and milk for the little one and a coffee for you."

"I must not miss the stage."

"Don't worry. You've a good half-an-hour to spare."

Lucinda gazed into the baby's huge blue eyes. Poor little thing. What if the woman never came back? And what if she did? Would the child end up in the river? Desperation drove people to take extreme measures. Take herself, for example, fleeing her husband in the dead of night. A mad thought popped into her mind. Had Fate offered the perfect disguise? Denbigh would never think to look for a woman with a child.

The waitress bustled over with a basket of fresh rolls, a pat of butter, a cup of milk, and another of coffee.

Lucinda's stomach growled hopefully. Ignoring her own hunger, she broke off a piece of roll and dipped it in the milk. She touched the milky bread to the child's lips. The baby sucked at the soggy roll, then opened her mouth and took a bite.

Gracious. The child had a mouth full of teeth. She must be older than she looked.

"What's your name, little one?" Lucinda crooned. "I can't keep calling you child."

The little girl stared hopefully at the roll.

Lucinda handed her the bread, and the child proceeded to dip it in the milk. While she devoured her roll, Lucinda buttered another for herself. Washed down with coffee, it seemed like the most delicious thing she had eaten in years. The two of them munched in silence until nothing but crumbs remained.

The little girl sat up and gazed around. "Mama?"

The word clawed at Lucinda's heart. No child would ever call her "mother." Not a child of her own. She gazed at the tiny face topped by wispy blond curls and couldn't prevent a smile.

The child blinked back enchantingly.

"Sweeting, to me you look like a Sophia." The name she'd chosen for the daughter she'd once hoped to conceive. She tickled her under the chin. "Sophia, let us use the facilities, and unless your aunt returns, then it will be time to depart."

Hugo drew Grif to a halt at the top of Beacon Hill, inhaled air redolent with the first cut of summer hay, and gazed over the magnificent sweep of Kent countryside. Three weeks laid up in an army hospital followed by a storm in the Atlantic made one appreciate England's beauty.

A lark trilled liquid notes high above him. He squinted into the afternoon azure sky and, as he expected, saw nothing of the small bird making one of the sweetest sounds on earth. He couldn't remember when he'd last heard anything besides shouted orders, booted feet, and the crashing of cannon. Perhaps coming home wasn't so bad.

In the midst of bucolic beauty squatted the Grange. A fortified half-timbered manor in medieval times, its outline had been softened with sprawling stone additions and outbuildings by succeeding generations of Wansteads. Looking down on it from the rear, traces of its origins remained: a dip in the lawn the last vestige of the moat, the square core of house, and even the bricked-up arrow loops either side of the oriole in the library, once the solar. If he stared hard enough at the lawn alongside the tree-lined drive, he could make out the old tilting field where once armored knights charged at one another. A haven of safety. At least he'd thought so as a boy, before he learned the truth and hotfooted off to war.

His gut twisted at the painful reminder. For a moment he considered turning tail. He sighed. He had nowhere else to go. The Grange was a responsibility he'd avoided for far too long.

Shifting in the saddle to ease his aching thigh, he pulled out his flask and took a long pull of brandy. For a moment, he let the numbing warmth spread out from his belly. Then he pressed his heels to Grif's flanks, urged the stallion into an easy downhill canter along the edge of a fallow field, and entered Brackley Woods, an approach that would take him directly to the stables. They'd ridden hard from Portsmouth, but his eagerness must have transmitted through his hands and heels, because Grif, game as always, broke into a gallop.

A flash of blue, ahead and to the right. On a collision course. A child. His hands sawed at the reins, his body adjusting to the skittering halt. The child stopped dead in her tracks in front of Grif with a high-pitched screech.

The stallion reared and danced on his hind legs, snorting and trembling. Flashing hot then cold, Hugo brought Grif down hard to one side of the track. Cold sweat poured down between his shoulder blades as his mind took in the near tragedy.

A woman in grey dashed out from among the trees and scooped up the little girl. Chest heaving, her dark eyes accusing, the woman backed up. He'd seen nothing but terror for years. He hadn't expected to be the cause of it in the peaceful English countryside.

He leaped down, reaching to calm Grif with a pat on the neck, aware of his own slowing heartbeat. What was this woman thinking, letting a child roam free in these woods? His woods, no less. How dare she put a child in such danger?

The child pillowed her head against the woman's magnificent bosom, while the woman stared up at him. A large woman and unusually tall, she held herself proudly. Not a beauty by traditional standards, with her aquiline nose and prominent chin. But unlike the ladies of Spain and Portugal, her fair complexion reminded him of cream fresh from the churn. A faint blush of pink stained her softly rounded cheeks. What little he could see of her light brown hair was scraped back beneath a plain straw bonnet.

All lush swells and hollows beneath her high-necked gown, she had the kind of voluptuous flesh a man could sink into without fear of crushing delicate bones. The kind of woman whose softness would be a comfort during the long hours of the night. To any other man, he reminded himself.

He frowned as a wry smile curved her full lips. Did she find the situation humorous? Anger welled up, whether at her or his unruly response he didn't know. "You are trespassing, madam."

The woman drew in a deep breath and squared her shoulders. "I apologize, Lord Wanstead, if my daughter's sudden appearance caused your horse to startle." Her voice was low, pleasantly musical, and that of a woman gently bred.

And she knew who he was. "Madam, you have me at a disadvantage." He spoke in tones designed to keep her at a distance. It worked well, for she recoiled, cuddling the child closer. Yet when she spoke, her voice was clear and calm. "I am Mrs. Thomas Graham, my lord."

Married, thank God.

She gestured behind her. "We live at The Briars at the edge of your woods. This is my daughter, Sophia."

He'd never heard of The Briars. An unwelcome suspicion nagged at the back of his mind. "Where?"

She raised her strong chin in a gesture of defiance. "The Briars, my lord."

The child twisted in her mother's arms and pointed at Grif. "Horsy?"

Mrs. Graham caught the tiny hand in fingers encased in York tan. "Hush, Sophia." Her dark gaze returned to clash with his, bright with intelligence and mingled with wariness.

What did she fear? Him? His horse? Why did he care? He shook off the intrusive thoughts. "I suggest you keep more careful watch on your child, Mrs. Graham." He touched his hat and climbed aboard the now placid Grif.

She retreated further to allow him free passage. Dipping a curtsey, she lay a hand flat on the base of her throat in a strangely vulnerable gesture. "I'm sorry we disturbed you, my lord. It will not happen again. I wish you good day."

Whoever she was, he'd clearly made her nervous. Something he discovered he regretted. Blast the woman. He had no reason for guilt. He bowed. "Good day, Mrs. Graham."

He set Grif in the direction of Wanstead Manor, her magnificent figure lingering in his mind's eye like some glorious Rubenesque beauty. He rarely noticed women these days. Couldn't afford to notice them, for their sake. And a married woman to boot. Bloody hell. He reached for his flask and took a swig. Perhaps brandy would cure this nonsensical stirring in his blood.

As he broke out of the woods, he concentrated on his family home. Despite his ten years of absence, the beech trees seemed no bigger, their trunks no more knotted and twisted than when he left. He liked the idea of permanence, he realized with surprise, along with a sense of belonging he hadn't expected.

On the other hand, the shade-dappled lawn beneath the trees badly needed mowing, while ancient ivy encroaching on the rear windows gave the house a secretive air, as if it preferred to remain aloof from the rest of the world. He urged Grif into the stable yard. No one emerged to greet him. Where the hell were the grooms? Cursing under his breath, he dismounted and led the stallion into the first vacant stall where he proceeded to rub down his weary horse. Old Brown was going to get an earful about the lack of servants in his stables.

Having provided for Grif's needs, he picked up his saddlebag, crossed the cobbled yard, and stomped in through the side door. He tramped along the unlit passage. Weren't they expecting him?

He paused where the passage opened out into the old medieval hall. In the middle of the white-and-black tiled floor, a grey lurcher lay curled in the patch of sunlight streaming in through the stained-glass rose window above the front door. The dog lifted its head and bared its sizable teeth.

"Lady?" Hugo said, knowing he was wrong.

The stringy tail whipped back and forth sending dust motes flying.

Hugo's chest seemed to fill with a painfully hot lump. This was not the dog who'd been his constant companion as a lad, but it must be one of her get. In two quick strides he reached the dog's side and dropped to his haunches, his hand running over silky hair and knobby ribs. Melting brown eyes stared trustingly into his. "Well, well, and who do we have here?" He turned the collar and found the name engraved on the leather. "Belderone."

The dog pressed his forehead into Hugo's knee, whining and thumping his tail against the tiles as if in recognition.

"Well, boy," he said, his vision unaccountably blurring. "Here I am. Home at last." He pushed to his feet, smothering a groan at the twinge from his thigh. Damn, he needed a drink.

"Jevens," he called out, then thrust open the study door.

Nothing had changed. He could almost imagine his father glaring at him from behind the paper-strewn desk at one end of the room. He closed his eyes briefly to dispel the image and opened them slowly. Although the curtains were drawn back, the room seemed unkempt and full of shadowy corners. What the hell had happened here these last few years?

"Jevens," he roared and then swallowed as Jevens appeared at his side, wisps of hair hugging his balding pate like damp string, something else that hadn't changed.

"Welcome home, my lord." Jevens's fleshy jowls wobbled. His old pale blue eyes looked watery. "We were not expecting you until tomorrow."

Perhaps his early arrival accounted for the house's general appearance of neglect. Somehow, Hugo found that hard to believe. "I came across country. It was quicker." Hugo's thigh throbbed a reminder. "Do we have any brandy?"

"Of course, my lord." His face flushed. "I should have thought to ask."

Hugo waved off the apology, and the butler trundled to the cabinet where his father always kept his wine.

"And may I say how glad we all are to see you safely returned, my lord," Jevens said as he poured.

"It is good to be back. I met a woman wandering in my woods. A Mrs. Graham. Living at a place called The Briars?"

Jevens brow lifted a fraction. "The Dower House that was, my lord."

Hugo's heart stilled. "The Dower House?" No Wanstead woman had taken residence at the Dower House in over a century. They never outlived their husbands. But even so, letting out a house intended for members of the family seemed a little odd.

"Mr. Brown advertised it as The Briars," Jevens continued. "Mrs. Graham has lived there for about three months."

"What does her husband do?"

"Sadly, she is widowed, my lord."

"A widow? Brown leased the Dower House to a widow?" This was not good. Not when the widow was so damned attractive.

Jevens stared at him. "Yes, my lord."

"Ask Roger to see me immediately."

"Mr. Roger Brown retired, my lord. His son Ronald is now steward."

"His son?" The son had been naught but a youth when Hugo left for the war.

"Nice young fellow, very organized," Jevens said, with what seemed like smug satisfaction. "Wants to make lots of improvements, he does. Get the estate back to what it was in your grandfather's day."

Hugo lowered himself into the chair behind the cluttered desk, his mood lifting. "Good. The first business of the day will be to offer Mrs. Graham a good price for her lease. The woman is making altogether too free with my property. I want her gone." He wanted her lush body gone. Her magnificent breasts and accusing eyes gone.

Jevens stilled, his eyes round. "Gone?" he asked blankly.

"Yes." He flicked his fingers in the direction of the door. "Gone. The woman is a menace letting her child roam through the woods. I could have run her down."

The butler stood rigid, his happiness fading. "As you said, my lord, you will have to talk to Mr. Brown."

"Then send him in. By the way, why is there no one in the stable? Or is that another question for Brown?"

"I will inform Mr. Brown of your desire to see him, my lord. He is not expected until tomorrow." Hugo heard the unspoken 'and nor were you.' "Regarding the stables, Albert Farrow went to visit his daughter in the village. He will be back by nightfall."

"Albert? He is still working?"

"Yes, my lord. There's a few of us left. Cook—Mrs. Hobb, that is, Albert, and me. That's it, except for young Mr. Brown."

Why the hell had Father let the complement of servants dwindle to nothing? No wonder the house and grounds needed tending. He'd have a sharp word with this new steward of his, both about the lack of servants and the rental of the Dower House. He didn't want strange females on his property. He didn't want people bidding him good morning and looking to him to solve their problems, not when they looked like the voluptuous Mrs. Graham. He just wanted peace and quiet. He took a sip of brandy. Excellent. At least Father hadn't allowed his cellar to go to the dogs with the rest of the place. The doctor had given him a choice of brandy or laudanum when the pain got too bad. Brandy tasted a whole lot better.

"That will be all, Jevens. By the way, Trent, my batman, will arrive in a few days with my luggage and my horses. In the meantime, I will manage with what's in my saddlebag."

"Yes, my lord." Jevens's wrinkled face rearranged into a smile. "Dinner will be served at six." He shuffled off.

Hugo took another long pull of his drink and felt the heat slide down his gullet and warm deep in his belly. The ache in his leg began to ease along with the uneasy feelings.

Nothing about his arrival had been as he envisaged. He'd almost killed a child; a woman with a body to drive a man to distraction had taken up residence in his grounds; and the house and estate had drifted into disrepair.

He raised his glass in a toast. Welcome home.

He stared at his saddlebag on the floor where he'd dropped it when he entered. Perhaps he would take it upstairs and see what surprises the rest of the house held in store.

Three

HER HEART BEATING TOO FAST FOR COMFORT, LUCINDA took Sophia's hand. They wandered along the forest path. It was the near disaster that had her heart racing, not her enormous landlord on his magnificent stallion. It had nothing to do with the way his gaze had lingered on her body like a caress. A huge man, with harsh manly features and the body of a seasoned warrior, the Earl of Wanstead engendered the kind of admiration one might have for a well-crafted sword. Not the least bit friendly, he'd sat on his stallion like some knight of old defending his land. When he'd dismounted, his sullen glare and taciturn commands might have terrified her, had he not petted his horse with such a gentle hand.

The trees opened out onto a rolling vista. Lucinda and Sophia ploughed through long grass stretching toward the ornamental lake and its complement of hungry swans. Slowly, the rhythm of her heart slowed. She glanced up at the Grange. Hopefully, he would not resent this further intrusion. Surely, a simple walk across his land did no harm, and she'd promised Sophia they'd feed the swans today.

She sighed. He really was a beautiful man. Well, she wasn't blind or too old to appreciate a handsome man—from a distance. Her heart gave a little skip. A foolish flutter of appreciation. She choked down a laugh at the mad flight of fancy that he'd found her attractive. The heat in his gaze was all about anger. Obviously, Lord Wanstead had disliked her on sight. Never one to strike admiration in any man's breast, she found that his instant hostility rankled, just a little. To be sure, the man was a great surly bear and best avoided.

Too bad she'd not had the sense to avoid Denbigh. Her doting parents had been thrilled when the handsome nobleman asked leave to court her. Wanting to please them, to make them proud, she'd failed to look any deeper than his title and his charm. He'd fooled them all. And it would not happen again.

Sophia pulled free of Lucinda's hand and crouched at her feet. "Daisies," she said. She pulled the heads off two of the white flowers struggling through the grass.

Lucinda picked another one and held out the pink-fringed petals for Sophia to see. "Like this, sweetheart. So you have a long stalk." She smiled at the eager little face surrounded by wispy blond curls. "You try."

With a frown of concentration, Sophia bent over another cluster of flowers. This time she plucked the stem and a few blades of grass. "Daisy," she crowed and handed it to Lucinda.

"Good girl. Get another one." She dropped to the ground, sitting cross-legged with her skirts smoothed over her knees as she had in the old days at home with her younger sisters. How they had giggled and teased in their youthful innocence. She pushed the memory aside. Those days must be put aside, only to be brought out and dusted off at some time in the future, when she felt easier in her mind.

Sophia trotted back and forth, dropping the little flowers in Lucinda's lap one at a time. Lucinda pierced each delicate stem with her thumbnail and linked them into a chain.

"Find a big one," she said the next time Sophia arrived.

"Big one," Sophia repeated, opening her arms wide like an angler describing his catch.

Lucinda chuckled. "Not that big."

The child trundled off, carefully inspecting each flower for bigness until at last one met her requirement. She skipped back, her little black shoes twinkling from beneath the edge of her pale blue skirts.

"This?" she asked with a baby lisp.

Lucinda tickled her tummy. "Let me see."

Sophia giggled and hopped out of reach.

The stem looked sturdy enough. If it tore, they'd have to find another one to complete the daisy crown.

While Lucinda worked, Sophia wandered off. "Don't go too far," Lucinda called out.

A few moments later Sophia returned. "This?" She poked a yellow flower under Lucinda's nose.

"Oh, no, that is a buttercup. Look, it is yellow, not white. Can you say buttercup?"

"Budderup," Sophia repeated solemnly.

Lucinda smiled at the serious elfin face. Still far too thin to be her child, for all that people seemed to accept the story. "Clever girl. Lift your chin."

Sophia obliged.

Lucinda guided the buttercup against the baby-soft throat. "My, my, you do like butter."

The little head nodded emphatically. "Bread."

"Yes, bread and butter."

Sophia held out the yellow flower. "You do?"

Lucinda tipped her head back. "Is it yellow under there?"

Sophia peered closely, her baby breath warm on Lucinda's throat. "Lellow," she said, although Lucinda wasn't sure she knew what the word actually meant.

"Then I like butter, too." Lucinda pulled Sophia close for a hug. The sweet, honest feel of the child's little arms around her neck reminded her of all Denbigh had forced her to leave behind—her younger sisters, her parent's love and respect. She inhaled the child's scent. Don't think of that now. She had made a new life for her and Sophia. But what if her investments in the Funds lost money? Even a small loss could render her destitute, and then where would they be?

"Oh, little one, how can I take care of you when I can scarcely manage to look after myself?" Her voice cracked.

"Mama cry?" Sophia looked anxious.

"No," she said, with a sniff. "Just something in my eye. Look, sweet, here is your crown." She plopped the little wreath on the sun-bright curls. "You are a princess."

Sophia jumped up and down. "Pincess," she shouted. She twirled around, skirts flying with a smile like sunshine after grey skies and laughter so infectious that Lucinda jumped to her feet and swung the child in a circle, her own laughter spilling forth.

How lucky she was to find this child and to end up here in this perfectly idyllic backwater. She would not let a grumpy old earl spoil her day.

Hugo glanced around his father's chamber. No. Not his father's any longer. His. Thank God it looked clean enough, as well as dreadfully imposing with the large four-poster bed smack dab in the middle and the boar-and-roses coat of arms emblazoned on everything from the royal blue bed hangings to the carved chest of drawers. He couldn't recall ever setting foot in this room.

With a strange guilty feeling, he approached the connecting door to the countess's apartments, a suite of rooms he would never need to enter. The polished brass handle moved smoothly under his fingers. With his fingertip, he nudged the oak door open. He hesitated on the threshold of a chamber as familiar as his own. Nothing here had changed, he realized with a savage sadness. Even the air clung to her memory with a faint trace of Attar of Roses.

Had his father intended it as a shrine to its last inhabitant? It seemed unlikely. Or had he simply never set foot in here again? At least Father had the sense to never remarry. No. He had imposed that unpleasant duty on his son. And having tried it, Hugo would never attempt it again. He didn't care about an heir. He certainly didn't want any more deaths on his conscience.

Dust powdered the filmy fabric on the Louis the Fourteenth canopy. Hugo remembered burying his face in the delicate folds and his mother's soft command to take care.

He'd been such a clumsy lout. Carefully, he lowered himself to perch on the edge of the bed the way he had as a boy. Each day, he'd tell his mother what he'd learned with his tutor, while she lay on her bed in her lacy cap and frilled gown with a wan smile. God. How ill she'd looked, even on good days.

Two Wanstead women sacrificed on the altar of genealogy in his lifetime. No more.

His gut twisted as his mind peered through doors he'd bolted shut. He stumbled around the bed and out into the corridor, searching for happier memories. His steps turned east. The earl's suite of apartments lay in the west wing and looked out over the tree-lined drive. In the opposite direction lay the room he'd chosen for his own when he left the nursery.

He strolled along the connecting gallery, nodding to the grim ancestral portraits ranged along the wall and then ducked into a narrow passage dark with ancient panels and blackened beams. He must have had a reason for selecting this side of the house, the oldest remnant of the original Tudor mansion. Perhaps his dreams of knights in shining armor had led him here. He sighed. More likely a need to be as far as possible from his parents and their misery.

The door to his old room opened on another shrine. This time, his own. The wooden bed dented from battles with dragons occupied one wall. His desk, marred by the obligatory initials of boredom carved by generations of Wanstead lads with varying degrees of artistic merit, stood guard by the mullioned window. He ran his thumb over his own effort, recapturing his satisfaction that his grooves were deeper than any of the others and thus more permanent. The diamond windowpanes never allowed in much light even on the brightest day, he recalled, hence the buildup of candle wax on the desk. A black stain on the Turkey carpet reminded him of the day, at the age of thirteen, when he'd toppled the inkpot because his knees no longer fit beneath the desk. His tutor had called him a great ox. If he thought about it hard enough, he could feel the sting in the seat of his britches for that piece of clumsiness.

He strode to the window and stared down at the ordered rows of vegetables in the walled garden below. A movement on the unkempt grass beyond the wall caught his eye. The unmistakable and toothsome widow was frolicking on his lawn with her daughter.

Frolicking. Now there was a word you didn't expect to use at the Grange. Even from this distance, he could see the laughter on their faces as she spun the child in her arms, her skirts molding to long, strong legs and full curvaceous hips.

A stirring in his blood caused him to frown. He had no business noticing her curves. He should turn away, not leer at her through the window. She put the child down and their long shadows stretched across the waving grass as, hand-in-hand, they strolled toward a lake burnished by the sun to the color of copper.

Lust, urgent and sharp, bit at his flesh. By thunder, he would do something about this disturbing woman and the child who called up memories too painful to bear. He wanted the pair of them gone.

The chill emptiness in his chest seemed to expand.

He turned from the view outside to stare at his old bed and inhaled the smell of mildew. Not that it mattered. As earl, he would use his father's chamber.

He closed the door on his childhood with a firm click.

"You wish to buy back Mrs. Graham's lease?" Young Mr. Brown, a somber man of about thirty with an open expression and fine brown hair flopping onto his forehead, stared at him agape. Of middle height and weight, he stood in front of Hugo's desk as stiff as a swaddy on parade. Unlike a private in His Majesty's army, however, his voice held a tone of distinct animosity.

Hugo lifted a brow. Most of his erstwhile troops would have recognized the gesture as a herald to frosty anger. Apparently, Mr. Brown thought nothing of it, for he continued speaking.

"She paid in full for a year, with an option to renew. I would be going back on my word."

"A word you gave without consulting me," Hugo responded in a voice as mild as scabbarded steel. "You exceeded your authority."

Brown visibly swallowed, his prominent Adam's apple bobbing above his stock. "I did what I thought best for the Grange, my lord, which I believe is my responsibility. Mrs. Graham is one of your best tenants."

The rush to defend the woman took Hugo aback. Did the steward have more than a professional interest in the young widow? Hugo discovered he didn't like the idea. "Is that so?"

"Indeed, my lord. She has even taken up teaching at the Sunday school in the village."

And Hugo was the ogre for tossing her out of her home. "I am quite prepared to give her time to find a new property to rent."

Brown's lips thinned. "Meanwhile, where does your lordship suggest I obtain another tenant willing to pay such a high price for a house with so little to recommend it?"

Sarcasm? By Hades, this self-righteous young man needed some army training. Perhaps then he'd learn the wisdom of obeying a direct order without question. What the hell had happened to England these past few years? Hugo glared. "The same place as you found Mrs. Graham, I presume." He laced his voice with enough ice to freeze the Thames.

The intrepid Mr. Brown took a step closer to the desk. "Her husband was killed in the war. She came here for peace. Surely you of all people can understand."

The words rocked Hugo back. A soldier's widow? He got up and went to the window. He stared at the tangle of weeds in the middle of the drive. In his mother's day, it had been a rose bed. "I see."

"She thought Blendon an ideal place to raise her daughter."

Hugo turned and caught raw condemnation in the fellow's eyes. Young Mr. Brown, the son of the steward who had served his family for years, found him lacking. No doubt he'd also found the old earl lacking. He narrowed his eyes. "Just what is your connection with Mrs. Graham?"

Brown frowned. "I don't understand, my lord."

"How shall I put it, Brown? You er…seem very interested in this woman." There. Cards on the table. He preferred to do business that way. No sneaking around picking up gossip and rumor.

Brown stepped back, his jaw slack. "My lord?" The color ebbed from his face, and indignation shone in his eyes. "Mrs. Graham is a gentlewoman. The estate needed the rent to pay the servants and buy supplies."

"How can that be?"

"Because your father decided to invest his money at the racetrack."

Apparently, Brown didn't soften his punches either. Hugo took the blow in the soft place in his gut, felt the sickness of lack of air, and breathed deep. Damn. What the hell had Father done? Well, no one ever accused Hugo of being unfair. Strict about discipline, hard on liars and laggards, but never unjust. If Brown was telling the truth about the desperate state of affairs, and he had no reason to lie, then he had been right to lease the Dower House. "Very well. I will accept your advice."

Brown blinked. "My lord?"

"However, please inform Mrs. Graham that she and her child are to stay out of the woods and off my property."

The tension in Brown's shoulders dissipated. A cautious smile broke out on his face. "I will make your wishes known, my lord. I am sure you will not regret your decision."

One less regret would not make a ha'porth of difference. "I am sure she will be grateful for your powers of persuasion, Mr. Brown. Now sit down and give me the rest of the bad news." He gestured to the chair in front of his desk. "Tell me why there are no crops or animals in my fields."

Color leached from Brown's face. He dropped into the chair. "As I understand the matter, not long after you joined the army, his lordship suffered a financial reversal on some horses he bought."

Horses. His father's passion. "I see."

"Yes, my lord." Brown inhaled. "Apparently, he tried to recoup his losses at the Newmarket races."

With a strong sense of worse to come, Hugo rolled his shoulders. Did he really want to know? "What happened?"

Brown tugged at his collar. "Badly dipped, I'm afraid. The fear of your demise and a dislike of your cousin drove him to the marriage mart. He entertained lavishly in London, my lord, with a view to finding a bride."

Hugo sat bolt upright. "What?"

The steward swallowed. "He paid out a lot of blunt on the enterprise. I understand negotiations were all but complete when…when he…"

"Dropped dead. Served him bloody-well right." A chill settled over the room. Hugo leaned back and stared at the low wooden ceiling embossed with the sixteenth-century coats of arms of every noble house in England. "You old dastard," he murmured. "Knowing what could happen and still…" he shook his head.

"I beg your pardon, my lord?"

Hugo brought his gaze back to the steward. "Now what the hell do we do?"

The man gave an embarrassed cough behind his hand. "His lordship might have been on to something, my lord. There are City gentlemen, bankers and such, or manufacturers from the north country, who would be only too glad to embrace a scion of English peerage in their families, along with a golden hand-shake, so to speak."

Hugo stared at him. "You would sell me off, like some prize bull? No, Brown, I think not."

The steward looked distinctly disappointed. "I am sure we could get a very handsome settlement. You being a war hero, as well as an earl."

Hugo brought his fist down on the polished wood. "No," he roared. "Mention it again, and I'll be looking for a new steward. Understand?"

Looking suitably crushed, Brown ducked his head. "Yes, my lord."

At last the fellow was listening. "Good." He snatched up the decanter of brandy and slopped brandy into a glass. He swallowed it in one swift gulp. Raw heat burned his gullet. "Now tell me just how badly off I am. Straight from the shoulder."

"It's difficult for me to say, my lord. Not being privy to all of his lordship's dealings." His ears turned red at Hugo's sharp stare. "I believe there may be some debts of honor outstanding."

"I see." He had come home for peace, only to discover he'd been unknowingly involved in a war at home. Father, it seemed, had won the first battle.

"I could sell off my carriage horses. Trent is bringing them down. I'll let the hunting box go. There may be some jewelry of my mother's to be sold."

Brown shook his head. "I believe the jewelry is gone. As for the horses, the fastest way for a gentleman to let the world know he is in dun territory is to get rid of his stable, my lord. Something your father discovered."

A feeling of impotence welled up in Hugo. He slammed his fist down on the desk. "Dammit. Don't sit there telling me what can't be done; offer me something useful."

"You need an infusion of funds. That was one reason I leased the Dower House to Mrs. Graham. She paid the lease a year in advance. More tenants like her would be a godsend."

"Mrs. Graham seems to be a paragon of all virtues."

Brown opened his mouth.

Hugo raised a hand. "Never mind."

"If your lordship would consider taking out a loan?"

"More debt?"

Brown grimaced. "If the money is used wisely, if we have a good harvest…"

"None of it a certainty." Hugo rubbed the back of his neck. "How much would it take? Do I have credit at the bank?"

Brown pushed a document from the corner of the desk to the center. "A year ago, I prepared a similar report for your father, my lord. He refused to look at it and became quite incensed when I suggested that we let a couple of fields to the squire for hay and another to Mr. Masters at High Acre for grazing sheep. I believe he didn't want it known he was badly dipped."

Written in a neat careful hand, most of the figures on the paper were red, all except the number beside Mrs. Graham's name. It wasn't a question of tolerating her presence, for Christ's sake. He needed her money. A powerful blow to his pride. He felt like an idiot. Heat scalded his face as he stared at the damning numbers. He straightened his shoulders. "Very well, Brown. I appreciate your honesty and your help. Take me through your suggestions."

Lucinda grasped her umbrella tightly in one hand and Sophia's little fingers in the other, all the while valiantly ignoring the damp creeping up her skirts and the wet petticoat wrapped around her calves.

"Sophia, darling, try not to step in the puddles." She guided the child onto the dryer verge, while sheltering her from the rain.

The little girl peeked up from beneath her pink bonnet with a mischievous grin.

"I mean it," Lucinda said with a shake of her head. Unfortunately, she could not resist a smile of her own. Sophia loved to splash in puddles. Sad to say, these puddles were filled with bottomless mud and stretched the half-mile between her and the row of stone laborers' cottages huddled at the end of Mile Lane. His lordship really ought to do something about this lane. It needed drainage. Never had she seen anything so ill-kept on her father's estate. She peered through the drizzle at the leaden sky, half-minded to turn for home. The other half of her mind, the half that knew where duty lay, pressed her forward.

The sooner she accomplished the task of bringing succor to those less fortunate, as the vicar had phrased it, the sooner she could go home to a nice hot cup of tea and a warm fire. Flaming June had forgotten to blaze.

With mud increasingly heavy on her half boots, she plodded on. Only the first cottage in the terrace showed signs of occupation, she realized as she neared her goal. The others seemed to have been abandoned, shutters swinging free, doors open to the weather. A waste of perfectly good housing when there were so many homeless in the city. She rapped on the wooden door. A young lad of about thirteen with a shock of red hair, a freckled snub nose, and big green eyes, opened the door a crack. An odor of musty damp wafted out along with a trickle of smoke.

The boy's eyes popped open as he took in his visitors. Sophia ducked behind Lucinda's skirts.

"Is Mrs. Drabet home?" Lucinda asked.

"Aye," the boy said.

"Good," Lucinda replied. "I am Mrs. Graham. The vicar asked me to call to see how your mother does. May we come in?"

"Who is it, Tom?" a tremulous voice called from inside.

"Some lady from the vicar," the boy called back, seemingly reluctant to open the door any wider. "She wants in."

It wouldn't take much strength to push past the boy, who had arms and legs the circumference of willow twigs and a painfully thin chest. But even the poorest of folk were entitled to believe their homes were castles, Mother had always said.

"I brought gifts for the baby," she said with a smile at the lad. "And bread and cheese for your mother."

The boy's face lit up like a candle in a well. Bribery worked so much better than force.

"Can she come in, Ma?" he yelled. "She brought sommat for the baby."

After a short pause, the voice came back in a weak whisper. "Yes. Yes, I suppose so."

Not a very warm welcome, but a welcome nonetheless.

The boy threw back the door. Lucinda ducked beneath the lintel and stepped inside. The cottage was very similar to those on her father's land, a single living room downstairs sporting a few sticks of home-made furniture, a curtained-off scullery at the back, and a ladder leading to the family sleeping quarters in the loft.

Mrs. Drabet, a woman who had been pretty in her day, sat on a low stool by a pitifully small fire in a black-ened hearth. Cradled in her arms, she held an infant, red of face and wrinkled beneath tufts of orange hair.

A truly beautiful sight.

Lucinda's arms had never felt so empty, useless appendages on an equally useless body. The room blurred as if a fog had rolled in from outside or the chimney had started to smoke. Liar. Babies always brought forth her tears. She blinked hard.

Finger in her mouth, Sophia crept forward. "Baby," she whispered. She touched the baby's head with her other hand. "Pretty," she whispered. Beside Sophia's healthy pink skin, the infant looked a little blue.

"How do you do, Mrs. Drabet. I am Mrs. Graham." Lucinda smiled at the wilted mother. "And this is my daughter, Sophia. The vicar asked us to call in. He wanted to come himself, but he had an urgent call to Mr. Proudfoot."

The woman raised her gaze from the child in her arms and nodded. "Old man Proudfoot won't be pleased for the reminder he ain't long for this world, but it's a good thing, the vicar callin' in an' all."

Lucinda glanced around for somewhere to deposit her basket. Despite signs someone had tried to sweep the dirt floor recently, the cottage definitely smelled of damp. Too damp for a baby and a new mother. She frowned at the water trickling down alongside the window.

"The roof only leaks when it rains," Mrs. Drabet said. "I usually sweeps in here every day. Dick said he would bring 'ome fresh straw later, if he could filch a bit from the Red Lion stables." She gasped and covered her mouth with her hand. "I mean borrow it."

"Does Lord Wanstead know your roof leaks? Surely he will have someone make the repairs?"

The woman shook her head. "My Dick told Mr. Brown about it last winter, but he couldn't do naught. His Lordship's orders. I mean the old earl, like. Dick said it were better to say naught to the new lord, in case he says we can't stay here no more." The words contained no rancor, only dull resignation.

Lucinda stared at her. "Not stay here? Isn't Mr. Drabet employed by his lordship?"

Mrs. Drabet shrugged and hugged the baby close as if to protect it from bad news. "There's been no work for nigh on two years. No pay, neither. Everyone else left and went up north, but Dick was hoping sommat would come along." The baby gave a thin wail, and she rocked it. "I couldn't travel, not expectin', I couldn't. Dick's been helpin' out at the Red Lion. Puts a bit of bread on the table for the lad here."

No wonder the vicar had been so anxious for someone to visit this family today.

"We ain't seen hide nor hair of his lordship since he came back," Mrs. Drabet said.

Nor had anyone else. Since her encounter with Lord Wanstead in the woods three weeks before, no one in the village had seen his lordship. Not even in church. He seemed to have gone to ground. The gossips hinted he didn't like company. Some even said he was a bit of a hermit. How dare he leave his people to starve? Especially such a tiny baby. She swallowed her words. Railing about the lord of the manor would only serve to upset the fragile Mrs. Drabet.

"Do you really have bread and cheese in there?" the Drabet boy asked staring at the basket.

She set the basket on the plank table pushed against one wall. "I do, and a few little gifts for the baby. I hope you do not mind, Mrs. Drabet? Miss Crotchet made a nightdress, and there are some nice bits of flannel for swaddling, and a knitted blanket from Annie Dunning. The bread is fresh baked this morning. The vicar sent a round of cheese and Mrs. Peddle a flagon of stout. That last is for you, Mrs. Drabet, to set you up."

The woman's eyes grew rounder with each word Lucinda spoke. "Well, I never. It's all that there vicar's doin'. I said to my Dick, he's a good man." She cocked her head on one side. "Needs a wife, he do. T'ain't right for a vicar to live alone."

Others had made similar suggestions. Mrs. Dawson, the squire's wife, in particular. Lucinda had simply ignored the hints and retained her half-mourning attire as a form of defense.

She glanced from the smoking hearth to the Drabet boy eyeing the bread and cheese with his hands clasped at his chin and looking like a hungry squirrel. "Do you have more fuel for the fire? It really is chilly in here for the baby."

"There's some wood at the back door," Mrs. Drabet said, "But it's got to last us through next winter. I shouldn't be having a fire, 'ceptin' the baby looked chilled first thing this mornin', poor little mite."

Poor little mite indeed. The blanket would help, and so would the food. "Send your boy down to The Briars tomorrow," Lucinda said on a whim. "I have some chores he can do in exchange for some kindling and a bucket of coal. In the meantime, young man, stoke up this fire."

After a longing glance at the items on the table, the boy knuckled his forehead and shot off.

Oh, heavens, by tomorrow she would have to think of something for the lad to do. She glared at the dark trail of moisture winding down the stone wall. Or Lord Wanstead would have to find the boy's father employment. Now that was an interesting thought.

"I'll bid you good day, Mrs. Drabet," Lucinda said. "Please do not forget to send the boy down tomorrow. Come along, Sophia. We have another call to make."

She stepped out, careful to close the door quickly to retain the fragile heat. Next they were going to call on an unthinking landlord who allowed his people to live at the edge of starvation. Just the image of the blue-lipped baby started her blood boiling all over again.

By the time they reached the Grange, the drizzle had ceased, but Lucinda's mood was as black as the clouds rushing toward the horizon.

They met Albert crossing the stable yard. He raised a set of grizzled brows, the wrinkles in his forehead joining with those on his weathered bald head to form what looked like a miniature plowed field above two curiosity-filled black eyes. "Good day, Mrs. Graham. Miss Sophia. How be you this day?"

"Good afternoon, Albert. We are well, thank you. Is his lordship at home?"

"Got back from Maidstone an hour ago, he did. None too happy, if you ask me."

Lucinda winced. Could she put off her visit for a day when she might find his lordship in a better mood? Never put off until tomorrow, what can be done today—the gospel according to Mother. "I'm glad to find him in."

"Aaah. Well, there you'll be lucky most times. He don't go much beyond the estate. Would you like me to take care of the little lady here while you visits his lordship? Take her to see the horses?"

Sophia, who was flagging after their protracted walk, gave a little hop. "Horsy."

So much hope blossomed in the child's face that Lucinda didn't have the heart to say no. Besides, it would be easier to talk to his lordship if she did not also have to keep an eye on a bundle of mischief. "If you are sure you have time?"

Sophia grasped the gnarled hand held out to her. "Naught else to do, Mrs. Graham, except watch the hay settle in the manger, so to speak. Not 'til the rest of the master's horses arrive."

And no doubt the horses would be better kept than the people who lived on his land. The thought stiffened her spine and propelled her toward the iron-studded front door. She lifted the circular knocker and banged twice.

A few moments passed before the door swung in to reveal an aged butler who peered at her through pale rheumy eyes. "Mrs. Graham," he said.

Everyone knew everyone in Blendon. "Mr. Jevens," she replied. "I'm here to see Lord Wanstead."

"His lordship is not at home," the butler said, without a great deal of conviction.

"Nonsense. Albert informed me he returned from Maidstone an hour ago."

The sagging skin on the butler's red-veined face flushed. "I mean he is not at home to visitors, Mrs. Graham."

It was all the excuse she needed to turn tail and run. "Is he ever home, Jevens?"

The faded eyes warmed to a faint twinkle. "No, Mrs. Graham. Never."

"Then let us consider this a business call, shall we?" She stepped forward and into the hall, brushing past the old gentleman, who tottered backward. Now he would be quite truthful in saying that she pushed her way in, should his lordship think to enquire.

"Where is he?"

"In his study." Jevens nodded at an oak-paneled door leading off what had once been a medieval great hall. The stone fireplace at one end was big enough for a man to stand up in. A suit of Cromwellian armor guarded the bottom of a great carved staircase blackened by age, and an enormous iron chandelier hung from the hammer beams overhead. Magnificent and draughty and… she raised a brow…exceedingly grimy. Why, she couldn't see her reflection in the mirror for the layer of dust on its face.

Jevens made no move to announce her.

If that was the way the wind blew, she would announce herself. Her footsteps rang out on the flagstones as she approached the door. Pausing to run her hands down the front of her gown, she composed her expression into pleasant but firm friendliness. The last time she had smoothed her skirts outside a door had been the last time Denbigh raked her over the coals. The recollection struck like a slap to the face. She drew in a quick breath. In those days, she had been nervous, afraid of saying the wrong thing. Since then, she had taken her life into her own hands. The coming interview might not be pleasant, but she wasn't afraid, even if her knees did feel a little weak and her heart pounded. Good gracious, you'd think she was about to beard a real bear in its cave.

She rapped on the door.

"Come." The voice on the other side was deep, pleasantly so, resonant, and very male.

She inhaled a quick breath and strode in.

Little outdoor light penetrated the room despite the open shutters. A candlestick lit the seated figure at the desk. With his head bent over a scattering of papers, the flame casting gold highlights among the dark brown of his hair, Lord Wanstead continued writing.

Lucinda closed the door.

"Yes?" Lord Wanstead said. He raised his head, blinked, and rose slowly to his feet. The pen slipped from his hand. His glance traveled from the hem of her waterlogged gown to her head in one swift pass, stopping when their gazes clashed. Heavy brows slowly lifted in question. Green eyes splashed with brown, eyes the color of cool summer forests, stared. The expression in their depths really did remind her of a bear, the one she had seen as a child at Astley's amphitheater, puzzled and wary, as if waiting to see what trick the world would play next.

The gaze hardened and darkened to the color of evergreens in winter. Lucinda's heart thumped against her chest as if it would prefer to be anywhere but in this room with this apparently angry male. "What the blazes—"

"Mrs. Graham, my lord," she said, annoyed at the quaver in her voice. "We met in the woods some two weeks ago. I am the tenant—"

"I know who you are, Mrs. Graham. What I don't understand is how you found your way in here." He left the desk, heading for the fireplace and the bell pull, no doubt intending to have her thrown out. An enormous grey dog emerged from behind the desk hard on his heels. Its white fanged smile and lolling pink tongue looked far more welcoming than its master's expression.

"Belderone," Wanstead said. "Sit."

The dog sank to its haunches.

"If I could beg your indulgence, my lord. There is a matter of some importance I must address with you."

He stopped and turned, his dark brows lowered in a frown, his full lips a straight uncompromising line. "What is it, Mrs. Graham. A mouse in your pantry? Some shelves you wish installed in the D—at The Briars? Mr. Brown handles those requests."

She stripped off her gloves and removed her bonnet. "Perhaps if we could be seated, we could have a civilized conversation." Dash it. Not the right thing to say to a man in his own home, a home that looked as dark and dingy as a medieval castle. She inhaled a steadying breath and made for the chair in front of the desk, keeping a wary eye on the dog. When neither master nor dog indicated any objection, she sat down.

Wanstead stumped back to his large padded armchair. The dog rested its head on his thigh, while he picked up the pen and ran the feather through strong, square fingers. A shiver ran down her spine, as if the delicate fronds had touched her skin. "Do you require tea, Mrs. Graham?" he asked.

After tramping about in the rain in sodden skirts for half the afternoon, the thought of a cup of tea sounded lovely, but the edge in his tone warned her off. "No thank you. I'm here in regard to the farm worker and his family who live in the cottage on Mile Lane."

"What business are they of yours, may I ask?" The growl in his voice and the lowering of his head made him seem more bear-like than ever, a somewhat confused bear.

Tall as she was, large as she was, this powerful male made her feel tiny and vulnerable and just a little bit breathless in a strange fluttering kind of way.

"The vicar asked me to visit Mrs. Drabet this afternoon with some things from the ladies of the church for the new baby."

"Drabet," he said. "Dick Drabet? Good lord. I haven't thought about old Dick for years."

"That much is apparent, my lord."

A flicker of shame darkened his eyes, and he glanced down at the papers on the desk. "I am a very busy man, Mrs. Graham. Please get to the point."

A rude, overbearing, busy man. "My lord, the Drabet family is living in conditions not fit for animals, let alone humans, and especially not a baby."

The stiffening of his shoulders, the flush high on his cheekbones, along with a spasm of fingers around the pen, signaled she had gone too far. Hadn't she learned not to point out to any male his shortcomings? Apparently not.

She cringed inside, shriveling against the chair back as if somehow she could make herself small enough to disappear beneath the rug and creep away like a mouse. An apology sprang to her lips, but her dry throat refused to utter a word.

A lump of granite would not have looked more impenetrable than Lord Wanstead's expression at that moment. She found it disconcerting, nerve-wracking. "You are here to tell me that a building on my property needs attention?"

"Y-yes." Put like that, it sounded dreadfully impertinent.

"I had no idea," he said.

"Well you wouldn't. You have barely left your house since your return. Did you know that the other two cottages in that row are empty, and if you do not do something soon, they will fall down?" Amazed at her temerity, a pulse beating heavily at her temple, she waited for his roar of outrage, for the threats men used to keep women in their place. Bluster, she reminded herself, posturing.

He shook his head, tossing off her baiting words. "I have been busy." Once more his gaze flicked to his papers. "I haven't had time…"

Time? What did he do for the hours he spent locked up alone in this mausoleum of a house? It, too, needed attention. For once, her questions remained where they belonged, behind her teeth. She pressed her lips together just to make sure.

His gaze rose slowly to her face, as if seeing her for the first time that morning, as if until now she had been an annoying insect, not worth a second look. He looked weary, even a little shaken, as if something had cracked through his iron reserve.

She suddenly wished she had been a little less damning. "If there is anything I could do to help…"

Eyes shuttered, he straightened. "No. Thank you. I believe you have done quite enough."

An obvious dismissal. And yet she had the sense that if she could just reach out to him, they would connect on some deeper level. Such nonsense. She shot to her feet. "Well, my lord. I really should not keep you from your urgent affairs. I bid you good day."

He looked as if he might say something more, then rose and bowed with precise correctness. "Good day, Mrs. Graham."

The dog's tail thumped on the carpet raising a small cloud of dust.

No invitation to call again, she noticed. But she had done her duty. No one could do more. At least, not without hitting the taciturn man over the head with a shovel and making him go and fix the roof himself.

She swept him a deep curtsey, perhaps a little over-done, but it suited her mood. She sauntered out of the room, if not in good order, then at least with her dignity intact. Only when she marched up The Briars's front path with Sophia in tow did her blood cool. Though whether it was meeting Lord Wanstead again or the excitement of standing up for what was right that had it simmering in her veins, she had no idea.

Four

THE NORMAN CHURCH HAD STOOD IN THE VILLAGE OF Blendon since around the time William the Conqueror arrived on England's shores. Jammed into the front pew in solitary splendor, Hugo felt his shoulder blades tighten. It was as if every gaze in the small congregation bored into his back. He didn't begrudge them their curiosity. After all, bad landlords ruined their tenants as often as good ones brought prosperity, as Mrs. Graham had so forthrightly pointed out. Damn the woman.

A few rows back, the know-it-all widow sat with her daughter. The hairs on his neck stood at attention just thinking about her calm, steady gaze. He smiled grimly as he recalled her bravery in the face of his gruffness a few mornings before, a mother hen standing up to a fox.

In front of him in the carved oak pulpit, the vicar, a tall reed of a man with a shock of black hair and skin as white as parchment, read the lesson. Rather than the usual noble son suffering through his duty, intensity colored his resonant voice and his soft blue eyes warmed when he glanced at his flock.

Hugo had met this man somewhere before.

The simplicity and the encouraging words of the lesson soaked into his weary heart with a burgeoning sense of hope. Something he barely remembered, if indeed he had experienced it at all.

The congregation rose at the end of the service, and he heaved himself to his feet, wincing at a crippling stab from his thigh. As tradition demanded, he led the exodus, foiling the pain in his leg with a brisk stride. He ran the gauntlet of shy grins on scrubbed shining faces and the bobs and touches of forelocks of those waiting for him to pass. God, sometimes he envied them their simple lives.

He returned their acknowledgments with a nod, including one to the somberly clad Mrs. Graham beside her daughter. Many of the rows were sparsely filled, he noted. Unless someone did something about bringing prosperity to this corner of Kent, soon there would be no one left to work his land. Damn the bank in Maidstone requesting more time to consider a loan and asking all sorts of awkward questions. He might have to go to London, to Coutts, for a loan.

Damn Father and his quest for another heir.

Squinting against the glare after the filtered light in the nave, he emerged into a perfect summer day with blue sky, fluffy clouds, and birds twittering in the trees. A cool breeze kept the temperature comfortable, unlike Spain in the summer. Yes, on the whole, he was glad to be back in England. A pleasant if surprising realization.

The vicar popped up in front of him with his hand out. "Good to see you again, Lord Wanstead."

The man must have run all the way from the vestry. Hugo shook the dry, firm hand. He did know this man. He dredged through his memory.

"Pasty," the vicar said with a deprecating smile. "We met at Eton."

"By thunder, Pasty Postlethwaite. You were two years behind me. I've been wracking my brains all morning trying to remember. I knew it wasn't the army."

The younger man nodded. "No. George, the next brother up, had the privilege of that service. I was always destined for the church. Oh, and I go by Peter now."

Other members of the congregation poured out of the church, their faces expressing a curiosity Hugo had no wish to satisfy.

"I'm glad you decided to join us today," Postlethwaite said.

Another person twitting him about his solitude? Hugo decided to let it go. "Call in at the Grange, Peter." Hugo headed down the steps. "We'll sink a bottle and chat about the old days."

Postlethwaite acknowledged the invitation with a nod and turned to greet his flock.

Hugo strode for his gig. A hearty voice called his name. Inwardly Hugo grimaced, but swung around with a smile. "Squire Dawson. How are you?"

He waited for the grey-haired gentleman, rotund and dressed in an old-fashioned frock coat, to catch him up. They shook hands.

"More to the point, how are you, dear boy?" The squire looked Hugo in the eye, the high color in his fat cheeks more noticeable than Hugo recalled. "Heard you were wounded?"

"A scratch," Hugo said. He tried not to fidget under the piercing gaze of an old family friend. "How are Mrs. Dawson and Miss Dawson?" There. That didn't sound too forced.

"Fine, fine. Making a stir in London. You know what the ladies are."

Hugo nodded as if he did know. "And Arthur? What news of him?"

The squire's jovial expression faded. Anxiety replaced the twinkle in his eyes. "Young varmint. I don't understand him, my lord. Never have. Never will. Got himself mixed up with the Bow Window set, most of them Prinny's men by all accounts. A more useless bunch of dandies I never heard of."

It seemed a shame that the Prince Regent's particular friends would be thought of so badly. "He'll get over it," Hugo said, albeit without much hope. "He's young yet."

"And wild. Pity you left. You used to be a good influence on him. He was right miffed when you joined the army without a word to anyone."

Hugo felt the familiar flood of shame at his cowardice. "Father didn't object."

"Your duty was here, learning to take care of the estate, raising the next heir." The accusation hung like a bad smell beneath their noses.

Hugo steeled himself to bear the elderly man's recriminations in silence. Mrs. Dawson's ambitions with respect to her daughter and Hugo were well known in the county, if totally out of the question on several fronts. He hoped to God she'd fixed her eagle eye on some other far more worthy and available prospect. He'd never harbored romantic feelings for Catherine, regarding her more as a very young sister. And as Father had so aptly said, far too delicate for a man of Hugo's size. It was as close as Father ever came to revealing the truth.

The squire pursed his lips. "No need to poker up, my boy. I've known you all your life. What is done is past, and I'm not one to cry over the might-have-beens. If I was, I'd be weeping over that wastrel son of mine."

Hugo refrained from comment.

The squire settled his hat more firmly on his head. "Come to dinner next Saturday. The ladies will be back from Town. Mrs. Dawson would never forgive me if I didn't issue the invitation." He clapped Hugo on the shoulder.

The thought of engaging in futile small talk, of hours spent in the company of Mrs. Dawson, robbed some of the brightness from the morning.

A frown gathered on the squire's florid face. "At least you and I can have a sensible conversation. No doubt Mrs. Dawson will invite the pesky vicar and Mrs. Graham to make up the numbers."

The prospect of another battle of words with Mrs. Graham glowed like a lighthouse on a foggy night. Suffering a slight pang of guilt at his change of heart, Hugo nodded. "I shall look forward to it."

"Good man. I have a new hunter I want you to take a look at. I wish you good day, my lord."

The old squire stumped off to his waiting mount. Hugo climbed aboard the gig drawn by an old gelding who went by the name of Bob. Trent's arrival with the horses from his hunting box would be most welcome. It would not do for a Wanstead to be seen driving such a disgraceful equipage for any length of time. Some of his creditors might indeed start to wonder about his financial stability. Pasty—no, Peter—gave him a nod of farewell over the heads of the crowd, which included Mrs. Graham. In the midst of a knot of women milling at the bottom of the church steps, she was conversing with an elderly lady while her daughter clutched her grey skirts. Unlike himself, the buxom Mrs. Graham seemed very much at home in the village of Blendon. A red-headed boy dashed to her side, jumping up and down to get her attention. Would it work for him, Hugo mused, if he also jumped up and down in her face?

After listening head bent to the boy for a moment, Mrs. Graham glanced up and caught Hugo's eye. She looked surprised and pleased.

Aah. The lad must be a Drabet. The Drabets always tended to have red hair.

Hugo felt a flush rise up his neck. So now Mrs. Graham would think him a weak-willed ninny, a man she could wrap around her interfering thumb. He wouldn't mind her wrapping those strong shapely legs around his waist. He imagined their creamy flesh, their generous plumpness, and almost snarled. Idiot. One little encouragement and he'd have her continually tinkering in his affairs. A very bad idea. The meeting in his library had made it perfectly plain that he did not have the power to resist her allure. He'd been so fascinated that he'd let her make her demands without a single word of protest.

The gig creaked into motion at his crack of the whip. He needed to make his disinterest in the widow very clear.

He could not let her believe she held any attraction. Dinner at the Dawson's would be the perfect opportunity.

A sense of anticipation lingered in the Dawson's azure and gold drawing room. Seated beside Miss Dawson, a diminutive brunette with a peaches-and-cream complexion and lips a rosebud would envy, Lucinda kept her gaze fixed on her hands clasped in her lap. Mrs. Dawson, gowned in chartreuse silk with a matronly cap on her grey coiffure, chattered like a magpie, while the rotund squire paced among the Louis the Fourteenth furniture.

A stage set for the arrival of the conquering hero. Or a prospective bridegroom. The wry thought did little to sooth Lucinda's nerves about renewing Lord Wanstead's disturbing acquaintance. Each time she remembered their brief encounter, her stomach completed another round of somersaults. Seeing him in church, the autocratic nobleman with no more than a stiff nod for his lowly neighbors, had done nothing to still her flutters. If anything, they were worse after seeing the way he towered over the vicar, his virility and size displayed to a dreadful effect on her pulse.

Then, as she heard from Tom about the repairs to the leaking roof, she'd caught Wanstead watching her. Thinking about that dark glance sent heat rushing up her face all the way to her hairline.

She fanned a hand in front of her face. "What hot weather we are having for June." Lucinda almost groaned at the fatuous-sounding remark.

"Yes indeed," uttered Miss Dawson with a gentle smile. "Between the rain."

The squire pulled out his watch, shook it, and then trundled to the carved armchair beside his wife. It was the only solid-looking chair in the room. He lowered his bulk onto the dark blue cushion. "Too much rain, if you ask me. The wheat is rotting on the stalk."

A knock sounded beyond the drawing room door. Mrs. Dawson raised her head, like a hound at the halloo. "Who can that be?"

"Mother, it can only be one of two people, Lord Wanstead or Reverend Postlethwaite." Miss Dawson's voice lacked any of the irritation that jangled Lucinda's nerves.

"Yes, but which of them is it?" Mrs. Dawson said.

"We will soon find out, wife," Mr. Dawson said, lumbering to his feet. "You may be sure of that."

"Lord Wanstead and Reverend Postlethwaite," the butler announced.

The newcomers couldn't have looked more different. The pallid vicar had the look of a monk who spent his days cloistered with books. Broad-shouldered and athletic, the sun-bronzed Lord Wanstead reeked of hours spent in strong sunshine. The crinkles at the corners of his eyes spoke of a man used to gazing at distant horizons. The set of his mouth above a square-cut jaw indicated he rarely liked what he saw in those far-off reaches.

"You came together?" Mrs. Dawson asked as the two men entered the room.

The vicar gave a deprecating wave of his hand. "We met on the doorstep."

Squire Dawson rushed forward, hand outstretched. "I'm grateful for it, gentlemen. Now we'll have some decent conversation."

Outdoors, Wanstead's magnificence had inspired Lucinda's admiration. In the confines of the room, among the gilt chairs and spindle-legged tables, he overwhelmed. She repressed a shiver. Fear? Or something far more dangerous—like attraction? Surely not.

"Come in, gentlemen. Welcome." Dawson said. "Wanstead, you know my wife, of course, and my daughter."

"Indeed." He bowed over Mrs. Dawson's hand. "It is good to see you again."

The earl's voice rumbled in the depths of his wide chest. Lucinda felt the vibration in the pit of her stomach, as if his baritone had the power to strum some chord deep inside her body. She steeled herself against its unsettling effect.

Miss Dawson seemed similarly afflicted, since a rosy hue infused the young woman's cheeks as she held out her hand. "Welcome home, Hugo."

"I can see you are well," he murmured.

"Let me introduce Mrs. Thomas Graham," Dawson said.

A stride brought Lord Wanstead to her chair.

The man positively loomed over her. Her fingers disappeared within his palm, and though he held them lightly, she felt his warmth through her cotton gloves, felt the physical manifestation of his strength, and felt oddly delicate, a most unnerving sensation full of melting and weakness. She stiffened her spine. "My lord."

His gaze remained distant, much as it had when she cornered him in his study, as if he neither knew her nor wanted to make her acquaintance. "How do you do."

She hadn't exactly expected him to be effusive after their last conversation, but his chill reserve acted like a dash of cold water. And yet beneath that stiff reserve, she sensed a deep loneliness, like a man cut off from the world to which he wished he belonged.

Behind him, the vicar was greeting the Dawson ladies.

"Mrs. Graham has only recently come to the village," the squire said.

"Mrs. Graham and I already have a passing acquaintance," Lord Wanstead said. "She is my tenant."

"You have met Mrs. Graham already?" Mrs. Dawson called out, her gaze narrowing in on him and then flicking to Lucinda.

"I wasn't sure you wished to recall our brief meeting, my lord." Lucinda murmured.

Lord Wanstead's eyes darkened. "I could hardly forget. I believe I owe you an apology, Mrs. Graham. I was not the politest of landlords."

To her mortification, Lucinda's heartbeat quickened, making her sound breathless when she replied. "I believe neither of us were particularly polite, my lord."

"What is this?" Mrs. Dawson said. "Sit beside me, Wanstead. I cannot hear with you blocking the middle of the room."

Lord Wanstead inclined his head and strolled to take the fragile seat beside his hostess as ordered, while the Reverend Postlethwaite made his bow to Lucinda with a smile and a murmured greeting. He claimed the empty chair between Lucinda and Miss Dawson.

"How are you, Mrs. Graham?" The Reverend's pale face seemed flushed, his voice hoarse, as if he suffered some sort of fever. While he did not glance Miss Dawson's way, his nerves in the presence of the beautiful woman on his other side were painfully obvious.

Lucinda managed a smile. "I am well, sir. But you seem a little out of sorts."

His flush deepened. "No indeed. Just a trifle warm from the walk."

"Come, now, Wanstead. How did you meet Mrs. Graham?" Squire Dawson boomed from his place at the hearth.

In trepidation, Lucinda waited for a tale of her interference in his private affairs. It would take little more than a word on his part to set the Dawsons against her.

"We met in Brackley Woods," Lord Wanstead said. "I almost ran down Mrs. Graham's child."

"Oh, my goodness," Miss Dawson said.

"You exaggerate, my lord," Lucinda said, gratitude warring with surprise. "Sophia startled his lordship's horse. He is too fine a horseman to come close to riding anyone down."

"Your confidence in my abilities is flattering," Wanstead said with a narrow smile.

Apparently he was not going to mention her foray into his private domain. Lucinda crossed her feet at the ankles and toyed with the strings of her reticule, like some sort of nervous debutante.

Mrs. Dawson rapped him playfully on the knee with her fan. "Now that you are back, sir, I hope we will see more of you here at the Hall. Catherine is certainly looking forward to your company, aren't you, my dear?" She arched a brow in her daughter's direction. "You should ride together, as you did in the old days."

A brief pang tightened Lucinda's heart. Not because she envied the young woman her riding companion, definitely not that, but because her own finances did not stretch to keeping a horse.

"Mama, it was Arthur, not me, who rode with Hugo. I was still in the schoolroom."

"Well, my love," the squire's lady said with a bright smile, "you are in the schoolroom no longer."

Miss Dawson colored. "Mother, please. What must Hugo think?"

Lord Wanstead clearly sensed a noose closing around his neck because he unconsciously tugged at his collar. "I regret that I will have neither time nor inclination for pleasurable pursuits. The estate demands all my attention."

"Glad to hear it, my boy." The squire said. "I can't think what your father was about letting things arrive at such a pass."

"Really, Mr. Dawson," Mrs. Dawson said. "Surely you are not going to start talking business in my drawing room."

The squire scowled. "All I said was—"

"Hugo, we heard you were wounded." Miss Dawson said. "Are you quite recovered?"

Lord Wanstead shifted in his chair, faint color staining his cheekbones. "It was nothing. Merely a scratch."

"At Bussaco, wasn't it?" the vicar asked. "My brother wrote it was a dreadful affair."

Lord Wanstead nodded. "Indeed."

A man of annoyingly few words. Although longing for news of her brother's regiment, Lucinda remained silent, not wishing to arouse questions about her eagerness for information.

"Dinner is served, sir," the butler said from the threshold.

"Wanstead, you will take Catherine's arm," Mrs. Dawson proclaimed. "Postlethwaite, be good enough to escort Mrs. Graham."

The couples organized to her liking, Mrs. Dawson sailed into the dining room on her husband's arm. Catherine and Lord Wanstead exchanged grimaces like old friends and followed suit.

Old friends? Or something more? They certainly made a striking couple, the tall hero soldier and the petite English rose. Another pang? What could she be thinking? Mrs. Dawson had every reason to set her ambitions high with such a beautiful daughter. Lucinda would not begrudge the sweet Miss Dawson her prize.

The vicar proffered his arm, and they brought up the rear.

A monstrous table ran the length of the paneled dining room, and the meal proceeded much as Lucinda expected. The guests were forced to converse with their immediate neighbors, if they did not want to shout to those opposite across an epergne laden with pink roses flanked by branched candelabra the size of ponies. Clearly Mrs. Dawson had set out to impress her noble guest.

The vicar engaged Lucinda and Mrs. Dawson in conversation regarding the parish and mutual acquaintances at the hostess's end of the table, while the squire entertained Lord Wanstead and Miss Dawson. And yet Lucinda had the strangest sensation the earl was paying more attention to the chatter at her end of the table.

The first course consisted of jugged hare and a roast of pork from the squire's own stock, accompanied by fresh peas. It reminded Lucinda of meals at home, when the table seemed to bow beneath the weight of the platters distributed from end to end.

Family meals with the Armitages were serious affairs. Mother would take offense if so much as a potato or a scrap of roast went uneaten. Father's hearty command to eat up echoed in her ears.

A surreptitious glance at his lordship, a man she expected to enjoy his dinner, found him filling his wineglass, a deep furrow between his brows. For such a large man, his preference seemed neither wise nor healthy. Dash it. His well-being was none of her concern.

After a remove of aspics and jelly, a second course of game pie, a calf's foot, and a side of beef arrived, accompanied by spring greens and a dish of assorted vegetables. Lucinda accepted a serving of beef and buttered parsnips from the vicar and passed the platter to the squire. She sampled the meat. Cooked to perfection, it melted on her tongue. Delicious. Her appetite sharpened. She forced herself to eat slowly, instead of like a pig at a trough as Denbigh had always described her at mealtime. Not that she lacked for manners. Mother would never have allowed any lack of etiquette. She just had a hearty appetite, which, as Denbigh had been swift to point out, stuck to her bones. An unfortunate Armitage family trait, according to her husband.

During a lull in the conversation, the vicar raised his voice to reach the far end of the table. "Lord Wanstead, what do you hear from the Peninsular?"

Lucinda could not prevent herself from leaning forward.

Wanstead's dark gaze focused on her face before moving to the vicar. "Very little."

Lucinda tried to contain her disappointment at his repressive tone and the brevity of his answer.

"Wellington is outmatched when it comes to Napoleon," the squire declared. "That is what they are saying in the newspapers. Mark my words, Bonaparte has his measure. The country is going to the dogs, sir."

"I think you will find that Old Hooky knows what he is doing," Lord Wanstead replied.

"Old Hooky?" Miss Dawson said with a laugh. "Surely you are not referring to Viscount Wellington?"

"It is a term of the greatest respect, I assure you," Lord Wanstead said.

"I hear it refers to his nose." Mrs. Dawson said. "Not respectful at all, if you ask me. Not that the Wellesleys can hold a candle to some of England's far more noble families." She glanced pointedly at Lord Wanstead.

"The Wellesleys have earned their honors, Mrs. Dawson. Not had them served up on a platter," Lord Wanstead replied calmly.

It seemed he had not entirely entered into the spirit of Mrs. Dawson's matrimonial game. At least, not yet. The thought unaccountably lightened Lucinda's spirits.

"Who is taking care of your child this evening, Mrs. Graham?" the vicar asked.

Once more Lord Wanstead's gaze turned her way.

"Annie Dunning, my housekeeper, agreed to stay with her this evening."

"A good woman, Mrs. Dunning," the vicar said. "She will be another sad loss to the community."

"Is she leaving?" Miss Dawson asked in her soft voice. "You know her, Hugo. She is Albert Farrow's daughter, married to the blacksmith's youngest son, Samuel Dunning. The Farrow family has lived in Blendon and worked at the Grange all their lives. The Dunnings, too."

"She will go if her husband can find work in the north," Lucinda answered. "She has no choice."

Postlethwaite frowned. "Everyone is leaving the countryside, lured to the cities by the promise of work."

"Rubbish, sir," the squire said from the head of the table. "This country runs on its farms. Always has."

"I beg to differ, sir," the vicar said. "The war brings great profit to the manufacturers in the north. Their wages are higher than anything offered by the landowners."

"Unfortunately," Lucinda said, "without skills, country people often fall into bad company rather than employment."

"Many men get taken up by the recruiters to serve in the army," Lord Wanstead said. "Lord knows we need them."

"War," Mrs. Dawson exclaimed. "And politics. That is all you gentleman think of. I'll hear no more of it at my dinner table, if you please."

"I apologize, Mrs. Graham," Lord Wanstead said. "I should have recalled that such discussions would be painful to you."

Lucinda stared at him blankly. Of course, her supposed soldier husband. Unable to meet his direct gaze, she looked down at her plate.

The butler entered with the dessert, a huge bowl in the center of a silver tray. He set it in the middle of the table.

"Floating island pudding," Miss Dawson said, her dark eyes laughing at her dinner partner.

"I remembered it was always a favorite of yours, Wanstead," Mrs. Dawson said with obvious satisfaction.

"And Arthur's," Miss Dawson added.

Lucinda hadn't had floating island pudding since she left her family home. The creamy scent seemed to transport her to another world where she had felt happy and loved. She couldn't wait to taste it.

"I thought I might find Arthur here this evening," Wanstead said, as the butler filled their dishes.

"He promised to attend my birthday ball at the end of the month," Miss Dawson said.

"If he can drag himself away from London," Mrs. Dawson added. "Do you plan to catch the end of the Season in London, Lord Wanstead?"

"I have no desire to go to London," Lord Wanstead said.

Mrs. Dawson beamed her approval. "Then it is settled. You will attend our ball."

Lord Wanstead had the look of a man hoist with his own petard. Lucinda repressed a smile. She could not help but admire Mrs. Dawson's tactics, even if they were quite shocking. She tasted her pudding. It was just as delicious as it looked. She wondered if Annie Dunning knew how to make the rich dessert.

"I have eaten more than my fill," Miss Dawson declared.

"You don't eat enough to keep a sparrow alive these days," her Papa said with a worried frown at her half-full plate.

No wonder she kept her slender figure. She hadn't touched more than a mouthful of each dish. And yet when Lucinda tried such tactics, she only felt ill. She certainly never got any thinner.

"You need to keep your strength up, Miss Dawson," the vicar urged, his expression intent. "Think how disappointed you would be if you were not well enough to attend all of the festivities."

Lord Wanstead narrowed his eyes. "Festivities?"

"We are planning a village fête," the Reverend said. "To raise funds for the church and possibly to hire a school teacher. Mrs. Graham suggested we think about opening a school in the village."

"I had no idea there were enough children in Blendon to warrant a school." Lord Wanstead said.

"There certainly are not." Mrs. Dawson said with some asperity. "Educating the poor only leads to trouble."

Lucinda's heart sank. Unwittingly, Lord Wanstead had played right into Mrs. Dawson's fears. "There are quite a number of children on the farms nearby, in addition to those in the village. With less and less work in the county, many are lured to London in hopes of employment," she said. "If they were educated, then they would be more likely to find something suitable."

"You speak as if you have firsthand knowledge, Mrs. Graham," Lord Wanstead said. "Did you live in Town before you came to Kent?"

Every eye at the table swiveled in her direction. She flashed hot, then cold. Stupid, stupid blunder. Why could she not keep her foolish tongue still? "I simply state what I have read in the newspapers, my lord."

"And yet you speak with some passion on the matter," Wanstead observed.

"Surely it is a subject that should engage the passion of anyone who cares about the human condition, my lord?"

"Well said, Mrs. Graham," Postlethwaite said. "But you see, Wanstead, we are somewhat stymied in our plans. The village green is nowhere near large enough to accommodate people in sufficient numbers to ensure a large enough profit."

"There is lots of room on the lawn in front of Grange," Squire Dawson said with a glower at his wife.

Lord Wanstead looked slightly stunned. "Surely you are not suggesting…"

"Of course not," Mrs. Dawson said.

"It would be for a worthy cause," the vicar said.

Lucinda threw him a grateful glance.

Lord Wanstead's gaze traveled from her to the vicar and back, assessing, weighing. Lucinda's palms felt suddenly damp. A flush crept up her face, hot and uncomfortable. She placed her spoon and fork on her empty dish and dabbed at her mouth with her napkin.

Mrs. Dawson snorted. "Why would anyone want a parcel of yokels tramping across their grounds, not to mention the unsavory characters such things always attract. Don't listen to them, Wanstead, or you will find yourself inundated with the worst sort of people. I refused to have them at the Hall. Ladies, let us adjourn to the parlor." She rose to her feet.

The gentlemen followed suit with much scraping of chairs on the wooden floor.

"We will leave the gentlemen to discuss their politics and wars over their port." Mrs. Dawson said. "I do hope, Lord Wanstead, you will join us for cards afterwards. And you, too, of course, Vicar."

The gentlemen nodded their assent, while inside Lucinda groaned. She had hoped to make her escape immediately after dinner. But cards would be impossible without an equal number, and it would be rude to leave her hostess in such a fix.

How she came to be partnered with Lord Wanstead in a one-sided game of whist against the elder Dawsons, Lucinda wasn't quite sure. Her refusal to be persuaded to play the pianoforte had been her undoing, she supposed. It left the vicar, who cheerfully acknowledged disinterest in gambling, to join Miss Dawson in singing a selection of ballads, their voices mingling in pleasant harmony at the other end of the room.

The squire laid the first card in what Lucinda hoped would prove to be the last hand of the evening, since she and Lord Wanstead were significantly ahead. She followed his lead with a club.

Mrs. Dawson laid a king of hearts.

"What are you thinking, wife?" the squire muttered, as Hugo laid a trump.

"Mrs. Dawson could do nothing else," Lucinda said, having endured an evening of such remarks with growing impatience. "The king is the lowest heart she has left in her hand, while Lord Wanstead has only trumps."

Lord Wanstead raised a brow and stabbed her with a piercing stare. "Very astute, Mrs. Graham."

She winced. Why could she never remember females were not meant to be able to count? "It is simply a question of keeping track of what has gone before."

Mrs. Dawson gasped. "Everything?"

"Mrs. Graham is an absolute whiz with numbers," the vicar said from across the room. He beamed to the company at large. "She helped me enormously with the church accounts."

"I'm only too glad to assist, Vicar," Lucinda said.

Lord Wanstead cast her a lazy glance from beneath lowered lids. "Then I for one am glad that you are my partner, not my opponent."

"I'm not cheating, if that is what you think," she replied.

"I suggested no such thing, Mrs. Graham," his lord-ship drawled.

He did not sound annoyed. In fact, he seemed to have mellowed as the evening progressed, but after the amount of wine he had drunk, she wouldn't want to stake her life on his temper. She remained silent.

"I must say, your knowledge is uncanny, Mrs. Graham," the squire said jovially.

Lucinda glanced down at her hand with a sigh. Once again her reputation as some sort of oddity was assured. Why could she not be like every other woman of her acquaintance and profess no knowledge of anything except the price of muslin and the latest style in hats? Why had she said anything at all? Absently, she rubbed her collarbone and wondered if she should lose in order to appear normal. Why did she care if Wanstead thought her an enormous freak of nature?

Lord Wanstead picked up the trick and laid his last card. A trump. "Personally, I prefer chess to whist. Do you play, Mrs. Graham?"

"A game of strategy, my lord? Yes, I played as a child with my brother."

"I didn't know you had any family living," Mrs. Dawson said. "Where do they reside?"

Words turned to gravel in her throat. She placed her card on the table, a high trump, using the pause to gather scattered wits. "My brother lives in the north." Blast. Too vague, too evasive. "In Yorkshire."

"Would you not find it more convenient to live closer to your family?" Wanstead's tone was idle, but the tension in his body gave away his interest.

A sudden longing for her family pierced her heart, a pain so sharp that for a moment she couldn't speak. She drew in a steadying breath. "I prefer to live here."

Mrs. Dawson's next card hovered above the table. "You will not find a better county in which to live than Kent, nor a better village than Blendon." She dropped the ace of hearts on the table.

The squire groaned. "That's it then. We lost again, Mrs. Dawson." He wiped his damp brow with his handkerchief. "A very good game, indeed. Anyone for another hand?"

"I regret it is time I went home," Lucinda said. "I promised Annie I would not be late." In truth, she should not have accepted Mrs. Dawson's invitation. Only the vicar's request for support in seeking Mrs. Dawson's agreement to host the fête at the Hall had tempted her to take so bold a step. Unfortunately, Lord Wanstead's presence seemed to make her feel so much more uncomfortable than she usually felt at social occasions. Perhaps because he noticed too much and listened too well.

She rose to her feet and held out her hand to her hostess. "Thank you for a very pleasant evening."

Mrs. Dawson's eyes widened as the gentlemen stood.

To her chagrin, Lucinda realized she had played too grand a lady for the widow of a mere lieutenant. She bobbed a suitably humble curtsey to her hostess and, in no time at all, had made her farewells and retrieved her wrap.

The butler ushered her out of house and into warm evening air smelling of earth washed clean by rain. Beyond the circle of light cast by the porch lantern, the night drew around her like a comforting cloak. Free from prying questions and curious stares, tension streamed away. She let go a sigh of relief. Never again would she let herself be wooed into company. As always, her eagerness had been her undoing. Composure firmly in place, she strode down the squire's gravel drive.

Footsteps crunching behind her brought her to a halt. She whirled around. Her heart picked up speed and rattled in her ears. The approaching bulk outlined by lamplight could only be one person. "Lord Wanstead," she said.

"May I drive you home in my gig, Mrs. Graham?"

How had he extracted himself from Mrs. Dawson's clutches so swiftly? And why? Her pulse stuttered, not in fear precisely, but definitely trepidation. "I wouldn't dream of troubling you, my lord. Please don't leave the party on my account."

"No trouble, Mrs. Graham. Come." He took her elbow, a light guiding touch of fingers and palm, without significant pressure, yet commanding. The warmth from his hand seemed to infuse her skin, spreading from where he touched her arm all the way across her shoulders. To shake off his hand would seem churlish, so she turned in the direction of the stables and quickened her pace.

His hand fell away as he matched her steps. The gig stood waiting in the courtyard with a groom at the horse's head. He must have sent word to the stables before setting out on her trail. Clearly a man of strategy.

If she had realized he would follow, she would have tried to avoid him. To refuse his escort in an open gig now would seem distrustful, especially for a woman alone at night. He assisted her into his vehicle, his hand firm in the hollow of her waist, his height and strength reinforced by the ease with which he helped her up, as if she weighed no more than the tiny Miss Dawson.

She forced herself to ignore the attendant trickle of heat in her veins, the pleasurable shimmer of awareness accompanied by shortness of breath. Her nervousness was a perfectly reasonable reaction to a man who a few short days ago had glared at her in anger.

She settled her skirts and straightened her spine, keeping close to her side of the seat.

He leaped up beside her. "I hope you will forgive Old Bob, here," he said, setting the horse into a steady plod with a flick of his whip.

"It might be faster to walk."

She felt him shift. Her stomach sank. Denbigh hated the swift banter she'd engaged in with her brothers.

"It might be faster if I got between the traces," he said, his voice amused, not tight or fierce or any of those other warning signs of temper. "But I don't want to insult Old Bob, even if he does look as if he'd prefer to ride. It is, after all, a fine evening for a leisurely drive."

"I appreciate your thoughtful offer," she lied.

"If not the means of carrying it out?" He gave a crack of a laugh. "Don't answer that, Mrs. Graham, if you please. My sensibilities cannot stand another of your set-downs."

Was he teasing her? The trickle of heat turned into a river of fire. Her insides tightened and pulsed in a most alarming manner. She shut her eyes, seeking an inner source of calm only to discover her mind churning like an ocean in a storm. Inhaling a quick breath, she caught the scent of his cologne, bay, the faintest hint of lemon, and deeper tones of the man himself. She clutched the side of the carriage like a lifeline and tried to ignore the warm mountain of man at her side. "I would not dream of criticizing your conveyance, my lord, since I have none myself."

"Forgive my levity. A widow, living on an army pension with a young child, must not have an easy time of it."

His quiet murmur sounded sincere, caring. Her heart seemed to still. She squeezed her eyes shut for a brief moment, gathering strength. The man was a menace, a wolf in bear's clothing. "I manage. There are many worse off. Take the children infesting London's streets, for example."

His head turned toward her, but she could not make out his expression in the dark. "We are back to that, are we?"

She clenched her hands, caution advising her to subside into silence, to admit defeat the way she had with Denbigh, yet knowing she would not forgive herself if she did. "Why won't you let the vicar hold the fête on your lands? Annie Dunning tells me that your grandfather always did so."

"Now you mention it, I recall something of the sort." He sounded surprised. "I haven't recalled it for years. My mother didn't like the fuss and bother after my grandfather's death. She wasn't well, you understand," he added quickly. "I do recall having a splendid time as a small lad, though."

"It would be a wonderful way to begin your tenure as earl. With your support, we are sure to get a good turnout. No doubt all the gentry in the county will also want to welcome you."

"Kind of you to think of my welfare, Mrs. Graham." He heaved a sigh. "Before I know it, they will be parading their eligible daughters under my nose."

A smile forced its way to her lips at his gloomy tone. "A daunting prospect indeed."

"Terrifying. I'd sooner face Marshal Ney." He chuckled, a warm deep sound in the dark.

With studied nonchalance, she leaned against the seatback, ignoring a tingle of awareness that seemed to raise the hairs on her arms and the back of her neck. Awareness of him as a man. Of his heat dashing against her side in waves, of his interest in her as a female. She couldn't remember a time when she felt quite so alive, or so much a woman. Sadly, her body lied.

"Mrs. Graham, I must thank you for bringing the Drabets' plight to my attention," he said. "I also apologize for my rudeness."

His voice sounded hoarse, as if used to barking orders rather than delivering apologies.

"I am grateful you were able to have the roof repaired so quickly," she said.

He sighed, a sound all but drowned in the beat of hooves and the creak of wheels. "It is but a temporary patch. Their cottage will need a new roof before the winter. The whole terrace needs extensive work, as you so rightly pointed out."

"An expensive proposition, but worthwhile, I should think?"

"I don't believe I knew a Lieutenant Graham," he said so abruptly she jumped. "What regiment?"

A typical male ploy, to go on the attack as a form of defense. Her brothers and Denbigh were masters of the art. "The Buffs." At least that practised lie came readily to her tongue.

"A fine regiment," he said. "They did a remarkable job at Oporto."

"So I understand." She hesitated, not wanting to be too specific, though she had read the obituary in *The Times*. 'Lieutenant Thomas Graham, age twenty-five, late of the Buffs, killed in a minor skirmish at Avientes'. The family home was inherited by a distant relative, her man of business had discovered. "It was shortly after that…"

"I beg your pardon," he said stiffly. "I should not have brought up so painful subject. I wondered if I might have met your husband. I did not. I am sorry for your loss."

Guilt wracked her at the lies piled upon lies. The breeze tugging at the wisps of hair around her face seemed suddenly chill. "I prefer not to discuss my husband." Her voice sounded colder than she had intended, almost bitter. She pressed her lips together.

Another awkward silence ensued while he apparently digested her words. He must think her a veritable harpy. She let go a breath. "I apologize for my sharpness. It is a difficult subject for me."

"No indeed. Forgive the intrusion."

She relaxed her hands, unclenched her jaw. He would not question her any more about her husband. He was too much of a gentleman to pursue an unwelcome topic.

The dark outline of Brackley Woods took shape, and off to the right a lamp twinkled a greeting. The Briars came into view, a square, comfortably solid shape among the shadows of the forest, a haven from probing questions. The gig halted at the gate in the low privet hedge. "Here you are, Mrs. Graham."

"Thank you, my lord." She gathered her skirts and alighted before he had a chance to leap down to assist.

At the gate, she looked back.

Hugo raised a hand in farewell and watched her glide up the front path. The porch light cast her Rubenesque figure into delicious relief, a shadow painting in graceful motion, a feminine sway to curvy hips. The sight held his gaze far longer than it ought.

A fascinating mixture of opposites, Mrs. Thomas Graham. Sharp-witted and soft-hearted. Outwardly subdued yet strong in her passions, direct of gaze yet secretive. Unremarkable in repose, her face glowed with an inner beauty when she spoke of matters close to her heart, like the fête or her child. While there was nothing wrong with her answers to his questions about her history, she weighed each word carefully as if she feared to trip over her tongue, unless the heat of her argument caused her to forget. The army had taught him enough about men who lied and cheated to recognize avoidance, if not downright bouncers. He found he didn't like to think of her as deceitful.

Mentally he shrugged, urging Old Bob into motion. So the curvaceous widow had secrets. Provided they caused no harm to his friends and neighbors, they were none of his business. A woman with a child had little chance to damage anyone, unless, he thought unwillingly, this desire of hers to raise money masked an attempt to line her pockets. She certainly bore watching. Unfortunately, he feared his interest lay not in her past but in the alluring sway of her skirts and the thought of the warm soft flesh beneath.

Damnation. Had he lost his mind? He needed a drink. A nightcap of brandy would reduce the ache in his leg along with the other ache he thought he'd learned to quell.

The rooms on each side of the front door were in darkness Lucinda noticed as she stepped into the house. A chink of light under the door at the end of the passage steered her steps in the direction of the kitchen. The sound of a male voice gave her pause. Annie was entertaining? She pushed open the door.

Two worried pairs of eyes stared at her, Albert on one side of the table, a mug of tea clenched in his gnarled fist, and Annie on the other. The normal coziness of the small stone kitchen with its gleaming copper pots, old-fashioned stove, and scrubbed wooden furniture seemed lacking.

Albert hauled himself up to his feet. "Good evening, Mrs. Graham."

"Mrs. Graham," Annie said, her voice full of relief. "Thank goodness."

Lucinda's stomach dropped away. "What has happened? Where is Sophia?"

"The lass is fine," Annie said in comforting tones. "Tucked up in her bed. It is not her that has us in a pelter."

Relieved, Lucinda plunked onto a chair. "Then what?"

"Perhaps you'd like a cup of tea," Annie said, pushing to her feet with a grunt and rubbing at her lower back. She reached down a cup and saucer from the dresser shelf. "While Pa tells you all about it."

Lucinda bit back her impatience. A show of anxiety might lead to questions she dare not answer.

Annie poured the milk, then the tea. Lucinda accepted her cup with a smile pasted on stiff lips. "Now, tell me what has happened? What is so important it could not wait until morning?"

"It's Pa," Annie said, her round cheerful face clenching in a rare frown. "He's brought news from the inn."

Lucinda held her breath, her heart too loud in her ears, her fingers tightening around the cup handle.

Albert's corrugated lips pursed as if to contain his excitement. "Remember when you asked our Annie to let you know if any strangers came asking for you?"

Lucinda's stomach churned. Surely too much time had passed for anyone to track her to this small corner of Kent? She set her face into an expression of polite enquiry. "Did someone ask?"

Albert nodded. "There was a Bow Street Runner at the Red Lion this evening, asking Old Peddle if he'd seen a heavy-set woman traveling through here or staying nearby."

The blood seemed to drain from Lucinda's head, leaving her weak and dizzy. She sipped her tea to disguise her panic, her thoughts refusing to form any order. "What did Mr. Peddle say?"

"I pipes up that the widder Mrs. Graham and her little girl came to Blendon three months or more gone."

"What I wants to know, Mrs. Graham," Annie said, "is why he said anything at all?" She glared at her father. "People coming here, asking all manner of questions. What right have they got?"

"Women," he muttered under his breath. "Stands to reason, don't it? If I hadn't mentioned Mrs. Graham, Peddle would've. An' he might forget that she wasn't traveling alone, see? He mightn't think to mention Miss Sophia at all. 'Cause, if he was looking for a lone woman, he wasn't looking for Mrs. Graham, here, was he? Even if she is…" His weathered face flushed as he turned his bright gaze on Lucinda. "But it do seem a bit odd, you mentioning that someone might come looking?"

Despite his advanced years, Albert was far too clever for his own good. Lucinda kept her face calm. "What did the Bow Street Runner say after that?"

Albert slurped a mouthful of tea. "Makes a good cuppa, my lass. He don't say nuffin'. He looked mighty disappointed. He finished his heavy wet, called for his horse, and off he went."

Fighting to remain upright, Lucinda nodded as if it all meant nothing at all. But if this man had really been sent by Denbigh, would he be satisfied? "He said nothing more?"

"No." Albert scowled. "That fool Peddle did mention as how you was on the big side. To my mind, the Runner lost interest the moment I mentioned your daughter."

Lucinda curled her hand around her cup. Damn Denbigh, if it was him, for continuing the hunt. "You are sure he left?" she asked Albert.

"Aye, Mrs. Graham." The old man hesitated. "Are ye in some kind of trouble with law?'

Lucinda swallowed. "I have done nothing wrong. As I told Annie when I first came here, my husband owed money. To some very bad men." She couldn't help how breathless she sounded. Just the thought of someone sent by Denbigh invading her new life sent bone-deep shudders through her body. "I gave them everything belonging to his estate. What I took belonged to me." At least that was the truth.

"You should go to the authorities," Annie said.

"How would I ever prove what is mine and what was his? It isn't possible."

"She's right, lass." Albert swigged the rest of his tea. "Looks like I said the right thing. I'll keep a sharp eye out for that there Runner. But I don't think he'll be back."

If Denbigh had eliminated Blendon from his search, then it might even be the safest place to stay. All she could do was hope Albert was right. If she wasn't safe buried in the depths of the English countryside, she couldn't imagine where she could hide.

Five

DAYLIGHT DRIBBLED THROUGH THE STUDY WINDOW onto a ledger covered in what to Hugo looked like hieroglyphics. Numbers mingled with lists of items in crabbed handwriting. He lifted his gaze to his tearful cook's face, and horror pitched his stomach to the floor, a sensation not unlike the one he'd experienced when faced with a battalion of French. In fact, right now, he'd prefer the French.

He pointed to a particularly disturbing entry. "What is this? Three pots of poison?"

Mrs. Hobb's head with its frizzle of grey curls leaned closer to the page. She scrunched her face. "I think it's raisins, sir. Raisin jelly, that would be. His lordship, your father, liked a bit of raisin jam with his game."

"Well that is a relief."

She cracked a watery smile. "It's a mess, my lord. And no mistake. I'm sorry. I did me best. It's just that the Missus always did it." She meant Hugo's mother. "After that, Mrs. Huxtable took it on. I never learned how. When she left, the old earl didn't seem to care much so I…" she waved helplessly at the ledger. "I didn't dare tell young Mr. Brown it had gone all wrong in case he turned me off."

Damn young Mr. Brown and his organized mind. Hugo sighed inwardly. No. That was unfair. Mr. Brown had done his best. Just as Mrs. Hobb had tried to do hers. This was Father's fault for not hiring a competent housekeeper.

He patted her shoulder. "Nevermind, Mrs. Hobb."

"I suppose you're going to get someone to replace me," the old woman said.

He really should. He gazed at her worried face, its color high from years working over a hot oven. "Not at all. I'll sort this lot out, and then we'll start from scratch."

Her tears dried in an instant. "You're a good man, your lordship. Like your mother, you are."

Look what goodness had got his mother. An early grave.

Damn it. If he didn't get a handle on the household accounts, more money would slip through his fingers. They'd already had an extra delivery of coal they didn't need and could ill afford. It was piled behind the stables waiting for space in the coal cellar. "Run along now, Mrs. Hobb. Leave it to me."

The old woman hobbled out, a hand to her furrowed brow. She really ought to retire, which meant Hugo ought to provide her the means to do so. He just couldn't afford to pay her off and hire both a cook and a housekeeper. Not until he sorted out his finances.

He pulled the ledger in front of him, turned it upside down and discovered that indeed some of the entries had been written that way, too.

Bugger. This was such a waste of his time. There were a myriad of things on the estate demanding his attention. Important things like deciding what to plant and where, and raising the capital to buy seed and animals. If young Mr. Brown caught him doing Mrs. Hobb's accounts, there'd be hell to pay.

The pain in his thigh rode muscle and bone all the way to his back teeth. He massaged his leg in an attempt to deny the call of the brandy decanter at his elbow. If he drank before lunch, he'd be finished by supper. He stared at a patch of blue sky through the small clear space left by the ivy. He needed to get beyond the four walls pressing in on him. For clarity of thought, he needed exercise and the wind on his skin. He'd ride out, take a look at the hay in the top fields, and see if it was ready for cutting before having another go at these wretched accounts.

Hugo galloped Grif home through Brackley Wood, the earthy smell of warm forest reminding him of the better days in Spain. Grif tossed his head playfully, and Hugo let him run, keeping a sharp eye out for low branches.

The trees stopped short at a clearing. Somehow, he felt as if some sixth sense had drawn him to this place. Utter rot. Yet he reined Grif to a walk.

On the clearing's far side, nestled against a thicket of hazel and fronting onto the lane, lay the Dower House, recently renamed The Briars. A picturesque blaze of color filled the flowerbeds within the low privet hedge. He hauled in a quick breath at the sight of a statuesque figure in a straw sunbonnet and high-necked grey gown strolling down the path to the back gate: Mrs. Graham.

She halted and looked at him over the hedge, her gaze coolly assessing.

Why would she not stare? Atop Grif, he was as obvious as a moving mountain. He touched his crop to his hat and walked the stallion closer. "Good afternoon, Mrs. Graham."

A small face peeked out from behind her hip-skimming skirts—the daughter he'd scared half to death the first day they'd met. He frowned, and the face disappeared.

"Good afternoon, my lord." Mrs. Graham sketched a curtsey. The inherently regal grace of her movements struck him anew.

"Lovely day," he said. Tongue-tied dolt. Surely he could say something more original.

"Indeed," she replied with the flicker of a smile he might have missed if he hadn't been looking for some softening in her expression. "It is wonderful to be out of doors at this time of year."

That dealt with the weather. Now what?

They gazed at each other across a gulf bridged by birdsong and the rustle of a breeze in the nearby forest. The translucence of her skin begged his touch. Awareness of the milky skin of her throat and the soft slope of her shoulders leading to the rise of bountiful breasts thickened his blood until he was sure he heard it pumping through his veins. The plain bonnet, banded in black ribbon, and the dove-colored gown couldn't disguise her generous proportions, but they did seem designed to keep all comers at bay. He found it fascinating, alluring, almost…virginal. His cock gave a happy little pulse at the thought. Hell fire.

Grif pranced dangerously.

Hugo cursed under his breath. What the hell was wrong with him? He might not have eased himself with a woman for months, but he was no adolescent boy with out-of-control urges. Since the death of his poor benighted wife, he'd thought there wasn't a woman on earth who could tempt him down the path of lust. Two innocents' deaths on his conscience were more than enough for any man. His ardor cooled with satisfying speed.

The little girl shot forward and held out her arms, saying, "Up."

Grif showed the whites of his eyes. "Steady," Hugo said to the horse.

Mrs. Graham scooped the child into her arms. "I'm so sorry, my lord. Sophia, no."

"Up," the child said again, waving her little hands.

"What does she want?" Hugo asked, working Grif's bit.

A smile transformed Mrs. Graham's face from plain to glowing. "Albert Farrow put her up on Old Bob the time she visited your stables." A worried frown chased the smile away. "Not that she goes there often."

Hugo the ogre. He clenched his fists at the unexpected pang of regret. The stallion danced sideways. He dismounted before the animal did some real damage. "Are you going out?" Another doltish question.

"I am going to the vicarage for tea. I really should not delay." She settled the child on her hip.

"Allow me to accompany you. Even in daylight, it is dangerous for a woman to walk alone in the woods."

"Mr. Brown assured me the shortcut to the village was quite safe."

Brown would. "Nevertheless, one never knows what might occur." He fell into step beside her.

"I suppose you are right. There may be riders galloping hell-for-leather down any one of these paths."

Spirits unaccountably soaring, he smiled at the faint flush on her high cheekbones and the nervous flicker of her tongue over the curve of her full lower lip. "Indeed. Therefore I must insist."

She sighed, a faint expulsion of resignation, but made no further attempt at demurral. Apparently this female had no intention of plying her wiles to keep him at her side. Something tightened in his chest. Pleasant surprise? Or pique? He didn't care to investigate.

They strolled along the cool path winding through the trees. A dove cooed softly somewhere in the pale green canopy. A thrush warbled. A bee blundered by in a hum of wings. With some surprise, Hugo recognized his mood as contented. Had he at last acknowledged the Grange as his home, despite his youthful declaration of hatred? Or was it the deep calm of the woman at his side that stilled his restless spirit? Neither seemed a likely explanation.

"And what is the purpose of your visit to the vicar?" he asked, hoping he did not hear a note of envy in his tone.

"A meeting regarding the village fête."

Her low voice strummed at a chord deep in his belly. "I see?" he said, struggling to command himself into some sort of attention to her words and not her voice. "A worthy cause, I am sure."

The ivory cheek on his side bloomed roses. She lowered her head, the brim of her bonnet obstructing his view of her expression.

A life force thrummed in his veins. The air smelled of green things and new life tinged with her lavender perfume and unique female scent. He'd forgotten the heady pleasure of making a woman blush and the excitement of the chase. It never occurred in the sort of commercial transactions to which he had become accustomed.

"I like to think I can help," she said. "Unfortunately, Mrs. Dawson is completely opposed to the idea." She glanced up at him, barely disguised hope in her gaze.

Her eyes were dark blue, not black, and edged in grey. He'd never seen eyes of that hue before, though the haunting pain in their depths was as familiar as his own face. His stomach clenched at the memory of the pain he'd caused and of his cowardice.

Dammit. When would he learn that he couldn't ride in on his charger and solve people's problems? He'd be just as likely to make them worse.

The child lifted her arms. "Up."

"Determined little thing, isn't she?" he said seeking distraction from his sour thoughts. "Come on then, missy." He whisked the child out of Mrs. Graham's loose hold and tossed her into the saddle.

"Is the horse safe?" Fear tinged Mrs. Graham's voice, her eyes huge as she reached for the child.

Real fear. Justified fear. The kind of fear any woman would feel around him if they knew the truth. He tasted bile.

"Grif is fine all the while I have his bridle." He sounded gruff and defensive when he had intended to reassure. It seemed to work, though, because she let her hands drop to her sides.

He gripped the back of the child's coat. "How's that?"

She kicked her little feet with all the bravado of a Household Cavalryman. "Go."

A chuckle forced its way up from his chest. It felt good as it scraped his throat. "Great heavens, Albert has been teaching her tricks."

"I'm sorry, my lord."

He hated how uncomfortable she sounded. "Don't apologize, Mrs. Graham. The child is a credit to you. Lots of bottom."

"He really is a fine animal." She reached up and ran her hand down the stallion's cheek.

To Hugo's surprise, Grif accepted her touch, much as Hugo would have accepted her fingers caressing his own face. God. He'd let her touch him anywhere she wanted. Her hands would be cool and gentle, light as a butterfly. And they would be firm and strong when—

He glowered. Had he been without a woman so long he would project his lust onto a widow who deserved nothing but respect? He stamped down hard on the flicker of fire in his veins. It died to a slow burn.

She must have thought his anger directed at her because she reached for the child the moment they arrived at a fork in the path, one leading to the village, the other to the Grange. "We really should not impose on you further."

Now he'd frightened her off. Damned good thing, too.

"You will be quite safe from here," he replied, pleased to note he sounded suitably distant, once more in command. He lifted the child down and placed her in her mother's outstretched arms.

She set the child on her feet. "Say thank you, Sophia."

"No," the little girl shouted. "Horsy." She stamped her foot.

Mrs. Graham colored. "As you can see, she is fast becoming spoiled." She bent to face the child at eye level affording Hugo a view of her delicate nape caressed by fine tendrils of light brown hair. He wanted free access to that tender perfection. He fought a sudden feral urge to possess.

"Sophia," Mrs. Graham said. "No tears. If you are naughty, his lordship won't let you ride his horse again."

The little girl looked up at her mother, then at Hugo. She stuck a finger in her mouth.

Hugo nodded.

"Say good-bye and thank you," her mother commanded.

"Sank you," she said around the pink finger. "Bye bye." She waved her other hand.

Mrs. Graham raised her chin and fixed her direct gaze on him in a most fetching way. "Thank you for your indulgence. I really must hurry; it would never do to keep the denizens of Blendon waiting."

"The pleasure was all mine." Not nearly as much pleasure as he wanted.

A smile teased the corner of her mouth in a way he had not seen before, as if she guessed the direction of his thoughts and did not object, and that miniscule softening kindled heat in places he shouldn't be aware of in her presence.

"Give my regards to Reverend Postlethwaite," he said. "He has my deepest sympathy. At least in regards to the other denizens."

Laughter lightened her expression for the briefest of moments, and her dark blue eyes danced with points of light, like the reflection of stars in the sky at dusk. "I'll be sure to pass on your condolences."

Pride in his ability to make this reserved woman laugh held him enthralled. "Remind him of my invitation to drop by."

She nodded gravely. "I certainly will. I suppose you wouldn't reconsider the idea of holding the fête on the lawn at the Grange?"

Trapped. A brilliant maneuver. And one that deserved to be acknowledged. "I will give it serious consideration. I would, however, require a favor in return."

She recoiled a step.

So, she was not unaware of the attraction humming between them. He masked his delight behind a neutral expression. "My cook's household accounts are in a dreadful condition, utterly confused. Postlethwaite bragged you were good at that sort of thing. I wondered if you might assist Mrs. Hobb in sorting them out?"

She blinked and angled her face away, staring off into the distance almost as if…as if disappointed at the innocence of his request. He smiled wryly to himself for wishful thinking.

"Are you saying, my lord, that in exchange for assisting with your accounts, you will consent to hold the fête on your property?"

Dear God, persistent and not very trusting. "Yes. A foolish idea. Forget I mentioned it."

A triumphant expression crossed her face. "It is too late to go back on your word, my lord. When shall I meet with your housekeeper?"

When indeed. The glint of excitement in her gaze made him want to laugh like a fool. Instead, he looked away, recalled the miserable state of his affairs, and wished he'd never strolled down this particular path. "I would need positive results before I made a final commitment. Are you agreeable?"

Could he be more unreasonable, more discouraging? He thought not.

She nodded. A half-smile curved her full bottom lip, and her soft round cheeks blushed a delicate shade of rose and tantalized his very being. It was as if a veil had dropped away from some lush eastern beauty, and yet it was only the briefest of smiles replaced instantly by a questioning frown. "Would Wednesday be soon enough?"

"As good as any other day, Mrs. Graham." He executed the sharp bow of a crusty old soldier.

"Then I bid you good afternoon, my lord."

Dismissed, like a junior officer. Hugo had to admire her style. The woman would put Wellington to shame. He swung up onto Grif, careful to show no sign of pain, and watched her saunter along the path with Sophia's hand in hers. Her hem swished with each motion of those exquisitely rounded hips beneath the straight fall of her gown.

The ache in his groin joined the dull throb of his thigh, fueling a flare of anger. What had he been thinking? Hadn't he learned anything at all? Women of gentle birth must be kept at a distance. After what he'd done to his wife, he wasn't fit to touch a decent woman.

What was so fascinating about this one? Was it her magnificent body or her no-nonsense air or the glimpses of passionate depths that crumbled his vows? Did the knowledge she, too, had suffered a loss so deep she could not speak of it bring her closer in spirit? Or was it her air of secrecy? If he stripped bare her cloak of mystery, would she lose her uncanny allure?

He wanted to bare everything.

The image had him as hard as a rock.

Devil take it.

Six

IN THE SMALLER OF THE TWO BEDROOMS ON THE FIRST floor of The Briars, Lucinda bent over the sleeping Sophia and pressed her lips to a delicate blue-veined temple. Eyelashes feathered on the child's delicate cheeks, and a tiny bubble moistened the rosebud lips. So tender, so precious, and so terribly vulnerable.

After so many years of praying for a child, to have had this little angel placed in her arms seemed like a gift from the gods. Once false move, and she might be ripped away. The visit of the Bow Street Runner showed just how delicate a thread held her world together.

After a final twitch of the bedclothes, she picked up the candle and hurried downstairs to the kitchen. Beneath the rack of shining pots, a scarlet-cheeked Annie looked up from rolling out pastry. She raised a brow.

"She's asleep," Lucinda said. Marmalade, the orange ball of fluff who'd arrived, all skin and bones, at their door one morning, clawed his way up her skirt. She freed him from the fabric and rubbed her cheek against his soft furry face. "She shouldn't wake for an hour or so. I will surely be back by then." She deposited the kitten back in his basket by the hearth. "I really shouldn't impose on you like this. You have enough to do."

"Ho hum, Mrs. Graham. Your little lass is no trouble at all. I'll get this pie cooking, and when she wakes, she can help me make some jam tarts with the leftover dough. I'm right glad to have found this work, 'til my Sam gets his first wages."

"He has found work, then?"

"Not yet, more's the pity. The vicar's been sayin' there might be work at the Grange now his lordship is working the land again, but there's no sign of it."

The other woman's worried expression pulled at Lucinda's heart. If only she could offer hope, but unless there were more horses on the earl's estate and more farm implements in need of repair, there wasn't enough work at the local smithy to support an extra man with a growing family. Annie was right; there was little sign of improvement at the Grange. All Lord Wanstead seemed to do was ride around on his stallion or hide out in his study. He was no better than Denbigh, who spent all his time gambling.

"Sam is a good man. I'm sure he will find something before the child is born," she said.

Annie spread her fingers over her swollen stomach. "I hope so."

The gesture twisted what felt like a sharp blade in between Lucinda's ribs. She would never know the joy of carrying a child in her body. She'd tried every remedy known to woman. The red hartshorn suggested by her mother hadn't worked, nor had inhaling the fumes from catmint as advised by her doctor. She had wanted to try an electric bed, something that one Harley Street doctor had advertised, but when she had suggested it to Denbigh, he'd taken it as an insult to his manhood.

Why pine for something that could never happen when she had Sophia and she had her freedom, both impossible dreams only a few short months ago.

"I've lived in Blendon all my life," Annie said. "I hates the thought of leaving. And I'll miss your little one when I goes."

"Oh, Annie, we will miss you, too."

Dabbing at her eyes with the corner of her apron, Annie sniffed. "Isn't it time you left? His lordship will be wondering where you are."

Truth to tell, and despite the increasing patter beneath her breastbone, Lucinda was looking forward to the afternoon immensely. The chance to glean detailed information about her brother's regiment in Spain beckoned seductively. And the chance to spend time with *him,* a little voice whispered. A voice she detested.

She retrieved her coat and hat from the coat stand beside the back door. The sound of a vehicle outside gave her pause.

"Who's that, then?" Annie asked.

Lucinda ran from the kitchen to the parlor and drew the curtain aside. "Why, it is Albert with the gig."

"Well now, there's what I call considerate," Annie said lumbering into the room. "His lordship must be very keen on that there invention."

"Inventory," Lucinda said, her knees feeling wobbly. Was Wanstead worried she would fail to keep her appointment? The flutters she'd been denying ever since lunch seemed to have turned into a bevy of grasshoppers jumping around in her stomach.

She glanced at her reflection in the mirror and saw the truth, a plain and plump pretend-to-be widow grateful for a crumb of attention from a handsome soldier. Her stomach headed for the floor. Whatever the reason for the warmth in his gaze, it had nothing to do with her and everything to do with the poor shape of his accounts. There must be another way to convince him to host the fête without the torture of looking at something as tempting as fresh cream cakes and knowing she couldn't taste. Why, it was worse than Denbigh's diet of dry crackers and vinegar. Unfortunately nothing had occurred to her so far, and if she failed to appear, he would no doubt simply disappear back into his lair and be glad of the excuse.

Never had she seen a man so desperate for company. Loneliness lurked amid the wintry bleakness of the front he presented to the world. He tried to hide it with bluster and gruff questions, but she wasn't fooled. She knew too much about desperation.

Oh, yes. The fête would not only be good for the villagers, but it would be good for him, too. Her feelings about him did not matter one whit. Indeed, she must not have feelings. This was not about her. It was about helping the people of the village. She took a deep breath and headed for the front door.

"Don't you worry about the little one," Annie said.

Lucinda wasn't worried about Sophia, not one little bit. It was her own peace of mind that seemed to be in danger.

Inside the Grange's hall, the ancient Jevens took her pelisse. "Good afternoon, Mrs. Graham. His lordship is in the library."

Lord Wanstead stuck his head out of a door. "Ah, there you are at last."

Her pulse gave a strange little hop as if the grasshoppers had found their way into her veins. She clasped her hands at her waist, holding down a nervousness she had not felt since she emerged from the schoolroom to attend her first ball.

"Ask Mrs. Hobb to join us, please, Jevens," Lord Wanstead said. "And bring tea for Mrs. Graham."

"At once, my lord."

Lord Wanstead gestured for her to enter.

As Lucinda passed by him into the library, she inhaled the enticing aroma of bay and warm male. She forced herself to focus on her surroundings. Leather-bound books lined two walls from ceiling to floor. Lucky man. The only reading material in her London townhouse had been *The Gentleman's Magazine* and *La Belle Assemblée*.

"Please, be seated." He indicated one of the overstuffed chairs by the unlit fire. Chairs large enough for his big frame. Comfortable for her, too. She imagined him sitting here of an evening, cigar in hand, reading a book or a newspaper. Or playing chess. A game was in progress on a fine mahogany board in front of the hearth. Black seemed to be on the run. She shook her head at the offered seat. "I would sooner get straight to work, your lordship. I have to be back when Sophia awakes from her nap."

His firm lips pressed together, whether in annoyance at her blunt speaking or disappointment, she could not be sure, indifference replaced it so quickly, but once again a sense of his loneliness swept over her. Anyone would be lonely living in a house that echoed with the lack of human presence.

She repressed a shiver and pointed to the table by the window containing writing implements and a ledger. "Is that where I am to work?"

"Yes, indeed. Please sit down. Mrs. Hobb will be along momentarily."

She took her place at the table.

A moment later, Jevens marched in with a silver tea tray. Behind him tiptoed an elderly woman with crisp grey curls, gaunt, wrinkled cheeks, and a tin box under her arm.

"Set the tray on the table," Lord Wanstead ordered. "Mrs. Hobb, sit down. Listen to Mrs. Graham. She is here to help."

With Wanstead looking like a surly bear and issuing commands in parade-ground voice, was it any wonder the poor woman seemed scared out of her wits?

Lucinda gave her a welcoming smile. "Yes, do sit down, Mrs. Hobb. I assume those are the receipts in that box? You can set them between us." Jevens set the tea tray at her elbow. It contained three cups and saucers in addition to a fine silver tea service. She glanced over at his lordship. "Would you like some tea, Lord Wanstead?"

"No, thank you." He sat on the white side of the chessboard. "I am sure I can leave everything in your capable hands."

She blinked. It had been a long time since anyone described her as capable, not since she used to help her father with his business affairs. A warm glow spread out from the center of her chest, rose up her neck, and heated her face. Good lord. He'd made her blush. Again. A slight smile kicked up one corner of his straight stern mouth, deepening her heat.

Swiftly, she turned her attention back to pouring the tea. Mrs. Hobb's hands were trembling so hard that Lucinda was not surprised when the elderly lady made no attempt to pick up her cup.

Opening the card-covered ledger at the spot where a red ribbon marked the last entries, Lucinda barely repressed a cry of dismay.

Beside her, Mrs. Hobb gave a little moan. "It's a terrible mess, ma'am."

"Do you think you can make head or tail of it, Mrs. Graham?" Wastead asked.

She turned in her seat and met his hard piercing gaze over the rim of a glass full of brandy. He tossed the whole thing off in one swallow. She tried not to wince. "It will be fine if we take it one step at a time." She flipped through the earlier pages until she found columns of neat figures and readable entries. "See. This looks like a good place to start."

"Oh," Mrs. Hobb cried. "That's from a year ago. It is going to take hours to put it straight."

"Take as much time as you need, Mrs. Graham," his lordship said. "I will be eternally in your debt."

She might be here for all eternity. "I doubt we can complete all the work in one afternoon. We will see how far we get and then decide what is to be done next."

In no time at all, she had a page of her own entries written, debits and credits reconciled to receipts. The clock in the hall struck three. An hour had passed already? Lucinda straightened her back aware, of a knot between her shoulder blades. Mrs. Hobb looked ready to drop. "I think that will be enough for today," Lucinda said.

"Yes, Mrs. Graham. Thank you." Mrs. Hobb popped up to her feet. She made a grab for the tray and whisked out of the door.

"My word," Lucinda muttered. "I had no idea she was so spry." She stacked the receipts they'd matched against the entries in the ledger into a pile.

A soft deep chuckle behind her made her jump. Her heart pounded wildly against her ribs. Dash it. She'd forgotten all about him. He'd come up behind her without her noticing and now leaned over her shoulder, warm and large and very male. "How bad is it?"

She struggled to get her breathing under control and turned to the page where she had started to enter everything over again. "Quite bad," she admitted. "You see some items have been paid for twice and others not at all, or at least not so far…"

He bent his dark head closer, the better to follow her pointing finger.

Much too close. She nudged the book in his direction. He didn't take the hint. His shoulder all but brushed against hers, his breath stirring the air at her cheek. From the corner of her eye, she observed the unyielding angles of his face, the large manly nose and fierce jutting brow, combining to create stark, unrefined male beauty on a magnificent scale. Yet beneath his aura of cool self-sufficiency, which gave the impression of a man in control of himself and his world, there permeated a strong sense of sadness.

It was none of her business. "There are so many mistakes that I wonder you do not find yourself under the hatches, quite honestly."

"Mr. Brown has managed to hold the creditors off, I gather."

She closed the ledger and frowned. "You don't think he…"

"That he has been cheating me? No. My father played deep. He kept his steward in ignorance of his state of affairs by handing cash to Mrs. Hobb to pay the most pressing bills while he drained the estate of every penny."

She swung around in her seat and stared into his shadowed gaze.

He gave a short, bitter laugh. "Don't ask me why. And things are not in such a bad case they cannot be put to rights. But I do need to know who is owed what. I would very much appreciate it if you would keep what I have told you in confidence."

Trust. It sparked to life a place she thought Denbigh had killed, the eager part of her spirit thirsting for approval and respect. She managed a shaky smile. "Yes, of course."

Impatient strides carried him to the chessboard, and he stared down at it blindly. Perhaps he already regretted his frankness.

She packed the receipts neatly in their metal box, closed the ledger, and rose. "When would you like me to continue with this?"

As if he had not heard, he stood in the middle of the room, alone like some castaway on a storm-swept island, staring down at the chessboard.

The black pieces shone like ebony, while the white were ivory. "A magnificent set," she said, joining him.

"It was my grandfather's. I have another in the study that I brought back from Spain."

Unthinking, she moved the black rook three squares, cutting off his queen.

"Nice move," he murmured. He moved a pawn, forcing a retreat or the loss of her queen. She tapped her chin with her forefinger. "Now you do have me in a pickle. Unless…" She moved her king, dropping into the chair to study her next move.

He moved his knight and sat down, leaning back and regarding her from beneath slightly lowered lids. She suddenly felt like a rabbit being eyed by a keen-eyed wolf who couldn't make up his mind if he was hungry or just wanted to play. "Your move." His deep voice caressed skin suddenly sensitive. A shiver rippled across her shoulders. Her limbs softened. She could hardly breathe in a room that seemed strangely airless. A pulse beat hard and raw in her feminine core.

This had to stop. She had no right to be attracted to this man. And marriage had proved she was as much a woman as the chair on which she sat. She should never have touched the chess piece, but having done so, she needed to finish the game quickly. Trying to ignore the intensity of the gaze directed at her face, she tracked the consequences of each possible move. Only one held the slightest chance of winning. Or she could concede, let him think her a fool. Even as it occurred to her, she knew she would not give up. She'd win or lose fair and square.

She played her usual cautious game, Lord Wanstead countering her moves aggressively but with none of Geoffrey's recklessness to give her an advantage. While they played, they chatted. She learned about his taste in books and discovered him to be as familiar with Shakespeare as she. He quizzed her about the plays she'd seen. Careful to give the impression of a small northern playhouse, she waxed enthusiastic about Mr. Kean at his best as Richard III and Mrs. Weston in her famous role of Portia.

Each time he reached forward to move a piece, the sharp scent of his cologne deepened by undertones of virile man filled her nostrils. Each time she caught his glance, she fought to ignore her stomach's betraying flutter of female appreciation. With each passing moment, the chord of awareness between them stretched tighter.

"What really made you settle in this part of the country?" he asked.

Taken aback by the turn in the conversation, she hesitated. To hide her confusion, she moved her bishop a little too recklessly. "I saw the house advertised in *The Times*. It sounded perfect."

"You are a brave woman, Mrs. Graham." The hint of a smile transformed his stern face into something far too sensual.

She quelled the urge to sigh. "Brave?"

"Yes." He tilted his head on one side. "Managing alone with never a complaint."

She could not prevent the wry twist to her lips. "I have little choice in the matter."

A green gaze speared her like a well-honed blade. "You did not think about going north, to your brother?"

He didn't forget one thing she said. "No. We do not get along."

He shot a quick glance at the table across the room. "Fortunately for me, I think."

Again the hint of a heart-stopping smile and a flicker of warmth in his gaze.

Heat rushed through her veins. Her pulse jumped and then pattered wildly. She clasped her hands in her lap to hide their tremble. "I believe it is your move, my lord."

Unbelievably, he grinned, open, playful, and a menace to her heart. "Chess, you mean."

"What else would I mean?" she shot back, shoring up her defenses against this show of charm, knowing full well he referred to his rapier questions and her swift parries.

He moved his bishop to block her king. "Check."

The sheer daring stole her breath. She hadn't seen it coming. She had let him distract her concentration. Trapped. There were a few moves left, but all led to one place. His victory.

She tipped her king, conceding the game.

"Very gracious of you, Mrs. Graham," he murmured.

"Clearly I am playing a master."

He grimaced. "Played a lot of chess in the Peninsular. There wasn't much else to do in the winter besides hunt or gamble."

"You don't hunt or gamble?"

"Oh, I hunted." He gave a short laugh. "With meat in short supply, the odd hare turned a meal into a banquet."

"It's a hard life," she said, at once thinking of her brother and his brief letters home.

"Not so bad in winter quarters," he said. "Apart from the boredom." He gestured to the board. "Hence the skill at chess." His eyes crinkled at the corners, irresistible laughing eyes, a rare sight. A desire to touch those creases left her dizzy. "But you can't tell me you are a novice, Mrs. Graham. Good strategy that, with your queen. You gave me some anxious moments."

His generosity cracked another chink in the impenetrable wall around her heart. "Thank you, my lord."

"Perhaps I should give you a chance at revenge?"

The teasing light in his eyes served only to increase the tumult in her mind. Unsure how to answer, she offered a smile. His eyes widened and flared with heat, all traces of bleakness fleeing like fog on a hot day. She wanted to lean across the game, place her palm to the hard plane of his jaw, feel the warmth of his skin against hers, slide her fingers into the dark curls of his hair at his collar, and press her mouth to his. Inner muscles contracted at the thought of his firm full lips melding with hers.

His hot glance excited her in ways she'd never experienced, sparked violent fires in her blood and turned her insides to mush. Her husband's courtship had been a mere ripple on her youthful pond compared to this surging tide of sensation.

In an effort to avoid his challenge, she dropped her gaze to his beautiful mouth. The sensual lips curved in wicked temptation as if he knew exactly what she experienced deep inside.

He leaned forward a fraction, reached out, and touched her jaw with a soldier's calloused fingertips, his thumb grazing her cheek. A brief yet searing touch.

Her heart thundered. The blood seemed to ebb from her mind and flow to some place deep in her center. The desire to meet him halfway, to offer her lips to him, dragged at her spine. The slightest move in his direction would be all the permission he required.

Why? Why was he doing this? Did he think her a lonely, unattractive widow grateful for any signs of affection? This new game reeked of excitement and danger. She had the premonition that to lose might wound something far more important that her pride.

She drew back, out of reach and out of range of his hypnotic draw on her body. "I really must go." The words left her feeling drained.

He tilted his head, clearly puzzled by her withdrawal. "Routed, Mrs. Graham?"

A gentler jibe than perhaps she deserved. "Simply regrouping, my lord." She rose to her feet.

He stood up. "Come again tomorrow."

She shook her head. "The vicar has organized a meeting to discuss the fête."

"Friday then?"

This was her moment to refuse point blank. Wildness thrummed a beat in her veins hard to ignore. In this short hour or two, she'd forgotten her fears of Denbigh and her anxieties about the future. He acted like a drug on her system, addictive.

"I really cannot leave Sophia."

Pinpoints of emerald danced in his eyes. "Bring her with you."

She rallied weakly. "It really is not my place to be poking around in your private matters like this. It is different with the church accounts. The vicar is accountable to the parish officers. But this? It is much too personal. What you really need, my lord, is a wife."

He stiffened and went utterly still. Long moments passed. "I had a wife, Mrs. Graham."

Had? That meant... Her heartbeat slowed. "I'm sorry, my lord," she whispered. "I didn't know."

His eyes shuttered, leaving her on the outside and chilled. "Your sympathy is misplaced, Mrs. Graham, believe me. My wife was the one who deserved pity." His forbidding expression precluded the asking of questions, almost as if he wanted her to believe the worst—that he had somehow harmed his wife. A dire warning.

Even as she stared, nonplussed, he rose. Lurching off balance, he grabbed at the bell pull. The unsteady motions of a man deeply foxed.

She eyed the dregs in the brandy decanter beside his chair. He must have emptied it while she was engrossed with Mrs. Hobb. Was that the reason he found her of interest? Blurred of vision and mind, he didn't notice her faults? And yet he'd seemed perfectly lucid during their game. A sour taste filled her mouth. A lonely man in his cups seeking solace. No doubt he'd see her in a different light when the fog of brandy cleared. She should be grateful for that.

A chill enveloped her, as if the spark of life he'd fired had been snuffed out with a single puff. She headed for the door. "Please do not trouble your butler, my lord. I know my way." Aware of his furious frown, she scuttled from the room.

Mr. Jevens met her in the hall, her pelisse in his hand. Before he could speak, the library door swung wide.

With the light behind him, Lord Wanstead's features remained cast in shadow. He leaned against the door-jamb. "Jevens, require Albert to drive Mrs. Graham home and then bring brandy." His deep tones rang off the medieval rafters like a knight of old roaring at his minions. Well, knights of old were long gone, and she'd fought for and won her independence. "It is not necessary, my lord," she said. "I can walk."

"I know you can walk, but you will go with Albert." He retreated into his lair and banged the door shut.

"Better if we do as he says, Mrs. Graham," Jevens said shuffling down the side passage.

Oh, heavens, she had not said no to his request that she return on Friday.

Seven

HE NEEDED A WIFE. HAH. HUGO STARED AT THE PIECES won and lost in their close run game. Was she putting herself forward to fill the position? Somehow he didn't think so. Was that why he'd reacted so badly? God dammit. He didn't want a wife.

But he did want Mrs. Graham.

He wanted her on a most carnal level. Nay. While her voluptuous body called to him, the intelligence lurking deep in those mysterious dark blue eyes had him fascinated. Intelligence mixed with wariness. A strange and heady combination.

He didn't fault Mrs. Graham for her need for privacy, but her caution ran deeper than mere discretion. The hunted quality to her gaze when he questioned her too closely gave her away. It was as if she expected a cage door to slam shut with her on the wrong side of the bars.

Everything in him wanted to drive out the fear and leave the sparkle only hinted at when one of those rare smiles curved her lips. Fool. Making more of what ailed him than simple physical attraction. He hadn't been with a woman of Mrs. Graham's caliber in a very long time, and beneath her cool demeanor he sensed a smoldering heat. Like a charcoal burners' kiln, no matter how cool she seemed on the outside, fires hotter than Hades burned within.

Jevens entered with the brandy and a disapproving expression. "Will there be anything else, my lord?"

"No thank you." Aware of the tremble in his hand, he waited for the butler to withdraw before pouring a glass of steadying heat. He took a long slow pull and rubbed absently at his thigh. He flexed his knee a couple of times, seeking ease from the nagging pain. It felt worse than ever—hell, it looked worse. He'd probably have to see the bloody surgeon in London after all.

At the sound of wheels on gravel, he stared at the window as if he could see beyond his reflection to her upright figure in the gig and her calm expression beneath the brim of her plain bonnet.

It wasn't appropriate, but damn he adored her smile, the way her cheeks grew rounder, like succulent peaches. His own lips curved in response to the image. He would like to hear her really laugh. Not that he gave anyone much cause for laughter. Nor should he, if he remained true to his vow. Beyond anything, he must respect her loyalty to a husband who had given his life for his country. A pang of envy twisted in his chest. Envy for a dead man?

Possibly. He just wished he knew what put the fear in her eyes. Something from her past? This brother perhaps? Whatever or whoever it was, it had driven the life he occasionally saw in her eyes into hiding.

He shook his head. She clearly did not need his help. He had gone against his better judgment in allowing her to remain at the Dower House, and it should be enough.

It wasn't, though. Nowhere near enough. He would get to the bottom of what troubled her, even if it meant hosting the damned village fête.

As for him, a simple case of lust for a bosom fulsome enough to fill his hands to overflowing and the thought of a pair of soft creamy thighs clenching his hips must be ignored. He shifted in his chair and forced his mind in other directions. Breaking through her barriers of reserve would require as much planning as a military strategy. It would take time.

His thigh throbbed and burned. The doctor said the leg needed time to heal. He needed time to discover what had Mrs. Graham looking over her shoulder. He poured a snifter of brandy and sank deeper into the cushions.

He didn't have much money, but he certainly had plenty of time.

"Good morning, Mrs. Graham."

Startled, Lucinda straightened from her task of cutting roses to take indoors.

Booted and carrying a whip, Lord Wanstead stood the other side of her hedge. Her pulse faltered and skipped in the stupidest way. She frowned. "I did not hear you ride up." Not a warm greeting by any means. But then she didn't feel particularly friendly. She felt skittish, nervous, out of breath.

He grimaced. "I drove my carriage." He slapped his whip against his thigh.

"Was there something I can do for you, my lord?"

"Yes," he said. "It is a fine morning, and I have something to show you."

Her mouth fell open. "You do?"

He grinned like a boy caught with his hand in the biscuit barrel. "I want to show you the field. For the fête."

The glimmer in his eyes started a hum along her veins and flooded her skin with very pleasant warmth. The very real effort she made to quell the sensation did not prevail.

She shook her head. "Far better you take Reverend Postlethwaite, my lord."

The pleased expression faded. "My hosting the fête was your suggestion."

"The vicar is in charge of the committee."

"I would appreciate your endorsement for my idea," he said with a gravity she did not quite trust. "You see, I remembered that my grandfather always used the bottom field near the stream when he hosted the fête."

So this was how he had contrived to avoid opening his home to his neighbors. "I see."

He looked rather deflated at her grudging tone. "It's a good spot. Not so far for the villagers to walk, you see. Take a look before turning up your nose."

But if she started gallivanting around the country-side with his lordship, people were sure to talk. She had already risked far too much by offering to help his housekeeper. "I have many matters requiring my attention today."

"I know. You have your committee meeting this afternoon. You will want to discuss my suggestion with them."

Dash it. Did he have an answer for everything? "But Sophia…"

Annie stuck her head out of the back door, caught sight of his lordship, and turned as red as a beetroot. "My lord," she gasped and ducked an awkward curtsey, her rounded belly making it impossible to do much more than bend her neck. "I heard talking and wondered who was out here. I'm sorry if I interrupted."

"Mrs. Dunning, is it not?" Lord Wanstead asked.

Annie beamed. "Yes, my lord."

"Are you able to care for Miss Sophia for an hour or two? Mrs. Graham and I have some business to conduct."

Lucinda stared at him. The arrogant rogue. She was supposed to be a respectable widow, not some flighty debutante out driving in Hyde Park. She opened her mouth to refuse.

"Yes, my lord," Annie said. "You go, Mrs. Graham. I'll take Sophia to the village; she can play with the twins."

Dash it all, would no one stand up to him? "I have to attend the meeting this afternoon."

"Well, there you are then," Annie said. "I will take care of the little one, as we arranged, and his lordship can drop you off at the vicarage."

Sophia squeezed past Annie. "Twins?" she said, with a brilliant smile.

Lucinda gave a sigh of exasperation. They were all against her. How could she deny a look like that on a child's face? "Very well. I will get my shawl." She hurried inside, giving Annie instructions as she went.

Back outside on the front doorstep, she halted at the sight of a matched pair of ebony horses and a high-perch phaeton waiting in the lane.

"Oh my," she breathed.

Lord Wanstead chivied her forward. "They arrived last night." He patted one of the shining flanks.

They were magnificent specimens with glossy coats and deep chests. "They are beautiful. I had no idea you owned such fine animals. You are a good judge of horseflesh, my lord."

He gave her a sharp stare. "Apparently so are you, Mrs. Graham. Since I knew Albert couldn't care for them at this time in his life, I sent them to my hunting box during my absence."

This bear seemed to lack teeth or claws or whatever they used to rip things apart. At least when it came to those he cared about. "How thoughtful of you, my lord."

He frowned. "Common sense."

Kindness, even if he wouldn't admit it. The more she got to know him, the more she realized the gruff exterior hid a gentle soul. "If we are going to look at the grounds and be back in time for the meeting, we must make haste."

The teasing glance that had so unnerved her on Wednesday rested once more on her face. "Allow me to assist you."

While she guessed his intent, she didn't quite believe he could lift her so high until she took flight with his hands around her waist. It felt wonderfully feminine. As she let her hands rest on those broad, broad shoulders and felt the sinew and muscle ripple beneath her fingers, she momentarily forgot the past, the mistakes, the pain. She smiled down at him.

He winked, and she felt herself blush like a schoolgirl.

As he set her on the box, a grimace of pain tightened his lips. She followed his progress around the carriage with narrowed eyes. He definitely hadn't been drinking. She would have smelled the spirits on his breath. Even so, an odd jerkiness interrupted the flow of his natural athletic grace. A well-disguised limp? One that had worsened since his arrival? He was proud enough to hide the effects of his wound.

He climbed up beside her and took up the reins.

"Does your injury still bother you?" she asked.

A startled expression crossed his face. He busied himself turning the carriage in the lane and urging the horses out at a smart clip. He made the whole exercise look effortless. Having watched Geoffrey learn to handle the ribbons and having once tried her own hand at it, she could only admire his skill.

The carriage turned onto the road bounded by the Grange wall on one side and a hedgerow on the other and headed toward Blendon. As they bowled along, she fought to ignore his strongly muscled thigh alongside hers, his broad shoulders taking up too much room, and the lemony scent of his soap that scrambled the thoughts in her brain and turned her insides to warm porridge.

"Does it bother you?" she asked again, for something to say as a distraction from those unruly sensations. "Your wound?"

He shrugged. "It gives me a bit of trouble on wet days," he said. "And when I've been sitting too long."

And no doubt gave him a twinge when he lifted someone the size of a pony, even if he was too polite to say so. Was the wound the reason he staggered occasionally? Not the brandy? "Should you seek the advice of a doctor?"

"A rather personal question, Mrs. Graham." The chill was back in his gaze.

She clutched her reticule tighter. "It is altogether too personal to show up at a single woman's house and take her gallivanting around the countryside in what I've heard young men in London call a lady-killer. However, here we are."

"Do you know much about what young men in London say?"

There it was again, the careful probing. Once more he had her on the defensive, and in order to avoid her question to boot.

"Even those in the north have heard tales of the great metropolis." Her brothers had talked of little else as they chased their manhood.

"Really. From whom?"

"My husband."

He stared straight ahead, lips pressed together in a thin straight line.

Reminding him of her widowed state served as a checkmate, apparently. She tucked that knowledge away and leaned back against the well-sprung seat, enjoying the warmth of the sun on her face and inhaling air scented by new-mown hay and sweet clover. The light breeze stirred the profusion of frothy wild parsley growing along the verge. Blackbirds and sparrows serenaded from the hedgerows.

He turned off the main road and entered what appeared to be a cart track. The brambles reached out to scrape the paintwork on each side of the carriage while an arch of beech filtered golden rays onto the shady track.

"How pretty," she said. "Where does it lead?"

"You'll see."

Back to the gruff answers. Better that than probing questions. "No doubt. And yet I would like to have some idea of where I am headed."

"Why?"

"You said it wasn't far from the village, and yet we seem to have turned in the other direction."

"Suspicious and bossy," he muttered.

"I beg your pardon?"

"I said not only are you suspicious, you also like to rule the roost." He sent her a sidelong glance as if to test her reaction, but the twinkle in his eyes took the sting from his words.

The horses halted at a dead end bounded by trees on three sides before she could think of a suitable retort. Somewhere in the distance she heard the sound of running water.

"This is as far as we can go in the carriage," he said. "The rest of the way will be on foot."

She grabbed onto his last words the way Sophia reached for a biscuit. "I am sure the ground is far too damp for walking."

"Nonsense." He sounded altogether too smug, and she glared at him as he helped her down. Although he didn't hold her longer than was needed to set her on her feet, on his release the heat from his hands lingered on flesh that once crawled at the feel of a man's touch, yet now seemed to regret the loss. A shockingly pleasurable sensation and one she must not notice.

He fished around under the seat, producing a hamper and what looked like a rolled-up tent.

She frowned. "What is this, sir?"

"I would hate for you to miss your lunch."

He cast her an innocent look. Having grown up with four brothers, it didn't fool her one little bit. For all her attempts at distance, he was clearly as aware of her reactions to him as she was herself and had decided to push her to the limit.

She repressed the urge to laugh at his bold maneuver. "The ground is far too damp for eating out of doors."

He waved the bundle in his other hand. "Groundsheet and blanket." Those wicked green sparkles were dancing in his eyes again. He was so sure he'd won. "A trick I learned in Spain. Sleeping on bare ground leaves one stiff and sore by morning."

She shuddered. "I can imagine."

He laughed. "Most of the time we billeted with the townsfolk."

"Yes, my b—Tom wrote to me about how bad those billets were, especially if the French used them first."

He did not seem to notice her slip of the tongue. "Wrote to you, did he? Then you know a good deal more about it than most people in England. They seem to think it is all a glorious adventure."

"I have no such illusions."

A breath of disgust hissed through his teeth. "Damn my runaway tongue."

He looked so contrite, almost miserable, that she couldn't help but nod.

He held out his hand. "Would you care to take my arm?" The return to formality chilled her as if the sun had disappeared behind one of the lazy clouds drifting across the blue sky. While her mind told her to welcome it, a tiny ache squeezed her chest. This had to stop. No matter how much she might wish for things to be different, she had nothing to offer this man, or any other.

"I can manage, thank you." She followed his broad back over verge and stile and along a path skirting a copse of hazel and birch.

The trees ended at an open space which in her younger and fanciful days she might have labeled magical. Bounded on one side by a babbling brook and shielded from the lane by the stand of trees, an expanse of emerald grass spread before them like a carpet. A small wooden bridge with a basket-weave handrail led across the stream to a Romanesque-looking summerhouse.

"Oh, yes," she said, circling. "This is perfect. We could set up the booths there against the trees. Over there we could have games, you know, three-legged race, egg and spoon, that sort of thing for the children."

Hearing his sharp intake of breath and a curse, she turned to look at him and was shocked by the pain in his expression.

"I'm sorry. Here I am babbling on, and your leg is hurting you. You should have let me carry some of that stuff."

"Stuff?" He looked blank for a moment and then placed the hamper and the bundle on the ground. He wiped a hand across his eyes as if to clear his vision. "I'm sorry. What were you saying?"

He must have wrenched his leg again. Since he seemed disinclined to discuss his distress, she could only ignore it. "I was simply waxing poetical about the beauty of this spot and deciding where we ought to set up the various booths and events."

"Peddle can set up over there," he said, his face assuming its normal stern lines. "Lots of shade and far enough from the water that no one will fall in."

"We would need an awning," she said, "in the event of rain. We wouldn't want water in the ale."

The strain around his mouth disappeared. "No, indeed." He looked at the river speculatively. "And if it is hot, perhaps some of the young 'uns might want to bathe." His eyes widened and he shook his head. "No. Probably not a good idea."

He was thinking about what they would wear, she just knew it. She wanted to laugh. The sound sat in her chest like a bubble waiting to burst. She refused to set it free. "I agree. But what we might do is have a rope pull from bank to bank. How about the Grange against the Hall?"

"I suppose so," he said looking dubious. "I doubt if Jevens or old Albert would be up to it, but Trent and Brown might, and perhaps Drabet now he's working in the stable."

So that's how he'd solved the problems of the little family at Mile Lane. She put her head on one side and pretended to measure him with her gaze. "A man of your size would probably make a whole team by yourself."

"Hey," he said with a short laugh. "No mocking folks who didn't have the sense to stop growing."

"But you are right," she went on, "Mr. Brown and Trent would make a good team."

Lucinda strolled around the perimeter, pointing out the suitability of this spot and that. Lord Wanstead seemed content to wander by her side. He bent over and plucked a stem of grass, placed it between his thumbs, and blew. It made a loud and rather rude noise.

"Not exactly music," she said.

He did it again, longer and louder, and then to the rhythm of reveille, his cheeks puffing out in the most ridiculous way.

The giggle she had repressed burst free and once she started laughing, she couldn't stop. She pressed her hands over her ears. "No more. If you don't cease this instant, I will…"

He dropped his hands and looked at her hopefully, rather like an overgrown puppy. "Eat lunch?"

As if joining the plot, her stomach gave a little gurgle. She clutched a hand to her waist. "Lunch it is."

"Thank God," he said fervently. "I was not looking forward to Mrs. Hobb's face if I returned to the house with nothing eaten."

Lucinda sobered. Would everyone in village know about this picnic?

"We'll eat under the oak tree. The grass seems a little less damp," Lord Wanstead said. He glanced back over his shoulder. "That is unless you prefer another spot?"

"The tree is fine," she said.

He spread the canvas and blanket, set the hamper in one corner, and gestured with a sweep of his hand. "Please, be seated."

Lucinda knelt at one edge. Picnicking in the woods with a bachelor could cause a scandal of the worst sort in such a small village, and yet as a widow, her reputation wouldn't suffer like that of an unmarried miss. If only she were really a widow.

He dropped down beside her and opened the lid of the basket. "What do we have here, I wonder?" He poked around. "Wine. Bread and cheese and cold roast beef. A couple of pasties. Some pickles. And, yes, apples and raisins."

The hamper seemed bottomless. Mrs. Hobb wasn't much with accounting, but as a cook she excelled. "She must have thought you were getting up a party, not feeding two people."

"Water," he said, picking out a jug and setting it beside her. He lifted a bottle. "Wine?"

"Water for me, please."

He opened the flagon. She dug out two sturdy pewter goblets and handed them over. He filled one and passed it back. It hovered inches from her chest, the bowl almost disappearing in his fist.

She reached for the stem.

Their fingers grazed. Bare skin, instead of cotton gloves. A sensation like hot sparks skittered up her arm. She gasped, snatching her hand back as he let go.

The goblet dropped. He caught it before it landed, diamond-bright droplets flying. Dark blotches spread on the blanket between them.

Shadows swirled in the depths of his eyes. A muscle jumped in his jaw.

Clumsy idiot. Denbigh's scornful tones echoed in her ears. She steeled herself for Lord Wanstead's anger.

"Damnation."

She flinched.

He snatched up a napkin and dabbed at the damp spot. "Are you...? Can I...?"

He leaned forward, the white square of linen aimed at her lap where pearly beads of moisture were sinking into the grey wool fabric.

"Oh," she said, heat and cold shooting through her at the thought of him mopping her up. "No really. It is quite all right." She whisked the napkin from his hand and brushed the drops away.

He retrieved the goblet. "I really must apologize for being so awkward. Let me see if I can make a better job of it."

The earl might not have her dandy husband's exquisite address or his elegant wardrobe or incomparable good looks, but he had a warrior's courage to accept responsibility for his deeds. A flame-like warmth danced in the pit of her stomach.

"There," he said and held out the glass.

"Thank you." She smiled.

For a moment he stared at the wine and then seemed to think better of it. He filled the other goblet with water.

"Let me pass you a roll and some beef," Lucinda said, putting them on a plate and handing it to him.

"Thank you. I should have brought a tray."

"I beg your pardon?"

He took a huge bite out of his roll, chewed thoughtfully, and swallowed. "A tray. A flat surface for the glasses. Then it wouldn't have spilled."

"No harm done, my lord. It was only water."

His gaze dropped to the basket. "You are right. It could have been red wine." He looked as if he wished it were red wine.

She bit into a meat pie. The golden crust melted in her mouth, the meat and potatoes spicy and with just the right amount of gravy to make the whole thing deliciously moist. She closed her eyes. "Mmmm."

"That good, eh?"

Oh, God. He would think her disgustingly greedy. Most young ladies picked at their food. In the Armitage household, appreciation for a good meal had been demanded. She returned the pastie to her plate and raised her gaze to his face. "Excellent."

He didn't look revolted or nauseated. Quite the opposite. "They are good, aren't they?" He sounded pleased. "I asked Mrs. Hobb to make them specially. May I have one?"

She passed one over, and he popped the whole thing in his mouth, nodding as he chewed. "Oh, yes. Just as I remembered. The best pasties in England."

She opened her mouth to remark on those made by her mother's cook but stopped herself just in time. Instead, she took another bite of pastie. "They are very good indeed."

"Try the sliced ham. Home cured."

Shaved into the thinnest of slices, the ham did indeed look delicious. She spread pale yellow butter on the white crusty bread and added two slices of ham. She peeked into the basket. He leaned forward. "What do you want? Mustard or horseradish?"

"Oh my," she said. "You thought of everything. Horseradish, please."

He handed her an earthenware jar. "Here you go." He helped himself to ham.

They ate to the sounds of the brook splashing over rocks, birdsong, and rustling leaves. He devoured the food as if it might be his last meal, while it was all she could to swallow, her heart felt so strangely full.

He picked up his glass and downed the water in two gulps. As his throat muscled convulsed above the snow-white linen, she could not help but notice the powerful neck, the shoulders a lion would envy, and the breadth of his chest in his skintight coat. Her stomach rolled, long and slow, giving the sensation of falling from a great height. She forced herself to look at the scenery, the stand of birch, the glimpse of water beyond the green bank, yet even when he did not fill her vision, she was acutely aware of his nearness.

No, her mind warned. To encourage him was wrong. She was living a lie. She snatched up her goblet and held it between them like a shield, sipping the water to cool her fevered blood.

"Tell me, Mrs. Graham, did you have a happy childhood with picnics and such?" The deep voice sounded wistful.

Memories flooded into her mind. Picnics on the lawn at the Armitage house had never been quiet affairs. There were always too many children. Nine to be exact. And most of them younger. Mother had always sat in the middle of the circle and made sure everyone ate every crumb until the children felt so full, they thought they might burst. Lucinda didn't mind the quiet, but she did miss her parents and sisters and brothers. Leaving her country home, where everyone was loved, no matter what their size or shape, had been a huge mistake. She realized it now, too late, but at least she had found her own little corner of England.

"Blissfully happy," she said.

His eyes widened. "Blissful?"

She gazed across the clearing to avoid that piercing gaze. Had she said too much? Shown too much of her longing? And yet denying her family was one betrayal she could not endure. "Yes. Blissfully happy." She gathered up the remaining bread rolls and put them in the basket.

"I envy you, then."

She swung around to face him full on, suspecting sarcasm. "You?"

"It seems ridiculous, doesn't it?" He sighed.

"Were you not happy as a child?"

"I wasn't unhappy, I suppose." He frowned, the bottle of wine paused above the basket. "There were some good times. I think my father and I were a little too much alike." He jammed the bottle into the hamper.

"Oh. That's just like…" She almost said Jonathon's name, "my brother," she finished. "But Mother kept the peace."

"Are you like your mother?"

"Do you mean good at keeping the peace?" She recalled Denbigh and her too frequent hot words. "No." Her shoulders tightened at the memory. She searched for a new topic, anything not to talk about her past. "What made you decide to join the army?"

A slight wince crossed his features. "It's a long story. What about your husband? Did he like army life? How could he bear to leave you?"

Back to her again. She tried to ignore the way his gaze searched her face or the curl of dark silky hair on his collar, and concentrated on her answer. "A soldier must go where he is ordered, my lord."

"Did he know about the child before he left?"

"No. She came as a complete surprise." She smiled. "But a very welcome one."

"I can only wonder at your courage, raising a child alone." His voice deepened to a seductive murmur that zinged through her veins and vibrated deep in her chest. Warmth spread through her limbs, like the tendrils of a fast-growing vine in spring, unfurling in hot little bursts.

"I do my best." The tremble in her voice further destroyed her composure.

"I'm surprised you don't return to the bosom of your blissful family."

Her mouth dried. She swallowed. "Things have changed."

"Was it an easy birth?" he asked.

Startled, she stared at him.

"Your child. Did you have a difficult time?"

Good Lord, what else would he ask? How to answer? "While it really isn't a suitable topic of conversation, I can say that Sophia's arrival was unexpectedly swift."

"You are fortunate indeed." He leaned back against the tree and closed his eyes, relaxed, less intimidating, perhaps even vulnerable. Shadows and sunlight chased across his face with the sway of the branches above. The lines on his brow and bracketing his mouth eased. What caused the grim visage he presented to the world? The pain of his wound? In repose, he had the look of a man who had endured suffering too great for the human spirit to survive.

The urge to smooth away his frown, to kiss those unsmiling lips filled her with longing. He was not for her. Another woman would have the joy of bringing him happiness, if he ever let anyone through that gruff barricade. She traced his strong features with her gaze: his mobile mouth, the noble nose that fit his face perfectly, the intelligent brow. If she had met him before she met Denbigh…would life have taken a different course? Would she have seen this man's solid worth against Denbigh's glitter of dross?

Would he have paid her any attention with all the slender, elegant women in London? Honesty won out over dreams. No, he would, not unless he also needed to marry a fortune.

He must have felt her staring, because he opened his eyes. Green fire danced in the gaze clashing with hers. Darkness warred with flickering heat, and fire won out. A faint smile curved his mouth, making him look younger and less careworn. He rolled toward her, propping himself on one elbow, his hard warrior's body inches from her thigh and hip.

Conscious of her mouth's sudden dryness, she licked her lips. Her heartbeat quickened. Warmth trickled through her veins from her head to her toes in slow languid heat. The air around her seemed to crackle. Life tingled through her body, as if she had awakened from a long sleep to find every muscle, every nerve humming.

Eyelids lowered, his gaze dropped to her lips. He leaned closer.

Move away, Lucinda.

His breath grazed her ear. A shiver ran down her spine. The delicious tremor stirred her heart and sent flutters of sweet ache pulsing in her core. A small cry sounded deep in her throat.

His dark head dipped and his lips grazed hers, warm, velvet soft, enticing.

The pounding of her heart, the sound of her shallow breathing filled with the scent of lemon and bay, drew her into his orbit. Every inch of her skin seemed to burn with a fire her instincts told her only he could quench. Her breasts tightened with the desire to press against his hard wall of a chest. Her hands, at first braced against his shoulders, slipped around his neck, her fingers sliding through the silk of his hair.

Never had she felt such melting in her bones.

A warm hand cradled her nape, his mouth moving against hers, his tongue teasing, encouraging. She parted her lips. As his tongue entered her mouth, desire flared out of control. She turned into him and arched against him, gasping for breath, her heart fluttering wildly. She drank of his sweetness. His strength surrounded her like the walls of a castle. The thunder of his heart echoed her own and joined with it, until they seemed to beat as a single organ, one note, one cadence, one song. Softening the kiss, he stroked her cheek and then ran the hand down her throat and across her shoulder blades. Her very soul rejoiced.

The warm pressure of his hand moving in circles on her back mimicked the gentle strokes of his tongue, drowning her will and her conscious thought. The heel of his hand kneaded her ribs, his thumb grazing the underside of her breast.

She froze. A bucket of ice water could not have chilled her blood so fast.

He drew back, his gaze searching her face, at first puzzled and then hardening to bleak.

For once, words, her only defense, failed her. Nothing in her life had prepared her for the firestorm of desire battling the fear of pain. In the strength of her want, she had all but forgotten her inadequacy. She swallowed and dropped her gaze to the blanket, to the remains of their feast. With swift jerky movements, she stacked the plates and placed the glasses back in the basket. Anything not to have to look at him, not to see the scorn in his eyes, not to plumb the depths of her humiliation.

Hugo pushed himself up to a sitting position and placed his goblet in the basket. He'd set out to win her trust and lost control. How the hell had that happened after all he knew about himself? He tossed the ham in the basket.

She'd looked so beautiful, her color high, her gaze mysterious, her lush breasts inches from his chest. The knowledge that beneath the full grey skirts lay mouth-watering soft, sweet flesh had driven him over the edge. Now she looked close to tears. Damn it to hell. Since when could he not control his baser urges? On campaigns, he'd gone months without even seeing a woman and hadn't wanted to tup the first female across his path; now he was acting like a rutting beast. Men were animals, and he was worse, knowing the damage he could do.

"I owe you an apology," he said. "I should not have—"

She cut him off with a wave of one dimpled hand. "It was a mistake. Let us forget all about it."

Uncomfortable warmth heated the back of his neck. He felt like a schoolboy dismissed for some prank. She had been a willing participant. At least, in the beginning. He'd got a bit carried away, but she had responded to his kisses with enthusiasm.

For now, he would spare her blushes. Next time he would take things more slowly. Next time? Even as his body responded with anticipation, he knew there must not be a next time.

He quelled the urge to smash his fist into the tree.

He forced himself to his feet and helped her to hers. "What do you think?"

She glanced around the field and nodded. "Yes, my lord, it will do very well."

Eight

SHELTERED FROM THE BLAZING SUN BY A SHADY TREE and seated with the other ladies on the organizing committee, Lucinda watched Lord Wanstead march across the patch of vicarage lawn. No sign of hesitation marred his stride today. She tried her best not to notice the way his blue coat hugged his brawny shoulders or the way his pantaloons stretched over his muscular thighs. After dreading and dreaming of their next meeting by turns, she perched on a chair whose cushion seemed to contain a frightened hedgehog, while her stomach engaged in what felt like somersaults.

With a beaming smile on his narrow face, the Reverend Postlethwaite surged to his feet. "Welcome, Lord Wanstead. You found time after all."

"Good day, Vicar." Lord Wanstead clasped the other man's outstretched hand, his jaw set with all the determination of a man ordered to undertake an unpleasant but necessary duty.

"Let me introduce you to the committee," Postlethwaite said.

Lord Wanstead nodded. "I should be delighted. Please ladies, do not get up."

"You know Mrs. Graham, of course."

Lord Wanstead took her hand and bowed with crisp military formality. "Indeed. How are you today, Mrs. Graham?" Piercing beneath his dark brows, his forest-green gaze raked her face.

She controlled the urge to flutter her lashes and grin like an idiot. "Very well, thank you, my lord."

The vicar moved around the circle. "This is Mrs. Peddle." The gaunt innkeeper's wife ducked her head.

"And Miss Crotchet." The plump seamstress bridled like a schoolgirl, her bright-flowered cotton gown at odds with the tributary of wrinkles on her powdered cheeks.

"I am well acquainted with Mrs. Trip," Lord Wanstead said, with a small bow to the miller's spouse.

How kindly he greeted these people who were not quite of his world. Gruff he might be, but not too high in the instep to treat these worthy ladies with respect. A whole new sensation filled Lucinda's chest, warm and large. Pride?

"Wonderful." The vicar rubbed his hands together. "We just need the Dawson ladies to arrive, and we will be complete. Please, my lord, take a seat."

It didn't exactly surprise Lucinda when Lord Wanstead took the vacant chair at her side. His glance had returned to her more than once during the introductions in what looked like a plea for help.

Since the other ladies seated in the semicircle had the glazed look of chickens faced with a fox, she assumed none of them had noticed anything untoward in his behavior.

"We were just going over where we are with our plans," the vicar said. "Mrs. Peddle tells us that the brewer will deliver the casks of beer two days ahead."

Mrs. Peddle pursed her tight lips and nodded.

"Mrs. Trip, how are plans for the baked goods?" the vicar asked.

"Ah," said that doubty lady. "My William has promised ten bags of flour. And Mr. Bell has ordered sufficient currants and sugar for ten dozen Eccles cakes and ten of pies. Eccles cakes sell for a penny a piece. Pies for tuppence. He'll split the profit fifty-fifty."

"I say," the vicar said. "That is generous. That will go a long way to help with the church roof."

"Another leaking roof?" Lord Wanstead said.

The three village ladies stared at him as if an oracle had spoken.

"Oh, yes," Miss Crotchet said. "The hangings in the vestry are quite ruined. Lord Wanstead...The other Lord Wanstead, I mean your father..." She turned bright red, and her voice trailed off.

"What Miss Crotchet is trying to say," the vicar interposed kindly, "is that your father and St. Mary's last incumbent were at odds. The late earl withdrew his support of the project at a crucial moment and so it is in rather worse shape now than it might have been."

Lord Wanstead frowned. "I am sorry to hear it."

The ladies stared at him expectantly, as if they thought he would offer to pay for it out of his pocket. "That is our purpose for holding the fête," Lucinda said.

The vicar nodded. "May I say how much we appreciate your permission to use the water meadow, Lord Wanstead?"

The earl visibly relaxed. "Mrs. Graham reminded me that my grandfather used to hold a similar event there years ago."

Every eye turned toward her. How generous of him to give her credit. The warmth of his gaze resting on her face gave her a funny tingling feeling across her breasts. It sent a flood of warmth to her face. Not again. After the embarrassment of the picnic, how could she respond to a simple glance with such wanton heat? She lifted her chin. "Thank you, my lord."

The vicar turned his angelic beam in her direction. "And how are plans for the children's games coming along, Mrs. Graham?"

"Very well indeed, Vicar," she managed to reply with a semblance of calm despite Lord Wanstead's steady scrutiny. "I sent word to the man in Maidstone about the merry-go-round, and he agreed on the date."

The sound of a woman's laugh floated out of the whitewashed thatched house. Those with their backs to the mansion swiveled in their chairs as two fashionably attired ladies stepped through the French doors into the garden. The diminutive Miss Dawson in primrose muslin, her fair complexion carefully shaded by a white silk parasol, floated across the lawn accompanied by her mother, who was wearing a green-and-red striped walking gown and a haughty expression.

Once more the vicar leaped to his feet. This time he rushed across the lawn to greet the newcomers. "Mrs. Dawson, Miss Dawson," he called out. "Here you are at last."

Miss Dawson picked up her pace. "I'm sorry. Are we late?"

Lord Wanstead came to his feet with what Lucida could only describe as an expression of genuine affection. "Miss Dawson. Well met."

Miss Dawson must be the reason he'd attended the meeting today. Lucinda's heart grew heavy. Her ploy to bring him out of his shell had resulted in the desired effect. Something sharper than a hedgehog quill seemed to work its way between her ribs. Envy? Unlikely. She'd no reason to envy any young woman.

Miss Dawson, her dark eyes twinkling, cast him a gentle smile. "Wanstead, I must say I did not expect to find you here."

Gripping her green parasol with one hand and the Reverend's arm with the other, Mrs. Dawson arrived, puffing and blowing at the final burst of speed.

Lord Wanstead bowed in her direction. "Mrs. Dawson, good afternoon."

"Wanstead," Mrs. Dawson said with a narrow look first at Lucinda and then at him. "A bit out of your element, are you not?"

Lucinda glared at her. At any moment, he'd feel unwelcome and return to his cave.

"Mother," Miss Dawson exclaimed. Laughter lit her expressive face and eyes. The beauty of her elfin face deepened the insidious pain around Lucinda's heart, when the sight of Wanstead's answering smile, the curve of his lips, and the crinkle around his eyes should have cheered her. How could she be so selfish?

Postlethwaite looked from Lord Wanstead to Miss Dawson. His animation seemed to dwindle. "Perhaps we can get back to our business? Please, ladies, take a seat."

The vicar's housekeeper arrived with a tea tray and set it on a small wicker table.

"Mrs. Dawson, I hope you will do us the honor of pouring?" the vicar said as the servant left.

"Certainly." Mrs. Dawson bestowed her agreement like a knighthood.

While she poured, the vicar caught the newcomers up with what had gone before. "In addition to the children's games, I'm told by Mrs. Peddle that some of the men would like to have feats of strength. We will need prizes."

"And a greased pig," Mrs. Trip said.

Mrs. Peddle wagged a work-worn finger. "That's all Lord Wanstead needs on his land. A bunch of drunken louts chasing a greasy pig all over the place."

"What about a greasy pole?" Lord Wanstead asked.

"Too much grease, if you ask me," Miss Crotchet said and giggled.

"Then what about a rope pull instead?" Lord Wanstead sent a swift glance Lucinda's way. "Across the river."

"That might cool them louts off a bit if it's a hot day," Mrs. Peddle admitted with a grudging upward tilt to her hard mouth.

"Archery," Mrs. Trip said.

"You would think of that," Miss Crotchet said. "Your son is a whiz with a bow. I'd like to see a baking contest for the ladies."

"And a prize for the best preserves," Mrs. Dawson threw in, no doubt thinking of her own cook's strengths.

Now that they had a decently sized location, ideas flew like shuttlecocks around the circle. The vicar wrote them down on a sheet of paper, and Lord

Wanstead, while mostly silent, nodded his general approval with a hint of a smile on his straight lips.

Lips that had kissed her so pleasurably. Lucinda daren't even look at them. Every time she thought about that kiss, her stomach gave a little hop.

Dash it. She must stop thinking about the picnic. While seeking his help with the fête had been a good idea, it now left her with the task of sorting out Mrs. Hobb's accounts. Not that the accounts were a problem. Rather, it was the thought of running into him every time she called that had her in a tizzy. Fortunately, he had been absent from home when she had returned on Friday as promised, called out to one of his tenants to discuss business. She'd been grateful for that absence, yet stupidly disappointed. After having lain awake half the night worrying what she would do if he tried to kiss her again and tormented by her body's protest when she was sure he would not, it had all seemed rather deflating.

"What about pony rides for the children," Miss Dawson said smiling at Lord Wanstead over the rim of her cup and bringing Lucinda's thoughts back to the here and now.

Lord Wanstead balanced his cup on his knee. Miraculously, it stayed there. He turned to Lucinda. "Mrs. Graham is organizing the children's games. What do you think, Mrs. Graham?"

"I think that would be fine," she murmured.

Miss Dawson swiveled in her chair to look at her full on with a tiny frown on her alabaster forehead. "You know, Mrs. Graham, every time we meet, I have the strangest feeling I know you from somewhere else? Did we meet in London, perhaps?"

Lucinda's stomach pitched. They had never met, but Miss Dawson might have seen Jonathon in Town. Everyone said they looked remarkably alike. Darn it, now Lord Wanstead had his ear cocked for her reply. She shook her head. "If we had, I would recall, I am sure. I spent very little time in London before my marriage." And no time in polite company, once Denbigh had made his disgust obvious.

"Nasty horrible place," Mrs. Peddle muttered. "I went there once. Couldn't breathe for the smoke. Couldn't hardly see a hand in front of my face, neither."

"I would love to go to London." Miss Crochet breathed, her smile achingly wistful. "Think of the culture. Why, my cousin often sees the King or a member of the royal family go by in their carriages."

The vicar clapped his hands. "Ladies, please, back to the task at hand. If we are to have all these games, someone has to organize them."

"I can look after the pony rides," Miss Dawson said with a bright smile at Lord Wanstead. "Fairy is a bit long in the tooth, but she is fine for small children."

"You still have that fat old thing?" Lord Wanstead asked.

"She is not fat," Miss Dawson said, then laughed. "You always were rude about poor old Fairy."

"You always gave her too many treats."

While they bantered back and forth with the ease of long-standing friends, Lucinda wanted to slink away unnoticed and leave them to it. Instead, she straightened her spine and fixed a calm expression on her face. Miss Dawson would make a beautiful countess. Elegant, charming, and ravishingly beautiful. And he would be a kind and respectful husband. A perfectly happy ending.

Then why did she feel as if a canyon had opened in her chest?

"I will look after the archery," Mrs. Trip said. "Trip will help."

"I'll be too busy making sure Peddle doesn't give the beer away to be of much help on the day," the innkeeper's wife said.

The conversation flowed around Lucinda like a river passing a boulder. She tried to maintain an expression of interest.

"I'll put up a notice about the baking contest," the Vicar said. "I will send it to all the nearby parishes."

"And preserves," added Mrs. Dawson.

"Yes, yes, of course. Preserves." The vicar scratched busily on his paper.

"I'll arrange for the pig and the grease," Hugo said. "Trent can help organize the men for the event."

There. Now he was joining in, just as she guessed he might if something caught his interest.

"And I will ask a couple of ladies I know to help with the stalls," Miss Crotchet said.

"Excellent," the vicar said. "It looks as if we will need one or two more meetings and everything can be finalized."

"Well, miss," Mrs. Dawson said turning to her daughter. "If the house is to be ready for our guests, we must go and prepare."

"Guests?" Lord Wanstead enquired with a raised brow.

"Yes," Mrs. Dawson said. "Arthur is bringing friends from Town for the ball. The fête seemed like a perfect addition to the entertainment."

People coming from London? Lucinda's pulse

picked up speed. Stupidly, she had expected only members of the local society to attend the squire's ball.

"Ah yes," Lord Wanstead said. "I recall you mentioned something of the sort." He looked as horrified as Lucinda felt.

"I have your promise to attend, Wanstead." Mrs. Dawson patted her daughter's knee. "Very popular with the gentlemen, my Catherine. You will have to claim your dance early if you do not wish to be left out in the cold."

Miss Dawson cast Lord Wanstead a pained smile. He grimaced in sympathy. The canyon in Lucinda's chest seemed to deepen.

"If you wanted to make yourself useful, Wanstead," Mrs. Dawson was saying, "you could invite some of the gentlemen to stay with you. Otherwise they will have to stay at the inn."

Lord Wanstead stiffened, no doubt thinking about the dreadful state of his housekeeping arrangements.

"Nothing wrong with the inn," Mrs. Peddle snapped. "My accommodations are perfectly fit for the gentry. Not that I want a bunch of rackety young gentlemen staying, I'm sure."

"They don't have to stay in the village," Miss Dawson said gently. "Maidstone is only a half-hour away by carriage."

"The Grange is less than ten minutes away," Mrs. Dawson said. "It would be most obliging of you, Wanstead."

Lord Wanstead's complexion darkened, his gaze becoming unreadable. "I have absolutely no interest in obliging anyone," he drawled, changing from fellow well-met to arrogant nobleman in the blink of an eye. Lucinda couldn't help but admire his strength faced with such a daunting adversary.

Mrs. Dawson glowered. "As your father learned to his cost."

A shocked silence fell on the group.

"Don't bother to deny it, Wanstead," Mrs. Dawson charged on. "Your duty was here. You put your father through a dreadful time going off like that." She shot a sharp glance at her daughter. "Not to mention the rest of us."

Lucinda's jaw dropped. Hugo had jilted Miss Dawson and married another?

Miss Dawson's face turned red and then white. She shot Lord Wanstead an apologetic glance and rose to her feet. "Mother, it really is time we left."

Was it guilt Lucinda saw in Lord Wanstead eyes, or anger? She tried to focus her gaze anywhere but on him.

"Indeed," Mrs. Dawson agreed with a sniff and a rustle of skirts as she stood.

The Reverend Postlethwaite rose with her, as did Lord Wanstead. Both men looked ready for murder.

"Don't bother to see us out, Vicar," Mrs. Dawson pronounced, twirling her parasol. "Call in at the Hall tomorrow. I want to discuss your idea for a church organ."

Lord Wanstead and the reverend remained on their feet as the two ladies trotted across the lawn. Suppressed fury glittered in Lord Wanstead's eyes as he glanced at the circle of faces gone suddenly blank. When his gaze reached Lucinda, it speared her with a silent accusation. She refused to look away. If he had

r. somehow wronged Miss Dawson, it was up to him to set things right. Perhaps this ball of Mrs. Dawson's would be the perfect opportunity.

"Well, really," Miss Crotchet finally whispered.

"I think I must be going, too," Lucinda said. She managed a smile. "I promised to return home long before now. Good day, everyone."

She fled for the safety of her cottage, her mind a fragmented whirl.

"Oh, no." Lucinda moaned as smoke poured from the stove. Coughing, throat and eyes stinging, she snatched up a cloth, grabbed the tray of biscuits, and pulled it clear. The hot baking tray hit the metal rack she'd placed ready on the table with a clang. She flapped her towel to clear the air.

Sophia tugged at her skirts. The sky-blue bow, a match to her dress, flopped amid her soft yellow curls. "Biscuit?"

"Wait a minute, sweet," Lucinda said, lifting the shortbread onto a plate before it got any worse.

"Mummy burn?" Sophia said.

Head on one side, Lucinda regarded the charcoal edges with a flicker of amusement. Annie had given her detailed instructions before she left for her day off, but it was years since Lucinda had spent any time in the kitchen. The Armitage cook had let her and her siblings play with the dough, but Lucinda couldn't recall making anything edible. "Actually, they are not too bad if I cut off the singed edges."

The little girl held out her hand and wiggled her fingers. "Biscuit?"

Lucinda caught the hot little hand in hers and dropped a kiss in the palm. "You cannot be hungry; we had lunch only an hour ago." The longing glance Sophia cast at the biscuits cut Lucinda's heart to ribbons. Perhaps the child remembered her hungry days in London "Soon. I promise. We have to let them cool or you will burn your tongue. By the time I have made the tea, they will be ready."

Sophia tilted her head on one side, her chin starting to quiver.

"No crying, sweet. I promise they won't be long. Now be a good girl and play with Marmalade for a while. I don't want either of you under my feet while I boil the water."

Sophia trotted around the kitchen table and hunkered beside the kitten stretched out on the hearth rug.

While she waited for the kettle to boil, Lucinda scraped the charcoal off the biscuits. "I was right not to go to the vicarage today," she said placing a ragged-looking finger of biscuit on a clean plate. She picked up another burnt offering. "Miss Catherine Dawson will be perfect for his lordship." A hot lump seemed to fill her throat. She swallowed it and forced a shaky laugh. "She is having guests come down from London for the fête, you know. If he doesn't choose her, there is sure to be someone suitable at the ball."

Sophia looked up from tickling the kitten's tummy. "Mummy cry?"

Lucinda wiped the stinging drop of moisture from the corner of her eye. "It is the smoke." She crossed to the window and opened it wider, gulping down a lungful of fresh air along with a measure of calm before returning to the table.

She shouldn't be thinking about Lord Wanstead. Her decision to resign from the fête committee was the right one. She had quite enough to do taking care of Sophia without involving herself in the vicar's projects. He had agreed with her decision. Too readily, Lucinda thought with a glower at the steam emerging from the kettle. She filled the pot and set it on the tray.

Sophia looked up from the cat. "Walk?"

"Maybe later." Lucinda set out the plates and cups. "If it stops raining." She carried the tray into the parlor and set it on the piecrust table in front of the hearth.

Trotting behind her, Sophia climbed up on the sofa and leaned over the back, staring out at the rain. "Man coming."

"What man?" Lucinda's stomach dipped. Not the Bow Street Runner? She rushed to see for herself.

"Horsy," Sophia said, pointing.

At the sight of the burly figure tying his horse to her gate in the pouring rain, a thrill shot through her. Lord Wanstead.

She watched him stride up the path between the borders of purple heart's ease. Why was he here? He should be at the vicarage, meeting with Miss Catherine Dawson.

"Oh Lord." What if he wanted to come in? A mixture of panic and hope left her unable to move. The house reeked of burnt biscuits, and she hadn't a decent piece of cake to offer until Annie returned from the market in the morning. Perhaps she shouldn't answer the door? If only her heart wasn't beating so hard, she might be able to think.

And that was another thing. If she was as cold as Denbigh had said, why did she glow like a furnace every time his lordship entered her line of sight? Dash it. What should she do?

Sophia stared at her. "Man coming."

"It is Lord Wanstead. Come away from the window, Sophia dear. It is rude to stare at people."

She removed her apron and ran back to the kitchen to hang it up. Standing in the passage, she smoothed her hair and adjusted her cap while she waited breathlessly for his knock.

Sophia's hand crept into hers, and the child looked up in puzzlement.

"Be a good girl, Sophia. He's a very important man." Their landlord. That must be the reason for the disconcerting tremble behind her breastbone.

The loud rap made her jump.

She took a deep breath, wiped her damp palms on her skirts, and opened the door. "Lord Wanstead. How can I be of service?" Her voice sounded breathy and hoarse from the smoke.

He looked taken aback, no doubt expecting a servant to answer the door. Then eyes the color of a storm-tossed ocean and equally as angry pinned on her face. "I want to know why you weren't at the meeting this morning?"

"I didn't have anyone to care for Sophia," she said as calmly as she could around the thudding of her heart.

"Postlethwaite said you resigned."

She tried for a light bantering tone. "My presence isn't that important, my lord."

His frown deepened. "Not important?" His voice growled as if he had swallowed grit, or a bear. "After you pressed me into attending these wretched meetings with your talk of serving the community, your lectures on civic duty?"

She blinked. "Nothing is left undone. Miss Dawson is to take my place organizing the children's games. She has more resources at her disposal. A pony, money for prizes...eggs."

One shoulder against the doorjamb, his head lowered to avoid the lintel, he looked like a puzzled bull ready to charge. "There are eggs at the Grange."

She glared back. "They are your eggs."

"And that is a problem?"

His anger buffeted her like a gale. She held her ground in the face of its fury. "There is no problem. You donated your land. Miss Dawson is in charge of the children's games. Everything is arranged."

"You were the only reason I agreed to the use of my land."

A strange melting weakened her limbs. She stiffened against it. "I am sure you will be just as generous with Miss Dawson." Oh God, was that bitterness she heard in her voice? Briefly, she squeezed her eyes closed in mortification.

He frowned. "What is that supposed to mean?"

Tears—stupid, hot, and wet—emerged from nowhere to choke her throat. "I mean for the sake of the villagers."

Sophia popped up in front of her. "Mama cry?" Her lower lip trembled.

"By thunder, madam," Lord Wanstead said. "I simply came to ask you why you were not at the meeting. Can we not discuss this like civilized people?"

Civilized didn't seem to fit Lord Wanstead right at this moment. But she had been rude keeping him standing on the doorstep. She managed a stiff smile. "It is my housekeeper's day off, but Sophia and I were just about to take tea if you would care to join us?"

He visibly relaxed. "Tea would be most welcome." He peered over her shoulder. "Someone is baking?"

"Not very successfully, I'm afraid."

Sophia hopped on her toes. "Biscuits, mama?"

"Please, my lord, step in out of the rain."

As he ducked beneath the lintel, water sluiced from the brim of his hat onto the floor. "Damn," he said under his breath.

She pretended not to hear and glanced past him out of the door. "I don't have a stable for your horse, I'm afraid."

"I can assure you Grif and I have suffered worse conditions."

A pang of sympathy invaded her heart. "I can well imagine." She gestured him into the parlor and closed the front door behind him. "Please, won't you sit down?"

He chose the more solid-looking sofa. Even seated, he seemed to fill the room, not so much because of his size, but because of his virility. He belonged outdoors, not in the confines of a lady's drawing room. And if weren't for the shadows in his eyes, she might well have believed his mask of invincibility.

Nine

OBLIVIOUS TO EVERYTHING EXCEPT THE COMING TREAT, Sophia hopped up beside him and smoothed her skirts over her legs. The sight of the enormous Lord Wanstead seated next to the delicate, fragile child who showed not a whisper of fear brought a smile to Lucinda's lips.

"Tea and biscuits," Sophia said and nodded for emphasis.

"Excellent," he said.

Lucinda winced. "The biscuits are a little charred."

"Oh, that's a relief," he said. "I thought the chimney was smoking and I'd have to poke around up there." Crinkles fanned from the corners of eyes dancing with mischief.

"I wouldn't ask you to do so before you had your tea."

"Very kind of you, I'm sure." A faint smile curved his lips.

The tension in Lucinda's shoulders eased. The worst of the storm seemed to be over. Not that she'd been fearful, she realized with surprise. For all his size and strength, she didn't think he'd hurt her. Not physically or with cruel barbs. His anger flashed like a summer storm, all noise and bluster, but with little damage.

"I'll fetch another cup," she said, and hurried down the passage.

On her return, she was surprised to find Wanstead and Sophia staring straight ahead like soldiers on parade. She sat down beside the tray. "Milk, my lord?"

"Yes, please."

"Milk please," Sophia said and folded her arms across her chest.

Lord Wanstead folded his arms.

Sophia crossed her ankles. Lord Wanstead crossed his.

He must find the small sofa terribly uncomfortable for his large frame.

Lucinda added a small amount of milk to two cups, half-filled the third, and then poured the tea. The rising steam filled her nostrils with fragrance.

Spoon paused above the sugar bowl, Lucinda watched in fascination as Sophia's actions became more and more outlandish, and her smile grew and grew, while his lordship seemed completely oblivious to the huge blue eyes fixed on his face.

Sophia wrinkled her nose. He wrinkled his right back. Sophia frowned. He frowned. She uncrossed her ankles; he uncrossed his. Sophia let out a trill of laughter, something Lucinda had never heard from the child in the presence of strangers. Twisting in his seat, Lord Wanstead tickled her ribs until she collapsed in a heap of giggles on his knee.

Why had Lucinda ever thought him a bear? He was more like a naughty boy.

"Enough, you two," she said, not bothering to hide her smile. "Sit up straight, Sophia, or you will spill your tea."

Lord Wanstead wagged a finger. "Be a good girl."

"You be good," Sophia retorted.

Lucinda held her breath, waiting for a gruff reply, but Lord Wanstead stiffened his body, put his hand on his knees, and assumed an angelic expression. "I am being good."

Sophia copied him.

The child liked him. A great deal. A sweet pang invaded Lucinda's breast. She liked him, too. Far too much. She carried two cups to the sofa and handed Sophia her tea.

"Hot?" the little girl asked.

"No, it has lots of milk. It won't burn you."

She handed a cup to Lord Wanstead and then offered the plate of biscuits. Sophia eyed the golden fingers with their sadly ragged edges, her hand hovering over the plate.

"They are all the same size, sweet," Lucinda said. "Come, choose the one closest or his lordship will think you have no manners."

Sophia peeped at him from under her lashes and then grabbed one from the bottom of the pile.

Lord Wanstead caught another as it fell. "Thank you, young lady," he said. "Very kind of you, I'm sure."

Sophia giggled and then took a huge bite of hers, crumbs scattering far and wide. Lord Wanstead took no notice. He popped the whole of his biscuit in his mouth. Sophia's eyes widened in fascination.

"Uh, oh," Lucinda said. "Another trick for her to try." She set the plate back on the table and returned to her seat.

"She has nice manners for such a small child," Lord Wanstead said. "Quite charming." He smiled.

How she loved these rare glimpses of his gentler side. She smiled back, her heart full of something so soft and achy she wanted to hug him. "I try not to crush her spirit by asking for more than she can understand."

"You are doing a fine job, Mrs. Graham. Now tell me why you abandoned the village fête—and me—to the denizens of Blendon."

The hint of steel in his voice demanded an answer and struck a small chord of guilt. "I didn't abandon the fête. I passed all my information to the vicar after church on Sunday. Miss Dawson had so much enthusiasm for the project that I thought it would be better in her care."

He frowned. "Or I might be better in her care?"

Heat rushed to her face and then drained away at the implication that she had a right to his care. "That would be presumptuous of me, my lord."

"Not presumptuous, Mrs. Graham. Misguided."

"I don't understand."

"There seems to be a general mistaken impression that I have some interest in Miss Dawson."

Lucinda got up and took Sophia's cup and saucer. The little girl rested her cheek against his massive arm and blinked like a sleepy owl.

"Sophia, would you like a nap?" Anything to get away from this topic of conversation.

Sophia snuggled closer, the little traitor.

"Let her rest," Lord Wanstead said. "Well, Mrs. Graham, is that your understanding?"

"My understanding is of no consequence."

"It is, if the next message I get is that after tomorrow you will no longer assist Mrs. Hobb with her accounts. Apparently you think she can manage the rest."

She was beginning to feel like a butterfly caught in a net. "I believe one more session is all that is required."

"Thus you satisfy the spirit of our agreement? I think not, Mrs. Graham." The jolly giant who had played with Sophia had been replaced by the hard-eyed warrior. This was a man who knew what he wanted, rode forth, and took it. The thought sent a shiver down her spine. An oddly pleasurable sensation.

She resisted it. "I agreed to straighten out your household accounts. I have done so."

"Then it seems I got the worst of the bargain."

"Why is that?"

He shrugged. "Your work is finished in two or three afternoons, something you must have known. Meanwhile, I am cursed with this fête nonsense for weeks. Hence, I came off worst." A wicked look glinted from beneath slightly lowered lashes. "Unless you are willing to make up for your obvious perfidy by repeating our game of chess."

The manipulating rogue. An answering smile caught her by surprise. She tilted her head. "You asked Mrs. Hobb how more much time I required, did you not?"

He had the grace to look a little guilty, despite his shrug.

"You want me to play chess with you? Why?"

"Because you are a damnably fine player." Color rushed into his face. "I beg your pardon. I mean you play very well. Also because I enjoy your company."

The declaration resonated in her mind and her heart like the crescendo of a sonata. It stirred emotions she thought she'd successfully buried. "It would not be fitting. Ask the squire. Or the Reverend Postlethwaite. I am sure either one of them would be glad to oblige."

"We are adults, both previously married. Where is the harm?"

Clearly he was talking about more than a game of chess. No matter how tempting, she could not let him charm her into doing something so outrageous. And besides he completely misunderstood her situation. He thought she was a merry widow. Even if she weren't married, she had nothing to offer such a virile man. "I'm sorry, my lord. I may have given you the wrong impression. I am not looking for male companionship. All I care about is providing a home for my daughter and living here in peace."

"If you wanted peace, why draw others into your grand schemes for improving the world?"

"Is wanting to improve the lot of others so wrong?"

"There you go again, answering a question with a question. You are hiding something, Mrs. Graham. When I asked Mr. Brown about you, he also avoided my questions. Is there perhaps something between you and my steward?"

The accusation felt like an arrow to her heart. What kind of woman did he think her? "You are insulting, my lord. I think you should leave."

He glanced down at Sophia. "I thought I made a pretty good pillow."

"You are as comfortable as a bed full of rocks," she shot back.

He laughed. Actually threw back his head, and a laugh rumbled up from his chest.

The sight and sound robbed her of anger, not to mention destroying the wall she'd been trying to build between them. In its place she found a desire to rest her head on his other shoulder and admit defeat.

"Mrs. Graham, let us call it *pax*. You don't like me making insinuations about you, any more than I appreciate you drawing incorrect conclusions about myself and Miss Dawson. We are childhood friends. Nothing more."

Friends whom rumor expected to marry. Everyone in the village, not to mention the county, assumed she was waiting for his return from the war. If so, it seemed she might be doomed to disappointment. Unless her mother managed to outflank her victim.

"You wanted me to provide my land for this fête," he continued. "I want you to take my place on the committee and to play chess with me one evening a week. Is that so very much to ask in exchange for my inconvenience?"

She narrowed her eyes. Was this was all about him wanting to crawl back inside his shell?

The full mobile mouth curved in a smile. "Please, Mrs. Graham."

Her insides melted like a candle left too long in the sun. Right there at that word and that smile. The man had the charm of a Lothario when it suited him, and she lacked the power to resist. "Very well, I will continue to serve on the committee and assist Mrs. Hobb with her accounts. Afterward, if time allows, we will play chess."

He breathed a sigh of relief. "Thank God that is settled."

Sophia stirred and rolled over on her back, her head resting on his thigh.

A large fingertip touched the end of a golden curl. "Perhaps she should go to bed." He lifted the child as if she weighed less than a feather. Indeed, in his arms she looked no more than a fragile doll.

Lucinda reached out to take her.

He shook his head. "Where does she sleep?"

"Upstairs, on the first floor."

In two strides he carried her out of the room. With the child cradled in one arm, he mounted the bottom step. A breath hissed through his teeth. His step faltered.

Heart in her throat, she reached out. "Let me take her."

"I've got her. Don't worry, I won't drop her." Beneath the impatient tone, she heard embarrassment.

It would injure his pride to say more. More than his pride would be hurt, if he dropped Sophia on the stairs, but Lucinda trusted him not to harm his precious burden. Trust. The word tasted sweet. She gestured for him to go ahead and followed him up the stairs, squeezed around him in the doorway, and drew back the sheet.

He laid Sophia down as if she was more precious than gold. Lucinda struggled with the images in her mind—the fierce soldier, the gentleman, the tender father, the lover…She forced the last thought away, but the flutter beneath her heart refused to subside.

Bitterness soured her mood. Her body always lied. No matter what she thought she felt, she was incapable of satisfying a man. A fraud.

While she pulled up the covers and tucked them close around Sophia's tiny form, he glanced around at the meager furnishings, the lacy curtains at the window, the little wooden doll on the dressing table. "You are a good mother, Mrs. Graham."

Lucinda put her fingers to her lips. "Let us go downstairs before we wake her." Not that the child would wake. Sophia slept like an angel.

He followed her down the stairs and then glanced back. "Those stairs creak. I'll ask Brown to see if they need repairs and ask him to add a balustrade."

Lucinda had bemoaned the lack of a handrail every day since coming here. "I can't afford to pay more for the house, so I would not bother if I were you. As is, I agreed with Mr. Brown."

His gaze swept the small parlor and his lips compressed. "I'll speak to Brown about it in the morning."

"Really, my lord, it is not necessary." She smiled. "Thank you for your help with Sophia. You will make a wonderful father one day."

"No children for me, thank you." A dull flush stained his face. "I don't mind them when they are like your little girl. It is babies I dislike." He grimaced. "Squalling infants."

Remembering Geoffrey's reaction to their younger siblings, she shook her head at him. "You soon become accustomed, and they grow up far too quickly." An expression of yearning softened his expression. The warmth emanating from his large body washed up against her like a warm current.

His gaze dropped to her mouth, his huge chest rising and falling with each intake of breath. Her heartbeat quickened to match the rhythm. A tremble ran down her spine.

"Sophia is fortunate," he said softly.

"She's a darling," she whispered around the constriction in her throat. She wanted to step back, to increase the tingling space between them, but found herself trapped by the intensity of his eyes.

He placed a hand on her shoulder, and heat scorched her skin through her gown. "I know how hard you work to keep your family together, Mrs. Graham. You should not belittle your efforts."

With his lips but inches from hers, sensual, tempting, and velvet soft, she tried to laugh off his praise but managed only a smile. A dark lock of hair fell forward on his broad forehead. She wanted to brush it back from his face, to smooth his brow, to press her lips to his cheek. Instead, she inhaled a ragged breath. "Sophia is my joy and that makes everything so much easier."

"You would sacrifice a great deal for someone you love."

She shook her head. "I don't know about sacrifices. I only know I need to take care of Sophia."

He leaned closer. His face filled her vision, the rugged chin, the aquiline nose, the emerald glitter in his eyes. His hand left her shoulder, leaving an instant of chill, until it cupped her jaw with blessed warmth. His breath, warm, scented with cookies and tea, fanned her lips. The light touch bestowed shimmers of sensual longing, a feeling unlike anything she'd ever known. She could not stop a shiver of pure pleasure. A symbol of her desire.

She inhaled shallow breaths, seeking air and the courage to refuse. The attraction between them was as undeniable as it was hopeless. She should stop him now, before he learned the disappointing truth.

He swooped down, slanting his mouth to brush hers, soft, warm, dry, and delicate as a whisper. It felt unbelievably right.

Time had no meaning as the ocean of physical sensation rocking her gently, swooping her to unknown heights, crashing down around her like surf in what was no more than a second of contact. An excited pulse thrummed deep in her core, rippling outward.

Oh God, what was she doing? She jumped back.

He tipped his head in question.

The answer trembled on her parted lips. She resisted the urge to touch them with her tongue. "This is wrong."

"You can't deny the attraction."

Her face flamed in shame. He must have sensed her instant arousal to his touch. Yet it meant nothing, a false coin.

"Let us call it a mistake, my lord." From beneath lowered lashes, she looked for his temper to show. After all, she had behaved no better than a harlot, only to reject him.

Clearly puzzled and definitely chilled, he offered a sharp bow. "Indeed, Mrs. Graham. I apologize for once more misreading the situation."

The growl in his voice and the hurt deep in his eyes made her feel cruel, heartless, and horribly alone. Life was just so confusing. All she had desired was a quiet life with Sophia until he came along with his shadowed eyes and tantalizing touches.

By her own rash actions she had destroyed her peace.

She stretched out a hand and then let it fall. "Please. No apology is necessary. The misunderstanding is my fault." Now she was talking again when she should be silent.

But it was her fault for marrying Denbigh and for not having the courage to see it through. Then again if she hadn't run from her marriage, she would never have met Lord Wanstead. Life seemed full of the strangest pitfalls, and somehow she managed to fall into all of them.

"Let us not argue about who is at fault," he murmured, his lips wry. "Suffice it to say, I will do my best not to impose on you again."

His voice contained the same harsh quality she'd heard the first day he spoke to her. Sadness burned in the back of her throat. She could do nothing to change her circumstances no matter how much she hated the lies.

"Do we have still our bargain, Mrs. Graham?"

Unable to follow his train of thought, she blinked.

"You will return to the committee as the Grange's representative? I have informed the vicar you will."

Impossible man. He had no idea how much it would pain her to see the beautiful Miss Dawson and know she would one day be his countess. Eventually, he would succumb. She'd seen it happen time and again on the marriage mart.

But she had enjoyed her part in planning the fête. She had felt useful, needed, something she hadn't experienced for a very long time. "Yes, we have a bargain," she whispered staring at the top button of his plain grey waistcoat.

"Good." He stuck out his hand.

His grip was firm and warm as his hand enveloped hers. Then, in a courtly gesture he brushed the back of her hand with his lips, warm and soft and infinitely gentle.

Heat traveled through her blood in delightful waves. Her head spun as if she had spent too long on the merry-go-round. And fool that she was, she desperately wanted him to kiss her again.

He raised his gaze to her face, his eyes hard, flat, and impenetrable. As with stained-glass windows, light shone through the greens and browns but gave no hint of what lay beyond. He pressed his other hand over the burning spot on her knuckles and squeezed lightly. Mine, the gesture said.

Before she could snatch back her hand, he let it fall with the barest hint of a smile. A smile that turned her insides to blancmange.

"Thank you," he murmured.

She managed a stiff nod. "Good day, my lord." She gestured to the door.

"Good day to you, Mrs. Graham. I look forward to our chess game on Wednesday."

Her mouth dropped open. He opened the door in one swift, smooth movement, stepped outside, and closed it behind him.

Trembling with the storm of conflicting emotions, she remained where she was until she heard hoof beats gallop out of earshot. With knees weaker than Sophia's tea, she sank onto the parlor sofa. The excitement buzzing in her veins terrified her. This must stop. Today. Then why did she feel so light, so joyous?

Remember, her mind warned. Her response was no different than the foolish reactions of a starry-eyed girl in her first season. To see the same disgust in Wanstead's eyes that she had seen in her husband's would be more than she could bear. She hugged her arms around her waist, feeling suddenly cold.

She had never said a word about going there on Wednesday. How could he make such an assumption?

One game of chess. Where was the harm, provided she made it clear they could be no more than friends? And he had only agreed to host the fête because she had asked him. She hugged the thought like a warm blanket.

Once the fête was over, she would end their bargain.

"Jevens said I would find you here, Mrs. Graham."

Lucinda's breath hitched in her throat, and she swung around from the library shelf. "Lord Wanstead." His coat of dark-blue superfine and his starched white linen set off his stern, rugged features to perfection. Her mouth seemed to fill with what felt like two centuries worth of dust. "I didn't know you were home. Mr. Jevens said you wouldn't mind if I selected a book from your exceedingly fine library."

He glanced around. "My grandfather collected most of it. Did you find something to your taste?"

She held up the green leather-bound volume. *Macbeth*.

"Ah, the bard. Of course. You said you liked his plays."

He'd remembered. "I hope you do not object?"

"Please, help yourself whenever you wish. It is a pity for so much reading material to go to waste."

"You don't read?"

"I do." He flashed her a wicked smile. "I prefer chess."

When she made no answer, he strode to the window and looked out across the sweep of tree-lined drive. "My ancestor built this part of the house in the sixteenth century."

A harmless enough topic. "It has been in your family all that time?"

"Yes. Somehow we managed to survive Henry the Eighth and Cromwell." He swung back to face her, a smile changing his face from serious soldier to boyish charmer.

Blast her sudden shortness of breath. "Fortunate indeed." Lucinda's own ancestors had been loyal to the Stuarts and had lost everything until the Restoration. How she would love to share her own family's history, her own pride in her forefathers. She twined her fingers together. "Was there a reason you sought me out, my lord? I have finished my meeting with Mrs. Hobb."

He cocked a brow. "I would rather like to ask your opinion on a matter of taste and good sense. You seem to be blessed with plenty of each."

"I, my lord?"

"Yes. Come with me." He strode for a door at the end opposite from where she had entered. His long legs had carried him halfway down the passage by the time she reached the hallway.

She trotted to catch up. "Where are we going?"

"Hurry up," he tossed over his shoulder.

Dash it, if anything he had increased his pace. Curiosity rampant, she picked up her skirts and flew behind him down a passage lined with portraits in crisp Tudor ruffs or dripping in Stuart laces, along with one stern looking fellow in unrelieved black. No doubt Cromwell's man.

Wanstead disappeared at the end of the corridor, the juncture of the Tudor house and the newer wing. She charged around the corner, skidding to a halt to avoid a collision with a massive obstruction. Him.

She sucked in a much-needed breath. "What—"

"This way." He threw open the door of the chamber. A bedroom? She hung back. "If you will excuse me, my lord, I think it is time I went home."

He glanced into the room and back at her. "Oh. I fear you have a wicked mind, Mrs. Graham."

From the heat in her cheeks, her face must have turned scarlet. Had he guessed that she had done nothing but dream of the feel of his hard body pressed against hers since the morning of their picnic? Did he know that she had been disappointed when he hadn't kissed her more thoroughly yesterday? She gave him a glare and marched past him into the room, the book against her chest her only line of defense.

Hot, her pulse jumping, she glanced around. A canopied bed occupied one end of the room and a lady's dressing table and stool the other. "What did you want to show me?" Her voice sounded breathless.

Small creases furrowed his brow. "I was thinking of installing one of the new-fangled water closets and a bath in this room. What do you think?"

"It would have to be a large one." Oh, her foolish tongue. And her ridiculous blush.

He didn't appear to notice, apart from a glint in his eyes. "Large enough for two, I hope."

A vision of Lord Wanstead in a tub lit a fire in her stomach she couldn't control. She tried to keep her voice steady and her thoughts focused on the discussion. "But if I am not mistaken, this is the countess's chamber. Will you do away with it all together?"

"I don't see why not." He moved past her to stand at the foot of the bed. The light from the window outlined his granite jaw and the planes and valleys of his square face. "Since I don't have a countess."

It sounded as if he thought that was a good thing. She found herself in agreement and felt her heart lift in pure selfish joy. She closed her eyes for a second, trying to get a grip on her seesawing emotions.

"And anyway," he continued as if unaware of the havoc he was causing, "my chamber is more than big enough for two." A wicked smile transformed his face from stern to rake in a flash.

Her body felt a languorous yielding. She clenched her fists against the insidious melting and was unprepared when he snaked out a hand and pulled her close.

He gazed down into her eyes, the smile still on his lips and a question in his eyes. He brushed the hair back from her face with a hand that shook very slightly. "What do you think?"

Heat from his body warmed her, seeping into her bones. The scent of lemon and bay filled her senses. She longed to lean against his shoulder, to accept the protection of his manly strength, to open her heart and her soul to this unexpected gift of something wonderful in her life.

She pressed her palms against his chest, unable to take her gaze from the lips hovering close to hers with their promise of heaven and, if she was brutally honest, their pathway to pain and humiliation. "Please, my lord, let me go."

"Do you fear me after all, Mrs. Graham? I had not thought you a coward."

The razor edge to his voice gave her pause, his ability to read her thoughts frightening. Yet his eyes showed nothing but kindness. Powerless to free herself, she gazed up at him. "I must find you presumptuous. I am a woman alone, but I am not fair game, my lord."

"Call me Hugo. Are you happy living alone?"

The request and the swift question sent her mind scrambling to follow his train of thought. "I like it well enough." She frowned at him. "Most of the time, my lord."

"Hugo." He gazed down at her, not threatening, but not relaxing his hold either. "Would you not prefer the warmth of companionship at day's end?"

The implication mirrored the sensual cast of his mouth and the warmth in his eyes. She'd heard enough of the rakish ways of her husband's friends to understand his intent. He wanted her. And God help her, she wanted him, too, with every fiber of her being. Never had she felt desire of such undeniable strength. Her heartbeat quickened with a mixture of excitement and dread. An overwhelming longing to agree left her mouth dry and her chest aching. Fortunately good sense prevailed and the word "yes" remained firmly stuck in her throat.

He sighed, a heavy sound in the quiet room. "You remain loyal to your husband's memory, no doubt?" The soft baritone deepened seductively. "Surely he would want a better life for his child than living in pecuniary circumstances?"

He had of course noted the meager furnishings in her house, her modest lifestyle, and her outmoded gowns. The offer represented a financially secure future with no ties or obligations along with the comfort of his arms. A prospect she found very tempting. With him. If her family ever found out…Or if Denbigh learned of her whereabouts…Her mind twisted and turned like a child lost in a maze, every avenue blocked by the image of her husband. Yet all she could think of was the feel of his arms around her, the storm of passion weakening every strand of moral fiber in her body.

But if she agreed, if she threw caution to the winds, what kind of lover would she make? His scorn would shatter her soul.

"I can't," she choked out.

He released her and stepped back. "Once more you leave me envying your husband, Lucinda." His gaze searched her face. "Why? I know you are attracted to me. Your kisses show it even if your words do not. Why not exchange loneliness for what we can bring to each other?"

Too many lies lay between them. She settled on a truth he could not deny. "You need a wife and an heir. I will not stand in the way of your responsibility."

His expression lightened, his gaze searched her face. "If that is the only impediment, it is solved. I am not the kind of man to break his marriage vows. I do not intend to marry again."

The words rang with painful certainty. "But surely…an heir…"

He cupped her face with his warm, large gentle hands and bent his head close to hers, his lips curved in a smile. "As I told you, I do not want children. I have an heir. A cousin."

She searched his eyes, seeking truth, and found heat and desire and yearning.

He swooped down. Their lips molded as if they had been designed to fit. She desired him. Wanted him. The force of her desire shook her body like the tremors of an earthquake. Never before had she felt such a powerful want. Was it real? If there truly was a woman hiding inside her, this man would set her free. Or he would confirm nature's cruelest trick. Dare she find out?

If she did not at least try, she would suffer regret for all time.

A pulse-beat of passion in her core fired her blood. She had never felt so warm and willing. Her heart thundered hope. She flung her arms around his neck and arched against his solid length, tracing the seam of his mouth with her tongue.

He opened his mouth to her pressure with a groan.

"Lucinda," he murmured.

Hugo, my love, her heart whispered.

Ten

ARMS WARM AND AS STRONG AS STEEL BANDED AROUND her shoulders and under her knees. He swept her off her feet, a most unnerving sensation until he settled her in a gentle embrace. Safe. Secure. Cradled against his massive chest, she felt delicate, treasured, and unbelievably feminine.

I *can* do this. The thought took her breath away, leaving her dizzy with longing.

She cupped his strong jaw, the stubble on his chin grazing her palm. Desire darkened his eyes to the color of mysterious forests.

Her heart beating unbearably fast, she lifted her mouth to meet his lips. Locked in a breathless, mindless kiss, she relaxed in his hold. As he strode into his chamber, the combined sounds of their breathing filled her ears. She ran her hands over his shoulders and tangled her fingers in the hair at his nape, smooth and silky, so different from his strong hard body.

At the side of the huge four-poster bed, he lowered her gently to her feet. A hot shivering sensation ran across her shoulders and down her spine as he captured her face in his hands, raining small kisses on her eyelids, the tip of her nose, and each corner of her mouth.

Too slow. She didn't want time to think. She attacked the buttons on his coat.

A low groan vibrated deep in his throat.

As he stepped back, his chest rose and fell with breathing as shallow and ragged as her own. He peeled off his jacket and ran a fiery glance down her length. With the flash of a wicked smile, he unknotted the tapes of her gown and pulled them loose. He frowned when the fabric remained in place, but then found the pins and slid them free.

She wanted to see him also. Had to. Her fingers flew to his waistcoat buttons.

"Take it easy, love." His voice sounded hoarse.

Love. Softness weakened her muscles' ability to protest. Her insides felt loose and achy with a deep longing.

He shrugged clear of his waistcoat and tore off his cravat, unbuttoning the throat of his shirt with nimble fingers. Dark hair at the base of his throat attracted her gaze. Without thinking, she reached out to touch the springy curls, coarse and very male. She cast him a hesitant glance. Would he think her too forward? He stared back, his eyelids drooping over stormy greens and browns, his mouth sensual.

Boldly she placed her hand flat on his chest, absorbing the heat and the pounding of his heart.

He drew in a sharp breath.

She smiled.

"You little wanton," he teased, with obvious delight.

He liked her touch. And she adored the feel of crisp curls over warm skin. She slid her fingers deeper into the open neck of his shirt and found the curve of his muscled chest, not soft but hard and warm, roughened by hair.

He caught her exploring hand and lifted it to his mouth, kissing each finger, all the while gazing into her eyes. "Your turn," he whispered.

A pulse fluttered between her thighs as her body turned to hot liquid with streamers of fire running through her blood. Desire. Lust. Something deeper she dare not name.

He lowered his lips in her throat and inhaled a deep breath through his nose. "You smell delicious."

Lightly, he drew her bodice down, exposing her chemise and stays. He groaned, his lips moving to the rise of her breasts thinly disguised beneath the sheer cotton fabric. He pulled the drawstring undone and unlaced her stays with practiced ease, tossing them aside when they fell loose.

On a sharp indrawn breath, he cupped one breast, lifting and kneading. His thumb circled her nipple, a hard nub pressing against the chemise's thin fabric.

Steeled against pain, unable to breathe, she felt nausea roiling in her stomach. She stilled. She couldn't do this. She adored his kisses and the heart-pounding excitement of his embrace, but she hated the pain he would inflict.

He looked up from watching his hand and stared at her, desire a glaze on his face. "What is it, love?"

Guilt as bitter as bile rose in her throat. He would think her the worst kind of flirt. Shaking her head, she closed her eyes to hide her shame. "I'm sorry." She brushed his hand away and crossed her arms over her scantily clad bosom, all ten acres of it, suddenly, horribly aware of her near nakedness.

"Did I hurt you?" The raw anxiety in his voice drew her gaze to his troubled face.

"It is me. My fault." She retreated, her buttocks encountering the edge of the bed. Nowhere to run. She turned her head and stared at the blue and gold counterpane. "I can't do this."

He didn't move, but she felt his gaze on her face. "You make no sense. The way you kiss me…" He reached out to touch her jaw with his knuckle.

Against all her training, she flinched. He snatched back his hand.

Rigid, he stared at her.

Even though she didn't dare look, his tension crashed against her with the fury of waves dashing against a cliff. The cold, hard unfeeling rock of her. Cringing inside, she straightened her shoulders. "I'm sorry."

"Your husband hurt you." His voice was flat and cold and empty. "Didn't he?" He stared at the circular scar on her collarbone. "Did he do that to you?"

Miserable, ashamed, wanting to flee his inquisition, she nodded. "It was an accident," she whispered. "He'd been drinking. He didn't mean it." If only she believed it.

"He didn't mean to burn you with what? A cigar?"

The ice in his tone terrified her. "I made him angry when he was drunk. I should have known better."

He let go a long, slow breath. "Dear God. Drunk or sober, angry or not, no man has the right to deliberately hurt a woman."

He placed a hand lightly on her shoulder. Her skin absorbed his heat like ice in spring sunshine. "I swear, I would never do anything like that." Anguish tortured his voice, cracking it.

She bit her lip and stared into his eyes, seeing sorrow and deep regret, as if he blamed himself for what had happened when it was all her fault.

"I know you wouldn't hurt me. Not on purpose. But I…" Clutching her chemise close across her breasts, she half turned her shoulder so she did not have to see his face and read his pity. "There is something amiss with me. I freeze up. I don't like…it."

He drew her chin toward him with gentle fingers, forcing her to look up at him. The furrow between his straight brows deepened, and his eyes watched her closely. "You like kissing well enough."

Heat infused her cheeks. "That's different."

His glance dropped to her chest. She hunched her shoulders.

"Did he hurt you when you made love?"

Oh God. She couldn't take any more. "Please, my lord, Hugo. Let me leave."

"Just answer me this one thing, Lucinda. When he took you to bed, did it cause you pain? Not just the first time, but each time you lay together."

"Yes." Her heart clenched so tightly she thought it would never beat again. "He said…I was…am…frigid." She flicked a quick glance at his tight expression. "He couldn't rouse me, no matter what he did. In the end, he didn't even remove his clothes. He just did his duty and…" her voice broke.

"And what did he do to rouse you? Hurt you?"

The pity in his murmur shattered the dam she'd built to contain her rage, to hide her humiliation. Words ripped from her tear-filled throat. "He said it was the only way to make me feel anything."

"He enjoyed your pain and fear." Ice filled his flat voice. "It's a bloody good job he is dead, or I would kill him myself."

"He always begged my forgiveness afterwards. Blamed me, because I could not respond."

"The bastard." His hands cupped her face. "Some men are pigs. He did it to please himself, not you. Lucinda, did you not sense something wrong? Talk to your mother? Other women?"

"He was my husband. He threatened to tell everyone about me, if I ever said a word." She lowered her lashes, avoiding his gaze, knowing he would despise her weakness. "I didn't want people to know I was…like that." Frigid. Cold. Unfeeling.

"I don't believe it. You are a woman brimming with passion. I sensed it the moment I met you. This…man robbed you of joy and pleasure. Don't live your life thinking pain is all there is between a man and a woman."

"What if you are wrong?"

He tipped her chin with one finger, forcing her to meet his compassionate dark forest gaze. "I know by the way you feel in my arms, the way your response fires my blood. But you will never know for sure unless you try again." He lowered his head, not touching her with his hands, and pressed his lips to hers, warm and soft, infinitely tender.

Instant heat flamed across her skin. She parted her lips to the gentle flicker of his tongue against the seam of her mouth. She darted her tongue into his open mouth, and her body clenched at the sound of his quick indrawn breath.

Their tongues tangled and danced in the hot, wet cavity of his mouth. Nowhere else did they touch. Her body yearned to yield against his hardness. She pressed into his chest. A groan vibrated his ribs, and the heat of his hands hovered above her back. The muscles in her shoulders ached for his touch. Thoughts suspended, she lost herself in the sensations swamping her body.

His breathing shortened, his chest vibrating with the thunder of his heartbeat.

She closed her eyes and drifted on the tumultuous tide of desire, learning his mouth, how each sweep of her tongue made him purr like a satisfied lion, and how her core pulsed at the sound. She longed for the feel of his arms around her.

Weak-kneed and dizzy, she clutched at his sweat-slicked shoulders and with a breathless laugh drew back.

Control etched lines around his mouth, but a smile tilted the corners of lips moist from her kisses.

"Your kiss has me on fire," he said, his voice raw. "But I'll do nothing without your leave. You lead the way."

"Hold me," she said.

He spread a hesitant, questioning hand against her spine.

In answer, she molded into him. He wrapped his arms around her, cradling her against his chest.

She nuzzled his neck, inhaling the scent of lemon and bay and man. She kissed the pulse beneath his ear.

He caressed her back, her sides, her rib cage. The heel of his hands brushed the undersides of her breasts.

A shiver skittered down her back. Fierce desire jolted her core and beaded her nipples. She gasped.

He loosened his hold, pulling away with raised brows.

She'd never seen her husband unclothed apart from sly peeks when he was dressing. And he was nothing like this magnificent male, all power and mystery.

"Take off your shirt. I want to see you." She tried not to wince at how brazen she sounded.

He visibly swallowed, then nodded stiffly. In a blur of movement he whipped the fine lawn over his head and stood still and silent.

A golden torso of muscle and bone and sinew met her wondering gaze. A bronzed god of war. But unlike any statue, this warrior god lived and breathed and gave off palpable heat. She gazed in awe at the sculpted curves beneath a mat of hair on his chest, at the flat copper disks with their hard nub in the center. He clenched his fists and the muscles in his arms bunched. He said nothing, didn't move.

She pointed to the white line that arced through the hair above the rise of his breast. "What happened?"

"A saber cut," he said.

"And this?" Her finger hovered over the crown-sized scar in his side.

A deep ragged breath defined his ribs. He shrugged. "Spent shot."

She raised her gaze to his impassive face. "You might have been killed."

"Yes." He arched a brow "Touch me—if you wish."

Her fingers tingled. She licked her lips and stared at the

vertical line of dark curling hair dividing the rows of hard ridges on his stomach. Desire flooded moisture to the apex of her thighs. She flattened her palms on the swells and hollows of his chest, felt his nipples pearl against her sensitive skin. She scrunched her fingers amongst the rough hairs and he groaned low in his throat.

She jumped back.

"For pity's sake. Don't stop," he pleaded. "It feels wonderful."

The rough edge to his voice sent waves of pleasure rushing outward from her core. She reeled from sensations she couldn't comprehend. The certain knowledge that she had the power to move him gave her the strength to continue. She caressed the satiny skin of his shoulders.

His hands came up to cage her waist, heavy, warm, comfortable, and steadying. He stroked her back in rhythmic circles, brushing the sides of her breasts until their peaks tingled and burned for his touch.

Fingers trembling, she explored the contours of silken muscles, of arms tensed beneath her hands, the heat of his flat, hard stomach. He sucked in an audible breath, his gut hollowing, as she traced the line of hair to the waistband of his breeches.

"Lie down with me, Lucinda," he murmured against her hair.

"Yes." Had she spoken the word out loud?

She must have, for he swung her up onto the great bed in a smooth easy motion and stretched out beside her.

He bent his head and she met his kiss half way, spearing her fingers though his hair, pressing her thigh between his legs, and giving in to a fog of mindless desire.

One hand cupped a breast.

The mists parted, and she tensed.

"Hush," he murmured against her mouth. "I promise it will not hurt. If you tell me to stop, I will."

Wanting above all things to believe, she managed the smallest of nods.

He smiled and dropped a kiss on the corner of her mouth, on her cheek, and her chin, lowering his head until all she could see were the dark waves of his hair.

He pressed his mouth to the rise of her bosom through her chemise. Against her will, her fingers dug into his shoulders. She forced herself to lie still.

"Ah, sweetheart," he said on a sigh. "Don't suffer me in silence. Tell me what you want."

The chill of the air against her damp skin where his lips left their hot, wet brand left her feeling bereft. "I like it," she gasped.

"And this?" he asked. He dipped lower, stroking one nipple with his tongue.

"Yes," she whispered.

He repeated his attentions on her other breast. A delicious heaviness weighed down her limbs. Languid, she caressed his back, enjoying the shiver of his skin beneath her fingers.

He covered her nipple with his hot, wet mouth. Delicious warmth ran outward. Then he suckled.

Fire blazed along her veins. Her bones dissolved. Desire spiked to unbearable heights. "Oh, sweet heaven."

Her body became an instrument, his to play, to draw sweet music from its depths. Her mind filled with a wonder and awe so vast that the world disappeared.

His hands slid up and down the scale of her body, touching, caressing, drawing forth notes of unimaginable sweetness, sliding down her ribs, drifting over her outer thighs, whispering a song at the back of her knee, gliding in the heat between her legs. She opened herself, giving him access, and his hand pressed down on her mons.

Unutterable joy. She cried out, arched her back, and tilted her hips seeking more. Eyes closed, she drowned in the music of his touch. Nothing mattered but the magic of his wicked mouth on her breast and his hand tormenting her damp swollen flesh.

He raised his head. She moaned her disapproval.

"My God," he breathed. "You'll be the death of me. I need to see all of you."

For a moment she stared blankly, and then he tugged upward on the hem of her chemise. She raised herself to help him strip it off. Exposed to his gaze, she felt a wave of heat burn her cheeks, horrible and hot. She crossed her arms over her breasts as if that would somehow make them less obvious.

"Lovely." The reverence in his low voice and his expression eased her awkwardness.

Defiant, she let her hands drop away. "Hardly lovely. My nose is too big, my chin too square, and there is altogether too much of me."

Hugo's gut twisted at the wry smile on her lips and the shadows in her velvet blue eyes. Shadows he had mistaken for secrecy, not pain. He brushed the hair back from her temples and kept his gaze fixed on her face. "You are gorgeous. Don't let anyone tell you otherwise."

Lashes swept down, obliterating the thoughts in those dark eyes for a moment, and then she stared up at him. "There is nothing wrong with my eyesight, my lord. I can see what others see when I look in a glass."

Wounded, but brave. It pained him more than if she had wept. Keeping his gaze clinical, he scanned her length, from her lips full from their kisses over her bountiful breasts. His gaze traveled to the dusting of light brown curls below the lush swell of her belly. Fine and damp, they hid little from his gaze. His gaze swept across her wonderful thighs. He drew in a shuddering breath. "Dear God," he whispered, "so white, so strong…" He groaned at the image in his head of those curvaceous limbs wrapped around his hips, cradling him softly.

"I would see all of you, too," she said in a husky whisper.

He grimaced. "I am not a pretty sight, I'm afraid." He chuckled.

Lucinda reached for his pantaloons and fumbled the buttons of his breeches. "I won't fear what I can see."

"Let me get rid of the boots," he said, turning and sitting on the edge of the bed. They hit the floor with a bump.

Lucinda watched in fascination as he peeled the tight fabric down his firm narrow hips over firm round buttocks and long muscled legs. She ought not to look, but could not drag her gaze away. The man was a miracle of male beauty.

He turned to face her, his erection curving up towards his navel from a nest of dark curls, his stones hanging large and fleshy at its base. The head of his erection was dark with blood, the shaft knotted with blue veins. Rampant, huge, and terrifying.

A breath caught in her throat. She edged back.

He knelt on the bed, took her hand, and pressed a burning kiss to her palm. "Your passion did this to me. It won't hurt you," he said. "Not if I'm careful. Not if you are ready."

He guided her hand between her legs, pressed her fingers to her slick swollen flesh, and rubbed them lightly against her cleft. A little burst of pleasure made more moisture flow.

"You are not cold or frigid. You are hot, wet, and ready for me," he whispered. "Prove it to yourself. Let me inside."

Temptation stronger than any she'd ever felt surged through her veins. If she didn't agree, she would never know for certain. "Yes."

A sigh gusted from his chest. He captured her mouth in a blazing kiss and eased her shoulders back against the pillows. "Just one more thing, sweetling." He reached over and opened the drawer in the table beside the bed. He drew forth a clear, crystalline envelope and pulled out what looked like one rather damp finger of a glove.

She recoiled. "What is that?"

"Protection."

At her blank look he smiled. "It will keep you safe."

Safe? From what? Dare she trust him? She nodded.

He fitted it over his erection and tied a narrow red ribbon close to the base in a bow.

"Pretty," she said, her laugh strained.

He growled something, and dove in for a kiss.

One hard heavy thigh pressed down on her legs, his knee nudged until she parted her thighs. The lust that had died to a simmer flared to life in hot demand for satisfaction.

This time, her body urged. Now.

His hand roved the contours of her thighs, hips, and stomach plucking the strings of tension, vibrating chords until sensations shot back and forth at dizzying speed. One hand cupped her mons while the other adored her breast. His hot mouth suckled.

Pleasure flowed over her. The sensations built to unbearable heights. At any moment, she would fly off the edge of some dreadful precipice. His finger slipped inside her, moved, and pressed against soft yielding flesh. It felt good, but not enough. She clenched around him. He groaned and shifted to lie between her legs, the head of his erection nudging her inner thigh.

This was the part she hated the worst, the sharp intrusion and the grinding pain. He had promised not to hurt her. Dare she trust him? Lord knew, she wanted to.

One finger still inside, he pressed against her pulsing flesh with the heel of his hand and circled. More sweet agony of pleasure. But still not enough. She lifted her hips, demanding more.

He inserted another finger and she gasped at the increased tension, winding her hips to encourage him deeper. Instead, he withdrew. No. She clenched muscles she never knew she had to hold him fast.

"Dear God, you are killing me," he whispered withdrawing his hand.

She cried out a protest.

His face hung above her, the cords in his neck standing out, his expression taut. "Take me inside you," he said in a hoarse whisper. "I can't hold off much longer."

Trust, her heart said. "Yes," she said. "Please." Hurry. Before I change my mind.

Hugo saw hope shining from her eyes amid desperation. Humbled, his vision blurred even as his mind shrank from the weight of responsibility.

Lust pooled blood in his loins, emptied his mind, and urged him to bury his cock to the hilt in her slick hot channel. Reason struggled with the demand of need and won by a whisker. He must make things right for this woman. His woman.

He dipped his head to drink the sweetness of her mouth. The heat of her response scorched his lips. The magnificent breasts grazed his chest, begging for his touch, his mouth. He buried his face in their warm valley, filling his palms with firm full flesh. He licked and nibbled and teased, suckling gently, her mewls of longing a choir of angels to his ears.

Gently he eased his engorged shaft against the opening of her passage. Slippery with her moisture, it slid inside her welcoming heat. Home, his body demanded, his hips pressing forward. Slowly, his mind reminded. He clenched his jaw, held still, and gazed into her face.

Her eyes widened and then cleared, like a midnight sky in the Spanish mountains. She lifted her legs, wrapped them around his hips, and pulled him deeper into heaven, her soft, yielding flesh beneath his body better than anything he had imagined.

In slow, steady strokes, he drove into her, each time a little deeper. Her hands roamed over his shoulders, her nails dug in his back as she lifted her hips to welcome him in. Never had a woman urged him on so sweetly or driven him so high. His arms shook with the effort of holding his weight, and his heart thundered in his ears, but the sweetest sound of all were her cries of pleasure.

His cock jerked, and his balls tightened rock hard at the scent of her arousal. He could not hold back. Her muscles clenched and quivered around his shaft, milking him and draining him. Control gone, he drove deep and hard. Her moans of release mingled with his shout of triumph.

Only by willpower, did he prevent himself from collapsing on top of her. He tried to breathe around the pounding of his heart, tried to still the tremble in his arms. He gazed down in wonder at her rosy lips and her closed eyes, her lashes a dark crescent against her pale skin, her breath coming in gasps. Silky brown hair spread across the pillow like the halo around a full moon. Bliss blurred her features.

He eased out of her. She stirred and looked up with a weary smile.

"Sleep," he said and rolled on his side. He pulled her close, content to hold her until the real world intruded.

His woman. So fragile. So hurt. He had plumbed the bottom of her wary silence and discovered a treasure beyond compare. Suddenly the future did not look so lonely…if she would accept the little he had to offer.

Eleven

THE BONE-MELTING HEAT OF BLISS SLOWLY RECEDED from Lucinda's limbs. Steady breaths against her cheek. Another body's warmth. Hugo. Wonderful, strong, gentle, compassionate Hugo. The man had given her a gift as precious as life, her womanhood.

She opened her eyes. Surrounded by royal blue bed hangings and secure in his arms, she desired nothing more than to snuggle closer and sleep away the day. Safe.

How safe would she be if he knew she was another man's wife? If he discovered that the man he despised could snatch her back on a word? Lies for her protection felt like a millstone around her neck, dragging her into the depths of deceit against a man who had brought her such joy. A flood of shame chilled her to the bone.

She pushed back the sheet and rose on one elbow.

Hugo raised his head, his hand warm on her back. "Awake already, sweetheart?"

Dark hair tousled, his eyes half open, he looked sensual and handsome and good enough to eat. The urge to stay shocked her. "I must go home."

A smug smile curved his lips. He looked younger, less careworn, almost boyish in his wickedness. "Move into the Grange. Then you won't have to dash off."

"Move in?"

"It would be more convenient."

By allowing him to make love to her, she must have made him think she'd agreed to be his mistress. The thought of lying beside him night after night, free to kiss him, to bring him pleasure, sharing his bed and his life, was madly tempting. And completely out of the question.

In the throes of passion, she had not thought ahead. "No."

His smile faded. Eyes wistful, he stroked her arm. "Was it something I did?" His teeth flashed white, and he leaned forward and nibbled her ear. "Or something I didn't do…yet."

Pure unadulterated lust shot straight to her core. She steeled against the urge to bury her face against his wall of a chest, to let him fire those wonderful feelings banked within her all over again, to forget her responsibilities to Sophia, to her family, to herself.

"It has nothing to do with you." She leaned over and pressed a swift kiss on his mouth. His arm encircled her shoulders. He deepened the kiss, and for one brief, ecstatic moment she melted into him, letting heat and the rising tide of passion claim her very soul.

The power he exerted over her body left her terrified. She shoved his shoulder and his hand fell away, just as he'd promised. "I do not think it is a good idea."

A pang twisted in her heart at the hurt in his eyes.

He lifted her hand, bent his head, and kissed the inside of her wrist sweetly, gently. It felt like a promise. "Don't decide now. Give it some time."

Why could she not have met this man first? How could she deny him out of hand? The knowledge that she would never know this bliss of flesh and heart and mind again tore at her will. "I will give you my answer next Wednesday."

"Wednesday? That is almost a week." The words came out a disgruntled growl.

The sullen curve to his mouth brought a smile to her lips and a wicked thought to her mind. "Why not give the servants Wednesday evening off to help prepare for Saturday's fête? It will give us a chance to talk without interruption."

He swung his legs over the edge of the bed and cast her a thoughtful glance. "I hope it is not only talking you have in mind."

The man had a quick wit. She repressed a sudden giggle. In heart-stopping appreciation of his magnificent physique, her gaze drifted down his torso and landed on his thigh. She gasped. A painful-looking red rash spread like a spider web around an ugly oozing scar below his hip. "Dear sweet Lord. What is that?"

He scowled and covered it with the counterpane. "It is nothing."

"It looks dreadful. You need to see the doctor." She tugged at the cover.

He held it fast. "A surgeon assured me it would heal in time."

She opened her mouth to protest. The words died at the darkness in his expression. Suddenly, she didn't feel quite so safe. Sheet wrapped around her, she stumbled off the bed and snatched up her chemise.

A hand lashed out and caught her.

In fury, she stared at tanned fingers grasping her wrist as if it was no more than a twig, then raised her gaze to his face.

He dropped her arm as if it was hot. "I'm sorry I snarled at you."

She blinked. An apology? But hadn't Denbigh apologized each time he caused her pain. Her gaze fell to her wrist. Not a mark marred the skin, no red fingerprints, no bruising, no pain. Hugo was not Denbigh. He had proved that. "I'm sorry also. I overreacted." She touched his shoulder. He turned his head and dropped a gentle kiss on her fingers. Desire bloomed. Tension mounted. She laughed, shaky and breathless and full of longing. "I really must go home, or Sophia will feel abandoned."

His smile returned, more wicked than ever. "What if I were to say you are abandoning me?"

An unruly chuckle bubbled in her chest. She shook her head. "I promise to give you an answer on Wednesday, when we will discuss what you are going to do about that." She pointed to his leg.

He gave a soft groan but said nothing more, seemingly content to sit back against the pillows, watch her dress, and help find her hairpins among the bedclothes.

To Hugo's horror on the following Sunday, the churchyard looked more like Hyde Park at five in the afternoon than a sleepy parish church. A garden of

flower-covered bonnets adorned the church steps and
cascaded onto the yew-lined path among the grave-
stones, Postlethwaite flitting from blossom to blossom.
White robes flapping, he had the look of a demented
cabbage white butterfly.

Where had the Dawsons dredged up all these people?

The local congregation looked equally bemused.
They hovered at the margins of the squire's party of
fashionable guests, regarding them with sidelong
glances. Only Lucinda seemed incurious about the
influx of visitors. He frowned. While he didn't expect
her to mingle with strangers, he had thought he might
manage a few words with her after the service. But
there she was, slipping out of the side gate, her plain
straw bonnet and muted grey a stark contrast to the
fashionable women gathered around Catherine. He
preferred her plain bonnet. It let the beauty of her
spirit shine through.

He toyed with the idea of running after her and
dragging her back for moral support. Excellent idea.
A good way to make her decide against moving into
the Grange.

The impulse to locate his carriage and flee the chattering mob filtered through his mind. He squashed it.
As a leading member of the community, duty required
he greet his neighbor's guests. With the same grinding
in his gut that he got before a battle, he took a deep
breath, fixed his gaze on Squire Dawson's checkered
waistcoat, and forged into the fray.

In no time at all, he was hemmed in by the nodding
blooms and beaver hats above a host of smiling
youthful faces. The squire introduced him around. For

once his facility with names eluded him. Nothing distinguished one from the other except the colors of their gowns or the heights of their cravats. Five or so pairs of eyes riveted on him as if anticipating some miraculous pronouncement. It might not have been so bad if the squire hadn't introduced him as a hero.

"Well met, Hu," murmured a voice at his elbow. "Didn't expect to see you in this mêlée. I thought you avoided this sort of thing." The cultured drawl provided a welcome diversion.

Genuinely pleased, he stuck out a hand to the short, fair-haired man who'd appeared at his side. "Dawson. I heard you were coming back for your mother's ball."

Arthur grimaced. "More of a repairing lease."

"Run off your legs?"

Arthur glanced around and lowered his voice. "Hush, man. D'you want m'father to hear? I'll drop by and see you later." The anxiety in the younger man's icy blue eyes belied the cynical cast to his mouth. It reminded Hugo of the expression green officers got when they realized that the army on the hill opposite numbered three times the one at their backs. If Hugo wasn't mistaken, the poor sod was well and truly under the hatches.

If Arthur hoped Hugo had blunt to bail him out of a sticky situation, he was going to be disappointed. By leasing a field to a neighboring farmer, Hugo had barely scraped enough cash together to buy next year's seed. He might, though, be able to offer a bit of advice to the young rakehell. "Come by tonight, after dinner." Company might keep his mind off Lucinda and her answer.

"It will be late," Arthur warned. "I have to do the pretty with that lot or Mother will throw a fit." Arthur gestured to the party now moving down the path to their vehicles.

"I'll wait up," Hugo said. His empty bed held no allure.

The tremble in Lucinda's hands wouldn't stop no matter how many deep breaths she took. She smoothed the sheet over Sophia and dropped a kiss on her sleeping daughter's cheek.

Arthur Dawson was Miss Dawson's brother. Why hadn't she recognized the last name before this? It wasn't until she saw the blond young man beside his sister at the church that she'd remembered. She pressed her fingers against her lip to muffle her cry.

She lifted the candle and headed downstairs. Dawson was a recent addition to the Duke of Vale's sycophants, the dissolute young men who hung about him with besotted expressions. Unlike Denbigh, Dawson wasn't one of Vale's inner circle. He existed on the fringes, a puppy awaiting a pat on the head from the great man. And that made him dangerous. He would surely leap on any opportunity to gain Vale's notice, including her betrayal.

If he recognized her. Hope battered at the door of her mind. They had never been formally introduced, though she had seen him once or twice from a distance. But if she knew his name and his face, he might well know hers.

She stumbled down the stairs to the parlor. Hot wax dripped on her hand. She winced and placed the candlestick on the table. Blendon was her home, her life. Oh God, she'd even found a man who honestly seemed enamored. What to do? She sank onto the sofa.

Her discreet enquiries at the churchyard this morning had led her to believe Dawson would soon tire of a sojourn in the country. 'A wild youn'un,' Mrs. Peddle had said. 'Breaking his mother's heart,' Miss Crotchet reported sadly, 'when he used to be such a nice little boy.' 'Balks at his mother's bridle,' another opined.

Please, God, don't let him stay. The silent prayer echoed in her aching skull. Could she possibly hide from Dawson until after the fête?

A fashionable fribble like Arthur Dawson was unlikely to pay attention to a matronly widow with little beauty to draw a wandering eye. Unless something or someone brought her to his notice. The mistress of the local earl might well stand out from the crowd.

She squeezed her temples with trembling fingers. Think. One step at a time. She took a deep breath. The time to panic was when he showed signs of recognition. If she took care not to attract his notice, kept her distance from the Dawsons and their party— and Hugo—she might bring it off. Hugo would guess she'd made up her mind to refuse his offer. It couldn't be helped.

The fates had decided to force her hand regarding Hugo. A cold and empty future stretched ahead. Better that than returning to a life of misery. It would have come to this in the end. After all, few men kept a mistress forever.

She clung to that belief.

Arthur slumped in the chair opposite Hugo. He nursed his third brandy of the night, glaring morosely into the golden liquid. His tale of woe hadn't been much different than that of the younger officers in Hugo's regiment—losses at the gaming table, tailor's expenses he couldn't afford from his allowance, along with the underlying anxiety about letting his family down. In the army, young men had less time to get into the kind of trouble available in London. On the other hand, young officers distracted by such foolishness died.

Hugo sipped his wine with reverence, letting the numbing heat trickle down his gullet and pool in his stomach. It numbed the throb in his thigh along with the urgent ache for Lucinda. So she intended to take him to task about his leg. She really was going to be the death of him. The thought made him want to smile.

Arthur leaned forward, his eyes intent. "Explain it, Hu. One moment, you were returning from university and my mother was bragging what a nice couple you and Catherine would make, and the next you'd joined the army. What the hell happened?"

"Happened?"

"Why did you run for the hills? Our family not good enough for the Wansteads?"

"Christ. Was that what she thought? There was never an understanding between Catherine and me. I never thought of her as anything but your little sister. Lord, she was barely out of the schoolroom when I left." Having finished school, all he could think of was getting away from the Grange, from his father's black looks and his mother's tears. He'd thought only of escape and had run right into the truth at the cost of another's life. After that, he'd thrown himself into the thick of the battle.

Arthur cocked his head on one side. "I must say I did think it was a bit of a hum, but the way my mother talked, you'd have thought you were engaged."

Hugo sat up straight. "Now listen to me—"

"No need to fly up in the boughs, old boy." Arthur waved his goblet in Hugh's direction. "Come to think of it, she had the poor girl tangled up with a duke this past season, and the duke only danced with her once." He shook his head. "I really wish Catherine would stand up to her more."

"Like you do?"

Arthur shot him a glower. "My mother does not order my life the way she does Catherine's, I assure you."

"I have never seen your sister look as beautiful as she does right now," Hugo said. "I am sure the right man will come along."

"Well, you could be right." Arthur swirled his brandy glass, staring at the resultant whirlpool ruminatively. He drained it in one gulp. "She is as happy as a grig since she got back from town." His gaze dropped pointedly to his empty glass.

Hugo leaned forward, filled Arthur's outstretched goblet from the decanter, and topped up his own.

Arthur settled back in his chair. "I say though, Hu, did you have to ruin *my* life?"

"What in hell's name are you talking about?" Hugo pushed up from the chair. Pain shot up his thigh. His head swam. He froze halfway to his feet.

Arthur put up a placating hand. "Good God, man, sit down. I jest."

"You never could hold your wine." Hugo flopped back, his skin hot and sticky from the sudden burst of agony. "I thought you planned on joining the navy, following in the footsteps of that uncle of yours?"

Arthur's mouth turned down. "That's what I mean. It was all set."

"So…what happened?"

The dandy leaned back and crossed one leg over the other, booted foot swinging. His top lip curled. "The navy is too much like hard work, old boy." He raised his glass in a silent toast and swallowed deeply.

This was not the Arthur he knew. "I quite see your point." He inhaled the rich aroma of brandy. "There's also the problem of getting shot at."

The cynical man about town gone in a blink, Arthur shot bolt upright. The golden eyebrows lowered over a sullen glower. "Do you think I'm afraid?"

A twinge of unexpected pain in the region of his chest snatched at Hugo's breath. He'd lost any number of men he called friends and seen lives broken beyond repair, all observed as if from a great distance. None of it meant anything after what he'd done to his wife. Until now. Shocked, he clutched the stem of his glass. Aware of the skin tightening, white across his knuckles, he unclenched his fist. "If you are not afraid, then you are a fool."

"I wanted to go. Me. You never gave it a thought, to my knowledge. Do you want to know what happened? The day m'mother heard you were wounded that first time and everyone was saying how the earl's property would go to some distant cousin if you died, she vetoed my joining."

"So that's what this going off at half cock is all about. Resentment."

"Dammit, Hu. You have no idea what it's like. Escort your sister here; sweeten up some old lady there. I'm nothing but a puppet on a string. I begged for a commission, but Father refused to allow my uncle to put up the ready. He told me to enjoy myself on the Town. And that's what I'm damned well doing." He drained his glass.

"It sounds more enjoyable than marching for three days and three nights, wet from arse to tit, with no food in your belly and your men ready to shoot you. The last time that happened, some idiot drew the map wrong, and we had to march all the way back."

Arthur stiffened. "I can handle a bit of discomfort."

"Then there's the task of scraping your best friend's brains off your sleeve," Hugo said mildly and watched Arthur turn a pale shade of green. "Not to mention using the bodies of your men as ladders to breach a wall."

Arthur swallowed then rallied. "Vale says you heroes are all alike. You want all the glory for yourselves."

"If you think that any of that resembles glory, you are a fool. It's nothing but a cesspit. This Vale chap sounds like an idiot."

"He is not. He's a great go, a pink of the ton and a Nonesuch to boot. You must have heard of him."

"Well, I haven't." Hugo eyed the brandy bottle wondering if another glass would make it easier to put up with Arthur's nonsense.

"I'll introduce you to him the next time you are in Town."

"Who?"

"The Duke of Vale."

The hero worship that Arthur had once directed at Hugo now shone for this other man. Against his will, he felt the loss. "I suppose he is the reason you are driving your parents to distraction."

He knew he'd gone too far the moment the words left his mouth. Arthur wasn't ready to face realities. Three sheets to the wind, he needed a gentle hand on the ribbons, needed to get the bitterness off his chest to a friendly ear, not practical advice. God knew Hugo had suffered enough of his father's criticisms to understand.

Slowly Arthur lurched to his feet. "God. You are just like them. You make me sick."

Damn. A couple of months out of the army, and already he was losing his ability to handle men, or in this case, high-strung boys. "I'm sorry, Arthur. I should not have said that."

Arthur straightened and looked him in the eye. He executed an unsteady bow. "G'night, Captain Lord Wanstead. Don't bother to see me out. I know the way."

He shambled to the door and closed it behind him with a bang.

Damnation. He'd made a mess of that. Now he'd have to spend a whole lot more time with Arthur undoing the damage.

Perhaps taking a more active part in the arrangements for the fête and drawing Arthur in with him
might get the rebellious young man out from under the
cat's paw. The plan had the added advantage of putting
Hugo in Lucinda's vicinity. He preferred the hell of
watching and not touching to not seeing her at all.

Wednesday. By dint of will, Hugo stopped from
rubbing his hands together and glanced around the
library. Everything was in readiness. The chessboard in
front of the fireplace. Big soft cushions scattered along
the sofa. Sandwiches nestled beneath a cloth on the
table, and a bottle of cold champagne and two glasses
discreetly rested in a bucket of ice beside the hearth.

For that last, he'd engaged Trent's aid. Apparently,
Jevens hadn't raised a brow at the request for the champagne, but Trent had smuggled in the extra glass.

Hopefully tonight, Hugo would make Lucinda
realize the foolishness of meeting in secret. God
dammit, there had to be some advantages to being an
earl. He didn't give a tinker's cuss what people thought
of his domestic arrangements. It wasn't as if he had a
wife to worry about.

He glanced at the clock. Almost six. She should be
here any minute. A pulse of anticipation thrummed in
his blood and stirred things lower down.

He frowned, a little unsure of her reaction. All week
she'd avoided his gaze when he met her by chance.
He'd seen her at the post office in the village on
Monday when riding out with Arthur to view the

field. She'd looked so pale at his approach that he'd asked if she was well. To his annoyance, she'd barely looked at him, and after a quick good morning, had scurried off. Damn, but he wanted her and the child with him where he could care for them. .

In a wild moment of pride he'd almost introduced her to Arthur. As what? The question had halted him, what with Lucinda's notions of propriety and Arthur's rakehell demeanor, he could imagine the awkwardness. He cursed. He certainly didn't want to give Lucinda a reason to balk.

Tonight he would follow his battle plan. He would woo Lucinda into his home. She had to agree. He couldn't live in a permanent state of arousal knowing she was flittering around in a nearby house where he couldn't get to her. He paced the carpet in front of the chessboard. He felt like he had at Eton when expecting sustenance from home, hunger building to unimaginable proportions.

He'd starved on the small portions they fed him at school. Only the arrival of cook's cakes and biscuits once a month had stopped him from stealing food from the kitchen. Or at least it had, after the humiliation of his first public beating.

This was a very different kind of hunger, sharper and more primal. It awoke a beast he wasn't so sure he could control. No. He had to remain in control. He could not risk making her fear him, even if she should. God. Courageous as he knew her to be, if she knew the truth, she would run away screaming.

He should tell her why he would never marry, why he could only offer a *carte blanche*. God that sounded so crass. Ugly. The truth was uglier. It might be better for her if she did stay away. He glared at the bishop and centered it on its square. He should not have sent Trent to fetch her. He should have gone himself. Then if she'd refused his invitation, her rejection wouldn't become public knowledge. On the other hand, if he went, then the neighbors might see her in his carriage and talk.

Damn. What a cesspit.

The crunch of wheels on gravel alerted him to the carriage's arrival. He parted the curtains a fraction. He watched Trent hand her down with a respectful demeanor and escort her to the front door. Good man, Trent. A good soldier, too. He could be trusted with any mission. The only servant on duty in the house tonight, Trent wouldn't interrupt unless Hugo rang.

He forced himself to sit in the chair opposite the door. It wouldn't do to appear too eager, like some untried boy. Faint heart did not win fair lady.

The front door banged shut. Decisive footsteps tapped on the flagstones in the hall.

Hugo leaped to his feet and swung the door open.

Eyes wide, she stared up at him. He divested her of her shawl and tossed it on the nearest chair. "You are late."

"Sophia—"

"It doesn't matter." He hauled her close, inhaled the faint scent of lavender, and captured her parted lips in a kiss.

The stiffness melted from her body. She leaned into him and clung to his lapels, her eyes closed, her breath warm on his cheek. He kicked the door closed with his heel and drank her sweetness. He felt his restlessness dissipate and the emptiness fill to overflowing. It wasn't enough.

He cupped her lush, rounded bottom, pulled her close, and tormented his body with her swells, the hills and valleys of her full soft figure. Lost all track of time, all thought, except of the female in his arms, the scent of her in every breath.

When she pressed a hand against his shoulder, he released her with reluctance.

Stepping back a fraction, she put her fingertips against her reddened lips. Her eyes swirled with emotions he didn't recognize.

He should not have rushed her. He got a grip on the powerful urge to swing her up in his arms and carry her upstairs. Don't rush your fences. His father's admonition to an impatient boy. Hell, he knew better. "Come," he said. "Sit down." He took her hand and led her to the sofa.

Straight backed, she lowered herself to the seat and perched on its edge. Her hands twisted in her lap. She stared down at them.

A lump of something cold sank to the pit of his stomach. He'd felt it before, in the heat of battle. Dread.

She raised her gaze. "My lord. Hugo. I have a confession to make."

Twelve

A WARY EXPRESSION DAMPENED THE LIGHT IN HUGO'S eyes and caused Lucinda to ease in a deep breath. No sense in beating around the bush. "I cannot move into the Grange."

A chill stillness seemed to descend on the room. A slight shift of his shoulders seemed to put miles between them. "Cannot, or do not wish to?" he asked coolly.

Breathless, she recited the words she'd rehearsed in the small hours of the night. "I like my life the way it is. How would I explain my position to Sophia…" She gentled her words with a smile through lips so stiff, she wasn't sure they moved at all.

He pushed up to his feet, strode to the console, and poured a glass of brandy. He took a deep swallow, staring at her as if he could read her thoughts. "There is something else troubling you. I feel it. Do you fear me?"

She jumped at the accusation in his tone, at his withering glance.

Dear God, what could she say that would satisfy him without giving too much away? "We hardly know each other. I…I just do not wish to rush into something I may regret later." As half-truths went, it made perfect sense.

"You fear I will abandon you or otherwise cause you harm?"

The words were flat and indifferent, and yet she sensed that the idea of her being afraid, her lack of trust, somehow wounded him deeply.

She could not let him think her reluctance was his fault. She shook her head. "I am not afraid of you."

His gaze raked her face. Unable to bear the bleakness in his expression, she glanced down at her hands, plucking at a loose thread on her reticule.

He crossed the room to her side, cupped her chin, and looked deep into her eyes until she was forced to lower her lashes or give away her heart. "If you do not fear me, then give me time to earn your trust."

He brushed his mouth against hers, and delicious shivers chased down her spine.

The prospect was all too tempting. But with Arthur Dawson wandering the neighborhood and her blushing like a schoolgirl every time she laid eyes on Hugo, it was far too dangerous. The young man would notice her sooner or later. "I don't know." Blast it, was that the best she could do?

"Let me help you make up your mind." He tipped her chin, angled her face, and with one hand at her nape, slanted his mouth over hers.

Just one kiss and she would go home.

The kiss deepened and went on forever. Her body tingled with desire. Just this one last blissful encounter, and then she would put an end to it, telling him that if he would not accept her word as final, she would take the only course left. She would leave Blendon. She didn't have a choice. She could not risk discovery.

Thought, reason, and common sense floated away on the rising tide of passion until she came to her senses, lying in the crook of the sofa's arm, panting with desire. Heavy lidded, she watched him rise and lifted her arms to bring him back, but he chucked her under the chin, tossing cushions from the sofa onto the rug in front of the hearth before striding to the door and turning the key.

Her heart knocked a steady rhythm against her ribs as if seeking escape. A lie. Her insidious longings, her need to feel wanted, held her captive. "What are you doing?"

"You'll see."

With a lopsided smile he caught up a bottle of champagne, pressing his thumbs against the cork with a sly glance in her direction. "I hope you don't object to a little nectar of the gods?"

How could she resist the devilish twinkle that replaced his frowns? She shook her head, a flutter of anticipation stirring low in her stomach.

The cork hit the ceiling with a bang. She squealed, then laughed.

He filled the two flutes to the brim, first with foam and then with golden liquid dancing in their crystal depths. He lowered himself to sit beside her and held the glass toward her mouth. She reached to take it.

He shook his head. "Close your eyes."

Surprised, but game, she parted her lips to drink. Cool bubbles burst in her face in a shower of mist. Instead of the edge of the glass, a warm finger moistened her lower lip. Instinctively, she licked away the bead of sharp-tasting liquid and opened her eyes. Shards of green crystal glinted amongst the brown flecks in his eyes, and her heart picked up speed.

He dipped his thumb in the wine, traced the seam of her mouth with cool liquid, and then swooped down to lick it away. His tongue heated her chilled skin.

"Umm. You taste like heaven," he murmured against her lips.

Pleasure hummed along her veins as if the bubbles from the champagne had somehow found their way into her blood and now sought an escape. Her eyelids drooped, weighted by desire. She let the sensation sweep her along.

When he lifted his head to drink from the glass, she felt a brief sense of loss and then smiled a welcome as he leaned forward to claim her mouth.

A froth of bubbles drizzled from his mouth into hers. Shocked and aroused by the strange sensation, she swallowed them down. Emboldened, she dove her cool tongue into the wine-flavored, hot cavity of his mouth. Delicious.

A groan vibrated his chest.

She pushed at his shoulder, laughing as she came up for air. "Where on earth did you learn such wickedness?"

He lowered his lashes, and his lips curved in a modest smile. "A soldier gets a broad education."

"I can see it now. Wellington's manual on bedroom strategy." She hiccupped. Good lord. Was she foxed on one sip of champagne? Or did the heady wine of lust pounding in her veins make her act like a giddy girl? She pressed her fingers to her lips. "Excuse me."

"There is more to come," he said with a roguish smile, "but you have to sit up."

Intrigued, she did as he bid. In a smooth motion, he rose and picked her up. She expected him to head upstairs to his chamber and threw her arms around his neck, inhaling his manly scent, kissing his jaw, nibbling his ear, and feeling the rasp of his shadow of beard against her cheek.

He stopped at the rug in front of the hearth and lowered himself on one knee. Though he tried to hide it, she felt him wince.

"Your leg," she cried out.

He grimaced. "A twinge. Nothing more."

"Perhaps we should not—"

"Oh yes, we should." His voice sounded rough, yet held laughter. He set her down beside the cushion and with swift tugs unlaced her gown. She helped him strip it over her head. Her stays and chemise swiftly followed.

He ran his hands over her shoulders and down her back, following the curve of her hip with long slow strokes that made her purr like a cat.

In only her stockings and shoes, she felt strangely naughty and dreadfully vulnerable.

"What about you?" she whispered. "Are you going to remain clothed?"

Like Denbigh.

The repulsive recollection chilled her to the bone. She stiffened. He must have seen it and interpreted it as fear, because he patted her shoulder as he might a skittish horse. "Easy," he whispered. He undid the buttons of his shirt. Muscles stretching and rippling, he removed his jacket and then divested himself of shirt, shoes, and breeches.

In fascination, she raised herself on an elbow to watch. She ran her fingertips across the warm flesh of hard flank and skimmed the bandage around the breadth of his injured thigh. The man was gorgeous.

He turned his head to look at her with a cocky smile and smoldering eyes.

Her core fluttered, her body clenched in a shiver of delight. She rolled on her side as he stretched out beside her, stroking the sculpted muscles of his beautiful chest and shoulders. When he leaned over to snatch up a wineglass from the hearth, her gaze drifted over the ridged stomach to his rampant cock, the proud proclamation of his virility.

The evidence of his desire. For her. Wild and wicked, female power surged in her veins.

"Feeling more comfortable?" he murmured taking note of the direction of her gaze.

She cast him a sultry glance from beneath her lashes and nodded.

It provoked an answering grin of appreciation. He held the glass to her lips, and she took a small sip at his hand. A tart burst of bubbles filled her mouth. He bent his head to kiss her cheek. His lips felt tender.

The room blurred as if a fog had rolled in through the window. How could she have such bad fortune all tangled with so much good luck?

"Lie down for me, sweet," he whispered. "On your stomach. I'm not done with you yet."

Pinpricks of anticipation ran down her spine and yet she hesitated, suddenly shy and unsure.

"Trust me, Lucinda."

The plea in his tone made her heart twinge. To show fear would hurt him. She did as he bid, her cheek pressed into the velvet cushion, her gaze fixed on his intent expression.

"Close your eyes," he commanded, albeit gently.

She let her eyelids drift closed. The heartbeat in her chest seemed to thunder. Blood rushed in her ears as she listened for movement, alert to his intentions. Her back muscles tensed against her will.

A splash of cold hit her spine. She gasped. A second later his hot tongue swept it away. She shivered. Her insides convulsed. "W-what are you doing?"

"Patience," he murmured, drizzling more cold liquid onto the small of her back, only to suckle it up in an instant.

Dear heaven, her insides were molten.

He drew circles with a moist fingertip at the back of her knees. As they dried, shivers ran across her thighs and buttocks. He blew on the sensitive spot, and shivers turned to heat. He continued to tease and torture her skin. Heat, cold, moist, dry until the tingles of electricity sparking through her veins had her reaching for fulfillment.

Pleasure, want, desire, he gave them to her as a gift of mouth and tongue and skillful fingers. She writhed and wriggled and gasped beneath one searing shock after another.

She wanted it to go on forever and wanted to beg him to end it. She rolled on her back, tugging on his shoulders. She might as well have tried to pull a mountain off its base. A supremely self-satisfied mountain, she saw from his face as he sipped from the flute and then dipped his head to suckle her breast.

Cold tightened her nipple. Pleasurable agony shot to her core. It tightened and clenched. She clawed his back, moaned her delight…and shattered.

Pulsing waves of gentle pleasure rippled through her body, followed by blissful heat. Her heart thundered. Breathless, mindless, she stared up at her tormentor.

A sensuous smile slowly curved his lips. His eyelids at half-mast, he looked boyishly proud and harshly handsome in the dim candlelight.

"I love the fire you hide beneath your prim and proper gown," he said. "Very erotic."

The woman in her purred with delight.

"And you?" she managed to gasp, glancing down at his still turgid shaft. "Will you not take your pleasure?"

"Oh, yes, my darling." He rocked his hips against her thigh. The head of his cock hot against her sensitive flesh, swelled and darkened. He reached for his jacket and pulled forth a crystalline envelope.

A condom. She forestalled him with a touch. "My turn."

A look of puzzlement and dawning hope crossed his face as, still staring into his eyes, she plucked the champagne glass from his hand and took a sip.

She ducked her head and gripping his rod lightly, kissed the engorged and gleaming tip. He groaned.

The liquid gushed down his shaft and over her hand in a cold rush. It disappeared into the dark thatch of curls at his groin. He drew in a harsh breath as she followed its trail with her tongue, sipping and licking, tasting the essence of him amid the wine. His hands convulsed in her hair.

Her pulse picked up speed. Would he reject her clumsy attempt?

He moaned. "God's bones. Where did you learn such a trick?" He sounded delighted.

She glanced up with a sultry look. "I wasn't sure it would please you…"

He swooped in for a swift kiss. "Woman, you drive me mad. Each time I see you, I want to put my hands on you. I inhale your perfume and can only think about the feel of your body against mine." He shook his head in bewilderment. "When I hear your voice I get so hard, I can't think of anything but being inside you."

She glanced down at his rampant cock with a naughty smile. "So I see."

He crushed her against his chest and angled her head to match his lips against hers, filling her mouth with his tongue and the empty places in her heart with the beating of his. She wanted to cry for the joy of it.

But he could never be hers. Not really. It was wrong not to tell him the truth, the nagging voice of conscience reminded. She thrust it aside. This was lust. Nothing more. No hearts, no souls, just the delight of male and female mating, something she would never have known without this man. She owed him this in return.

"Now," he said. "I have to be inside you now."

He sounded as desperate as she felt. "Yes. Now."

He quickly fitted the condom. With a gentle smile, she brushed his shaking fingers aside and tied the bow. She barely made it fast before he pressed her back against the cushion and thrust into her with a deep sigh.

The muscles of her inner passage tightened around the invasion. He held still, giving her time to adjust, to relax, to feel the slide of his heat against her slick inner flesh. With strong fingers pressing into her thighs, he lifted her hips, tilting her, opening her to his deeper penetration.

He drove home, to the hilt, his gaze on her face.

The bliss in his expression, the taut grimace on his lips filled her heart with tenderness. She clenched her legs around his hips and felt his muscles hard against her inner thighs. She caressed his shoulders, opening to his next thrust with an encouraging tilt of her hips.

"Dear God, you make me come too fast," he bit out.

"Really?" she asked, adjusting again.

"Little witch." He withdrew and pressed in and up.

A wild burst of pleasure ripped through her. She shivered with ecstasy, hovering on the brink of another shattering release.

Eyes glazed in passion he drove deeper, his neck corded, his breath exhaling in a groan with each pounding stroke. His buttocks clenched beneath her wandering hands

Again the subtle shift of his hips, the shivering abrasion and the wild burst of pleasure. Her inner muscles squeezed his shaft, clenching so tight that the dam inside her broke.

His rumbling groan of release joined her cry of pleasure and she flew apart, aware only of the slowing pulse of hips and cock, as he prolonged their shuddering climax.

For a long moment, head lowered, eyes closed, he hung above her, as if he had lost all of his strength.

Somehow she managed to lift her mouth to his, to brush his lips with a kiss.

His eyelids lifted. He returned the kiss with a sweetness that pulled at her heart and then rolled onto his side, drawing her into the circle of his arms, pressing her cheek against his rapidly rising and falling chest. To the sound of his heavy breathing, she drifted into a dreamless and bliss-filled doze.

The clock on the mantel struck ten. She jerked awake. "Is it really that late?"

His glance held a touch of sly temptation. "If you moved in with me, you would not have to rush away. We could play all night."

The temptation tore at her heart. "I'm sorry," she whispered.

He shook his head and smiled. "You have no need to apologize. Just think about it for a day or so."

"After the fête," she said, watching his face. "Until it is over, I cannot think of anything else."

His expression tightened, but he nodded. "If that will help you decide in my favor, then I agree."

"Manipulator."

"Procrastinator."

She laughed. Freely, openly, laughed at his nonsense. The way she'd laughed at home with her family. Tears burned the backs of her eyes. Foolish and wonderful.

They dressed in companionable silence, helping each other, giggling, becoming a little breathless and a lot aroused, when they should have been serious.

"I will ring for Trent to take you home."

While they waited, he poured himself a glass of brandy and stood staring out of the window.

"I wish you would not drink that stuff," she said.

His expression said she'd surprised him, before it turned politely blank.

"My husband became violent in his cups."

He put down the glass down on the nearest table as if it were hot. "I'm sorry. I wish you had said so before. I can easily do without."

Denbigh had said much the same thing after the accident with the cigar. He'd forgotten it was in his mouth, he had said, but there had been a mean glitter in his eyes. His sobriety had lasted less than a week.

"I don't expect you to change for me." Would not hope.

He came to her then, eyes full of tenderness. "There you go again, all stiff like the bristles of a hairbrush."

The image made her laugh. He folded her in a warm embrace and kissed her brow, then her nose, then her lips. The heat flared all over again. Only the sound of the carriage outside forced them apart.

"Damn, Trent," he said.

"No," she said softly, trailing her fingertips along his jaw. "I really need to go home."

"When will I see you again?"

"After the fête. When all of the fuss has died down."

He gazed at the ceiling as if seeking strength from on high. "Yet another week?"

She opened her mouth to suggest they not meet at all. He must have guessed her intent for he touched his finger to her sensitive lips. "Your wish is my command."

In that moment, she realized he would never accept anything but yes as an answer. If her final decision was no, she would have no choice but to leave Blendon and never see him again. The prospect left her entirely too empty, her heart ripped in two.

The sun kissed the Dingly Dell with gold. Good God. Hugo hadn't recalled his childhood name for this spot in years. All across the emerald sward, sweating farm laborers in shirtsleeves heaved on guy ropes, striped awnings on tent poles snapped in the breeze, and pennants fluttered. In two hours the Blendon village fête would be underway.

The happy, excited faces of the men and women who lived on his estate surrounded him. Lucinda was right. People needed a bit of fun to brighten their hard and oftimes dreary existence.

Thinking of Lucinda, he spotted her statuesque figure towering over the grim-faced Mrs. Peddle and a group of ladies at the archery target. In her somber grey gown with its starched white collar, she looked drab, dowdy, nothing like the passionate woman he knew resided beneath the cool reserve. He wanted to see her in jewel tones and silk, showing off that wonderful body, to see roses in her hair as well as her cheeks. He wanted to show her off.

A slight lowering of her lashes each time his gaze rested on her signaled her awareness of his regard. A secret message of desire and longing. It pleased him enormously.

After their last meeting, he'd arrived at a conclusion. It was time to bring the full force of the Wanstead charm onto the battlefield. If it had won his father the most sought-after beauty after the Gunning sisters, there was no reason why it would not win him the elusive Mrs. Graham.

This time her defensive line would not stand against his powers of persuasion. He'd storm her battlements one by one until she raised a white flag. Swinging his walking cane, he strolled to join her and the vicar and the other ladies of the committee.

"Not there," Mrs. Trip called out. "Can't you see that the sun will be right in the contestants' eyes?"

The bovine-looking lad moved the target three feet to the right.

Lucinda shook her head. "It can't go there. If they miss, the arrows might hit the children on the merry-go-round."

"Mrs. Graham is right," Hugo said.

All four ladies turned to stare.

Lucinda shot him one of those what-on-earth-are-you-doing-here looks females seemed to practice from birth, but then she remembered they were in company and sketched a curtsey. Damn, he hated the formality of it all. He'd much rather pull her close and kiss her generous mouth until she melted.

"Good day, ladies," he said.

"Good day, my lord," they chirped back at him.

"Why not put the target over there in the corner? Out of the way of everybody," he said.

"I thought it should be front and center to draw a much better crowd, my lord," Mrs. Trip said.

"Closer to the beer garden is best," Mrs. Peddle stated. "Good for trade."

"I agree with his lordship," Miss Crotchet said, then turned bright red.

"So do I." Lucinda suddenly looked a whole lot less frazzled. "There will be more room for people to gather and watch, and the sun will be behind the contestants."

Mrs. Trip pressed her lips together. "Well, if you think so, Mrs. Graham, then that's what we'll do." She raised her voice. "Fred. Pick that up and bring it along. We're taking it over there."

The long-suffering Fred wrestled the tar-dowsed target into his brawny arms and followed in Mrs. Trip's authoritative wake, wisps of straw scattering on the grass behind his every step.

"If he is not careful, there will be nothing left of that target," Lucinda observed.

Hugo smothered a laugh. "I am sure that will be the last time he has to move it." He touched her shoulder lightly. "Is there anything I can do to help?"

Miss Crotchet stared at them, her eyes popping open. "Oh, please do excuse me. I must see about the tables for the baking. Squire Dawson's men are sure to set them up in the full sun unless someone is there to put them straight."

"Aye," said Mrs. Peddle, her narrowed eyes fixed on the other side of the glade. "And if I don't keep an eye out for Peddle, he'll be giving away free samples to them as is helping."

Lucinda's eyes twinkled. "That would never do."

"I will treat all the helpers to one pint of ale, Mrs. Peddle," Hugo said. "Send the bill to Mr. Brown."

Mrs. Peddle's face lightened. "That's right gentlemanly of you, my lord. Right gentlemanly, indeed.

Excuse me while I go and tell that fool Peddle."

"Of course." Hugo gave her a nod.

Lucinda watched her stomp off and then turned her adorable face up to Hugo. A frown creased the space between her eyebrows. He found himself wanting to kiss it away.

"Did you do that on purpose?" she asked.

"Do what?" he said, avoiding her gaze by knocking the head off a daisy with the tip of his cane.

"Get rid of them."

"Mrs. Graham, what can you mean?"

"I thought you were going to help set up the rope pull and grease the pig."

"Ah. Well, when I told Trent about the plans, he volunteered to lend a hand. I need your opinion on another matter."

She glanced around.

The vicar, assisting Miss Dawson to tether her pony to the fence, caught Lucinda's eye and waved. Far too familiar, the Reverend Postlethwaite, Hugo decided.

"I think the vicar needs my help," Lucinda said.

"You can help him in a moment."

"I really can't think what else is needed. Everything we planned is in place and ready."

"There is something no one thought of."

She must have caught something in his voice, because she stopped looking around and stared at him. Yes. Now he had her full attention.

"What is it?"

"Come with me and you will see."

He wanted to take her hand. No. He wanted to put his arm around her shoulders and stake his claim in front of the world. Instead, he satisfied himself with a brief guiding touch on the small of her back. "This way."

He gestured to the marquee set up at right angles to the Peddles' stand.

Her frown deepened. "The trestles are all set up for supper."

"Yes." He lifted the flap and bowed. "Step inside and you will see what you missed."

The cool smell of canvas and crushed grass filled the cavernous space. Filtered light leaked through the canvas walls. As he'd instructed Brown yesterday, at one end of the tent the grass had been covered in sheets of wood nailed together in front of a raised dais.

Lucinda strolled to the center of the board floor and stared at the music stands and chairs on the platform. She twirled around, her face alight. "I do not believe it."

He tried to look innocent and failed miserably. His mouth insisted on grinning. "What do you not believe?"

"It is for dancing."

"After supper. The squire will have his ball, and the villagers shall have theirs."

She flew back to his side. "It will be the highlight of the evening. They will be so happy. Thank you." She leaned forward.

She aimed the kiss at his cheek, but he fielded it with his lips and caught her close.

For a moment, they clung together, her hands on his shoulders, his at her waist, like an old married couple, instantly in tune.

She pulled away. "Oh, goodness." She smoothed her gown, touched her hair, and glanced over her shoulder.

"We really shouldn't. Someone might see."

And that was her last bastion. He had a plan for that, too.

"The musicians will arrive at supper time."

A throat cleared outside the tent.

Lucinda retreated a step and stared at the wooden boards as if inspecting their joints.

Trent entered, a knowing smirk on his face.

Hugo wanted to smash the smirk into smithereens. "Yes."

"The squire is looking for you, my lord."

The tension leached from his shoulders. He should have known that Trent would watch his back. "Is he, indeed?"

"Yes, my lord. He was over by the stalls a moment ago, but he is headed this way."

"Thank you, Trent." He turned to Lucinda with a rueful smile. He couldn't remember smiles coming so easily. "So, Mrs. Graham, I assume this meets with your approval?"

Her lips were rosy and her cheeks flying flags of color. She looked delicious. Like a woman well kissed. A deep satisfaction settled in the pit of his stomach. Oh yes. He had a very nice plan for later.

"I think it is excellent, my lord," she said.

The twinkle in Trent's eyes said he didn't buy the inspection one little bit. He grinned and ducked out of the tent.

"Shall we, Mrs. Graham?" Hugo held back the tent flap.

"Yes, my lord." She dipped beneath his arm and out into the sunshine.

Blinded by the glare, Hugo blinked. Ahead of him, Lucinda seemed to turn to stone. Then Hugo saw reason for her consternation. Not only was the squire bearing down on them, but the whole Dawson family was tramping across the grass in their direction.

"By thunder, Wanstead," the squire roared. "This is like old times."

"Really, Henry," his wife said. "There is no need to shout. Wanstead isn't deaf."

Behind his parents, Arthur stuck out his tongue, while the diminutive Catherine smiled serenely.

"And there," Lucinda said pointing in the opposite direction, "is Annie with Sophia. I really need to speak to her. Please excuse me, my lord."

He couldn't actually say no, dammit.

As Hugo made his bows and shook hands with the squire, he was aware of Arthur's gaze following Lucinda's stately progress across the field.

"Who is she?" Arthur asked when Hugo squeezed his hand.

"Who?" Hugo asked, the back of his neck bristling.

"The woman you had tucked away in the tent."

"We were inspecting the tent," Hugo said.

"That is Mrs. Graham. She is a treasure. She has done most of the organizing," Catherine said.

Arthur glanced over to where Lucinda chatted with her housekeeper. "Have I met her somewhere before?" He frowned and shook his head. "Striking woman, and a snug armful for a man of your size." He cast a sly look at Hugo.

Hugo wanted to hit him, too. What he really wanted was to drag Lucinda back into the cool dark of the tent and keep her hidden, like a dragon protecting his treasure. He kept his fists firmly at his side, but God help him, his strategy for tonight had to work or he'd find himself demented and baying at the moon.

"Never mind that." Mrs. Dawson waved her sunshade to encompass the whole of the field. "Hugo, will all it be ready in time? I have guests from London expecting to spend a few hours here this afternoon before the ball."

"Mama," Catherine said. "It is quite obvious everything is in order. Is it not, Hugo?"

Dragging his gaze from Lucinda, Hugo glanced down into her vivacious expression. Good for Catherine. Standing up to her mother at last. "Yes. I am quite sure everything will be fine."

Thirteen

LUCINDA PICKED UP SOPHIA AND PERCHED HER ON her hip. She placed a hand on her damp forehead. "My word, child, you do feel hot." She wiped away the beads of perspiration with her handkerchief. It came away grubby. Darn it. It was one of the handkerchiefs she'd intended to keep for best.

Annie shook her head and smiled. "She's a mite overexcited, I'm afraid. We thought we'd come and take you home for lunch. You've been here for hours, and you hardly touched your breakfast."

Lucinda gave her a grateful look. "You are right." She brushed the damp tendrils from Sophia's temple.

Annie rested a hand on her belly. "She can't understand why I won't let her ride the horses." She nodded toward the makeshift paddock created by Trent and Albert.

"Horse mad," Lucinda said. "Annie, your father did none of us any favors by putting her up on Old Bob." Sophia would never have access to a horse, the way Lucinda had as a child, unless she did a whole lot better with her investments. They were doing outstandingly well, according to the last letter she'd received from her man in the City, but not well enough for expensive luxuries. Or unless she accepted Hugo's offer. The magic of his touch would be a whole lot easier to resist if she just had herself to consider. Denying Sophia her heart's desire seemed dreadfully hard-hearted.

The knowing expression on Mr. Dawson's face moments ago flashed into her mind. Life for Sophia would become far harder if he recognized Lucinda. But since he had not and he'd seen her several times, both here and in the village, perhaps he never would. A little flower of hope unfurled deep inside her. Perhaps she really had secured a second chance at happiness.

She set Sophia on her feet and took her hand. "Let us go for lunch. There is nothing more I can do. This afternoon is all yours, little one. Won't that be grand?"

A long line of folk waited to pay to get into the fête. Lined up with Annie, who had donned her Sunday-best bonnet and had her two little boys rigged out in new skeleton suits, Lucinda stood tall with the pride of accomplishment. Without a doubt, this year's fête would go down in the annals of Blendon's history as a resounding success. The money collected today would go a long way to help with the church roof, and there might well be enough to pay for a teacher one or two days a week. The day had also brought a spirit of community to the village, people caring for their neighbors, including Hugo.

"Bless me," Annie said, handing three pennies to the smiling verger. "I don't think I've ever seen so many people all at one time."

The field seethed with gaily dressed country folk and a smattering of townspeople from nearby Maidstone. The cries of the strolling hawkers competed with those at the booths for attention. Was it really only a few months ago that she had been afraid to step out of her townhouse, reduced to an ungainly freak by her husband's sneers?

They strolled between the rows of booths lined up down the center of the field.

"The vicar's flyers certainly seem to have done the trick," Lucinda said, grasping Sophia's tiny hand more firmly, afraid of losing the little girl in the crowd. She glanced down at Annie's twin boys. They had drawn closer to their mother's skirts, their eyes huge in their three-year-old faces. Good little lads. It would be a shame if their family had to go north to get work.

Sophia, the naughty little minx, tugged on her hand. "Horsy," she said.

"Don't you want to try the lucky dip?" Lucinda asked, pointing to the bran tub where a little girl with beribboned brown ringlets dove elbow deep in wood shavings fishing for her surprise. Behind her, a line of excited children waited their turn. They were good prizes, too, supplied by Miss Dawson.

The open-mouthed twins pulled Annie in the direction of a juggler.

"Horsy," Sophia said, her bottom lip pushing out.

"In a minute, sweetheart. Watch how the man catches the pretty balls. Isn't he clever?"

While Sophia regarded the juggler with a distinctly unimpressed expression, Lucinda scanned the crowds. No one she recognized at the paddock or at the ale tent. Then she saw him. Hugo. Large and solid and a full head above those around him. How handsome he looked, and cheerful, entirely different from the sullen man who'd arrived a few short weeks ago with shadows in his eyes and an unsmiling mouth. Had she put that warmth in his gaze? It hardly seemed possible, and yet something deep inside her knew it was true.

The crowd divided, leaving a clear path between them. She willed him to turn, to look across the space and see her. But it was Miss Dawson who held his attention. She laughed up at something he must have said, and he bent his head to hear her words. Then the break in the crowd closed, leaving Lucinda with a desperate urge to march across the trampled grass, hook her arm in his, and declare him out of bounds. As painful to her heart as lightning to the eyes, a thought flashed across her mind. She didn't have the right.

She was a runaway wife who must stay in the shadows, at best a mistress. A burning sensation crept up behind her eyes. Not tears. Not when she had every reason to feel thankful. She would not allow self-pity. Not now. Not ever. She sniffed. She rummaged in her reticule, found her handkerchief, and dabbed at her eyes before grasping Sophia's hand and turning away.

"Mummy angry?" Sophia asked.

Lucinda loosened her grip. "I'm sorry, darling. Of course I'm not angry. Come, let us join Annie and the twins." She ushered the little girl to the front of the crowd around the juggler.

Staring, but barely seeing more than a blur of colored balls, Lucinda bit her lip. What on earth was wrong with her? She had wanted him to rejoin his world, to take an interest in his estate and his neighbors, instead of playing chess alone. She should be happy, not feeling as if she had lost half a crown and found a penny. A nobleman had duties to fulfill, important responsibilities, and one of those included marrying and siring a son to continue his name. The knowledge had been instilled in her from birth. She must not become an impediment to his duty.

"Mummy," Sophia said, jumping up and down as the crowd clapped their approval and the juggler passed his hat for pennies. "Horsy. Now, please."

Here Lucinda was mooning over something she could not have like a spoiled child, when she had a cherished daughter who wanted her attention.

"Are you coming, Annie?" Lucinda asked.

"Wouldn't miss it," Annie said. "I can't wait to see what these lads make of sitting on a horse." If anything, the tousle-haired twins drew closer to their mother. "Cowards," Annie said with a grin.

"Mrs. Graham!" Lucinda swung around at the sound of her name.

A hot-looking lad puffed up beside her, his red hair sticking out in corkscrews from beneath his cap. "I've been looking all over for you."

Annie raised a brow.

"Oh, dear. What is wrong, Tom Drabet?" Lucinda asked. "I thought you were helping Mr. Peddle."

"You're wanted over at the butts," he said. "Come on. It's real bad."

Lucinda stared at him, her stomach sinking in a most unpleasant way. She did not want to go over there with Miss Dawson and her London friends. "The vicar is in charge of the archery contest."

"'T'were the vicar who sent me to find you. Please, Mrs. Graham, it's important. You must come." He dodged around a woman in a coal-scuttle bonnet and was off before Lucinda could question him further.

"Mercy," Annie said staring after the boy with an open mouth. "What could possibly have gone wrong? Perhaps one of the ladies has fainted. You know how the vicar relies on your help with the sick."

Sophia tugged on her skirt.

"Yes, darling," Lucinda said. "In a moment."

"If it's the vicar asking, you best go," Annie urged.

What excuse could she give for refusing? 'I don't want the Dawsons' friends to see me.' That would certainly raise some unwanted questions. And having seen them all at church, she knew she had never met any of them in her previous life.

"Go on," Annie said. "Stop your dithering, lass. Someone could bleed to death afore you gets there."

"In that case, they need a doctor, not me," Lucinda muttered. She handed Annie some coins. "Let Sophia ride all she wants. I'll be back as soon as I can."

"Don't you worry," Annie said. "Sophia'll be fine with me and the boys."

Lucinda gazed at her daughter's eager face. The child might be fine, but that wasn't the point. Lucinda had promised to spend the afternoon with her, and here she was running off to do someone else's bidding. She sighed and crouched beside her daughter, holding the child's impatient gaze with her own. "Mummy has to leave for a while. Will you stay with Annie?"

The bright blue eyes staring back at her glistened with the beginning of tears. Lucinda winced. "Annie will take you for a pony ride," she bribed.

Sophia glanced up at the housekeeper, who nodded. The tears dried up with a blink, and Sophia put her tiny hand in Annie's work-roughened one.

"Little wretch," Lucinda said with a laugh that caught in her throat.

She picked up her skirts and hurried after the Drabet boy, determined to deal with the crisis as quickly as possible and get back to her child.

On arrival at the end furthest from the target, she discovered two groups of people—the villagers and Miss Dawson's youthful guests. Both clusters eyed each other with wary glances, but not a drop of blood was in sight. She frowned. The contest should have started more than half-an-hour before.

Reverend Postlethwaite rushed up to meet her. "There you are."

"How can I help?"

"We are a lady short," the vicar blurted out.

"I beg your pardon?"

Mrs. Trip waddled up to join them. "We 'ad it all set. An open contest. Then him, there," she glared at the young Mr. Dawson, "says it should be them from London against the village, but we need an equal number of ladies and gents on each side. And our side is one lady short." She put her hands on her hips. "And there ain't no way out of it now our men lost their bout." She glared at the chastened-looking men's team. "We ladies 'ave got to win."

"Oh, dear," Lucinda said, at a loss as to why they had called her. "I do not know anyone——"

The vicar looked a little shocked. "Now, Mrs. Graham, surely you won't let the Blendon team down. I know you can use a bow. You told me so yourself."

Another occasion when her unruly tongue had leaped ahead of her thoughts. "Oh, I couldn't," she said. "I am out of practice, and I was never any good." It didn't feel quite right lying to the vicar. In fact, it felt awful. A blush crept all the way to the top of her head.

Mrs. Trip folded her arms across a generous bosom restrained within the confines of a sprigged cotton frock. "There ain't no one else in the village. We're done for."

"Mrs. Graham, please," the vicar said with an encouraging smile. "It is not about winning. It is about entering into the spirit of the day."

Lucinda stared at him. He wasn't going to let her off the hook. With a strangely warm but heart-rending pang, she realized that just as she had been trying to draw Hugo out of his shell, the vicar had tried to draw her into the community. If she failed them now, they might never fully accept her. God knew, she wanted to belong somewhere. Dare she stop fretting and looking over her shoulder and believe Denbigh was out of her life for good?

At a glimpse of Hugo headed her way with steady strides, her heart leaped in welcome. She forced herself to focus on the vicar's face.

"Mrs. Graham?" The vicar's smile broadened. "You will do it for Blendon, won't you?"

The rest of the villagers stared at her hopefully.

How could she simply ignore the people who had been so kind to her and Sophia? And anyway with expert Mrs. Trip on their team, it wouldn't matter if she lost the first round and had to sit out. She would attract far less attention than she was at this very moment. "Very well. I will do my best."

Mrs. Trip beamed. "I knew you wouldn't let us down, Mrs. Graham."

"Now we'll show them," the Drabet boy crowed.

A warm glow told Lucinda she had made the right choice.

"Bravo," Hugo said arriving just in time to hear her agreement. The gleam of quiet approval in his eyes turned the glow to a blaze. It infused her from head to toe. Her heart picked up speed in response to his closeness. Sure that every eye must be turned in their direction, she lowered her gaze to his shining black Hessians. "Thank you, my lord."

He stiffened and half turned away. Her ploy had worked, but it left her feeling bereft and the glow faded to a memory. From beneath the brim of her bonnet, she watched him march back to rejoin Miss Dawson and her party with an ache in her chest. Setting up a mistress into his house might well ruin him socially, as well as her, isolating him from his peers. She would not allow it.

"Listen, everyone," vicar called out. "Same rules as for the men, but the mark will be closer."

"Don't look so worried, Mrs. Graham," Mrs. Trip said. "I been practicing at the butts with my boy. You and I can beat them delicate little things." She nodded at the other team.

"I certainly hope so, Almira Trip," Miss Crotchet muttered.

The ladies drew cards for opponents to the claps of the crowd gathered behind them. Lucinda kept her face fixed toward the target, facing away from burning curiosity and unable to shake the nonsensical feeling that she had left the house in nothing but her shift. A too tight shift.

Mrs. Trip and the youngest of Miss Dawson's friends went first. Miss Abbott had come prepared. She wore a forest green archery gown with a jaunty hat *à la* Robin Hood. Miss Crotchet drew Miss Dawson who looked demure and modest in a simple white muslin trimmed with rosebuds.

Lucinda's opponent was clearly a diamond of the first water and no doubt this season's Incomparable judging from the way Mr. Dawson hung on her lips. A golden-haired beauty, she wore the latest Parisian wrapping dress of cambric tied beneath her bust by a blue figured ribbon. Her Wellington hat added inimitable style to a stunning ensemble.

In the face of such elegance, Lucinda felt dowdy in her best grey cotton gown. Envy stirred in her breast. She quelled it. No matter what she wore, she would never have either woman's style or elegant figure, but given the heat in Hugo's glance when it rested on her face, for once she didn't mind.

The first contestants stepped up, and to Mrs. Trip's evident chagrin, Miss Abbott won handily.

"Miss Abbott moves up the ladder," the vicar announced and scribbled her name on the chalkboard.

Next up were Miss Dawson and Miss Crotchet for the village. The seamstress looked exceedingly pale and fumbled with her bow as she moved to the line. "Oh, I should never have let you talk me into this, Almira Trip."

Mrs. Trip, obviously smarting from her loss, placed her hands on her hips. "You heard the Reverend, Liddy. It ain't about winning, it's about doin' the village proud."

"Come on, old girl," Mr. Dawson called to his sister. Despite her stiff posture, Miss Dawson made three creditable shots just off center. Although she grimaced and shook her head at her brother, she clearly was happy with her effort.

Such a nice girl, Lucinda thought. The kind of woman Hugo really ought to marry. A painful realization, but nonetheless true.

Miss Crotchet's first arrow dropped at her feet. She looked mortified. "I told you I could never do it." The vicar picked up the wayward flight and murmured some calming advice to the trembling Miss Crotchet.

"We need this win," Mrs. Trip muttered in Lucinda's ear.

Much to her credit, the nervous spinster lady, with much encouragement from the vicar, landed her final two arrows at the edge of the target.

"Miss Dawson moves up the ladder," the vicar announced.

The beauty was next, and she handed her parasol of blue shot silk to the attentive Mr. Dawson.

"If you can help Miss Crotchet, Reverend," Mr. Dawson said with a lift of his fair brow, accompanying Lucinda's opponent to the mark, "I can surely lend my aid to Miss Belle."

Miss Belle indeed, thought Lucinda dryly as the gorgeous young lady giggled shamelessly. As he pressed his cheek to hers to help her take aim, her shoulders shook with laughter.

The naughty minx. Lucinda narrowed her eyes. Someone should take the young gentleman aside and remind him of his duty before a harmless flirtation got out of hand.

"All set," Arthur said.

Miss Belle let fly. The arrow missed the center of the target by only a few inches. Lucinda raised a brow. Clearly the young lady had talent in more than one direction.

"I say, bravo," Arthur called out. A ripple of applause ran through the watching crowd.

Miss Belle's next two shots landed further from the center of the target than her first, but close enough to present a challenge. She cast Lucinda a tiny glance of triumph. A challenge that fired Lucinda's blood, no matter how she tried to ignore it.

"Mrs. Graham," Mrs. Trip said grimly. "Take my bow. It's a beauty. Normally I wouldn't lend it out. But we needs all the help we can get."

Horribly aware of every eye focused on her, Lucinda took the bow and stepped up to the line. Studiously avoiding anyone's gaze, she lined up with the target. She tested the string of the bow. It gave sweetly but cut into her cotton glove.

Miss Dawson must have noted her predicament because she rushed forward. "Take my leather glove."

Lucinda only had to glance at it to know it was far too small. "Thank you, but I am sure I shall manage perfectly well."

Miss Abbott stepped forward with a friendly smile. "We are closer in size. Use mine. I would not have it said that I took unfair advantage."

Such generosity, but Lucinda expected nothing less from Miss Dawson's friend. The glove felt tight, but she could clench her fist. It would work.

"Can I be of assistance?" Hugo murmured in her ear. He raised his voice. "It's only fair that you should have the same help as your opponent and not from Mr. Dawson." The possessive light in his eye indicated he'd murder the first man who offered.

Whatever could he be thinking? Didn't he realize how people gossiped? Or was he trying to force her hand? Whatever he had in mind, he was making her pulse beat too fast. Her breathing shortened to shallow gasps, and her knees felt more like pond water than bone and sinew. How on earth could she concentrate with him standing so close?

"Stand with one shoulder forward," Hugo said. "Take your time." He, too, leaned close to check her aim. The scent of his cologne filled her nose and reminded her of sensual pleasure in his arms. Sparks seemed to jump between them, like the air before a thunderstorm, setting off a chain of reaction down her spine. If he touched her, she'd burst into flames.

The rogue's eyes twinkled as if he knew very well what was happening to her body. Fortunately, he stepped back before her knees gave way. "Good luck." The gentle words steadied her as if his arms had gone around her in support.

She took a deep breath, checked her aim, adjusted for the breeze cooling one cheek, and fired.

To her surprise, instead of a creditable showing, the arrow hit dead center. The intervening years hadn't dulled her skill as much as she'd expected. If she fired wide now, they might guess she was doing it on purpose, and after all, there was at least one more round in which to lose.

She carefully fired the next two arrows close to the first.

Hugo caught her eye as a burst of applause broke out. He shook his head, pride shining in his eyes, and suddenly she stood taller. Being large sometimes had unexpected advantages.

"Well done," Mrs. Trip said on her return.

"Oh, my dear, you were brilliant, simply brilliant," cooed Miss Crotchet. "I had no idea you were so good."

"Beginner's luck," Lucinda said trying to hide her pride. After all, she could still fall flat on her face when she competed in the next round.

The vicar decided that as the only remaining member of the village team, Lucinda, would compete against the winner of the contest between Miss Abbott and Miss Dawson.

Miss Abbott easily beat Miss Dawson, who accepted her brother's teasing with equanimity and a wave of her hand.

The final round was between Lucinda and Miss Abbott, who went first. The proficient young lady clustered her arrows neatly around the center of the target.

All Lucinda had to do was be slightly worse and disappear into the crowd while everyone congratulated her opponent.

"Blendon's honor rests with you," Mrs. Trip declared grimly. "We lost the men. We can't lose this one as well." For once, the village martinet sounded close to tears.

Us against them. The need for the underdog to have his day. To feel respected. She had learned how it felt to be stripped of self worth under Denbigh's harsh tutelage. But this was just a game.

From beneath her lashes, she shot a glance at the only person who knew her husband, Mr. Dawson. Fortunately, engaged in stealing a rose from Miss Belle's hat, the besotted dandy was completely unaware of Lucinda.

She glanced at the villagers' anxious faces. She could not lose deliberately and let them down. Win or lose, as long as she did her best, she would satisfy her honor.

Firmly, she stepped up to the mark and nocked and fired her arrows in quick, smooth succession.

A groan went up from the Blendon contingent as the flights splayed out of the target.

"My word," the vicar shouted, running forward. "They are all dead center."

"Bloody hell," Mrs. Trip said, "where did you learn to shoot like that?"

"My brother," Lucinda said, unable to contain the elation in her voice.

A rousing cheer went up from the villagers. Reverend Postlethwaite handed her the engraved silver spoon as both teams gathered around her, the young ladies mingling with the villagers, everyone shaking her hand in congratulations until she thought her fingers would break.

The vicar clapped his hands together. "Time for the greasy pig contest," he shouted.

The crowd drifted away. The greased pig was always a favorite, particularly since the winner got to keep the pig.

"You never cease to amaze me," Hugo said, lingering at her side. "I have never seen a woman shoot as well, nor many men."

"A fluke," she said. "Beginner's luck." She waved a dismissive hand to forestall his questions.

He tipped his head to one side. "Why do I once more have the impression you are hiding something?"

"We are all hiding something, my lord," She let her gaze fall to his thigh.

He shifted uneasily. "Yes. Well. That was something I wanted to talk to you about, but for the moment I believe I am the lucky judge of the pig contest." He turned and marched off.

Lucinda let go a sigh. She had come through unscathed, and clearly Mr. Dawson had no inkling of her identity. Now if she could only make up her blasted mind what to do about Hugo.

By dint of keeping a wary eye out and with a little bit of luck, Lucinda managed to dodge Hugo and the squire's guests for the rest of the afternoon. Finally, even the stalwart Sophia began to flag.

"Me ride horsy," she said when Lucinda tried to interest her in bobbing for apples.

Lucida bent and smiled into her rosy face. She wiped the beads of sweat from the child's upper lip. "How about some lemonade?"

"Lemonade," Sophia said with a nod. "Then horsy."

Lucinda chucked her under the chin. "You certainly are one determined little lady. I think you take after me. Just be careful it doesn't lead you into trouble." She grasped the small, hot hand. "Let us find some shade and have a nice cool drink. Then we will go to the paddock."

They wove their way through the throngs around the booths and bought mugs of lemonade from a lad with a tray hanging around his neck. By the time they had finished the refreshing brew, they had reached the line of horses against the fence.

"She wants to ride again," Lucinda said to a weary-looking Albert.

"Come along then, missy," he said. "Up you go." He put her on the little pony.

He turned to look over his shoulder at Lucinda. "Why don't you go and watch the rope pull." He winked. "Master's on one of the teams. He do strip to advantage."

Instant heat flooded her face, and more perspiration dripped down her back. "Albert," she said in what she hoped were shocked tones and not those of an excited schoolgirl.

He winked and slapped the pony on the rump. "Go on. Have a bit of fun, Mrs. Graham. I'll look after this little baggage."

"I'm not a baggage," Sophia said. She kicked her little heels. "Go, Fairy."

Lucinda bit her lip. She would like to see the contest of strength. But surely Hugo hadn't really entered because of her teasing. Not with his bad leg.

"I'll just take a quick look," she said to Albert's retreating back. "To make sure he is all right."

She left the mugs with Mrs. Peddle and hurried to join the back of the crowd gathered on the stream's bank.

She worked her way forward until she had a view between two strapping farmhands. Her breath caught in her throat. On the far bank, with jacket discarded, throat bare, and shirtsleeves rolled up, Hugo was a mouthwatering sight. His broad brow glistened with a sheen of sweat as he straightened the thick piece of rope alongside the other men. The sight of rippling muscles beneath fine linen dried her mouth, and she didn't dare think about the speed of her heart.

He should not be doing this. It was utter foolishness when his injury wasn't healed.

One of the men moved aside. "Here you go, ma'am. Stand here," he pointed to a spot in front of him. "I can see over your shoulder."

She hadn't planned to get so close, but if something happened to Hugo, it might help if she was near. She glanced at the watching faces, all laughing and cheering the men, with no one observing her. Hugo spat in his palms and picked up the rope. The other men in his team did the same. Ribald and good-natured insults flew back and forth across the stream from one team to the other.

Trent joined the Grange team. He spoke to Hugo in low tones, as if remonstrating with him. Of course, Trent would know about Hugo's leg. She willed Hugo to listen to reason, but Hugo shrugged him off.

Her worries eased when Trent slipped in behind his master, forcing the man behind to back up a few steps. Trent would make sure Hugo came to no harm. She hoped.

She unclenched her aching fists. Hugo knew the risks; she should not worry so much.

"Are you ready?" shouted the squire, mopping at his brow with a spotted blue handkerchief.

The men nodded and leaned back on the cable. The two men at the back of each team wrapped the free end of the rope around their waists and dug a hole with their heels in the soft earth.

The rope, which up until that moment had been hanging in the water, pulled taut. A white handkerchief tied at its center dripped and then fluttered in the breeze. If the handkerchief went too far one way or the other, one team would end up in the water.

"Heave," the squire yelled.

Each man dug in his heels and hauled back. The strain made Hugo's thighs bulge beneath the skintight fabric of his buckskins. Lucinda could only imagine his pain. Stupid, prideful man.

Hand pressed to her mouth, she edged closer.

"Heave," Hugo roared at his team. They all pulled together.

The other team gave an inch.

"Heave," the other leader cried. Great heavens, it was Arthur Dawson. Who would have expected such a languid dandy to join in the fray? Mind you, he looked quite different stripped of his finery. Not a giant of a man like Hugo, but trim and well-muscled and grimly determined.

The yells of the crowd drowned out the cries of the men. The handkerchief wavered back and forth across the water, first one team taking control, then the other. The ground beneath their feet turned into a muddy swamp until they were slipping and sliding.

Faces red with effort, neck sinews corded, they pulled with all their might. The agony in Hugo's expression tore at Lucinda's heart. Couldn't they see his pain? She couldn't bear to watch any longer. She had to stop it. She started forward.

Then something happened. Somehow Hugo heaved, Trent gathered up the slack, and the Grange team jerked backwards. On the Hall's team, the anchorman, the blacksmith, lost his footing and started to slide.

Hugo's team hit dry ground and gripped. They fought their way back. One inch. Then another. Muscles in backs, arms, and legs strained with pure animal strength. Sweat poured from their agonized faces, their bodies parallel with the ground. Lucinda held her breath, certain that Hugo's leg would give out at any moment.

Then it was over. Dawson's team fell like skittles. A rout. They tumbled down the shallow bank into the water. Hugo's team landed flat on their backs.

Arthur Dawson lay in the water laughing so hard he took in a mouthful of water and came spluttering to his feet. Covered in mud, Hugo's team picked themselves up and jumped into the stream, splashing and whooping their victory. The men shook hands, slapping each other's backs and ducking one another.

Men. No better than overgrown children.

Laughing, his arm around Trent's shoulders, Hugo looked up and saw her. He grinned. He looked happy and alive, like a man who'd come home. Her heart expanded with joy. She smiled at him and shook her head.

He turned to shake Arthur Dawson's hand, but Dawson was staring at her, not at Hugo, a look of comprehension in his narrowed eyes.

Her heart stilled. What did he see? A pair of ill-suited lovers or a runaway countess? Her stomach churned. She wanted to run, but a fascinated horror kept her gaze riveted on the two men.

Dawson muttered something and jabbed an elbow in Hugo's ribs with a sly glance at Lucinda.

She had seen and heard enough of her brothers' lewd comments to guess at the tenor of Dawson's remark—it was not related to her name. Hugo's flush confirmed her suspicion. She felt ashamed.

Her heart slowing to normal, Lucinda eased out of the crowd. Idiot. What did she think she was doing staring at him like some lovelorn maiden? How low would she sink before she came to her senses? She had let herself be swept away by unattainable dreams. Wasn't it better to end their affair before she sank beyond redemption?

Suddenly, the sun did not feel quite so warm or the blue of the sky quite so bright. If she hadn't known the truth from the limp flags, she might have thought a chill wind had got up. She turned and wriggled through the crowd in search of Sophia. As she had promised, she would give Hugo her answer on Wednesday. The expression on Arthur Dawson's face had been the sign she needed.

At the paddock, Annie stood beside Albert with a flushed Sophia in her arms. "Poor little lass, she is tired and hot. I think we've all had enough fun for one day."

"I think you are right. I have never seen her look so exhausted."

"Why don't you stay for the supper and the dance as you planned? You know Miss Crotchet is relying on your help. I'll take this little one home with me." Annie rubbed her belly and laughed. "To be honest I'm mortal tired. More so with this one than any of the others."

"Oh, Annie, I should never have left you to care for Sophia all day. She can be such a handful."

Annie ruffled Sophia's hair. "Now then. She's no trouble and besides, she's spent most of the time with my da here. Plumb wore her out, he has."

Albert paused in helping a cherubic little boy with a helmet of black curls up onto the pony. He gave Lucinda a wink. "No trouble, that little one," he said and shambled off.

Sophia looked far from a handful at the moment. Her eyelids were heavy, and the day's excitement had left a scarlet flush on her cheeks. Yet Lucinda was sorely tempted to stay. Keeping busy would take her mind off the upcoming meeting with Hugo. And Annie was right; she had promised to help.

She glanced at the weary Annie, who looked almost as flushed as Sophia. "If you are sure?"

"I told you so," Annie said. "I'll just collect Janey and the boys from the Punch and Judy show and be on my way."

Lucinda watched Annie lumber through the crowds with Sophia's head on her shoulder. How lucky she and Sophia were to have such good friends. She'd almost lost the happy place she'd found for herself and her daughter by letting herself be talked into something she knew wasn't right. And not for the first time.

She and Hugo would return to being acquaintances. Nothing more. All she had to do was break the news.

Fourteen

HUGO PUT THE FINISHING TOUCHES TO HIS CRAVAT, AND
Trent held up his coat with a knowing grin. "I don't
think I've ever seen you this cheerful, Captain. Not
since I've known you."

"Not Captain any more, Trent, remember? And
what the hell do you mean?"

"You were whistling."

"I was?" He hadn't noticed.

Trent eased the tight-fitting black evening coat over
Hugo's shoulders with a grunt. "Yes."

His mood was light. Carefree. Coming to such a
momentous decision ought to give him pause, yet he
felt only the excitement of anticipation. He'd found
the perfect answer to the mistakes of the past. He stared
at himself in the mirror. He looked different, younger.
He smoothed his hair. He'd get a haircut in London.

"Looking forward to this ball, then, sir? It's about
time you did more than worry about the estate."

Hugo groaned. He was so focused on the future that
he'd almost forgotten why he was getting all dressed
up. "It should be a pleasant enough evening." He

noticed his voice lacked the enthusiasm of moments before. Damn Trent and his poking and prying.

Trent picked up two ruined neck cloths from the floor and headed for the pile of wet towels and dirty linens by the tub. "It's the widow-woman isn't it? Mrs. Graham?"

Tucking a small square of fine lawn into his tailcoat pocket, Hugo couldn't resist a small smirk. "I don't know what you mean."

Trent bundled the dirty laundry in a towel, his usually lighthearted expression turning somber. "You want to be careful with that one. She's probably got family somewhere waiting to pounce."

The niggling doubts he'd harbored scurried from a dark corner of Hugo's mind out into the light. He really knew very little about Lucinda's family. He shoved it back into the shadows, unwilling to examine it too closely. "You don't know what you are talking about."

"Something strange about her," Trent said with a flick of the washcloth. "Albert closes up as tight as an oyster round a pearl if I so much as ask a simple question."

Pretty much as Lucinda did. Hugo knew as much about her background now as he had after their first chess game. He didn't need to know about her past. He knew her. It was enough.

At his lack of response, Trent shrugged and carried the bundle of laundry to the door. "Will you need me anymore tonight?"

"No. Where are you off to?"

"I thought I'd call in at the village dance. The miller's daughter is reputed to have a roving eye."

The thought of Trent cavorting with a willing wench while Hugo did the pretty to the coy young ladies at the Hall dampened his spirits.

"Just watch your step, Trent. These are my people. My responsibility. Get a lass into trouble, and you'll find yourself wed before the froth is off the ale."

Trent paused in the doorway, a taunting grin lighting his fair face. "Afraid I'll cut you out with Mrs. Graham?"

He shut the door before Hugo could lob the hairbrush at his head.

A faint buzzing sound filled Hugo's ears. He wasn't afraid that Trent would cut him out. He had proved his loyalty in blood, but there would be other men at the village dance. Brown and the local farmers. One of them might tempt Lucinda with an offer of marriage before Hugo had a chance to firm up his own proposition. Why the hell she had refused the invitation to the squire's ball, preferring instead to remain at the fête, he didn't understand. She seemed happier rubbing shoulders with the villagers than mixing with the Dawsons and their guests. Stubborn do-good woman.

A wry little smile crossed his lips. He wouldn't have minded avoiding the Dawson's ball himself. He should have said no as he wished, instead of doing his noble duty.

Supper over and the remains of the meal cleared away by the village ladies under Miss Crotchet's watchful eye, the men moved the trestles and benches to the perimeter of the tent.

As one of the few single ladies present, Miss Crotchet had latched onto Lucinda at supper. Now they chose a table in the shadows farthest from the ruffians at the bar. Lucinda forced herself to lean back and watch the fun. Mr. Peddle was doing a roaring trade at the other end of the tent, while couples in their Sunday best and some of the older generation took their ease at tables. Beside her, a farmer with a nasal voice jabbed a pipe at the air for emphasis as he expounded on the attributes of his bull to his neighbor.

The orchestra had arrived as supper was ending and now played a merry country dance. Lucinda's foot tapped in time to the music. She'd forgotten how much she liked to dance, repressed it really, because the Duke of Vale despised dancing, and therefore so did Denbigh. And besides, the last time she had joined a set, her elegant husband had likened her to a heifer in a fit. She almost laughed. In this company, she'd look right at home.

Despite her smile, she could not help but recall how hurt she'd been at the time, how mortified and small inside she'd felt. A horrid sensation. Only now did she recognize how far she had retreated from public life after that day. A fortunate thing, apparently, or she might have met Miss Dawson, or one of her friends, in London. She had been right to flee, to take back her life, even if she had caused a scandal. And besides, a scandal only lasted until the next one came along. The only thing needed to make her happiness complete was to be able to see her family occasionally. A hopeless dream.

Miss Crotchet leaned close to make herself heard. "We were lucky with the weather today, Mrs. Graham." The lined face beamed and nodded, the little feather in her hair looking surprisingly jaunty. "And the vicar was so gracious in his thanks to the committee at supper."

Lucinda smiled. "Yes, he truly is a gentleman." Her gaze wandered to the lanky vicar chatting with a group of parishioners.

"I'm going to miss all the planning," Miss Crotchet said.

In those wistful faded eyes, Lucinda glimpsed her future. Seemingly a widow, but not free to wed, she would also be required to view other couple's enjoyment from a distance, like an outsider peering through a window. Once Sophia grew up and left home, Lucinda would be on her own. After growing up in such a large family, it seemed odd. Feeling kinship for the frail elderly lady, Lucinda reached over and gave her papery hand a squeeze. "I am sure the vicar will have lots more fund-raising ideas."

Miss Crotchet cheered instantly. "It was fortunate you managed to convince his lordship to let us use his land."

"He really didn't take much convincing." At least, not of the kind Miss Crotchet had in mind. A little burst of heat trickled up from Lucinda's abdomen. To cover her discomfort, she drummed her fingers on the tabletop in time to the Roger de Coverley now in full swing.

"Good thing he's more like his grandfather than his father, I'd say," Miss Crotchet continued in a conspiratorial voice. "Mind you, the old earl had his troubles, poor man."

Hugo had never spoken of his father. "Troubles?"

The elderly spinster lowered her voice and put her lips close to Lucinda's ear. "Women troubles. The countess. A prettier lady you couldn't hope for, but so delicate. According to her maid, he made her cry every time he went nigh her, the brute. She used to drive about the estate, bringing comfort to the poor and the sick, a regular saint." She nodded sagely. "After her death, I heard the old earl was thinking of marrying again."

Gossip. Lucinda put it down to fiction based on very little fact. It had been the same at home, the tenants always watching the inhabitants of the big house, putting their lives under a microscope and drawing their own, often wrong, conclusions.

"I am sure there are two sides to every story," Lucinda said firmly.

Mr. Brown, looking serious and just a little diffident, approached their table. He offered an awkward bow. "Will you do me the honor of a dance, Mrs. Graham?"

Miss Crotchet trilled a laugh. "Go on, Mrs. Graham. It'll be Christmastide before we see another celebration."

Wishing neither to hurt Mr. Brown's feelings nor give him untoward encouragement, Lucinda hesitated. She had gone into half-mourning, but would the villagers be shocked if she danced?

His serious brown eyes pleaded his case.

The band struck up a cotillion. "Very well," she said, rising to her feet and taking his warm, moist hand. She towered above the steward and made two of his slight frame, but he didn't seem to mind. In fact, he looked rather pleased with himself. He led her to the bottom of the first set. The numbers being even, they waited for the first couples to complete their steps, and then it was their turn.

Brown proved to be an accomplished if ponderous dancer and a little too enthusiastic in the turns. Still, not once did he tread on her toes or go the wrong way as happened with a couple of the men further up the set.

Breathless and laughing, she let him return her to her seat. "Thank you, sir, that was most enjoyable."

He bowed. "Thank you, Mrs. Graham." His neck flushed brick red.

"It is warm, isn't it?" Miss Crotchet said with a sly little smile.

Brown swallowed. "Yes indeed. Thank you again, Mrs. Graham." He turned and strode off clearly laboring under some strong emotion. Oh dear. Perhaps she should not have danced after all.

"My, oh my," Miss Crotchet said. "You are charming them out of the trees today. First his lordship, now Mr. Brown."

A flush as hot as Mr. Brown's flooded Lucinda's face. Some of the delight seeped out of the moment. Did Hugo boast of the conquest of his widowed tenant? She didn't want to believe it. She cast around for a distraction. "Look, there is Trent, his lordship's valet, at the bar. I wonder if he enjoyed the day? He certainly worked hard enough."

The handsome scoundrel had one booted foot on a bench and a flagon of ale in his hand. He leaned forward to whisper something in a pretty village girl's ear. Trip's daughter. A young lady with a less than spotless reputation.

"Oh my," breathed Miss Crotchet. "There is his lordship. Talking to the vicar."

Hugo? Here? Lucinda's body quickened at the mere mention of his name. She drew back into the shadows, afraid others would notice the intensity of her reaction.

"My, doesn't he look fine?" Miss Crotchet cooed. "Such a handsome figure of a man, such military bearing. How kind of him to drop in to see how we are going on."

The older lady cast a speculative glance in Lucinda's direction. She kept her expression blank and watched the lord of the manor visiting his peasants. She repressed the unkind thought. Hugo had done a great deal for his tenants and dependents today. He had no need to show his face to curry their favor, yet here he was mixing and mingling. More evidence that he no longer needed her to get him involved. Her heart contracted, even as her mind took pleasure in her triumph.

In deep conversation with the vicar, Hugo allowed his gaze to sweep the room. The moment it alighted on her, she knew for certain he'd been looking for her. He didn't single her out or dash to her side, but his lingering glance contained so much warmth, she could almost feel it on her skin. Her eyes drifted half-closed with pleasure, her lips curved in a welcoming smile. Swiftly, she caught her unconscious response, straightened her shoulders, and fixed her gaze on the dancers.

Out of the corner of her eye, she watched the two men shake hands. Good. He was leaving. If she was glad, why did her stomach dip in disappointment and then rise again as he circled the tent toward her?

Casual, bluff, and extraordinarily attractive, he traversed the tent, shaking a hand here, slapping a back there. The villagers in their turn greeted him with respect. The charming smile he bestowed on Mrs. Peddle at the bar didn't sit so well. Especially not when Mrs. Peddle actually simpered. He also had a few words with Trent.

From beneath her lashes, she watched him accept a mug of ale from the blacksmith anchorman on the squire's rope-pulling team and down it in one draft. The other man, who matched Hugo in breadth, looked as pleased as punch.

In just a few short weeks, the man had changed from sullen bear into charming man of-the-world. If only fate had been kind and they had met earlier. It would be wrong to continue their meetings and not tell him the truth. His anger at Denbigh's vile treatment had been palpable. What would he do if he knew Denbigh still lived? Might he think it his duty to send her back? A chill ran down her spine. Hugo would never betray her to her husband. Would he? She daren't take the risk.

The sadness she'd been ignoring all day welled up in her throat, clogged her nose, and burned at the back of her eyes. It didn't matter what she wanted or how she felt about him; she had to end it before it developed into something meaningful. The wave of pain that hit her heart told her what her mind refused to believe. For her, it had already gone too deep.

A sense of loss seemed to fill her with a strange sense of detachment. She forced herself to watch the dancing instead of his progress through the room, not sure she could hide her grief.

And then he loomed in front of her.

"Good evening, ladies," he said with a flash of white teeth and a small bow. "I trust you are enjoying yourselves?"

"How good of you to ask, my lord," Miss Crotchet gushed. "I was just telling Mrs. Graham, it is just like the old days."

He turned the full power of his warm gaze on Lucinda. Her heart clenched. She could not breathe. It was as if he held her close against his beautiful hard body. Her heartbeat thundered loud in her ears. "I didn't expect to see you here, my lord. I understood you were to attend the Dawsons' ball."

He stiffened slightly at the edge in her tone, an edge she really hadn't intended to show, but he retained his pleasant expression. "I thought this might offer more entertainment."

Was he mocking her? Farmers and laborers in homespun trousers cavorted on the dance floor. They were all hearty laughter and red faces, sweating in the confines of unaccustomed cravats and partnering women in outdated gowns. And there he was, magnificent in the finest black evening clothes, eyes glinting a challenge.

"Will you honor me with a dance, Mrs. Graham?"

Longing quickened her heartbeat before common sense took command. She opened her mouth to refuse.

A mere flash of bleakness darkened his gaze, but she caught it, even as he braced his shoulders and schooled his face into bland unconcern. A rejection would hurt his pride, no matter how much he would try to hide it. She hated the thought of wounding his feelings.

Wasn't that the reason she didn't have the strength to deny him in the first place? She always had been too soft. And besides, what harm would one dance do? She'd sat in the shadows all through her marriage, and now she wanted to dance. Her feet could barely remain still.

She placed her fingers lightly on his large warm palm, feeling the shock of his touch all the way to her toes. The hard line of his mouth softened as he brought her to her feet, his gaze one of warm approval, as if she'd done more than agree to dance. Her heart fluttered. Much more of this, and she would lose what was left of her mind and her resolve.

He led her to the orchestra dais as the set drew to a close, his military background apparent in the set of his shoulders, and the precision of his stride perfectly adjusted to hers. "A waltz, if you please," he commanded of the conductor.

A waltz? How shocking. Only the raciest of hostesses allowed the dance at their balls. Geoffrey had taught her one rainy afternoon while Denbigh had been off on a hunting trip. It was scandalous. And fun. Surely a country band wouldn't know such a thing? But after barely a moment's pause, the orchestra struck up the music.

Hugo pulled her into his arms and guided her into the steps as if no one else existed, just the two of them. Judging from his smug expression, he had planned this in advance. The man was impossible, as irresistible as a cavalry charge. And against her will, against what she knew to be right, she found herself loving every moment.

A smattering of exclamations rippled around the room. Some of the younger members of the party joined them on the dance floor. None of them danced as smoothly as Hugo. He had the grace and control of a warrior. Held firm in his embrace, her very bones seemed to absorb his strength.

Since this might well be her last chance to feel his arms around her, she would make the most of it. Indeed, she ought to be grateful they were in full view of the rest of the village. Given the way her heart was beating and the fire low in her belly, heaven alone knew what would happen if they were alone.

Liar. She knew only too well.

She glanced up at his harsh face, at the polite expression and the fire in his eyes, and knew he felt exactly the same. "You dance well," she said.

"As do you."

"You took a chance that I knew how to waltz." She glanced around at the handful of couples on the floor, one of them Trent with the boisterous miller's daughter, who seemed more inclined to polka.

He rumbled the rare chuckle that always caused her inner muscles to squeeze in a most pleasurable fashion. "After today's display at the butts, I am not in the slightest surprised at your many talents." His intent gaze fixed on hers contained a question she would never answer. "And besides," he went on, "Wellington insisted that all his officers dance. I could have got you through it, if required."

She glanced at Trent. "Did the same order go for batmen?"

"No. Trent's is a whole different story."

Lucinda didn't care about the valet. The music lulled her mind while her feet moved with the joy of dancing, and her sinful body simmered with sensual longing.

Hugo was a good and kind man, and he had come here tonight to dance with her. More important, he had given her the gift of her femininity. Her marriage hadn't failed because she was frigid. If her body's lustful demand right at this moment provided any indication, the case was quite the opposite. Making love to Hugo had become an addiction. The fact that she'd lost a piece of her heart in the process was, as Father would say, another of life's little tragedies.

The rhythm in his stride broke the tiniest bit. He winced.

"Is your leg strong enough for dancing?" she asked.

"Always concerned for someone else, aren't you? You worry about the villagers and the vicar's new roof, not to mention Sophia. Have you added me to your list of responsibilities?"

If only she could. "You need to see a doctor."

"Who cares for you, Lucinda?"

She jumped at the sound of her first name and looked around, but no one seemed to notice. "I am perfectly content. I have my home, my work in the parish, and my child."

"You deserve so much more, you know."

Not so long ago, she had started to believe she deserved nothing. And now she had taken all she dared, indeed far too much, but she would not regret one moment, not tonight.

They danced in silence. She could not help but be aware of his desire, the heat from his body, the feel of his hand at her waist—firm, strong, protective, the warmth in his gaze when his eyes met hers. And yet the forced restraint of being in the public eye gave her the sensation that they communed on a different plane, not bodies, but hearts and minds. The music ended all too soon.

Hugo bowed his thanks, and she swept a curtsey.

"Walk with me outside," he murmured.

Her mouth dried. Outside in the dark, where no one could see them, was a very different prospect than dancing before a room full of people. Her pulse raced and her insides clamored for attention, for his touch in her most intimate places, for the joy of mutual fulfillment. She swallowed in an effort to regain control of her voice. "Very well. I will meet you outside by the tree where we picnicked."

He escorted her back to her table and bid good evening to Miss Crotchet, who, far from seeming shocked by their dancing, looked, well…misty-eyed.

Lucinda watched him greet a few more people as he passed by their tables and saw him acknowledge the vicar's farewell before disappearing into the night. Should she join him? Or would it be best to slip away home? And what then? He would only search her out. There really was no avoiding him.

She gathered her shawl and her reticule.

"Leaving already?" Miss Crotchet asked with a sly little smile.

"I have to collect Sophia," she said, trying to repress any sign of anticipation, the patter of her heart, her shallow breathing.

Miss Crotchet's pale blue eyes danced with curiosity. "I'd offer to go with you, but John Cawfield asked me to dance the next Scottish country dance."

"Oh, please don't think of leaving on my account. As you said, there will not be another celebration like this for a while." Lucinda patted her bony shoulder. "Goodnight."

Miss Crotchet smiled. "I will see you in church in the morning. And there will be a few thick heads sitting in pews alongside us, I'll be bound."

On that note, Lucinda slipped out of the tent and into the starlit night.

With no moon, the shadows beneath the trees thickened to impenetrable. She peered into the dark, seeking a different and more solid shape, yet she jumped when his arm went around her waist and pulled her close.

The scent of bay and the smoke from a wood fire filled her nostrils. His lips, warm and velvet and very inviting, claimed her mouth. When he broke away to inhale, she leaned her cheek against his solid wall of chest and listened to the steady beat of his heart, relishing his protective embrace, committing it to memory.

"I wanted to do that at the end of our dance," he said. "I started to think you would not come after all."

"I had to take my leave of Miss Crotchet."

"I hoped it was something like that. I'm glad you agreed to meet me."

It would never happen again, once she gave him her decision. After tonight she'd have only memories. Regret hung over her like a shadow.

A couple emerged from the tent giggling and laughing.

"I don't think we should stay here," she whispered. "Someone might see us."

A sigh wafted past her ear. "Dammit. I hate this skulking around."

Soon he wouldn't have to worry about that anymore. A sense of urgency sent blood flying around her body. There was so little time left. "Do you have to leave for the ball soon?"

Another faint sigh in the dark. "It starts at eleven. The ladies need time to change their gowns. I must leave in a half-hour or so."

So little time, Hugo thought. Tomorrow he left for London.

The way she relaxed inside the circle of his arms sent his elation spinning out of control. She trusted him. God, he needed that from this woman. "Walk with me a little way."

She nodded.

He took her hand and guided her along the river-bank. Enveloped in warm night air, they strolled beside the starlit ribbon of water. Walking hand in hand beneath the arching universe with Lucinda. Could anything feel more right? A mantle of peace descended on his shoulders. A willow tree leaning over the chattering stream trailed fronds like fingers against the flow. Music wafted on a light breeze, fading in and out of hearing as if Pan darted back and forth to tease them with his merry pipes.

Thank God, he'd decided to drop in on his way to the Hall. Decided? Hell. He couldn't stay away. He swung her around.

She tipped her chin in question, cupped his cheeks, drew him down, and kissed his parted lips, soft and sweet.

He thought his heart might burst.

As she nibbled his bottom lip and swept his mouth with her tongue, reason fled. Blood, hot and heavy, pooled in his groin. Lust, never far below the surface in her presence, gripped him in iron claws. He squeezed her bottom, his fingers sinking into her soft flesh. She pressed against him, her breathing impatient, her hands caressing his neck, kneading his shoulders and his back. She burrowed against his chest, widened her thighs to take his leg between hers. He growled his pleasure.

His woman. The savage need to brand her as such boiled in his brain and his veins. He wanted her. Now. He caught himself up, hard. He must not take her here on the ground like some rutting beast. He pulled back, inhaled, struggled to think.

Her hands went to the buttons of his coat. Her breathing sounded ragged, desperate, wanting.

Undone, he backed her through the screen of willow and pressed her against the tree trunk.

The music of her whispered laughter clutched at his heart as she glanced around. "It is like a fairy bower."

And did he play Bottom to her Titania, an ass who would awaken and find it all a dream? He felt more like a starving lion. He nibbled her ear.

She sighed and tilted her hips, offering him heaven on earth. He took her mouth, hard, savage, and hungry.

She kissed him back and fought him for control, sweeping his mouth with her tongue. Her hands clawed at his back as if she would pull him inside her body. The desperate urgency in her kiss heated his blood to steam and fried every thought in his brain. He fondled one delectably full breast through her gown. She whimpered her approval.

His cock hardened to rock.

With a groan, he slid his hand down her ribs, spanned the hollow of her waist, and caressed the swell of her hip, her buttocks, the thigh pressed against his so sweetly. He needed to die inside her.

He must not let it go that far. One small taste of heaven, no more. He dragged her skirts up to her hips, skimming the butter-soft flesh above her stocking.

Her hand went to his erection and traced the ridge of its length through his satin breeches. He hung by a thread to fragile control.

Control. He must keep control. He hauled in a breath and raised his head, staring through the dark into a face full of shadows, inhaling the scent of lavender and peat moss and summer.

Her fingers petted his swollen cock. Too gentle, not nearly enough, he wanted to growl. He pressed her fingers against his hard flesh, closed them around his shaft through the fabric.

"Hugo," she whispered, "Can I…"

"God, yes." He ripped open his falls.

Cool fingers burrowed beneath his shirttails. Nails scraped his scrotum, a chilly palm closed around his heavy balls and squeezed. He couldn't breathe for the agony of pleasure.

Her leg lifted, hooked around his good thigh, leaving her open, vulnerable to his questing fingers. Wet, hot, her narrow passage welcomed his touch, pushed down on his fingers, tightened.

She wanted him. He needed to be inside her. All the way. To the hilt, just for a moment.

In one motion, he lifted her high, resting her back against the tree. He guided the head of his cock to her entrance, felt her heat and wetness. He could not go any farther without protection. He bathed the head of his cock in her generous moisture.

God dammit. He might not see her for weeks. Taking a couple of minutes of pleasure for himself would not hurt before he saw to her need.

She gripped his shoulders threw her head back and lowered herself onto his straining cock. Shocked, he couldn't move for pleasure. Heat enveloped his shaft. Flesh slid and joined, and thrust and squeezed. She'd driven him to her womb, deeper than any woman before.

She was the light in his darkness.

She nuzzled his neck, licked his ear, captured his mouth.

Waves of pleasure rocketed outward from his balls. They tightened to unbearable hardness. But bear it he must. He would not lose control. He would not risk anything so dangerous, not with his woman.

He shielded her back and head from the rough bark with his hands and drove deep.

She opened, accommodated, took his length with murmur of encouragement. He pressed harder, deeper, faster, barely withdrawing before the next stroke, pounding into her, and she onto him, setting a pace with the clench of her tight muscle around his yard.

Blissful agony held him on a tight rein.

Death beckoned.

Not yet. Not inside her and not until she met her end.

His hips pumped and drove; his cock begged for release. He denied it. Fought it. Held on by the shred of primal need to conquer.

She took him and gave back hard, raising and lowering her hips until his vision darkened to one small pinpoint of light in his mind, his only awareness, the place where they joined.

A soft moan sounded in her throat. The sweet sound drove him mad with desire. He covered her mouth with his, swallowing her cries, and was rocked by the trembles quaking through her body. Heat poured from her centre as her climax shivered and pulsed in her limbs and around his shaft. Her insides sucked at his cock.

He exploded. He filled her to the womb with his essence, his life force spurting, his body pulsing and vibrating. He swallowed his own cry of triumph against her lips.

They subsided in bliss and clung together against the tree, weak, panting, empty except for a deep languid heat. She kissed his neck and drooped around his shoulders, a heavenly burden.

It took all his strength to remain standing. He had never reached so high so fast or spilled with such force. His mind sharpened. Oh, dear God. He'd lost all sense of honor. He'd filled her precious body with his thrice-damned seed.

For all he knew, he'd killed her.

"Lucinda," he said. And stopped, his mouth full of nothing. What the hell could he say?

She rested her head against his chest. "Hugo, we have to talk."

Her regretful tone rang a faint warning bell deep in his unconscious mind. A more important anxiety filled his thoughts. Should he warn her of the danger? Would she hate him for what he'd done? Surely one slip would not do the deed?

"Mrs. Graham," a high-pitched voice full of panic called from back toward the music and the lights. "Mrs. Graham. Where are you?"

Fifteen

"THAT SOUNDS LIKE JANEY." LUCINDA SHOVED AT Hugo's shoulder. Her heart had slowed from fever pitch, but picked up again in painful rhythm.

Hugo lowered her to the ground and helped her straighten her bodice.

"Mrs. Graham? Where are you?" The shout ended on what sounded like a sob.

"Oh, God. Something has happened to Sophia. " She lifted her skirts and ran.

"Careful." Hugo grabbed her hand. "The path is this way." He guided her across the grass toward the tent lights.

"Janey," Lucinda called. "I'm here."

The girl rushed at her, wide-eyed and wild-looking, her cloak thrown over what looked like a nightgown. "Oh, Mrs. Graham," the girl cried. "It's Sophia. She is sick somethin' awful and calling for you. Ma sent to fetch you home."

How could she? Lucinda railed at herself. How could she be here when Sophia needed her? Her chest felt as if she'd fallen into a pond and couldn't draw breath, couldn't move her limbs fast enough.

Hugo caught her shoulder. "I'll take you in my carriage. It will be faster."

They ran to the edge of the field, dragging Janey with them. Lucinda pushed the panting girl up onto the seat and scrambled up behind her. Hugo untied the horses' heads and leaped in.

It seemed to take forever to turn the phaeton around in the lane. Surely it would be quicker if she ran. About to jump clear, she was forestalled by a brawny arm crossing in front of her.

"Easy." His calm voice steadied her. He flicked his whip. The horses broke into a canter.

She gripped Janey's sleeve. "What is the matter with Sophia?"

"A fever. Mother thinks it could be the measles."

Measles. Children died of the measles. She couldn't lose Sophia. Her mind emptied of rational thought as her every nerve focused on arriving, her body tense and rigid. Nothing breached the fog of panic as the journey went by in a blur. Was it minutes or hours before they arrived at Annie's cottage at the other end of the village?

The horses halted. Lucinda leaped for the ground. Somehow Hugo was there to catch her.

"Calm down," he said. "You are not going to help matters if you break your neck."

The words went into her ears, but she could not grasp their meaning.

"I'll go for the doctor," Hugo said.

That she understood. She nodded, pushing past him, and dashed for the front door.

Hugo urged the horses back to the Dunning cottage as fast as he dared, grimly aware of the doctor clutching the side of the carriage with one hand and his hat to his head with the other. Frustration clenched Hugo's shoulders. Perhaps if she'd moved into the Grange as he'd wanted, this would not have happened, or at least he would not feel so helpless.

"You were lucky to find me at home, my lord," the doctor said. "Another ten minutes, and I would have left for Squire Dawson's."

Did the man think Hugo wouldn't have dragged him from the ball? He clung to a thread of calm. Angering the doctor wouldn't help Sophia. "I appreciate you changing your plans, doctor. And of course I will drive you to the Hall after you see the child."

"If you continue to drive like this, my lord, I might even arrive there before m'wife."

Hugo slanted him a grin. "Send your bill to me."

"Like that is it?"

Damn. "Mrs. Graham is a friend. I simply happened to be on hand at the news of her daughter's illness."

"Hmmph."

Hugo didn't care what the doctor thought, so long as he aided the child.

They passed the Red Lion, its windows dark for once, with the Peddles raking in coin at the fête. At last, Hugo drew the horses to a halt outside the Dunning cottage. Please God, they were in time.

The doctor, overweight for his fifty years, huffed and puffed his way to the ground. "Damned contraptions," he muttered when his feet hit *terra firma*.

Someone must have been watching for them, because the front door spilled light into the lane just long enough to admit the heavy-set figure. If a calm mother of three was anxious, it didn't bode well for Sophia. He clenched his jaw and swung down, suppressing a bit of huffing and puffing of his own. Dancing, and what followed, hadn't done his leg one bit of good. In fact, his thigh burned like the very devil.

The world seemed to slip sideways in a sickening rush. What had been a perfect day had become a nightmare of an evening. First he'd lost control and now this. He wanted to beat something to a pulp or run for the hills like a bloody coward. He was always running. He'd run from his father, then he'd run the night he'd as good as killed his wife—Juanita. Tonight, he was staying right where he was. He would not let Lucinda down the way he'd let his mother and his wife down.

He went to his cattle's heads, tension in his back nigh unbearable, the horses' hot breath on his face. The smell of horse and leather in the warm night air reminded him of nights in Spain. Of the nightmares. God. He hadn't had one bad dream since he'd met Lucinda, but now he was living one.

He clenched his fists and pressed his knuckles against his lips to stem the stream of curses hovering on his lips. He wanted to storm into the house, to protect Lucinda from the doctor's words. All he could do was swallow his nausea, hide his weakness, and wait. But God dammit, he wished he could do more.

Light from the opening door blinded him for a moment.

"Lord Wanstead?"

Lucinda. He steeled himself to hear the bad news, to be her rock. "I'm here." He moved around the horses. "How is she?"

Her laugh sounded shaky. "The doctor sent me away. Too many questions." The sound of tears in her voice felt like a sword blade to his heart.

"Did he say anything at all?"

"She has a fever. He was listening to her chest but said he couldn't hear anything apart from my voice. I could not sit still, so I came out here."

Even in the dark he was aware of her fingers twisting, of the barely restrained emotions tearing her apart. He clenched his fists to stop himself from reaching out and pulling her close.

"Annie says there are all kinds of things it might be." She dashed a hand across her face. "Sophia is all I have." Her voice was thick and broken. "If anything…happens to her…I don't know what…"

"She will be fine." God help him. Children were such fragile things. So were their mothers. He repressed a shudder. If the child died… He pushed the thought aside. "I'll take a message to your family, if it would help."

She jerked back. "My family?" She reached for the side of the phaeton for support. "No."

He took a step toward her. "Surely they would want to be of assistance, to know?"

She drew back. "I am estranged from my family. I cannot…will not ask them for aid."

At a loss, Hugo slammed his fist against the panel of the vehicle and cursed.

She flinched and backed away.

He reached out. "I'm sorry. I'm not angry with you. I hate doing nothing."

She took his hand and brought it to her lips in a gesture so tender it almost unmanned him. "Your presence here means more than I can say," she murmured.

Without hesitation, he enfolded her in his arms and pressed his lips to her hair, his heart aching with the effort to contain something so large he thought it might split asunder.

Her body trembled with tears waiting to be shed. And yet her inner strength, her resilience, held her together. Distract her. It always worked well for his men. "Earlier, I was about to tell you that I am leaving for London tomorrow."

Her body stiffened.

He patted her shoulder. "I wrote for an appointment to see a doctor."

Her face tilted up. "About your leg?"

He nodded.

"I'm glad. There must be something they can do."

That she could even spare a thought for him in her current state shattered every wall he'd built around his heart. He gave her shoulders a brief squeeze.

Having said the words, he was committed. He forced the image of knives and screams out of his mind. "I won't leave until I am sure Sophia is well."

"Thank you, but it really isn't necessary."

Was she telling him he wasn't necessary when already he missed her? Odd how uncertain he felt with this woman.

The front door swung back, bathing them in light. Lucinda jerked away from him as if he was hot. That side of his body felt the chill of her absence, and his arm felt empty, useless. He clamped his jaw shut on a protest. He had no wish to keep her from her beloved daughter, nor did he have the right to join her in her suffering. Not yet.

"Mrs. Graham?" Annie called.

"I'm here." Lucinda hurried into the cottage without a backward glance.

Hugo stared at the door. It might as well have been the walls of Bussaco. For all his size and strength, he could not break through it. Instead, he lingered in no man's land, where he'd always been. Curse it.

Only a man who could offer love would be permitted inside that inner circle.

Love. The word had an ominous ring. He wanted companionship and physical comfort. But love? Was that the emotion filling to bursting a heart he thought he'd frozen out of existence? Or was it merely sympathy?

As tense as a drum skin, Hugo waited. Dammit. The child would be all right. Little Sophia had to get well. He refused to allow anything else.

He grabbed the horses' bridles and turned the carriage around. As he brought them to a halt, the door opened again and this time the doctor emerged. Annie waddled after him.

Chest tight, Hugo narrowed his eyes. The doctor better have a good explanation for his departure.

"How is the child?" His voice sounded as if he had swallowed acid.

"Too much sun," the doctor said. "And probably too many lollipops." He glared at a chastened Annie.

"She was having such a good time." Annie said. She threw Hugo a glance of appeal. "I thought she was just excited."

"Spoiled," the doctor said. He glanced at Hugo. "I have given Mrs. Graham detailed instructions. She seems intelligent enough to follow them. I will check back in the morning." He threw his bag up onto the seat. "Now, your lordship, you better get me to this party before my wife has my head on a platter."

"The child will be all right? You are sure?"

"Yes, my lord." His voice had the dry quality of a man pressed beyond patience. "She needs cool and quiet and a physic to help her sleep."

Hugo's breath left his body in a huge rush. The tension in his shoulders and jaw flowed away on a river of thankfulness.

The doctor heaved into the carriage. Hugo leaped up beside him.

"My lord," Annie called. "Mrs. Graham said to thank you and remind you to keep your appointment in London."

Mrs. Graham would. Damn her. He could not prevent a smile.

The table chilled Hugo's bare arse. His stones retreated inside his body like a couple of cowards. Hugo wanted to join them.

"Tut, tut," the highly recommended surgeon uttered. He poked at the center of the swollen red mess of Hugo's thigh.

Gritting his teeth, Hugo stared out of the window, peering between blackened chimneypots at what little he could see of clouds drifting across a patch of hazy blue rather than look at the tray close at hand where knives and saws and pincers lay ready for the surgeon, a navy man who'd sawn off more limbs than he'd had Sunday dinners.

A comforting thought.

London. He hadn't been here since his come-out. The past two weeks hanging about at Grillons for an appointment to see this doctor had been hell. His glance dropped to his jacket neatly folded beneath his breeches on the chair, remembered what was in his pocket, and smiled. At least he had not wasted those days.

The surgeon poked at Hugo's puckered and weeping flesh.

Hugo jumped. "God's teeth, man." He barely prevented himself from planting the surgeon a facer.

"You had better have a swig of this." The surgeon held out a brown glass bottle.

"What is it?"

"Laudanum. For the pain."

"You are going to operate now?" Hugo swallowed bile. At any moment his leg might be lying on the black-and-white tiled floor. He'd known this was a bloody bad idea. He shifted forward on the table, prepared to jump down.

"I wouldn't call it an operation," the doctor said. "I think there's something in there. I want to have a look. He picked up a scalpel and a pair of forceps from the tray.

Hugo bit back his instinct to decline the honor. "The last doctor said he'd removed all the fragments."

The surgeon's soft grey eyes shot to Hugo's face. "Ah. So you had more than one operation on this."

"Yes. Once at Bussaco, and again in Lisbon. Doctor Mullet recommended I come and see you if I had problems."

"Good man, Mullet."

"Not if he left something in there."

"Well, we won't know if you don't let me look. And I can tell you this, my lord. This is not going to get better unless we open it up. You are lucky you came now. In a month's time I would be taking this leg off. I promise you that."

Bloody doctors. Hugo wanted to howl his rage. "Fine. Look all you want. But I'm not having the leg off."

"Would you sooner die?" Two months ago, facing an endless empty future, struggling alone with his demons, he might have said yes. He didn't bother to answer.

"I have brandy if you prefer," the surgeon said, waving the laudanum under his nose.

And while he drifted in a drunken stupor, who knew what the knife-happy doctor would do. "Neither."

He clenched his fist and felt the scrap of fabric nestled in his palm. He'd found it on the grass after the fête, recognized the little blue flowers and the initial, and had intended to return it to Lucinda before he left for London. In an unconscious gesture, he lifted to his nose and inhaled its lingering scent of lavender and woman. His woman.

"Well, if you bloody well pass out, make sure you fall backwards or risk cutting an artery." The doctor handed him a strip of leather. "Bite down. And don't think about hitting me." The grim expression also held empathy.

"Saw a lot of action in the navy, did you?" Hugo asked.

The man's lips curved in a humorless smile. "Too much."

Hugo knew exactly how he felt. He stuffed the leather in his mouth and watched the scalpel approach his thigh. Of their own accord, the thigh muscles bunched.

The surgeon made a swift stabbing stroke.

Pain shot up Hugo's leg and straight to his gut. "Jesus. Hell. Bugger." The muffled words exploded from his throat.

"That the best you can do?" the doctor said. "You army types are all the same. A bunch of molls." He held a cloth against the flow of blood.

"You bastard." Hugo spat around the gag. He concentrated on breathing through his nose, instead of paying the doctor in kind.

"Sit still a moment longer, please, my lord."

The surgeon nudged the spectacles off his forehead onto his nose. "Magnifying glasses," he said, bending over Hugo's leg. All Hugo could see through the blur of watering eyes was the back of the doctor's greying head and the brown mole on his neck.

Another stab of pain. Christ. What the hell was he doing?

"Aha." The exclamation had an ominous ring.

"What?" Hugo squeezed out between his teeth.

The surgeon straightened. He whacked the cloth against Hugo's thigh and pressed Hugo's hand on it. "Push down on that."

He held up what looked like a thick hair or a short bloody piece of string. "Well, well. Look what we have here."

Hugo removed the damp strip of leather from his mouth and swallowed to moisten his tongue. "What the hell is it?"

"If I'm not mistaken its braid. Good quality gold braid, too. The cheap stuff would have caused a much worse mess."

"Braid?"

"Part of a uniform. Shot must have carried it in there. Not surprised Mullet didn't find it when he was looking for metal." A puzzled look crossed his face. "How the hell it got in your leg, I can't imagine. We usually find it in shoulder or arm wounds. Off the jackets, you know. I even found a button once, months after the injury healed. It had worked its way up to the surface."

Beau Bainbridge's braid. A picture of the handsome, laughing young lieutenant filled Hugo's vision. He wanted to puke.

"A cannon ball took the head off of the man beside me," he said tersely. "He'd pushed in beside me moments before it landed. By rights, I should have been the one to die."

The surgeon looked delighted. "That's it, then. You've been walking around with a bit of his uniform in you all this time."

Hugo swallowed the sour taste of nausea. Poor, bloody Beau. If Hugo had been a better leader, firmer with the lad, perhaps the boy might still be alive. Along with the rest of his men. Hugo dragged himself back from the smell of gunpowder and the sound of cannon. That part of his life was over, best forgotten, like so much of his history.

The surgeon dropped the bloody piece of braid on the tray. "All we have to do now is clean the wound and suture it, and you will be almost as good as new. Unless it becomes infected. Then we will have to have the leg off."

Did he have to sound so bloody hopeful? Hugo tensed, ready.

"Are you sure you don't want something for the pain? This is going to hurt."

"No."

The surgeon threaded his needle. "You know, if you had left this much longer, I would have been looking at gangrene. You had a narrow escape, my lord."

Then he had Lucinda to thank for his worthless life. And he'd found the perfect way to do it. It had occurred to him the night of the fête. Since she already had a child, she wouldn't hanker for another. He could marry her safe in the knowledge she'd never have to suffer the torment of a Wanstead bride.

He allowed a cautious hope for the future to blot out the pain of the past. He shoved the leather back between his teeth as the doctor began his gruesome work.

Two weeks after the operation, the pain had faded to a distant memory. Finally on his own two feet, instead of leaning on Trent, Hugo strode through the crowds on Bond Street with a spring in his step and a cheerful swing of his cane. Pedestrians parted around him, like a cavalry charge around a cannon. One more errand to run and one obligatory visit to a gambling hell with Arthur, and then he would go home. To Lucinda.

The anticipation of seeing her face when he asked her to marry him made him want to dance in the street. Now wouldn't that look fine? He grinned at the street sweeper who cleared his path across the road and flicked him a shilling. The boy pocketed the coin as if fearing Hugo would notice his mistake.

The alley he sought opened on his right. He picked up his pace until he found the sign he sought above a discrete shop door. *Mrs. Syms, Purveyor of Gentlemen's Needs.* The doorbell tinkled as he stepped inside.

"Good afternoon, sir," said the motherly middle-aged woman behind the counter. "How can I help you?"

"Condoms."

"Yes, sir. How many?"

"I'd like a standing order delivered to my house. A dozen."

"Yes, sir. Would that be every three months?"

Hell, he hoped not. "One month. Send the bill to this address." He handed the woman his calling card.

Her sagging face smirked. "Planning to keep the old soldier at attention and on parade on a regular basis then, sir?"

He stared into her knowing muddy eyes blankly, and then realized she was talking about his anatomy and not his former occupation. A grin spread across his face. "Yes. I am."

She wheezed a chuckle. "Want to take the first month's supply with you then, sir?"

"Good idea." He dug for his money.

"Don't worry about that, sir. I'll add it to your bill. The order'll arrive the first of every month without fail. If you find you need more, just send me a note."

More. "Perhaps I better make it two dozen. Just to be on the safe side."

"Ah. New romance, is it? I can't imagine a gent like you'd be opening a brothel."

"Good God. Certainly not."

"And I don't imagine you needs to be visiting one three times a day."

"Madame, that is none of your business."

The woman cocked her head. "And if she's your regular, she shouldn't be a'giving you the French disease. So you're using them to stop from havin' children. Mighty considerate of you," she glanced down at his card, "Lord Wanstead. It ain't every gentleman who thinks about the plight of his light o' love havin' his bastards."

Wife. She would be his wife. He almost patted the pocket with the special license he'd picked up from the Doctor's Commons before his visit to the surgeon.

The woman didn't seem to expect an answer, because she took a box from the shelf behind her and set it on the counter. "That should keep you going until the first order arrives. They come wrapped in brown paper, no return address, and marked personal and confidential. Is there anything else I can get fer yer lordship today?" She nodded at a glass case containing everything from pills offering increased stamina to dildos of every size.

"No. Thank you."

She ran her gaze over him. "Reckon not. You look like you got all the equipment you need."

Such was his mood, he didn't have it in him to take offense. "Good day, Mrs. Syms."

"Good day, Lord Wanstead."

Stepping out into the street, Hugo felt a trickle of sweat run down his back. Well, what did he expect? Ordering vast quantities of condoms was bound to incite a comment. One thing he knew, he didn't dare get anywhere near Lucinda without a supply. He would not repeat his mistake of that last night, no matter how aroused. He was not going to be responsible for yet another death.

When he reached the corner, the street sweeper had loped off. Probably off at the local inn, gloating over the crazy man who had thrown away good coin. He avoided a dollop of dung steaming on the cobbles, dodged a coal heaver's dray and a hackney bent on locking wheels like a couple of sparring bulls, and strolled back to his hotel.

One more night in this stinking noisome place, and he could get back to the Grange.

Home.

Suddenly, after all these years, he desperately wanted to go home. He could scarcely believe it, and it was all Lucinda's fault. He strode on, not caring who saw his idiot smile.

Sixteen

Trent brushed a piece of lint off Hugo's coat and stepped back. "Anything else, my lord?"

"No. Go off and enjoy yourself," Hugo pointed to the package on the bed. "Help yourself to a couple of those. Don't forget to put them in soak for a couple of hours."

Trent grimaced. "I hate using them. It's like bathing in Hessian boots."

"Better than having it drop off."

Trent's handsome face twisted in disgust. He scooped up a handful of the French letters and tucked them in his pocket. "Thank you, my lord."

A knock sounded at the door to the outer chamber Hugo had rented alongside the bedroom.

"That will be Mr. Dawson," Hugo said. "Let him in and you can go."

"Yes, sir." Trent saluted, then winced. "Sorry, my lord," he mumbled and strode off.

Old habits died hard, Hugo mused.

The deep rumble of voices came from the parlor, and then the outer door closed. Hugo gave himself one last glance in the mirror. In a coat of blue superfine and a fancy knot in his cravat, he should pass muster with Arthur's friends, even if he wasn't a fashionable fribble. He was too big to be a dandy so he'd settled for Weston's coats and well-cut beige pantaloons. He wanted a look at these friends of Arthur's, either to set the squire's mind at rest or warn Arthur off. Satisfied with his appearance, Hugo strolled through the adjoining door to find Arthur lounging in a chair with a fashionably bored expression. "Trent says you have nothing to drink in here?"

The thought of a good stiff drink made Hugo's skin clammy. "I don't." He shoved his hands in his pockets to stop them from fidgeting. "So where are you taking me tonight? Some hell, I think you said?"

Arthur's face brightened. He stood up. "This club is all the crack, I assure you. It only opened a few month's ago. Vale is particular about membership. It's taken me weeks to gain entrance."

Mentally Hugo sighed. This had all the markings of a very tedious evening. No doubt he'd be pulling Arthur out of the River Tick and carrying him home in his cups. But a promise made must be kept. He retrieved his hat and cane from the stand by the door. "Do we walk or take a hackney?"

"Walk," Arthur said. "It is not far. No point in cramming a man of your size into a stinking cab."

"My sentiments exactly." Hugo clapped him on the shoulder. "Lead the way."

Evening time in London. Despite summer's heat, dandies and drunks crowded the streets. Colorful prostitutes jockeyed for position on street corners, and the stink of offal and expensive cologne pervaded all. Thank God Almack's was closed for the season. Not that Arthur could have dragged him anywhere near the place.

They strolled through Mayfair's grimy dusk chatting about Wellington's exploits in Spain the previous month.

"How can you bear to miss the excitement?" Arthur asked. "Now the tide has finally turned." He colored. "Of course, you can't, not with your wound. But I wish I had a part in it."

The eagerness in the younger man's voice struck Hugo like a blow in the midriff. Bainbridge had that same excited glitter in his eye moments before a cannon shot ended his young life. "You are better off here."

Arthur shot him a look that said he thought Hugo dicked in the nob.

They turned on to St. James. Hugo frowned. "Why did you make such a mystery out of this? I'm a member at White's and Brooks's."

"Oh, nothing so stuffy as that. This way."

Arthur guided him into an unlit alley beside a tavern. Hugo grimaced as his boot sunk into something with the consistency of treacle. The smell of rotting vegetation hit the back of his throat. Typical London. The alley opened into a court, and Arthur rapped loudly in what sounded like code on a black door in need of a coat of paint.

"Good God, Arthur, what on earth have you got yourself into?"

"Nothing." He half-laughed. "This is my first time here. To be honest, I think it is one of Vale's jests. He'll have us all bellows-to-mend in under a week, call it a frightful bore, and head off for Brighton to visit Prinny."

Before Hugo could suggest they forget the whole stupid idea, the door swung open. A man with a face that looked as if it had been smashed flat by an anvil dropped from a great height peered out at them. The rubbery lips stretched in a smile that revealed toothless gums. "Evenin' Mr. Dawson."

"Good evening, Perkins," Arthur said, holding out his hat.

"What do you want?" Perkins asked. "Members only."

Instead of telling the cheeky bugger to go to hell, Arthur flushed. "His grace said I could join him this evening."

The man rubbed his jaw. "Aar, I remembers now. And this must be the friend you mentioned to 'is grace?"

With a look of relief, Arthur tossed his hat to the waiting meaty fist. "Yes, Perkins. Lord Wanstead."

"Big'un, ain't he? Heavyweight. Fists like 'ams. Don't s'pose you'd want to go a couple of rounds, would you, my lord?"

Hugo stared at the battered face. "I know you. Saw you fight once at Newmarket. Practice bout. Windmill Jack Perkins you were then."

"Gor blimey. That were years ago. You can't 'ave been more than a nipper." He stuck Arthur's hat on the nearby shelf.

"Well, Jack Perkins," Hugo said, "unless you've learned to keep your guard up since those days, I'd deaden your lights in under a minute."

"Aar, sir, but I'd do you a fair bit of damage in that minute, I would."

Hugo laughed. "To my ribs, you squirt."

Perkins jabbed with his right, blocked instantly by Hugo. "Gets the bigg'uns down to my level," Perkins muttered. "Anyways, 'is grace don't let me use me five's for anything except opening the door and takin' coats and castors, so give me yourn."

Divested of his hat, Hugo followed Arthur up a set of narrow stairs. They entered a room with curtains pulled closed and lit by a couple of lanterns hanging from the low, blackened ceiling. A haze of blue smoke hung in the air. Six men lounged around a long table covered in green baize.

At the head of the table, a harsh-faced nobleman with thin lips and eyes like polished steel beneath straight black brows glanced up at their entry. His gaze reminded Hugo of a hawk viewing its prey. "'Fore gad, Arthur. Is this behemoth your soldier friend?" The languid posture and bored tone seemed at odds with the intelligent gaze.

To his right, a fair-haired Adonis giggled.

Toadeater. The word popped to the forefront of Hugo's mind.

Arthur strolled to the head of the table. "Vale, let me introduce Lord Wanstead, lately a captain of His Majesty's infantry. Fought at Bussaco. Hugo, this is the Duke of Vale."

"Your hero worship is showing, Dawson," Vale said.

Hugo was surprised when the duke rose to a height that almost matched his own and held out his hand with an open smile.

"Wanstead," his grace said. "I've heard good things about you. Welcome to the Missing Countess Club.

That is Denbigh," he pointed to the fair-haired giggler who stared back with a sullen pout to his lips.

"Pettigrew," the duke continued the introductions.

The elegant dandy looking over Denbigh's shoulder executed a sharp bow.

"And these gentlemen are Otford, Sanderson, and Longfield." The men around the table acknowledged the newcomers with laconic greetings.

Vale gestured to the empty chair on his left. "Pull up a chair and sit down. Pettigrew there has run out of the ready. Now he is trying to help Denbigh lose his fortune."

The lantern-jawed Pettigrew pulled at his lower lip. "He don't need my help." Beside Denbigh's elbow lay a pile of vowels ready to join several more in the pool.

Since Hugo couldn't refuse without insulting a man connected to royalty, or without putting Arthur's nose out of joint, and because he'd steeled himself for just such an evening, Hugo sat. He refused the offer of brandy. Arthur, looking overly smug, slouched in the seat beside him with a full glass.

Vale pushed some chips into the pot. Longfield, a jolly country-squire sort of a man, folded his cards. "Too rich for me."

The play went on with Vale as banker.

"I don't usually get invited to play with Vale," Arthur murmured in Hugo's ear. "Not even at White's."

Just as well, since they were betting one hundred guineas a hand. Squire Dawson would be bankrupt in a night.

The game ended, and Denbigh scrawled on another slip of paper. "Curse you, Vale. Your luck is in."

"His luck is always in," Otford said, getting up and scratching at his unshaved chin. "I'm done up. Not a feather to fly with. I think I'll call in on Mrs. Bixbey. Perhaps one of her girls can get the old fellow roused." He winked lewdly. "Coming, Pettigrew?"

The other man swallowed the dregs from his glass and stretched his arms over his head. "Is it morning?"

"No," Hugo said. "It is early evening."

"Good God," Pettigrew said. "We've been at the table twenty four hours straight. Must be some sort of record, what?"

"No," Vale said. "I hold that at faro. Forty-eight hours in one sitting, five years ago."

"Did you win?" Arthur asked as wide-eyed as a schoolboy with a jar full of tadpoles.

Vale turned his blade-sharp gaze on Arthur, his eyelids drooping. "Why, I believe I did."

Longfield cackled. "Bankrupted a hopeful viscount, if I remember rightly." He paused, coloring. "Killed himself the next day, too," he mumbled and sent a sheepish glance in Vale's direction.

"The fool deserved it," Vale said, his voice full of frost.

Chilly silence permeated the room as if someone had left a door ajar on a winter night. Only Vale seemed unaffected as he stacked his winnings and pushed Denbigh's vowels into an untidy heap.

"Mrs. Bixbey or not?" Otford said.

"Certainly," Pettigrew said. He linked arms with his friend. "G'night all."

Vale waved a pale languid hand at their departing backs and dealt another round of cards, including

Hugo and Arthur in the play. "A shilling a point?" he said.

Hugo blinked at the huge drop in stakes.

"I say, Vale," Denbigh protested. "You can't be—"

Vale raised a brow, and Denbigh snapped his mouth shut.

Hugo stared at the duke. Was the lowering of the stakes for his benefit, or for Arthur's? Whichever the case, there was something about Vale that engendered unwilling respect. He hadn't liked the man on sight, but he knew men, and there was more to this one than appeared on the surface. A quick look at his hand showed all high cards. One round and he'd leave.

"Arthur said you were wounded?" Vale said.

Hugo blew out a breath. Alive when he should have been six feet under. At least, so he'd thought not two months ago. "A scratch."

Denbigh looked at his hand and groaned theatrically.

The corner of Vale's mouth curled in a sneer. "Got a good hand for a change?"

Hugo almost laughed. Vale, despite his dissipated air, was not nearly as foxed as the others. What the hell was a man like him doing with a bunch of idiotic wastrels?

Hugo laid down his jack of diamonds. "What did you call this club? The Missing Countess?"

Sanderson pointed at Denbigh. "He lost his wife."

"I didn't lose her, you bag of wind. She ran off."

"Legged it." Longfield said helpfully.

"Don't suppose you've seen her have you, Wanstead?" Sanderson said, with a taunting grin.

"He shouldn't have left her lyin' around," Longfield muttered into his brandy glass. "I wouldn't have."

"I did not leave her lying anywhere," Denbigh said, his voice pitched close to a whine. "The bitch slipped out in the middle of the night."

"Told you. He lost her." Sanderson sounded ready to argue.

Denbigh shot him a sour look.

Good God. Hugo stared at the handsome young man. "Why would you want her back, if she didn't want to stay?"

Vale cast Hugo a swift look. "Therein lies the rub, my friend."

"Her bloody father cut off the allowance." Denbigh's whine grew more pronounced. "Won't pay a penny 'til he knows where she is. I think he suspects me of doing away with her." He picked up his glass and waved it toward the door as if in a toast. "My missing countess. The fat, barren cow. Money was the only thing she brought to our marriage."

Pity for the poor maligned countess stirred in Hugo's breast.

"That's her," Denbigh said. "Thought the club should have her picture."

Hugo turned to raise his gaze to a painting suspended over the door behind him.

Time seemed to stand still. The portrait showed a buxom, aristocratic young woman, with strong features wearing a pale-blue gown cut low over a magnificent rise of creamy flesh. Her unmistakable midnight-blue eyes observed him calmly, the sweet smile on her lips untroubled. A tumble of light brown curls fell from her crown to one plump bare shoulder. Someone had pierced the picture below the left collarbone with a sharp implement, an ugly slash. The same shape as the scar on Lucinda's shoulder.

The room swung around his head until he thought he would throw up. Lucinda.

Words hammered against his skull. *Missing countess. Fat barren cow.* God dammit. This puling miserable idiot was her husband. The bastard who had hurt her. Alive.

It was as if a fourteen-pounder of solid ice had ploughed dead center into his chest, knocking the breath from his body and chilling him to the bone.

Vale stared at him. His eyes flicked to the picture and back to Hugo's face. Dear God. If the duke suspected...The desire to kill surged through his blood. His fists clenched. He'd kill every man in the room. Enveloped in rage and bitterness, somehow he kept his face blank. He had to get out of here fast, before Vale's rapier brain sliced through Hugo's smoke-screen of disinterest. If it hadn't already.

The blood rushing in his ears battled the sound of Arthur's voice. He was also staring at the picture. "Hugo, is—"

Hugo brought his foot down, hard. "Are we playing cards or not?"

"Bloody hell, Wanstead," Arthur said. "Be careful where you are putting those great hoofs of yours." He raised his gaze to the picture again.

Denbigh lunged across the table and clutched Arthur's sleeve, slopping wine on the green baize in glittering droplets like spilled blood. "Fuck. You've seen her."

Every eye in the disgusting place fixed on Arthur's ashen face. Arthur sucked in a breath. He glanced at Hugo.

Shut up, Hugo willed with his eyes.

Arthur must have read the message because he shook his head. "No. For a second I thought she looked familiar, but she looks like any other wife I've ever met."

Sanderson giggled and then covered his mouth. "No one has had so much as a whiff of her perfume since she left."

Hugo had. More than that. He closed his mouth on the bitter bile in the back of his throat, swallowed it down hard.

Denbigh subsided into his chair. "Curse you, Sanderson. I'm not worried. Vale said he would find her. And he will. Won't you, Vale?"

Sickening puppy. Couldn't even look for his own wife. Hugo crushed his cards in his hand to stop himself from wringing Denbigh's scrawny neck.

The sneer on Vale's thin lips deepened as he gazed at his friend. "You can guarantee, Denbigh, that I will make sure that your wife ends up back where she belongs, if it is the last thing I do." His voice held more passion than it had all evening.

The deuce. What game did Vale play in that particular hand? Suddenly, the brandy decanter at the duke's elbow looked exceedingly inviting. It filled Hugo's vision. He tasted the smoky liquor on his tongue. Numbness beckoned.

No. Not here. Not yet. A pain throbbed in his head in time to his heartbeat. He had to get out of here. He needed air, and he needed to think. "Are we playing or not?"

Vale drummed long white fingers on the table staring at Hugo as if he could see right into his mind and lay his thoughts bare. "I agree with you, Wanstead. If Denbigh wants to sit around crying in his wine, I for one have better ways to spend an evening."

Blindly, Hugo pushed a pile of guineas into the pot. "I'll raise you."

"You are a man after my own heart," Vale said. "Risk all or take all." He pushed forward a mountain of gold. "I'm in."

What the hell did he mean? Hugo squeezed his eyes shut in an effort to clear his head.

Denbigh scrawled his name on a vowel. Sanderson and Longfield placed their cards face down.

Arthur hesitated, then folded. "My hand is abysmal."

At least the twit still had an iota of sense left.

Vale raised a brow at Hugo.

Damn them to hell. It would kill him to give one penny to these bastards, but he had to get this game finished. He pushed ten more guineas into the center.

Vale stared at his cards and then back at Hugo. He placed his cards face down. "I'm out. Denbigh?"

The color drained from Denbigh's complexion. His Adonis face crumpled. "I was sure you'd win, Vale. I can't let some stranger off the street hold my vowels. I can't bloody well pay."

Vicious in victory, Hugo pushed to his feet. "Then do not show your face in society, because I promise you that by day's end everyone will know that you reneged on a debt of honor."

"You can't do that," Denbigh croaked.

Arthur tugged at his sleeve. "Wanstead, give him a chance to win it back."

Fury threatened his grip on reason as his sight grew red around the edges. "If you continue to play with these…reprobates who pass for men, you are a bigger fool than ever I thought, Arthur Dawson. If your father disowns you, you'll deserve it."

Arthur's jaw dropped.

Hugo scooped up his winnings, including Denbigh's vowel, and raced for the exit. From above the door, Lucinda gazed down, a vision branded into his brain.

Hard on his heels, Arthur grabbed Hugo's arm at the bottom of the stairs. "Hugo, old man—"

"Outside," Hugo muttered in what sounded like a growl.

Perkins handed them their hats, and Hugo stomped out into the alley.

"What the hell is going on?" Arthur glanced over his shoulder and kept his voice low. "That was Mrs. Graham. I thought there was something familiar about her when I saw her at the fête, but it wasn't until I saw that picture that I twigged. I must have seen her somewhere with Denbigh."

Hugo grabbed Arthur by the throat and squeezed until his eyes protruded and he started to choke. Hugo released him just enough for him to draw breath. "Swear you won't say one word to any of those bastards up there."

Arthur clawed at his wrists. "I swear it."

"Break your word and I will kill you." Cold to the bone, he watched Arthur gasp for air. "Understand?" He let go.

Panting, Arthur clutched at his throat. "I gave you my word. What the hell do you take me for, Wanstead?"

"A pathetic fool. Just like me." And apparently just like Denbigh. Oh, Lucinda certainly had some questions to answer.

She wasn't a widow. She had left her legal wedded husband, run away from her vows and her responsibilities, carelessly sowing lies and deceit. He couldn't reconcile the woman he knew with the picture forming in his mind. Anger ran hot, like a fire out of control, and beneath it the familiar ache of despair.

If he stayed angry enough, he wouldn't feel the pain of the weight crushing his chest.

A carriage drew up in the lane outside The Briars front gate. Kneeling on her bedroom floor, Lucinda looked up from packing the last of her trunks while Sophia napped. She pressed a hand to the small of her back. No doubt the vicar had decided to call. He often dropped by after church to discuss what they could do for the parishioners in the coming week. Today was as good a day as any to tell him she would be leaving at the end of the month.

She got up off her knees. Her head swam. A sour taste hit the back of her throat. Good Lord. Was she going to be sick again? She stood utterly still until the wave of nausea passed. She must have risen too quickly, or she needed something to eat. The babe in her belly seemed determined to make itself known in the most unpleasant of ways. A hand went instinctively her belly. It felt no larger than before, though her breasts were tender to the touch. Joy swept the nausea away. She and

Hugo had made a baby. She couldn't get over the wonder of it, despite the accompanying desolation that she would never see him again. She'd be gone before he returned from London.

The child would be a permanent reminder, but she would not inflict her desires on him. He had never spoken of more than a physical attraction. He'd been adamant he didn't want children. It was better that she left before he knew and felt it his duty to support her babe. And besides, once her condition became obvious, her position in the village would be untenable.

The sound of boot steps on the front path brought her to her senses. Whoever it was, she did not want them to wake Sophia. She ran downstairs and pulled open the door.

Her jaw dropped at the sight of the soldierly figure marching up her path two weeks earlier than expected. Hugo. Oh God. Why had he returned so early? If he came in, he would see she was leaving. And do what? He couldn't stop her.

Deep lines bracketed his mouth and furrowed his brow. He had the look of a man in agony. Her heart faltered. Something must have gone wrong with the surgery. She longed to rush into his arms and offer him comfort. Aware of Trent's curious gaze from the carriage box, she calmed her expression, hiding her panic. "Lord Wanstead. You were not expected back until next week."

"Trent," he called back to the servant. "Take the carriage back to the Grange. I'll walk home."

Trent slid over and set the vehicle in motion.

"My lord," she said. "Do you think it is wise to walk all that way so soon?"

"Oh, it is more than wise, Lady Denbigh." The words were said in a voice so low and so bitter that at first she did not comprehend. Then the import of her name glittered with the dreadful clarity of a bayonet about to strike.

He knew. The ground beneath her feet heaved. She clung to the doorpost. She would not faint.

Hugo closed the gap between them. His jaw flexed, as if it took all his strength to speak in quiet tones. "Nothing to say for yourself, Lady Denbigh?"

"I…" Words could not dispel the shattered hurt in his eyes, but she said them any way. "I'm sorry." It came out a broken whisper.

"Sorry." His eyebrows shot up. "Really? Do you know the position you put me in?"

Numb, she shook her head.

His fists opened and closed at his sides. "I was forced to lie to a man about his wife. Honor demanded I tell him the truth and I lied, just the way you lied to me. What does that make me?"

He hadn't betrayed her. She sagged against the jamb. Cool reserve shuttered his expression. A bitter smile curled his lips. She folded her arms at her waist. "I didn't mean—"

"You didn't mean what?" The sarcasm cut into her like a whip. "You didn't mean to fool us all? Do you know what I did in London?"

She eyed him warily. "Saw a doctor."

He fumbled in his waistcoat pocket, pulled out a ring in a flash of blue fire. "I bought this."

Heartsick, she stared at it and then raised her gaze to his face.

"A bloody wedding ring." He enunciated the words slowly as if they tasted of poison. Then gave a short laugh. "You certainly played me very cleverly."

She recoiled a step. "Please, Hugo. My lord. You don't understand. I wanted to tell you."

"What do I not understand?" The chill in his tone froze her rigid. "That you have lived in this house as an imposter? That you have lied to my neighbors and friends for months? I made a few enquiries about the missing Lady Denbigh before I left London. You don't have a child." Bleak remoteness filled his eyes, as if he had no idea who she was and didn't care. The cold stare hurt far more than his scornful words.

She backed up a step.

The next words were delivered as if ripped from his throat. "The wine-soaked dolt you married is seeking you the length and breadth of England. How long do you think it will be before he finds you here, living openly?"

He took a slow, deep breath as if hauling on some inner reserve of control. "Arthur Dawson knows who you are. At any moment, he might tell his hero, Vale, and you will be found. You must leave here at first light."

She swallowed, unable to speak for shock. "I…" She had nowhere to go. The new house wouldn't be vacant until the first of the month.

"God dammit. Don't you understand? As a peer of the realm, it is my sworn duty to uphold the law. You are found." He put his hand in his pocket and drew forth an envelope. "In here is a bank draft on Coutts. Use the money to get as far from here as possible,

Ireland, Scotland. If your family won't help you, it is the best chance you have."

He scrubbed a hand across his face and went on in a thick voice. "Mr. Brown will come first thing in the morning and drive you to London."

He held out the envelope.

Numb from his brute force tirade and scourged by guilt, she stared at the paper trembling in his gloved hand. When she made no move to take it, he tossed onto the floor at her feet. She raised her gaze to his face.

"Run, Lucinda," he said wearily. "Wherever you go, don't look back." He straightened his shoulders. "The only good thing about this whole debacle is that I understand you are barren. For that I thank God…If there was the slightest chance of a child of mine belonging to that disgusting piece of rubbish you married, I'd have to kill him. And hanging over a faith-less jade is not an end I wish to contemplate."

The agony of soul in his every bitter words cut Lucinda to the quick. She never imagined causing anyone such pain, least of all this man. But had she not done her best to discourage his advances? He'd pressed forward when she'd tried to deny him. He'd battered down her defenses. And now, like Denbigh, he placed *all* the fault at her door.

Fury ignited in a flash. Flames danced at the edges of her vision as words poured forth like molten lava. "Damn you, Wanstead. What I gave you, I gave freely because I desired you. Had you asked me if I wanted to marry you, I would have said no. But you didn't ask. Typical arrogant male that you are, you decided my fate. Well it was *never* yours to decide. I gave you my body, and God help me I gave you my love, but I did not give you control over my life."

She was yelling. She didn't care. "Even if I were free to marry you, I would not do it. I will never give a man that kind of power over me again."

A thin wail from above her head pierced the red fog in her brain.

"You've woken Sophia," she said, all but collapsing in a heap at his feet in tears as her rage evaporated like steam and condensed into loss. "I'll thank you to take yourself off."

"Likewise," he said. He raised his arm. She flinched and he laughed, a cruel harsh sound. He tossed the ring into the rose bed beside the door and strode down the path. At the gate he looked back. "Run far and run fast, Lucinda." He executed a stiff bow and strode into the forest.

For a long time Lucinda stared at the place where he'd disappeared among the trees. She felt completely empty inside, as if her blood had drained into the ground. She half expected to see a pool of red at her feet.

"Mummy," Sophia called.

"I'm coming, darling," Lucinda whispered. Hot tears cooled on her cheeks, and she tasted their salt with the tip of her tongue. The burden of his pain lay heavy on her shoulders. Until today, she hadn't realized how fragile he was beneath all that male pride. An unbearable ache filled her chest. She doubled over, arms clutched to her waist, sobs shaking her until she could not breathe.

This was what she had planned. To leave. To go her own way. To never see him again. But to part on a note of such hatred…

"Mummy."

Sophia. She had to think of Sophia. And the babe. She was having a child. Hers and Hugo's. It would be all she would have of him. She'd known that from the moment she knew she'd conceived. She pushed the door shut on foolish dreams of love.

The next morning, Mr. Brown arrived grim-faced and, to Lucinda's surprise, not alone. The Reverend Postlethwaite drove up behind him in his gig. Both men looked thoroughly uncomfortable.

Weary from lack of sleep and too many tears, Lucinda invited them in. Numb, she gazed at them side by side on the sofa as Mr. Brown explained that he had met the vicar on his way over and told him of the sudden high-handed termination of her lease.

So Hugo had decided to play the autocrat. Determined not to reveal the depth of her misery, she straightened her shoulders and spoke in brisk tones. "I hope his lordship did not blame you for agreeing to the lease in the first place, Mr. Brown?"

The young man swallowed. "No. His lordship was not of a mind to discuss anything."

Slack-jawed, the vicar looked from one to the other. "I don't understand why Lord Wanstead broke the lease. You have the right to stay, you know."

Both men fixed their eyes on her, awaiting her answer. She could not let Hugo appear to be the villain in her melodrama. "I had planned to depart at the end of the month, anyway, to be closer to my family." She winced inside at the lie.

"I thought you liked living in Blendon," the vicar said. Brown nodded his head.

"I did," she said. "I do. I—to be frank, there is someone looking for me. I do not wish to be found. His lordship learned of my situation in London."

Postlethwaite's eyes glazed, and he licked his lips. "Are you in some sort of legal difficulty? "

A gentlemanly way to ask if she was fleeing from justice. She hesitated. "I have committed no crime."

"I see," the vicar said, clearly not seeing at all. He shifted in his seat, his Adam's apple bobbing wildly.

Mr. Brown pulled a fat envelope from his coat pocket and held it out.

"What is that?" Lucinda asked eyeing the Wanstead crest in the corner.

"The refund due on the lease."

She took it and then rose to place it on the table, picking up the other envelope, the one Hugo had flung at her the day before. It contained a banknote for one thousand pounds, a great deal of money and more than Hugo could afford, she suspected. She handed it to Mr. Brown. "Return this to his lordship with my thanks." She didn't want his largesse. It felt too much like the paid-off mistress, and she would never think of herself that way. The return of the lease money was fair.

The vicar opened and closed his mouth a couple of times. He reminded her of a trout left on a bank, except his usually pale face took on a crimson hue. "Mrs. Graham, I am surprised his lordship gave you so little notice."

"You do his lordship an injustice," she said calmly. "He has done all in his power to help. As I said, I already have another house rented. It simply means I must stay in Town until it is vacant."

"London is a dangerous place for a woman alone," the vicar said.

He had no idea how dangerous. Her mouth dried at the thought of returning to the city. She clenched her hands together, trying to look calm and unconcerned, while her heart was racing out of control. It had done so all night as she tossed and turned the alternatives in her mind.

The vicar rose to his feet and paced the few steps to the hearth. He stood, feet braced apart, with his back to it. He rubbed at his chin. "You could stay at the vicarage for a few days."

Mr. Brown frowned. "Wouldn't that cause a good deal of talk?"

"I cannot possibly live at your house, Reverend. I am a single woman. What would your parishioners think?" What would Hugo think? He really could not think anything worse than he did already. She sagged back against her chair.

"It is no one's business but ours," the vicar said.

It would be Denbigh's business. He might arrive to drag her home at any moment. "The man who seeks me poses considerable danger to anyone who stands in his way. I cannot remain in Blendon."

The vicar narrowed his eyes, his gentle scholarly face for once grimly determined. "A few days. Until the end of the month as you planned. My housekeeper is exceedingly discrete, I assure you. No one need know, but the three of us, and one other person whom I would trust with my life." He turned a darker shade of red. "Miss Dawson." He uttered the name with such reverence Lucinda had no doubt about his feelings.

She bit her lip. "I believe Miss Dawson's brother may suspect the truth."

The vicar looked a little nonplussed for a moment, his brow furrowed. "Arthur Dawson is a scapegrace. But if it comes to a test of loyalty, Miss Dawson will keep my counsel. After all, she will become my wife."

The revelation startled Lucinda out of her numbness. "Oh goodness. Does her mother know?" His shoulders slumped, "Not yet." He waved a dismissive hand. "But Mrs. Graham, do I have your agreement?"

"You and the little one only have to remain indoors out of sight for a few days," Mr. Brown urged. "When it is time, I will drive you to Maidstone to catch the stage."

"There," the vicar said. "It is settled."

Neither of them knew the power of Denbigh's temper. Her hand crept to her collarbone, as if she could feel Denbigh's brand on her skin through the fabric. If he caught her and dragged her back to London, who knew what he'd do. One thing she understood: never again would he give her a chance to escape. "This man I speak of is violent. You might be in danger."

Mr. Brown looked dazed, then started to his feet with clenched his fists. "Tell me who he is. I'll deal with the blackguard."

"Take it easy, Brown," the vicar murmured. "Mrs. Graham, it is my Christian duty to offer sanctuary." The strain in his voice told Lucinda that he suspected the cause of her fear. He would know the risks, not just to his person, but to his career in the church. All she could do was count the blessing of such good friends and pray they'd never suffer Denbigh's retribution. Another reason not to impose on their kindness. But Denbigh would expect her to run. If he found The Briars abandoned, he might well leave Blendon to look elsewhere. "I feel as if I am putting you to a great deal of trouble."

"It is the least I can do after all you have done for the village," the vicar said.

"Exactly," Mr. Brown said.

A painful lump, hot and hard, filled her throat. Her vision blurred. Exhausted from lack of sleep, too tired to do battle any longer, she lowered her head in acquiescence. "I accept your offer of a place to stay until the end of the month."

Mr. Brown looked at her trunk in the middle of the floor and the valise beside it. "Is this everything?"

"Everything except Sophia who is sleeping upstairs. And the kitten. Can I bring him, too?"

"Of course," the vicar said. He rubbed his hands together. "The more the merrier."

"I'll take the bags, Vicar," Brown said. "Mrs. Graham, you fetch the child."

Within minutes, Lucinda was seated beside the Reverend Postlethwaite with a sleepy Sophia in her arms and the kitten protesting in his basket at her feet. She cast a tearful glance at the place she had made her home for such a short while. The flowers seemed to nod a farewell on the breeze. "I'm going to miss this house and the village."

Beside the gig, Mr. Brown followed the direction of her gaze. His lips thinned to a hard straight line.

"I'm to set two men to pull it down stone by stone. His lordship wants the clearing planted with trees.

An ache more painful than anything she'd felt in her life struck Lucinda dumb. How much she had wounded her bear if he intended to wipe out any trace of her existence.

Seventeen

"PLEASE, MRS. GRAHAM," MISS DAWSON SAID GENTLY. "Won't you sit down and take tea with me?"

Unless she wanted to appear dreadfully rude, Lucinda couldn't see how to say no. She perched on the chair furthest from the sofa. "It is kind of you to call, Miss Dawson, when I understand you still have company at the Hall."

Miss Dawson waived an airy hand. "Not at all. And besides, my friend, Miss Abbott, departed the day before yesterday, so I have no one to keep me company." She poured the tea and held out a cup to Lucinda, who got up to take it. Miss Dawson patted the cushion beside her. "Sit here."

Lucinda swallowed an impatient sigh and sank onto the sofa beside the tiny lady and tried not to take up more than her fair share of the seat.

"I was sorry to hear that Lord Wanstead forced you out," Miss Dawson said.

Deep inside Lucinda cringed. "It was a mutual agreement."

"More like mutual disagreement, I should think."

"Please, Miss Dawson, Lord Wanstead is not to blame for my departure."

Miss Dawson pursed her lips. "Postlethwaite has been reticent to say much about what happened. I assume you and Hugo argued. I was so sure the two of you were a perfect match. There must be some way to patch up your quarrel."

Lucinda held herself aloof, tears chained firmly beneath the outer composure she'd set in stone these past few days. "You mistake the situation. Mr. Brown leased the house without his consent. He requested that I find a new house to lease, since he had other plans for The Briars."

Sorrow filled Miss Dawson's expression. "It was the child, wasn't it? He always did express a dislike of children, one reason I would never consider Hugo as a husband." She covered her mouth with her tiny hand. "Should he ever deign to ask, I mean. Not that I wanted him to, nor did he ever show the slightest interest. Oh, dear, I am making a bumble broth of this."

"The vicar tells me you and he have an understanding," Lucinda said, taking pity on her embarrassment.

A wicked twinkle entered Miss Dawson's dark eyes. "Umm. It is more than that. Don't tell my mother, not yet. Not until Peter is firmly established."

Lucinda was unlikely to tell Mrs. Dawson anything, but she nodded.

"I can't believe it happened so quickly." She blushed. "Our falling in love, I mean. We met at the beginning of the Season and now await the right moment to give Mother the news." She sighed. "Unfortunately, Hugo's arrival in Blendon rekindled some of Mother's old dreams. I had hoped you and he might make things easier for us."

Lucinda blinked at her forthrightness. "You could not possibly have imagined that Lord Wanstead and I…"

"Good lord, everyone thought so. You two reeked of April and May on the day of the fête. Even Miss Abbott remarked on it. I could not have been more surprised in my life when Peter said you packed up the day Wanstead returned from London. Was it something he said? He can be a little gruff at times, but he has a good heart."

"I will never marry Lord Wanstead."

Miss Dawson pursed her pretty lips and tilted her chin. "Was your first marriage so dreadful? "

Faced with a sudden urge to reveal her whole history, Lucinda bit down on her lip until she thought she would taste blood. "I beg you not to question me further. Lord Wanstead and I have agreed it is best we do not see each other again. I have rented a house in another part of the country." In spite of every effort at control, her voice roughened and thickened until she was forced to blow her clogged nose.

Miss Dawson tilted her head on one side. "You really are a woman of mystery. I said that to Peter, after our first meeting. But I promise not to press you further. It is something I have to learn if I am to make a good vicar's wife."

To Lucinda's relief, the vicar chose that moment to join them. The Reverend Postlethwaite looked from one to the other with a fond smile. "Ah, tea time. Have you ladies had a pleasant conversation?"

Almost as pleasant as walking over hot coals.

Hugo stared at the headlines in his paper. *Wellington fails to advance.*

God-damned armchair soldiers. Did they think the general hadn't weighed all the odds? After winning some of the finest victories against France in decades, Wellington knew what his army could or could not do.

He flung *The Times* aside at a stab of pain in his temple. Squinting, he raised his head and watched dust motes dance in a sunbeam, gazing at the puddle of light it formed on the threadbare rug. Had she made it to safety? He should have gone with her and seen her settled, but in the face of Vale's obvious suspicions, he hadn't thought it wise. He curled his lip. Besides, if he knew where she was, it would be too much of a temptation to fetch her back.

His mouth dry, his palms sweating, he got up and strode to the console, the brandy decanter a magnet to the ache in his chest and the battle raging in his gut. No brandy. He'd promised.

Fuck. If he only knew for certain she had taken adequate precautions to ensure she could not be found. He rubbed the back of his neck. If only he'd kept his damned breeches buttoned, if he'd not reached for happiness he didn't deserve, none of this would have happened.

No. He shook his head. Arthur would have seen that portrait sooner or later. He'd done the right thing, chasing her out of Blendon, letting her go. Then why did he feel so blasted hollow.

Dammit to hell. Why did she have to be married?

He trudged back to the desk and slumped down behind it. He needed to work. Needed to get the estate in order. For what? Who cared? Let his cousin have the problems. He should rejoin his regiment and throw his useless weight into the war, now that his leg was as good as new. Anything was better than sitting in his empty house where every nook and cranny reminded him of Lucinda.

A knock sounded on the door.

"Come."

Jevens shuffled in. He held out a small square box discretely wrapped in brown paper. "A parcel for you, my lord. No indication of the sender."

A wave of grim humor crept over Hugo. The condoms. He didn't know whether to laugh or cry. Grown men didn't cry. They felt nothing. They smashed things or trampled them to the ground.

Instinctively his fingers fumbled in his fob pocket, played with the circlet of gold he'd retrieved from the forest floor, and traced the hard facets of gemstones the color of summer skies through the small scrap of cotton wrapped around it. A futile reminder.

"Burn it," he muttered. "Better yet, give it to Trent with my compliments." He'd have to send the old crone a letter canceling the order. He returned his gaze to the paperwork on the desk.

Jevens coughed. "There is a personage requesting audience, my lord."

Hugo didn't look up. "I told you I would see no one."

"So I told this person, my lord. But he refused to take no for an answer. This is his card."

Jevens handed Hugo a small white square of paper on which was written, *'Jerome Scrips, erstwhile of the Bow Street Runners. Investigations.'*

"What the devil?" Hugo growled. "Throw him out."

"I'm afraid that won't be possible." A trim middle-aged man with brown receding hair and a garish red waistcoat stepped over the threshold. "Don't blame your butler here, my lord. He did his best to keep me out, but I can be very persuasive when I've a mind."

The anger he'd been holding in check escaped his sleep-deprived brain. A wash of crimson obscured his vision. He pushed to his feet. "How dare you force your way into my house, sir? If you don't depart immediately, I shall have you arrested."

"Come now, sir. I'm just doing a job."

"I care nothing for your job."

"I think you does, my lord. All I wants is to ask you a couple of questions and I'll be on me way. It won't take above a minute or two." He looked pointedly at Jevens. "Preferably in private, yer lordship."

Hugo glared at the butler. "That will be all, Jevens. Ask Trent to stand ready in the hall." Not that he expected to need help tossing the smaller man out on his ear.

The Runner settled himself into the chair in front of the desk without invitation. Cheeky bastard.

Hugo slumped down in his seat. He plucked a pen from the inkwell, drawing it through his palm as if the feather-light brush on his skin might keep him from strangling the little upstart. "Well?"

"Until last week, you had a tenant at a house called The Briars. A Mrs. Graham?"

"Yes. What of it?"

"Where is this Mrs. Graham now?"

The feather crumpled inside his clenched fist. "How the devil should I know?"

The man looked like a beady-eyed sparrow spotting a worm. "Surely she left a forwarding address?"

Why should she? So he could write love letters? The thought drove the breath from his body. Was that why he felt so bloody numb? He loved her?

He forced his attention back to sparrow-face. "If she did, she would have provided it to my steward. He looks after that sort of thing."

"Where did she come from? She must have provided some sort of introduction?"

Hugo opened his mouth.

The man grinned. "I know, yer lordship. Yer steward. Can I speak to this 'ere steward of yours?"

"He is away from the estate on business," Hugo said. Take that, you nosey bastard. Hell. Now he would have to think up an errand for Brown.

"When's he due back?"

This young man was nothing if not persistent. While it would be impossible to keep him from questioning Brown, Hugo could at least forewarn the steward, giving him time to think about his answers.

"Mr. Brown will return tomorrow."

"Right, then. I'll take me a room in that snug little tavern in the village and call 'round to see 'im tomorrow." The cheery blackguard rose and bent in the middle as if he'd spotted a tasty morsel on the carpet. Hugo presumed the motion represented a farewell bow.

Hugo gave him a stare of cold indifference. "As you wish."

The man headed for the door. He turned back with a smile. "You know it could go very ill for this Mrs. Graham if the party that's seeking her doesn't find her soon. Very ill indeed."

"Are you threatening me?"

"Wot, me? And I ain't a one to make h'acusations, your lordship. Wot I say is, if the cap fits…"

Hugo returned the other man's gaze with indifference. "Good day to you, sir."

"Good day, yer lordship. The pleasure was all mine."

Hugo remained on his feet until he heard the front door close and the carriage pull away. Thoughtful, he sank back into his chair. Perhaps if she had taken his money, he wouldn't be quite so fearful. He hadn't slept for days worrying about whether she and the child had a roof over their heads. She'd been right to run from her husband, not cowardly. If he'd thought about her instead of his own selfish disappointment, he would have recognized the enormous courage it took for a delicately bred noblewoman to leave everything she knew and manage alone.

The image of her weak-livered, cork-brained, dissolute husband laying a finger on her again revolted him to the core of his being. His gut ached as if someone had planted a fist right in its middle. Dear God. He'd do anything to help her escape that fate.

Dammit. He didn't know where she'd gone.

"Jevens," he roared.

The butler creaked into the room. "Is something the matter, my lord?"

"Yes. Fetch Brown in here. Immediately."

Lucinda's stomach rebelled at the smell of cooking wafting into her chamber from the kitchen below. She ran for the bucket beside the bed and hung over it. Dry heaves racked her body. Mother never suffered for more than a week or two and hopefully she would be the same. Slowly, her giddiness receded. She wiped her face on the towel beside the washing bowl and then rinsed her mouth. Pray heaven it eased before the journey to Cornwall tomorrow.

And she must finish packing. Returning to the bed, she picked up her gown. Blinded by tears, she had no idea if she folded it properly or not, but she stuffed it into the trunk while dashing away the moisture tracking down her face with the heel of her hand. How ridiculous to be crying when everything had worked out for the best. It certainly would not do for Sophia to wake up and find her in tears. She sniffled into her handkerchief and then tucked it into her sleeve. She did altogether too much crying these days. It must be the babe.

Even so, the weight on her shoulders seemed to grow heavier. These last few months, her life consisted of nothing but partings. And she'd hurt Hugo dreadfully.

The little she had gleaned about him through the vicar did not bode well for his future. He had locked himself up in the Grange again, refusing to see anyone. The servants' talk had him abandoning the estate and returning to the war.

The wrong choices of youth carried a heavy price, but she had never intended hers to make others suffer.

Hugo's intention to offer marriage had come as a complete surprise. It was the one thing about his parting words she didn't understand. Although he had every right to be angry at her deceit, at her lack of trust, he'd spoken of nothing but a convenient arrangement, no stronger emotion than physical attraction. Even at the last, he hadn't said a word about love. Without love, a marriage meant nothing.

If only he hadn't wormed his way into her heart.

Packing done and the vicar out on calls, Lucinda sat idle, watching Sophia play with a line of tin soldiers ranged along the windowsill. A sharp rap sounded on the door.

"Man at the door," Sophia said, peering out.

Lucinda's heart picked up speed. Might Hugo have discovered where she was staying? Was it hope that made her heart beat faster? Or fear? "Who is it?"

Sophia moved the officer on horseback at the front of her line to the back. "Just a man."

Not Hugo, then. Disappointment dipping her stomach, she set her mending aside and rose. Careful not to be seen, she glanced out of the window. The caller was hidden by the porch, but no carriage or horse waited in the lane. It must be a villager seeking the vicar. They would leave soon.

The rap sounded again.

"Me go." Sophia scooted for the door.

Lucinda trotted after her. "No, Sophia. Come back."

Too late. On tiptoes, the little girl slid the bolt.

The door slammed back, missing Sophia by an inch.

"Be careful," Lucinda said, then stared.

Denbigh's blue eyes gazed back at her soulfully. "Darling. Thank God. I found you at last."

The breath left her body in a sickening rush. "What are you doing here?" She glanced around wildly. "Sophia, come here."

Denbigh flashed his charming smile. "You almost had me fooled, hiding behind the skirts of a child."

Fear filled Lucinda's mouth with what tasted like ashes. "What do you want?"

His smile hardened. "You, of course. I have come to take you home." He reached out.

She backed away her heart battering against her chest. "Sophia. Come here." If she could make it to the kitchen, she could run out of the back door and hide in the woods.

Denbigh raised a brow. "Is that any way to greet your husband?" He dropped to his haunches, his face on a level with the child's and smiled his angelic smile. "Sophia. Is that your name?"

Sophia nodded and stuck her finger in her mouth.

"Sophia, he's a bad man. Come here."

The child dragged her gaze from Denbigh's and made a move in Lucinda's direction.

Denbigh grabbed her little bare arm.

"Mummy?" Sophia said, her eyes huge, scared.

"Let her go, Denbigh."

Still grasping the child by her upper arm, Denbigh stood up. Cruel triumph filled his eyes and curled his finely drawn mouth. "Where did you find her?"

"It's none of your business," Lucinda spat back. "She's my daughter now. Nothing to do with you."

"Come with me willingly, and nothing happens to her. Cross me and…"

He reached out a hand to Lucinda. "You made me a laughingstock, disappearing like that. Your father cut off the allowance he settled on you, and the debts are piling up. Come home, now, today, and I'll say nothing more."

Black fear invaded her mind. It widened and deepened until she thought it would swallow her whole. She edged closer to the kitchen door.

Denbigh didn't move.

Sophia squealed and tried to pull out of his grip. He squeezed harder. Tears welled in the little girl's eyes.

"Let her go. You are hurting her," Lucinda cried out.

"No," Denbigh said. "It is you who are hurting her. One more step toward that door, and I will not be responsible for what happens to the brat."

She could not let him hurt Sophia. She took a step toward him, then another. She took his outstretched hand, felt his cold dry fingers curl around hers. Flinched as he pulled her close.

"You bitch," he whispered. "How dare you?"

The words drained her of all emotion, leaving her numb and cold. She was back in his power.

"Let her go," she whispered. "You promised."

His lips twisted cruelly. "You always were naive."

A hot rush of anger penetrated the dull fog that had closed in on her mind. "If you harm one hair on her head, I will find a way to bring you to justice."

A sharpness glittered in his gaze. "Your time away from me has made you bold, my dear." He let Sophia go. Weeping, she buried her face against Lucinda's legs.

"We will talk about your attitude later, wife," Denbigh said. "Hurry up. I have a chaise waiting down the lane."

"How did you find me? The Bow Street Runner?"

"I didn't hire a Runner. Perhaps Vale did. He had people out looking." He pushed her out of the door. She blinked against the bright sunlight after the gloom of the hallway. "No," he said with a smirk. "For once fortune glanced my way. A friend saw you at some ridiculous village fête."

Arthur Dawson. It could be no one else. The moment she recognized him, she should have run. Her shoulders slumped. It made no difference who had betrayed her. She was caught. Nothing else mattered.

Denbigh pushed her up the path to the gate, one hand clamped to her wrist, an arm about her waist.

The crying Sophia clung to her skirts. Lucinda reached down to pick her up.

Denbigh shoved the child aside.

"What are you doing?" Lucinda said, digging in her heels.

"Where's Wanstead? I hear he was sniffing around your skirts."

"It is a lie."

"Really? I heard all about you two lovebirds. The talk of the village."

He made what she shared with Hugo sound disgusting and tawdry. "Lord Wanstead was my landlord."

"He threw you out, didn't he? Found out what a cold bitch you are, I suppose."

Lucinda bit back a defiant reply.

His lip curled. "Cat got your tongue?"

She would never admit her feelings for Hugo to this man. As in the past, she lowered her gaze, hid her thoughts, and kept silent. He crashed her against the gatepost. On purpose. She grabbed onto its solid strength. "I am not leaving without Sophia."

"Oh, for God's sake. Where the hell did you find the brat? On the streets?"

Her stricken expression must have given her away because he laughed. "That's it, isn't it? You picked up a dirty little street urchin like you picked up the stray dog you foisted on your father when we were betrothed."

Horror closed her throat. Her words came out as a whisper. "You can't leave her here. I am all she has."

"Let the parish take her."

Again he shoved the weeping Sophia aside. She fell on the verge. "Mummy," she wailed. "Mummy," Her voice rose to a scream.

When Lucinda refused to release her grip on the gatepost, Denbigh bashed her knuckles. She swallowed a cry and let go. He picked her up, slung her over his shoulder, staggering under her weight.

Good. For once she was glad she was heavy. She kicked her feet, slamming her fists into his back.

He cursed but kept walking.

The jingle of bridles and the beat of horses' hooves sounded behind her. Relief rushed through her. The vicar had returned. He couldn't stop Denbigh from taking his wife. No one could. But she would beg him to care for Sophia.

"Good God," Denbigh muttered.

The hooves of four black horses entered Lucinda's field of vision, not the vicar's chestnut gelding.

"Am I glad to see you," Denbigh called out as the horses stopped. A footman jumped down to aid its occupant to alight.

Lucinda craned her neck and peered back over her shoulder. "Oh no," she whispered.

"I see you found your wife, Denbigh," the Duke of Vale drawled and flicked a speck of dust off his black coat.

Eighteen

THE IDEA OF SEEING LUCINDA AGAIN MADE HUGO FEEL lightheaded, even as the recollection of his verbal attack on her burned his cheeks. He shoved his remorse to one side. His feelings didn't matter in the face of her danger, though his lack of the right to protect her gnawed at his gut. He grabbed Brown by the lapels. "If you don't want me to part you from your breath, you will tell me where she is."

Damn. He was out of control. He released the man's jacket and stepped back. "I apologize, but this is important. Where is she?"

Brown shifted from one foot to the other. "I cannot be of assistance, my lord. It is Mrs. Graham's prerogative to inform you of her whereabouts."

Snotty bastard and bloody well right. Hugo swallowed his ire knowing any attempt to browbeat his honorable steward would result in failure. Hugo wanted either to strangle him or thank him for his loyalty. He settled for a chilly glare. "I just had a visit from a Bow Street Runner. Someone must warn her."

The color drained from Brown's face. "Here? At the Grange?"

"Not half an hour ago, threatening to speak to every person in Kent until he discovers her whereabouts. He knows she was living at The Briars."

The pallid cheeks flooded red. "It's your fault she is at risk. Do you expect me to trust you?"

Trust. The word hit Hugo like a blow to the solar plexus. For a long moment he could not speak.

Lucinda had trusted him once. Trusted him with her body and worse than that, her love if he believed words spoken in flashing-eyed fury. It wasn't until later, when he recalled her tirade, that her words had penetrated the mind-numbing rage. *And God help me, I gave you my love.* The words hammered in his head. God help him. He didn't want love. He simply wanted her safe.

Self-loathing and disappointment rose up to choke him like bile. All his life he had tried to protect the innocent. And failed.

He hauled in a deep breath. "I beg your pardon, Brown. Wherever she is, I believe she is in grave danger. If she left Kent, perhaps there is nothing to worry about, but if you know where she is, send her a message. Warn her to lay low. The man's name is Scrips. Apparently, his employer is not a man to give up easily."

Brown nodded. "I will tell her, my lord."

Tell her? Damn. Did he mean she was hiding nearby despite his warning? He kept his face cool and distant. "Very well."

"Will there be anything else, my lord?" Brown said stiffly. "Perhaps you would like my resignation?"

"No, I would not. I might have been a fool when it came to Mrs. Graham, but I am not a complete nincompoop."

Brown's stiff face softened. "You are no fool, my lord. We all thought very highly of Mrs. Graham. We were all hoping…" He tugged at his shirt collar and looked very much out of his depth.

Hugo nodded a dismissal. "Get a move on, Brown. Get a message to Mrs. Graham."

The steward bowed and ran.

Hugo rubbed his eyes to clear the blur from his vision, felt moisture on his skin. Lack of sleep, worry taking its toll.

Think. He paced the carpet in front of his desk. He hated inaction. He needed to know. He needed to impress on her the need for urgency. He buttoned his coat. He'd take his normal afternoon ride. If he happened to see Brown, it would be a coincidence. He snatched up his hat and strode for the stables. For the first time in two days, a renewed sense of purpose cleared his mind of the cobwebs of misery. The thought of seeing her one last time set his heart drumming. Dammit.

The urge to hasten tensing every muscle, he forced himself to saunter out to the stables. A quick glance through Brown's office window from the courtyard revealed the steward notably missing. Obviously, the man wasn't writing her a note. A grimace tightened his lips. As he feared, she was still in the neighborhood. No doubt he'd also find Brown's horse missing from its stall. He glanced around the barn.

"Good morning, yer lordship." Albert leaned on his pitchfork with a frown.

Trent emerged from the stallion's stall. "All ready to go, my lord."

Albert wagged a finger. "Take it easy on that beast. I just got the swelling down on that there right hock."

"I will," Hugo said. "Brown just left, did he?"

Trent jerked his chin in assent.

"Damn. I meant to ask him to ride up to High Acre to look at some cattle I thought we might purchase. I'll have to catch him. Which way did he go?"

"Blendon," Trent said, backing Grif out of his stall and bending to give Hugo a boost. "Went off in a bit of a hurry."

Hugo headed the horse out of the yard.

"Watch out for rabbit holes," Albert called out, the way he had when Hugo was a lad.

He waved his crop in acknowledgment and kneed the horse into a trot. Trent shook his head and disappeared into the barn.

Damned if Hugo didn't feel like a headstrong youth setting out on some wild adventure. Damned if it didn't feel good to be doing something worthwhile. Or it would, if he weren't filled with nagging fear for Lucinda's safety.

Grif's long stride ate up the ground. Hugo kept a sharp eye out for Brown. There. A dust cloud on the road ahead. Brown was certainly keeping his word about informing Lucinda right away, and with luck he wouldn't turn to see Hugo behind him. Keeping the man in sight, but not shortening the distance between them, Hugo followed him into the village. Lucinda must be at the Dunnings' place. It was an obvious place for her to go. And stupid.

He acknowledged a wave from Peddle rolling a barrel across the inn's cobbled yard.

Brown passed Annie Dunning's stone cottage at a fast clip.

Hugo frowned. Where then? The steward turned into the lane. Only one house lay in that direction. Postlethwaite had her. She'd be quite all right at the vicarage. He wasn't needed after all. The ridiculous desire to set eyes on her had sent him flying after his steward without thinking things through. And she'd been clearer than glass about never wanting to see him again. Hell. He'd sooner face the whole of Bonaparte's *Grande Armée* than stand in front of her anger for no good reason. A smile formed on his lips. She'd been magnificent in her anger, so proud and strong. She made him proud. If only he could set her free.

The thought burst in his brain like cannon shot. The means to make sure her husband never touched her again easily lay within his grasp. He wheeled Grif around. The phaeton would get him to London long before the Runner could get a message to Denbigh. A quarrel over cards or the outstanding debt, and the whole thing would be resolved.

Gripping her wrist, Denbigh set Lucinda on her feet. With his shoulder no longer pressed against her stomach, she managed a deep breath. Oh God. Vale. She twisted her arm in Denbigh's crushing hold.

A man in a red vest stepped out of the coach behind the duke. The Runner. Another enemy. Her heart sank. Three men against one woman. The miserable cowards.

The Runner frowned at the sight of Lucinda. "Too late, your grace."

Vale raised a brow. "Apparently so."

"I didn't expect to see you here, Vale," Denbigh said. "But I'd be damned grateful for the loan of your carriage. The bloody postboy is refusing to return to London unless I show him some blunt." He wrinkled his brow. "Unless you'd care to lend me a pony?"

A sobbing Sophia ran up behind them and wrapped her arms around Lucinda's legs. "My mummy."

Vale's other eyebrow shot to his hairline. "How utterly charming."

"You snake," Lucinda said. "I'm not going anywhere with either of you."

"You are my wife," Denbigh said. "Tell her, Vale. She doesn't seem to understand. She is my chattel, my property, just like my horse."

"And you treat me worse than your blasted horse," Lucinda yelled, her struggles hampered by Sophia's clutching arms around her knees.

Denbigh raised a fist.

Swift as lightning, Vale stepped forward. He captured Denbigh's wrist, his chest rising and falling with jerky breaths. "You fool. Will you chastise your wife in public? Do you think her family will not hear of it? What hope then for restoring your allowance?"

The high color in Denbigh's face faded. A sneer curled his lips. "I certainly don't want her to look worse than she does already."

Vale's gaze jerked to Lucinda's face.

She wanted to die of shame, to disappear into the dirt at her feet. Instead, she lifted her chin. "You knew what I looked like when you married me, Denbigh." If she didn't know better, she might have thought the expression on Vale's cold face held admiration.

"Stop arguing and get in the carriage," Denbigh yelled.

"Please, Lady Denbigh. You will find it more comfortable than a post chaise, let me assure you," Vale's low voice purred.

The Runner coughed. "Might be the best thing to do, yer ladyship. Afore we starts to attract attention." He gestured to a lone rider galloping up the lane.

Mr. Brown. Lucinda's heart leaped with the joy of recognition. Surely he would come to her aid if she delayed long enough. "I'm not going anywhere without my daughter."

Vale looked startled, but recovered his bored expression with no more than a blink. "I see no harm in taking the child."

"No," Denbigh said. "I'll not take some foundling off the street."

"Now, now, dear boy," Vale murmured placing a hand on Denbigh's shoulder. "We can sort it all out when we get to London."

"Aye," the Runner said, opening the carriage door wider.

Denbigh's chest rose with a lungful of air. His face flushed red. "Sweet Christ." He grabbed Sophia around the waist and flung her onto the verge. "I will not take that piece of horseshit into my house."

Sophia screamed.

Lucinda slipped under Denbigh's restraining arm

and fell to her knees beside the howling child. She pulled her close, rocked her against her shoulder. "It is all right, darling. Mummy is here."

"What is going on?"

Lucinda glanced over her shoulder at Mr. Brown's horrified face. "Mrs. Graham, are you all right?" He swung down from his horse. His gaze swept the circle of men standing beside the carriage.

Denbigh took one quick step to stand over Lucinda. "Sir, you have no business here. I am Viscount Denbigh. This woman is my wife, and I am here to take her home."

Mr. Brown's face, shoulders, and body all sagged. He lifted his hands from his sides in a gesture of helplessness. "I'm sorry." He grimaced and glanced at the Runner. "I came to warn you that this man visited the Grange."

"You are sadly *de trop,* my man," Vale uttered in bored tones.

Mr. Brown clenched his fists. "And just who might you be?"

A smile curled one corner of Vale's hard mouth. He made a magnificent leg. "I am the Duke of Vale. And whom might I have the pleasure of addressing?"

The steward seemed to shrink inside his brown coat. Lucinda wanted to smack the supercilious expression off Vale's face. "This is Mr. Brown. Lord Wanstead's steward."

"Pleasure, I'm sure." Vale said. "I suggest you take yourself off." He flicked open his snuff box and stared down at Lucinda cuddling the crying Sophia. "On second thoughts, you might want to take charge of the child."

"No," Lucinda screeched. She got to her feet. "Sophia stays with me."

Mr. Brown opened and closed his mouth a couple of times before managing to speak in strained accents. "This is clearly a family matter."

Her own panic forgotten for a moment, Lucinda's heart went out to him at the sight of his anguish. Confronted by such powerful opposition, what could he do?

Denbigh seized the moment to pull her to his side.

Sophia set up a high-pitched wail.

Denbigh drew back his foot for a kick. Lucinda stuck her shin in its path. Pain shot up her leg. She sank to the ground.

"Scrips," Vale snapped, "Hold the child. Denbigh, put your wife in my carriage."

The Bow Street Runner picked up Sophia, who screamed louder.

Denbigh grabbed Lucinda around the shoulders. She elbowed him in the ribs and heard his gasp with satisfaction. She kicked at him. Her soft slippers made no impression on his booted ankles and only served to stub her toes.

Denbigh captured her wrists, heaving her toward the carriage. She dragged her feet, clawed at Denbigh's fingers, and tried to bite his hand.

"She doesn't want to go," Mr. Brown cried. "Leave her be."

"Please, Lady Denbigh," Vale said. "I promise no harm will befall you or the child."

"Liar," she yelled through sobbing gasps for air. "Do you think I don't know what you plan?"

Above the pounding in her ears and Sophia's cries came the thunder of more hoof beats.

The huge black stallion reared to a halt. "What the hell is going on here?" Hugo roared.

Lucinda's heart crashed to her feet. Now Hugo would witness the truth of her marriage. Of all the things that had happened, this was the worst. She slumped against Denbigh's chest.

"Well, well. Look who has arrived," Denbigh said. "The man who stole my wife."

Bile in his throat, Hugo glared at the sniveling cur who held Lucinda's arms in a cruel grip. He wished for his saber. Or better yet, a pistol. He should have borrowed Peddle's musket when he stopped to ask him about the Bow Street Runner and learned of the sudden rush in carriage trade headed for the vicarage.

He leaped down and looped Grif's reins over the picket fence.

Denbigh tightened his arm around Lucinda's shoulders. "Have you come for your slut? I'm surprised you haven't tired of the cold-hearted sow. Take yourself off, Wanstead. You aren't wanted here." He gave Lucinda a shake, and she bit off a cry of pain.

The small stifled gasp made Hugo wince. He stepped forward, fists clenched. "Let her go."

"Stay back," Denbigh said. "It will worse for her if you come any closer."

Hugo let go a short breath and regained control. He stayed put. God dammit. He wanted to smash Denbigh in the face and then hang Arthur up by his thumbs. He glanced at the other men gathered around the shiny black carriage—the nervous Brown, the wary Runner, and the nonchalant but alert Duke of Vale. Three against two. Outnumbered but not impossible odds. Brown backed away. Hugo sighed. Three to one. He needed a plan of attack.

The pallor in Lucinda's cheeks and the way her gaze remained rooted to the ground like a beaten dog sickened him. He had to set her free of this bastard, no matter the cost.

Vale lifted an elegant brow. "Wanstead."

Hugo bowed. "Your grace. I assume Scrips *is* your man?"

The duke nodded.

Oh yes. Badly outnumbered.

"It seems Lady Denbigh is not willing to go with you, Lord Denbigh," Hugo said.

"My whore of a wife will do as she's bloody well told."

By force of will, Hugo held his surge of killing anger in check. "Divorce her." He flinched at the sound of Lucinda's indrawn gasp of horror. "Name me in your suit. I won't contest it."

Denbigh's finely molded lips parted in a parody of a smile. "What, and lose access to her money? D'you think I'm a fool?"

"If it is money you want, I'll pay you." He had the banknote he'd borrowed to help Lucinda.

"No," Lucinda cried.

The anguish in her voice cut him to the quick, but he could not let it stop him.

"You are a man after my own heart, Wanstead," Vale drawled. "I offered to pay for her months ago. Just before she fled."

Lucinda gazed at him with loathing. "What did I ever do to warrant such a disgusting proposition?"

A faint flush stained the duke's high cheekbones. "Darling, you captured my heart." He gave a nonchalant laugh. "What is left of it."

For some reason, Hugo sensed an underlying sincerity in Vale's rather cynical declaration. And something else was strange: the duke and his man had come separately from Denbigh, who seemed to have arrived in the post-chaise waiting further down the lane. Apparently Vale was playing his own game. Hugo tentatively revised his count of the opposition. "I'll double whatever Vale offered to pay," he said. "If she is barren, as you say, why keep her?"

"It's a good offer, Denbigh," Vale said. "You could even marry again and get your heir."

"How does he know it is not his fault we have no children?" Lucinda yelled and then cowered as Denbigh raised his fist.

"You…you bloody cow," he said. "How dare you?"

"Come to think of it," Vale drawled, "Lady Elizabeth isn't breeding either, is she?"

With absolute horror, Hugo watched Denbigh swing around to stare nonplussed at the duke.

"What the hell are you implying, Vale?" Denbigh said.

If she wasn't barren…Hugo's gut lurched.

Vale shrugged. "I'm no expert."

Denbigh looked murderous. "God damn you. Lady Elizabeth takes precautions. Do you think she wants a bastard?"

Relief held Hugo in thrall. God. That had to be it. He took one step closer to the distracted Denbigh, a foot or two closer to Lucinda. One hard snatch would free her from the other man's clutches. It would take but a second to mount her on Grif and get her away before Denbigh drew breath.

Denbigh must have caught the movement out of the corner of his eye because he swung around. "She's worth ten thousand pounds invested in the Funds," Denbigh said. "Have you got that kind of money? Cash."

"No!" Lucinda cried out. Denbigh gave her a shake.

Hugo tried not to blink at the enormity of the sum. A debt of that size would ruin him. He tried to keep his voice steady. "Not to hand. I'd have to sell some land."

"What about you, Vale?" Denbigh loosened his grip a little as he turned to the duke. "How much are you willing to pay to mount the fat sow?"

The color drained from Lucinda's face. She shrank away.

Blood roared in Hugo's ears. Red filled his vision. He shot out a fist. Denbigh jerked back. Hugo's fist glanced off his chin.

Denbigh cursed and tested his jaw with probing fingers.

Before Hugo regained his balance for another blow, Denbigh shoved Lucinda at Vale. "Hold the bitch."

The Bow Street Runner handed Sophia to Lucinda.

Hugo raised his fists and squared off.

Eyeing him up and down, Denbigh put up his guard.

"I am surprised," Hugo said. "I thought you only stood up to women and children." He threw a left jab.

Denbigh ducked and slammed a boot into Hugo's thigh. Right on his scar. Hugo staggered from the sudden agony.

Lucinda screamed.

Breathing hard though his nose, Denbigh grinned and landed a swift punch to Hugo's stomach. "Heard about your wound, old chap."

Hugo shook his head to clear the wave of dizziness. He feinted a right at Denbigh's ribs and caught him with an upward swing of his left, flush on the jaw. Denbigh's feet left the ground. He flew back and landed on his arse.

"Bastard," Denbigh said. "I wouldn't let you have her, if I was penniless."

"You are penniless," Vale pointed out. He tucked his snuffbox in his pocket and raised his quizzing glass. "Fisticuffs are so crude," he complained in long suffering tones. "A duel is far more gentlemanly, don't you know."

Denbigh touched fingertips to the blood running from his nose and glared up at Hugo. "I'll kill you for that." He dove a hand in his pocket and pulled out a pistol. "It doesn't matter what you say, Wanstead. She's my wife. Mine to do with as I please." A cruel smile twisted his lips. "Hit me again, and she is the one who will suffer."

The words stopped Hugo cold. "Coward."

"Try to see her, and I'll keep her in a rat-infested cellar, I have a nice one at Denbigh Hall," Denbigh said.

The expression of revulsion and horror on Lucinda's face made it clear she believed the threat.

Rage tore at Hugo's reason. He clung by a thread to his sanity. "Do you think her father will pay an allowance under those circumstances?"

Denbigh grimaced.

"Wanstead," Vale said. Hugo flicked him a glance.

"Have a care, Wanstead." The duke spoke softly, but his tone held menace, although neither he nor his henchman seemed prepared to go to Denbigh's aid.

Denbigh scrambled to his feet, brushing dust off his breeches. He shrugged. "Her father might pay more just to keep her out of the cellar. What do you think, Lucinda?"

"I think my father will do everything he can to set me free of you." Her words were boldly spoken, but her voice wobbled.

The pain in Hugo's chest intensified.

"Too bad you didn't think of that before, sweetheart," Vale said.

Hugo stared at him.

A movement at the corner of his vision caught his attention at the same moment the Bow Street Runner shouted. "Look out for the pop."

Hugo swung around. Denbigh leveled the pistol at the middle of his chest. "Say your prayers, Wanstead."

"No," Lucinda shrieked. "No, Denbigh. Please. I'll go with you. I'll do anything you say." She thrust Sophia into the Bow Street Runner's arms.

"Blimey," he said.

Hugo lifted his hands away from his sides. "Go ahead. Shoot. You will swing for it."

"Will I?" Blood dribbled down from his nose. He hawked and spat. "Vale will say it was self-defense."

"I will tell them," Lucinda said fiercely. "I will tell everyone what a coward you are, shooting an unarmed man."

"As will I," said another voice.

Postlethwaite. And dear God, Catherine, their faces white and shocked as they rushed out of the vicarage gate. Not exactly the place for two such gentle people. "Take Catherine back in the house, Vicar," Hugo said.

They didn't move. Damn. This was becoming a circus. Somehow he had to gain control before someone else got hurt. "You won't kill me, Denbigh," Hugo taunted. "You are too much of a coward."

Denbigh's head jerked around, his eyes blazing.

The Bow Street Runner put Sophia in the carriage. Good. Lucinda would be forced to follow.

Denbigh must have thought the same thing because he nudged his wife in the direction of the open door. Hugo put all his money on the duke taking care of her, no matter what happened next.

Lucinda didn't move. She seemed mesmerized by Denbigh's pistol.

"Mummy," Sophia cried out.

"Get in the carriage, Lucinda," Hugo murmured. From the corner of his eye, he saw Vale give the faintest of nods.

Dear God. He better be right about the duke. He took a step towards the pistol. "What are you waiting for? I tupped your wife."

Lucinda recoiled, her expression stricken. It hurt Hugo to cause her pain, but it worked because now all of Denbigh's attention focused on him. The earl drew back the hammer, his handsome face twisted in a snarl. "You bastard. You think if I kill you, I'll hang." His swollen lips grimaced in a death's head smile. "I don't blame you for any this, Wanstead." He nodded at Lucinda. "She's the one who must be punished."

"For God's sake, Denbigh," Vale drawled. "Put the gun down. I'm getting bored. Countess, get in the carriage if you have any care for this brat."

Denbigh shot Vale a wild glance. The pistol wavered.

Hugo prepared to spring. A figure in grey shot between him and Denbigh. Lucinda. Hugo thrust her aside with one hand, knocking Denbigh's pistol up with the other.

A shot rang out. And another. Denbigh faltered, a shocked expression on his face, then keeled over.

Lucinda collapsed.

Off-balance from his leap, Hugo felt as if he'd been struck through the heart. "No," he yelled.

Nineteen

HUGO DROPPED TO HIS KNEES AT LUCINDA'S SIDE, reaching her just before Catherine.

"Nice shot, yer grace," Scrips said.

"She's fainted, I think," Catherine said, kneeling on the hem of her pale blue gown and chafing Lucinda's hands. "Postlethwaite, there are smelling salts in my reticule. Find them please."

Postlethwaite knelt beside her and fished in the bag.

Hugo glanced from the clearly dead Denbigh to Vale leaning against the carriage, a pained expression twisting his features. "Thank you for your help, your grace, but you should not have killed him. You'll face a jury of your peers."

Vale managed a half smile. "Couldn't do much else, my dear. I don't think there is a judge in England who will blame me. Self-defense, d'you see."

"Self…" A drop of something dark and thick landed on the duke's impeccably polished boots. "Good God, man, you're hit."

"Yes," the duke said a gleam of mischief in his pain-filled grey eyes. "Devilish lucky, that."

"'Ere, yer grace," Scrips said. "Let me set my peepers on that there." He undid the duke's coat and peeled it off one shoulder. He unbuttoned the black waistcoat and revealed a white linen shirt mired red with blood and rent high on the shoulder. Scrips pulled out a spotted handkerchief.

"Good God, man," Vale said. "I hope that's clean."

"'Course it is," Scrips muttered, staunching the wound.

Hugo turned back to Lucinda. Her eyes were open, and she was staring at Denbigh's still form. "Is he dead?"

"Yes, dear," Catherine said. "Quite dead."

Lucinda shuddered and looked away. "Where is Sophia?" she asked in a whisper.

Sophia peeped out of the carriage door. "Bad man gone?" she asked.

Lucinda's laugh sounded so broken and brave and full of tears that Hugo found himself watching her through a watery blur.

Bloody idiot. He backed away, giving her room when everything in his being strained to take her in his arms. If he did, there would be no going back. Seeing her fall, the utter feeling of helplessness had left him rigid with terror and brought the truth into stark clarity. The duke, who had given his blood to save her, was the far better man.

The little girl hopped down the steps as Postlethwaite and Catherine helped Lucinda to her feet, while Scrips pulled a blanket from the carriage and threw it over Denbigh's remains.

Lucinda turned to the duke. "Thank you, your grace," she said stiffly. "I still don't understand why you did it, but thank you for your help."

Vale's hard eyes softened. "I knew what you suffered, my dear, only too well. I know you thought me lacking in finer qualities. You certainly surprised the hell out of me." He shook his head. "I thought you'd run to your parents after I made it clear what sort of country house party that idiot had planned."

"B–but you encouraged him into all that vice and dissipation. It was all your idea."

He winced as Scrips pulled the knot tight. "Guilty, I'm afraid. It was the only way I found to keep the bastard away from you." He closed his eyes for a moment. "I'm so very sorry he hurt you, my dear. If I hadn't been out of the country when he proposed, I might have stopped the wedding. I knew what he was, d'you see. Unfortunately, he didn't waste a moment with the nuptials once he heard about your dowry, and by the time I was back in Town it was all too late."

Hugo forced himself to watch Lucinda's reply, waiting for her to fall into her savior's arms. The Duke of Vale had proved to be what Hugo had known instinctively, a good man behind a mask, a man who had continued his quest to help a woman in jeopardy. He obviously cared for her. He'd risked his life for her, for God's sake. He was the kind of man Lucinda deserved—charming, wealthy, and clearly enamored.

Amazingly, she didn't move.

The duke's cold gaze flittered around the silent group, coming to rest on Hugo in question.

Aware of Lucinda's gaze fixed on his face, Hugo shook his head. He backed toward Grif at the fence.

The duke took a deep breath. A rare smile curved his thin mouth, turning his face from cynical devil to dark angel. "Lady Denbigh," Vale said. "I would be honored if you would agree to be my wife?"

Hugo turned, his jaw locked so tight his teeth ached, his heart picking up so much speed he had trouble breathing. What woman would refuse the wealthiest man in England and a duke to boot? And she shouldn't. After all she'd suffered, she deserved the best of life. All Hugo had to offer was a mountain of debts and a heart encased in ice. He would be little better than her dead husband. And besides, she'd already given him her answer. *I would never give you that kind of power over me.* She'd been right not to trust him.

Yet somehow he wasn't surprised when she shook her head. "You are too kind, your grace." Lucinda's clear soft voice broke through Hugo's attempt to block it out. "But I do not love you." She cast him a swift yearning glance.

He stamped out the flicker of hope. Love was a foolish foundation on which to build a marriage. It weakened a man and made getting through life impossibly painful. Love required a man's soul, and he'd left his in Spain, buried beneath the hot dry soil.

Give her time to think the duke's offer through, and she'd realize the advantages. If not, she'd return to her family. Hugo caught Grif's reins and unhooked them from the peeling fence. He thrust his foot in the stirrup and dragged himself into the saddle. He stared down at her from Grif's back, drinking in her slowly widening fathomless eyes, the way she lifted her chin, the sweet curve of her cheek. He forced words past his stiff lips. "The duke makes a good offer, Lady Denbigh. The best you'll get." He touched his hat and turned Grif down the lane.

Catherine rushed to Lucinda's side to put an arm around her shoulders, but Lucinda couldn't take her gaze from the broad back riding away. Hugo didn't want her. Her arms went around her waist at the sudden wave of nausea. She was carrying his child, and he didn't want her. He didn't know about the child. Perhaps if she told him…

And force herself on a man who'd rejected her out of hand after she'd as good as declared her love? What had happened? Before he knew about Denbigh, he had wanted to marry her. A sense of betrayal warred with confusion. Why was it different now that she was Denbigh's widow? She glanced at the draped form on the ground and shuddered. What had changed his mind? The duke's offer of marriage?

She had to know. She turned to Postlethwaite. "Can I stay here for a few more days?"

Postlethwaite's mouth dropped open. Catherine gave a gasp of astonishment.

The duke flashed a rather pained smile. "Your family has been worried sick since you disappeared, you know. They will be relieved to discover you are safe."

"You have spoken to them?" Lucinda asked.

"Scrips is their man. Your brother Geoffrey hired him. When I discovered we were on the same errand, we joined forces. The child threw us off track for a while."

"Geoffrey is in England?"

Vale nodded. "Scrips sent him a message yesterday. Your brother, possibly even your father, will no doubt arrive tomorrow, Lady Denbigh." Vale said. "They both agreed to support you against your husband."

"Coming here? To the vicarage?"

The duke raised a brow at the still stunned-looking vicar. "Can Lady Denbigh remain here until her brother arrives?"

Catherine shook her head. "I won't hear of it. Lady Denbigh, you will stay at the Hall until you feel well enough to travel."

Postlethwaite breathed an audible sigh of relief.

A feeling of numbness seemed to invade Lucinda's chest. Not even the news of her family's arrival pierced the strange emptiness.

"If you'll take my advice, your grace," Scrips put in. "You'll see a doctor as soon as maybe. Bullet's still in there. Have it out, or by morning you'll be cocking up your toes. We'll take a room at the local inn. I'll send the magistrate back to look at the body and take statements."

"Timely reminder, Scrips," the duke said on a weary sigh. "Hopefully the pesky inn will have rooms for us."

Scrips assisted him to the carriage. "They'll make room, yer grace."

"I'll ride ahead," Mr. Brown said, "have a word with Peddle, send for the doctor, and then ride for the squire."

"Good idea," Catherine said. "Father loves playing magistrate, and he won't be happy if you do not call him right away. Perhaps you would also request my mother to expect a guest?" She took Lucinda's arm. "I think you should come indoors, Mrs. Graham. I mean, Lady Denbigh. I think we could all use a cup of tea."

"And biscuits," Sophia said with a little hop and a smile on her tear-stained face.

Lucinda forced her gaze away from where Hugo had disappeared at the end of the lane and pulled

Sophia close to her side. "Yes. A cup of tea would be just the thing." And some time to gather her wits.

"Are you sure you are all right?" Catherine's gentle voice asked when tea was over and Sophia was tucked in bed for a nap.

Lucinda hesitated, looking into Catherine's sympathetic if puzzled eyes and drew a deep breath. "I do not understand why Hugo…Lord Wanstead left like that. What did I do wrong?"

Like a tiny bird, Catherine pursed her lips and slowly shook her head. "I can't help you, I'm afraid. His father was a harsh disciplinarian, a cold man, but Hugo was always kind and gentle, more like his mother for all he looks just like his father." Catherine looked down at her hands folded in her lap and sighed. "The army does seem to have changed him, made him stern and remote." She glanced up. "Except when he looks at you." She shrugged. "We've all changed. Look at Arthur. He never cared about clothes and gambling. Now he is a dandy of the worst sort."

"Hugo certainly seemed relieved when Vale proposed." The pain of that moment came back to strike another blow at her heart.

Catherine's eyes shone unshed tears. "I cannot think what to tell you."

Lucinda rose to her feet and paced in front of the hearth, her hands twisting her handkerchief around her fingers. After meeting Denbigh, had the disgust Hugo felt for her husband rubbed off on her? Could she ever be satisfied if she did not hear the truth from his lips? "I must speak with him."

"I could invite him to the Hall tomorrow."

"No. I have to broach him alone." Catherine's eyes widened, but Lucinda continued, "Today is Wednesday. I will go to the Grange after dinner, the moment Sophia settles." She would accost the bear in his cave, poke him with a stick, and see if she could make him roar.

Catherine caught at her hand and stopped her rapid steps. "You are very daring."

Lucinda smiled and shook her head. "With my parents arriving tomorrow, this might be my only chance. May I borrow a horse?"

Dark had fallen hours before Lucinda crept through the Grange's kitchen garden. She inhaled the scent of lavender on her way passed the rampant bush beside the path. Only reflections from the new moon glittered on the diamond-paned windows across the back of the house. No glow from within. The last time she had crept around in the dark, she had been on the run from London. That long ago night had brought her to Hugo.

Tense, breath held, heart pounding in her chest, she pressed down on the back-door latch. Perhaps she was wrong and Wednesdays were no longer the servants' night off.

Gliding across the kitchen, she felt the hairs on the back of her neck prickle as if she could sense someone watching. She stopped. The clock ticked on the mantel, and the banked fire cast a red glow over clean pots and polished tile. And not a sign or sound of any of the servants. At the hearth, Belderone lifted his great head, his black nose quivering.

"It is me," she whispered.

The dog thumped its tail once and let its head fall back to its crossed paws.

"Fine watch dog you are."

The door to the passageway creaked as she drew it back. She stopped, listening. Silence. She tiptoed into the great hall. Empty. Apart from a lantern beside the stairs, there were no lights and no sounds from the study or the library. She peeked through their doors just to be sure. No one.

Her heart sank. Could he have left so soon to rejoin the army? One hand gripping the cool balustrade, the other lifting her skirts high in readiness for flight, she climbed the stairs.

Outside Hugo's chamber, she paused. This room, too, appeared to be in darkness.

With fingers that shook, she turned the knob a fraction at a time until the latch slid back. Under her gentle pressure, the door cracked open. She waited. Listening. The bed, ropes creaked. A muffled curse. The sound of heavy breathing. Awake breathing? Or the deep breath of a sleeping man? She pushed the door a fraction wider. No challenge rang out, so she slipped inside.

Waiting for her eyes to adjust, she lingered at the door. The fastened back shutters permitted the moon to fling eerie shadows on the floor and the walls. Furniture slowly took shape, the armchair against the wall, the glint of a brass handle on the dresser, its mirror reflecting moonbeams onto the great bed.

Body taut, ready to run, she crept to the side of the bed closest to the door. Hugo's naked chest rose and fell, his eyes remained shadowed. Was he watching her, waiting to pounce when she drew close enough? The scent of soap and sleeping man assailed her nostrils, tempting and scary.

He rolled onto his side, punching at the pillow as if it contained rocks. Not so peacefully asleep, then. Would he be furious at her invasion?

What had triggered his rejection this afternoon? Had the cruel jibes of her husband made him see her through Denbigh's eyes as disgustingly fat? If so, by coming to see him, she was in for a hefty dose of mortification.

She crept closer. Stretched out in the center of the huge bed, his torso gleamed like polished pewter in the moon's cold light. A moonbeam grazed a cheek hazed with stubble, deepening the crease between his brows and hollowed his cheeks. He seemed so alone in the great bed.

He shifted. The covers slid down to his waist. He groaned and rolled away from her. Stock still, she waited until once more his breath evened out. She relaxed her shoulders and watched the wide chest expand with each indrawn breath. A beautiful man.

Her mouth dried at the sight of his powerful muscular body and the curve of his firm buttocks. How she'd missed him these last few weeks. Missed his touch, his heat, the pleasure of his flesh buried inside her.

She squeezed her eyes shut and remembered how she'd decided to say good-bye on the night of the fête, when as a married women she'd been wrong to carry on an affair. Circumstances had changed. Why then had he handed her over to the duke like a worn pair of shoes?

Had it been relief she'd seen in his gaze, or regret? If only she could be sure. She had to discover what had caused the breach, plumb its depths, even if he did savage her heart like a wounded bear.

On tiptoes, she merged into the shadows near the head of the bed, afraid he might see her, wishing he would. Scarcely daring to breathe, she stripped off her gown. Stays and chemise dropped to the floor with a whisper. Teeth clamped tight to prevent their clatter, she eased out of her shoes and stockings.

God, she felt cold. Anyone would think it was the middle of winter. Fright made her cold. Fear held her in its thrall. She knew the feeling too well, but never with Hugo. Perhaps he would roll over and see her, taking the final decision from her hands. Fingers clenched on the edge of the sheet, she waited. If anything he seemed to breathe more deeply.

Now. If she didn't do this now, she'd give in, the way she always had. For once she was in control of her life and she had to see this through to the end, no matter how painful.

Lifting the corner of the sheet, she perched on the edge of the bed and felt the cool linen against her bare thighs and buttocks. Slow, like thistledown landing on water, she slipped beneath the cover. The air didn't move as the mattress sank beneath her weight. She lay back on the pillow, stiff and straight, the way she had lain waiting so many nights in Mayfair. But in those days she had not been waiting for Hugo.

She wriggled deeper into the bed, warmed her hands beneath her armpits, and then touched her fingertips to his warm silken back.

His breath hitched.

She froze, remaining still until his breathing became easy and smooth. Was he imitating sleep, ignoring her presence in the hope she'd leave? She turned on her side and edged herself closer until they lay like two spoons in a drawer. His bottom fitted into her lap, pressed against her curls with a most pleasurable tickle.

She nuzzled his knobby spine, licked his skin, tasted salt and musky male. Hugo. She rubbed her cheek against his shoulder blade and ran her finger along the outside of his ear.

A breath hissed into the dark. His backside pushed deeper into her groin, firing sparks of pleasure at the outer lips to her entrance. Heat flushed her skin and desire tightened low in her belly.

She traced the smooth contour of his upper arm, trying to drum up courage. Hesitantly, she reached over his arm to rub his nipple with her thumb.

He growled low in his throat. The sound made her quicken and ache.

Hugo. Her bear. The thought made her smile.

He flipped onto his back. She jerked away, escaped being crushed beneath his shoulder by inches. He flung his arms above his head. Awake or asleep, he certainly wasn't protesting and now she had much better access to his glorious body.

When he made no further move, she dared to resume her exploration. This time she stroked the hard ridges of his stomach. They flickered beneath her palm, hard, warm, full of life, incredibly vigorous. She propped herself on her elbow and leaned over him to taste the nearest manly nipple. The rough hair tickled her lips and her tongue. The tiny bead stiffened to attention.

Interesting. She ran her palm over her breast and felt the nipple harden. She rubbed it against his bicep and shivered at the delicious sensation firing rockets of pleasure to her core. She bit back a moan of desire and raked his large body with a greedy gaze. He lay immobile; eyes closed, expression tight but not grim, legs spread wide, the sheet tenting at his groin.

Completely at her wicked mercy.

Touch him there, a naughty voice goaded. The bold idea jolted her insides. Desire heightened. She worked the sheet down until his mighty phallus lay exposed, curving up toward his navel in virile glory. She swallowed at the sight of a tiny bead of gleaming moisture at its dark tip.

In a sudden unexpected move, his hand came to his groin. She froze as he adjusted the dark-skinned sack beneath his rigid shaft, then his fingers encircle his straining member, stroking its length with swift jerks. The purple tip emerged to its fullest extent and seemed to swell with each downward stroke. He moaned with pleasure.

Instinctively, she reached out and curled her fingers around the hot base below his fist, feeling wiry curls against her hand.

He stilled, his hand falling to his side.

She held her breath.

His hips arched up, driving his cock through her closed hand, the hot velvet skin gliding against her palm. She squeezed. He groaned deep in his throat and deepened the thrust of his hips, covering her fingers with his, encouraging her to grip tighter, to follow his lead.

She darted a glance at his face. Was he really sleeping? His eyes remained closed, his lips parted, his chest rising and falling to the rhythm of her caress. It felt good, this slide of skin over a shaft of hot rigid flesh. Pleasurable. Her quim stirred with its own demand, tightening insistent longing.

This was wicked madness. She swallowed. She'd been insane to climb in his bed like a woman of the night. Did she really want to suffer more embarrassment? If he awoke and found her toying with his body as if she owned it, he'd be appalled by her wantonness. She released him.

Quick as a flash, he caught her around the waist, pulled on top of him, her chest against his thundering heart, his hand fumbling to bring himself inside her, his breath a harsh rasp in her ear. He wanted her. Even in sleep, desire etched deep lines around his mouth and heated his body to fever pitch.

And she wanted him. Just as flowers wither from lack of sunlight in winter, her heart had shriveled at the thought she would never see his face again or feel the magic of his touch. The tears trapped in her throat made it difficult to breathe.

She knelt astride him, nudged the tip of his hard male flesh into her wet, welcoming passage.

A breath hissed from between his teeth as if the heat inside him had been released in steam.

She lowered herself down his length, felt her insides stretching to accommodate his width and length. Closing her eyes, feeling the throb of his blood inside her, she pressed down until she could go no further.

His hands came to her hips, and he arched into her, pressing deeper, fraction by fraction, until she felt his stones against the cheeks of her bottom.

He let go the long sigh of someone who has come home to safe harbor. "Lucinda. Love."

The tears sprang to her eyes at the sound of her name coupled with the one word she longed to hear, even if he never knew it had crossed his lips.

She looked down at the place where they joined, where his body entered hers, their curls mingling and glistening damp. Desire forced her to rise, to create that wonderful friction. She squeezed tight in anticipation of the next downward slide.

"Lucinda!"

No dreamy voiced murmur, but a sharp shocked rumble.

She looked into his eyes, still hazy with sleep and lust and confusion.

"Hugo," she whispered. She drove herself down to the hilt, her back arching with pleasure.

"Ah, yes," he moaned. "I thought I was dreaming, love."

Love. This time he had said it while awake. Her heart sang, but her body demanded. She rose to its command.

This time his hands beneath her bottom helped her lift and then pressed her down, pushing his hot flesh deeper inside, until the head reached the mouth of her womb.

"Yes," she cried out, not sure she could stand so much pleasure, yet wanting more.

Together, they increased the rhythm, the slow upward slide until he almost withdrew, the hard, fast, downward rush to mindless delight. It seemed to go on forever, harder, faster, their bodies grinding together, one of his hands caressing each of her breasts in turn, her fingers tweaking his nipples, grazing them with her nails until he too cried out.

He raised his head to suckle on her breast. An arrow of tension and pleasure and pain shot to her core. She moaned her pleasure.

"Ah, God," he cried out. He lifted her clear and dove and rolled her over on her back. "My turn," he growled.

She smiled up at him, cupped his cheek in her palm, raised her mouth to his, touched her tongue to his lips, and tasted the depths when he opened for her.

"Take all of me," he said and drove home, hard and deep, to the hilt.

"Yes."

His hips pumped in a furious but gentle assault.

The wire pulling her skyward fought with gravity. She twisted and writhed to take him deeper, seeking the release hovering just out of reach. He slowed the pace, angled his hips until the pleasure grew so great her limbs were numb and her mind as empty as the universe.

"Now," he begged. "Come for me."

The wire broke at the desperation in his voice, flung her into the void vaguely aware of his cry of fulfillment and the weight of him as she sank into the mattress. Heated by bliss she had thought never to know again, she fell into deep sleep.

Hugo loved watching her sleep. He had lit the candle by the bed for just that purpose. The soft curve of her lips, the way her cheek nestled into his shoulder and her dimpled arm lay along the curve of her waist and hip. Here, in his room, they were one. He reveled in the feel of her here beside him and refused to think about her leaving. In coming to him tonight, she had merely prolonged their parting. Damn him for a selfish bastard.

He knew the moment she awoke, although she didn't open her eyes. Wariness tensed her neck, and her breathing hesitated for a second. "What are you doing here?" he asked.

Her delicate eyelids opened. Lashes tipped in gold from the candlelight framed fathomless, mysterious eyes. "We need to talk."

"What is there to discuss?" He said it flatly, firmly.

She rolled on her back, away from him. Good. The further apart they were, the easier it would be. He braced himself to be brutally honest.

"Why don't you want me any more?"

She asked it calmly enough, but the tears in her voice cut a swathe through his heart. He hardened his heart against the longing to comfort and kept his voice cool. "You lied to me. I dislike being made to look a fool."

She lay in utter silence for several long moments, as if listening for unspoken words. "That is the only reason?" She made it sound trivial.

"Yes."

"You are the liar," she said coldly. "I hear it in your voice. Let me guess. It was all right to offer to marry a widow you could hide away in the country." Her voice broke and she swallowed. Her hand went to her collarbone in a painful little gesture that struck like a dagger between his ribs. "But now, knowing who I am, you could not do that. You would have to be seen with me. I would make you ashamed."

His heart wrenched. He longed to reach out and take her in his arms, kiss away the tears that he knew without looking must tremble on the brink of spilling over. He forced himself to remain still. "The duke made you a very good offer. One I cannot match."

"A perfectly cold offer, without mention of love. I deserve more." The words were fierce and angry. They humbled him to the core of his soul.

He rolled on his side and cupped her beloved cheek in his palm. "Think about it. Give it some time."

She sniffed and subsided into silence. He felt as if he'd flattened something delicate and precious, crushed it beneath the iron hooves of a charger, or ground it beneath a boot heel. He clenched his jaw, determined not to beg forgiveness.

A small sigh of resignation stirred the air. The divide between them grew to gargantuan proportions. A crevasse too wide and deep to cross and too long to go around. Good, he told himself and ignored the growing ache in his throat.

"Don't you love me?"

The breath left his body in such a rush he felt dizzy. "I believe that two people can be drawn to each other to the point of madness," he said. "I do not believe in love." Daren't believe in it.

The crevasse widened and deepened. He felt it, even though she did not move a muscle. She was slipping away from him, just as he wanted.

"What you describe is lust. Love is intangible. The willingness to die so the other might live is the stuff of which love is made."

"Melodramatic nonsense," he mumbled, recalling his resolve of earlier in the day with a pang of guilt. Love was a dangerous and painful emotion when those loved were lost. It had been bad enough with his mother, and his wife and child, but if anything happened to Lucinda it would be ten times worse. Coward.

"Where are you supposed to be right now?" he asked.

"I beg your pardon?"

"Did you come here from the vicarage? I will drive you back."

She rolled over to look at him. He kept his gaze on the folds of blue velvet above his head.

"I am staying at the Hall. Catherine very kindly loaned me her horse."

"Have you no care for your reputation coming here in the middle of the night?'

"Not one jot." She sounded almost amused.

"It is time you returned, before someone misses you." Time for her to leave before the urge to take her again became too strong. The scent of her and their lovemaking filled every breath he took, and the knowledge that her glorious body reclined only inches away was diverting blood to his groin, making it far too difficult to think. And he needed every morsel of his brain to dodge her questions.

"So you do not believe in love?"

That kind of question. "No, I don't. And even if I did, I'm the wrong man for you. You deserve someone who can protect you. The duke saved your life this afternoon." He allowed himself a bitter smile and pulled his hand away, even while missing the warmth of her skin beneath his fingers. "In fact he had it all well in hand before I blundered along, if I'm not mistaken."

"I have to admit I was mistaken in the duke. Somewhat."

"As you are mistaken in me. I am not the man for you."

"Are you saying that because I made an error in judgment with Denbigh, I am not capable of knowing my own mind?"

"Good Lord. You are one of the most capable women I know. There isn't a woman of the *ton* I can think of who could make her own way in the world as you have."

"Compliments? They mean nothing, Hugo, when they hide the truth. There is something you are not telling me."

He wanted to lash out. To tell her to go to hell, to close the door on the world and lick the wounds she inflicted with every word. He feared only the truth would satisfy her. Only her knowing the kind of man he was at heart would send her away.

"You do not know me."

"I know who you are."

She sounded so heartbreakingly certain, he didn't know where he found the courage to continue. His voice thickened in his throat as if it were full of heavy fog. "I'm the kind of man who runs away. I ran from my father and abandoned my mother, and I ran from Spain. I am a coward."

"Everyone says you were a hero."

"The real heroes are dead. I, on the other hand, am a man who stands idly by while another saves his woman."

"Your woman?" She sat straight up, a curtain of long straight hair falling about her shoulders, framing her face and softening her features, her sumptuous breasts temptingly close to his face. With the sheets tumbled around her hips, she looked like a mermaid rising from the waves.

An unattainable goddess.

A highly distracting vision. "You are not listening. I had a crazed notion you had no one who cared about your welfare, that you could live here with me in this moldering pile and be happy. At any moment, I might find the bailiffs on the doorstep. You saw the state of the household accounts. Believe me, that is a fraction of what is wrong here. How can I let a woman with your prospects live in such squalor? Surely you must see it is for the best?"

"So you would give me away to the duke." She sounded resigned.

His heart thudded, unpleasantly slow, and a tremble shook him deep inside until he thought he might vibrate apart. He clenched his jaw. "You are not mine to give." He forced the words out to control the shake in his voice.

"And your child?"

Damn her. She knew his every weakness. "She will forget about me inside a fortnight. Tell Vale to buy her a pony."

She put a hand on her gently rounded stomach. "I wasn't talking about Sophia."

The bed seemed to slip sideways. "What!" He shook his head to clear his hearing.

"I'm expecting your child."

He threw himself out of the bed, his feet carrying him to the window and back. "No," he yelled in her face. "It is not possible. Your husband swore you were barren."

Eyes huge in a face the color of moonlight, she stared up at him. "He was wrong." She dragged the sheet up to her chin. "Is it so very bad?"

"Bad," he roared. "It couldn't be worse." He rubbed the back of his neck. "You are mistaken. Or…" He glared at her. "It is your husband's child and you are trying to pass it off as mine. Tell me. I won't mind."

She shook her head.

"God dammit." He prowled the room, reached the dressing table. "No," he yelled at his reflection in the mirror. He smashed his fist into the glass. It shattered into a million pieces, fractured and gleaming with pieces of himself reflected in the shards. "God dammit. No." He wanted to curl into a ball, to weep, to pray to the gods. He would not allow this a second time.

"Why are you acting like this?" she whispered.

Hunched up in the middle of Father's bed, her face as white as the sheet she clutched to her chest, she was staring at him as if he belonged in Bedlam. He did.

"I told you. I don't want children. Hate them. Get rid of it."

She recoiled. "You can't mean it." She shook her head. "You will get used to the idea." Tears trembled on the edges of her lashes.

He wanted to howl and smash everything in sight. Anything but face this. He swept his hand across the dressing-table top, scattering brushes and cologne and slivers of glass onto the floor with thumps and crashes and infuriating tinkles.

She scrambled back, pressing against the headboard and glancing wildly around.

"If you keep this child, you are as good as dead," he said. "I told you I was married before, didn't I? I told you about my Spanish wife."

She shook her head, her hair whipping across her shoulder. "You said you were married. Nothing more."

"I killed her. In nine months time you will be dead, too. Who will look after Sophia then?"

"Stop it," she cried. "You are frightening me."

"Not half as much as you are scaring me. Do you want to die?"

Dumbly, she stared at him, her eyes enormous, her bottom lip grasped tightly by her top teeth, the sheet shivered with the trembles of her body. She lifted her chin.

Oh God. What would come out of her mouth now? He steeled himself for bitter recriminations, disgust, hatred.

"Tell me what happened. Let me decide on the danger."

That he hadn't expected. Yet it would work. He could make it gruesome enough, dark enough, violent enough to frighten the bravest of women, and God knew Lucinda had courage.

He strode to the bed, still naked he realized. He perched on one edge, close to her on the pillows. He scrubbed a hand over his rough jaw and chin. "Where the hell to start?"

"At the beginning," she suggested in a dry little voice, a voice on the edge of breaking. But he couldn't think about that now. Would not let it bother him.

"I met Juanita at the officer's mess during the winter. All the boys were sniffing around her skirts. I wanted her the moment I saw her. Most of the Spanish women were fragile little things, but she…she was tall, sturdy, a lush armful. And she was alone, in need of protection. Juanita was no fool. She knew the other fellows would take whatever she offered and no strings attached. She was desperate, her family dead or disappeared, no money. At any moment she was going to succumb to an offer of a temporary liaison in exchange for food in her belly. To save her that and to keep her for myself, I offered marriage. Hell, Father had been nagging at me to marry since I left school."

A soft touch on his shoulder made him start. He glanced down at her soft white hand on his skin. The tension in his back eased.

"That was good of you."

He sneered. "Oh yes, very gentlemanly. Let us be honest. I had a strong case of lust." He ploughed on. "She accepted my offer, and we dragged a priest out of bed in the middle of the night."

"How romantic."

"I'd offered. I had to make good. I wrote home to tell Father what I'd done. I knew he wanted an English bride, but I didn't care. He was the one who insisted I join the army. Said I needed toughening up. If I'd figured out what he meant, I never would have married."

Her soft stroking ceased for a moment and then picked up its gentle rhythm.

"I got a terse congratulations and 'do your duty' from Father. Mother on the other hand babbled with joy. She urged me to get my wife with child as soon as possible and to let her know the moment I did. I thought it odd but was pleased there were no recriminations from her about my choice of a bride from the lower orders and a foreigner to boot. She said she was grateful. I should have guessed then."

"Guessed what?"

"That Mother's life hung in the balance."

"What do you mean?"

"Let me finish. Juanita got pregnant almost right away. She never seemed to worry and carried the child well while we moved from one disgusting billet to another, even sleeping under canvas. Everything seemed perfectly fine. Until it came time for the babe."

He shuddered remembering the blood and the screams. "The doctor said the baby was sideways. I had my doubts, memories, overheard snatches of my parents' fights. I ignored them. We were billeted in some ghastly stable with the horses. Hours, it lasted. All day and all the next night. In the end I couldn't stand it, her screams, her calling me every kind of bastard under the sun and deep inside knowing she was right. It was inhumane—abnormal, one of the camp women said. I left and got drunk. Bloody coward. When I came back, she was dead. Her and the child. I killed them by planting my seed in her belly. Can you not see? I have done the same to you."

He turned away from her and curled his body into itself, reliving those horrible hours, the dreadful realization that he should have known why his father insisted he marry the moment he reached his majority. His birth had damaged his mother's insides and a couple of miscarriages early on had made things worse. Rather than hate himself, his father had blamed Hugo when his mother refused Father her body. "Once I heard Mother yell at my father, 'All the countesses die in childbirth.' They did. Don't you understand? I knew the truth, and still I got her pregnant." His voice dropped to a whisper. "I will not kill another woman."

He buried his face in the pillow the way he had as a lad to shut out the sound of his mother's weeping and his father's curses, once more too full of horrible throat-choking emotion to speak. Slowly he inhaled a shuddering breath. "Later, I wrote to Father and said I was done. No more children. I was going to break the chain. God. And now this?"

He slammed his fist into the pillow. "I will not have another death on my conscience. Do you know what my father did? Do you have any idea? He said if I wouldn't give him a son, he would get his spare from Mother. Her letter chased me across Spain. She begged me to take another wife, to give Father hope. By the time the letter reached me, she was dead. God dammit. He killed her trying to have another child. She wasn't cold in the ground before he was looking for a new wife. Do you know what his last letter said? 'I always knew you took after your mother, but I did not think you were a coward. You are too soft for a Wanstead.' Well, I may not be a Wanstead in nature, but my seed is just as cursed."

"Hush," she whispered. "I promise you I am not going to die."

The stubborn set to her jaw sank him into despair. "I can't take that chance. I love you too much."

Her little gasp halted him. He'd said he loved her. He did. It was a heady feeling and one filled with fear.

She leaned her cheek against his back and felt her breath stir the air above his shoulder blade. A deep conviction filled his mind. He would not give life to another killer of females. "You must not have this child."

Silence. Not outright denial. What would he do if she would not listen to reason?

Unable to move, he lay there for a long time with her stroking his shoulder, petting his hair, and infusing him with a peace he never thought possible. He drew strength from her spirit, her courage, for he had none left. The hard knot of rage around his heart that had protected him slowly unraveled, leaving him vulnerable. There, deep inside, he discovered something new. Hope. A tiny grain of hope that perhaps with Lucinda life could be different. If only she'd listen.

When he finally found his voice, he rolled over on his back and gazed into her troubled eyes. "For my sake, and yours, you have to...I am sorry. I am too much of a coward to go through that again."

She sighed. "No, Hugo. I am sorry. My mother gave birth to nine healthy children. With or without you, I will bear this child. It is the thing I have longed for most in the world."

A groan tore up from his chest. "Is there nothing I can say?"

She shook her head. "And do not for a moment think I am going to marry the Duke of Vale."

He pushed the hair back from her face, stared into her midnight eyes, and saw she'd been crying. He'd made her cry, when all he wanted was for her to be happy. He imagined her managing alone, as she'd done all these past months. Even if her family supported her, the thought of her giving birth to his child filled him with terror, while it seemed as if she faced the unknown future with stunning calm. "You leave me no option."

Her back stiffened a little.

"Lucinda. I love you. I will not let you suffer alone. Will you marry me?"

She gasped and buried her face in his shoulder.

"Will you?" he asked again, knowing he was grinning like a mad fool, despite the fearful thunder in his heart.

"Yes. Yes." She raised her head and kissed his mouth, his cheek, his chin. "Yes."

"It is going to be hell."

She choked on what sounded like a cross between a laugh and a sob. "It will be fine, I promise."

A rap sounded at the door. They stared at each other. Exhausted, unable to face another human soul. Hugo glanced at the window, no sign of dawn. Too early for the maid to make up the fire, and besides she wouldn't knock.

"Quiet. Perhaps they will leave," he said. It seemed he was right. The knock didn't come again.

He pulled her against his shoulder and inhaled the scent of her hair, lavender and lovely woman. "I love you." He rolled the words over his tongue, and they tasted of honey. "I love you."

She grabbed his jaw, turning him so she could see his face. "You are getting very good at saying that. Perhaps I shall reward you."

He grinned. "What did you have in mind?"

Another knock, louder, more insistent. "My lord?" Trent.

"My lord, there's a gentleman downstairs to see you. He won't take no for an answer."

"Who is it?"

"A Lieutenant Armitage. The Tenth."

"Geoffrey?" Lucinda squeaked. "My brother?"

"Damnation. Now we are in the suds." He leaped out of bed, avoiding the broken glass, and grabbed his robe and slippers.

By the time he had them on, Lucinda had slipped into her chemise and gown. "I am coming with you."

"Not a good idea, sweet. He might shoot me the moment he lays eyes on you fresh from my bed. I would like a chance to explain." She glanced at her reflection in the mirror above the hearth and saw with pride that she looked thoroughly well loved, her mouth swollen from his kisses and her hair tumbled.

"No. You don't know Geoffrey," she said. "He is my closest brother. It will be better if I speak to him."

He sighed. "Stubborn wench. Very well, I will stand behind you."

She chuckled.

More knocks. Louder than before. "My lord. He threatened to come up here and break down the door if you aren't downstairs in five minutes."

Hugo threw open the door. "We are coming."

Trent recoiled a step at the sight of Lucinda. With a shake of his head, he turned and headed downstairs.

Hand in hand, they followed. Lucinda bit her lip. How wonderful that Geoffrey was here, and how awkward that he'd arrived to find her in bed with her lover. Her future husband, she amended. Her heart gave a joyful jump.

"I put him in the library, my lord." Trent said. "He seems like a rather hot-headed young gentleman. Cavalry. Jevens is still recovering in the kitchen with a brandy."

"Threatened him, did he?" Hugo said grimly.

"That doesn't sound like Geoffrey," Lucinda said.

"You probably haven't seen him when his sister's honor is at stake, my love. Let me do the talking."

He didn't wait for an answer, but opened the library door and stepped in.

Magnificent in his cavalry blue coat, the fur-edged pelisse hanging from one shoulder, Geoffrey stood in front of the hearth. He had his hat under his arm in true military style. Since she saw him last, he seemed to have filled out. He was almost as large as Father and heavier set than Hugo.

He glared at Hugo, his cheeks ruddy with good health and more than a smidgeon of anger. "Good of you to see me, Wanstead." Then his gaze fell on Lucinda, eyes widening, mouth dropping open. "Dear God, you are here. How could you, after all the worry you have caused us?"

"What?" she said, shocked and hurt by the critical words from the brother to whom she felt closest. "Who do you think you are coming here and telling me what I should or should not do?"

He rocked back on his heels, his mouth open.

Well, she had never been quite so forceful before.

Hugo put up a placating hand. "Leave this to me, Lucinda." He turned to Geoffrey. "I know this looks bad, but I have asked your sister to marry me."

Geoffrey dropped into the closest chair and ran a hand through light-brown waves. "Thank God for that. I don't know what I would have said if I'd had to give Mother this story."

"How did you find me?" Lucinda asked

"Miss Dawson."

Lucinda narrowed her eyes.

"I forced it out of her," Geoffrey said hurriedly. "I threatened a bit of murder and mayhem when no one at the Hall could tell me where you were, and she came clean."

Hugo put a careful arm around her shoulders and guided her to a couch. The gentle way he helped her to sit made her heart ache. "I'm not an invalid, you know."

Geoffrey stared at her. "What is wrong?"

"I'm carrying a child."

Her brother leaped to his feet. "What?" he thundered.

"Oh for God's sake, sit down," Hugo said. "We are getting married."

"Tell him about Mother, Geoffrey," Lucinda urged. "About how she has children like popping a cork out of a bottle and I am sure to be just like her."

Geoffrey's jaw dropped.

"How large were you when you were born?" Hugo asked.

"I don't recall."

Lucinda threw a pillow at his head.

"*Pax*. All right. Huge, according to our nurse. Why?"

"Hugo is afraid I will die in childbirth."

Geoffrey started to look a bit green about the gills.

She threw her arms around Hugo's waist and burrowed her head against his warm, comforting chest. He hesitated, then ran his hands down her back, stroking her hair.

"Tell him about Brandon, Geoffrey," she urged. "And how is he, by the way, and the girls? Are Father and Mother all right?"

Geoffrey put up a staying hand. "One question at a time, please. Everyone is in good health, but worried about you."

"And Brandon?"

Geoffrey looked a little somber. "He seems fine. I'm really not sure he is cut out for the army."

"I didn't mean, that," Lucinda said. "Tell him about when Brandon was born." She turned to Hugo. "Brandon is our youngest brother. He was enormous, according to Mother."

Geoffrey nodded. "He's taller than me. Our Mother is no lightweight, mind you. She couldn't be with a Papa as big as ours."

"I am just like my mother," Lucinda added.

Hugo shook his head. "It would kill me to stand around and watch you die."

She elbowed him in the ribs. "Then we would both be dead, and it would not matter one jot to either of us."

"Lucinda. That is sacrilegious," he sounded horrified, but there was the start of a smile on his lips and a gleam of hope amid the panic in his eyes.

Her heart settled down to a steady rhythm. It seemed that things might just work out all right if she could keep him calm. He folded her into his embrace, kissing her long and hard with a passion she thought she'd lost forever. When at length he came up for a breath, he stared down at her with a smile. "God, love, what did I do to deserve someone like you?"

"You are a good man, and I love you. I am glad we found one another."

His face grew serious, and he looked over at Geoffrey who was silently studying the toe of his boot. "I assume your father will give his permission."

A corner of Geoffrey's mouth kicked up. "Said he'd kill you if you didn't. He's at the inn with Vale."

"Good God," Hugo said.

"How is Vale?" Lucinda asked.

"He'll survive," Geoffrey said, and he gave her a look that said he didn't mean his wound.

She looked into her heart and found that she had never been the slightest bit attracted to Vale, even before he lured her husband into his orbit. "Do you think I could have a cup of tea?" She put a hand to her stomach, feeling just a little faint. "And a biscuit?"

Hugo suddenly looked anxious. "Do you want to lie down? Put your feet up?"

"No, Hugo. Do not start treating me like an invalid. I simply want something to eat."

He took a deep breath. "God, I hope you are right." She jabbed him with her elbow.

"Right. Tea and biscuits it is. By the way, just who is the father of that beautiful daughter of yours?"

"That's what I'd like to know," Geoffrey said frowning.

Lucinda laughed at their suspicious expressions. "Soon to be Hugo's daughter, too. And quite honestly, I have no idea. I found her."

"That sounds like a story for another occasion," Geoffrey said.

"Yes," Hugo agreed. "Trent?" he called out

Trent popped his head inside immediately. "Everything all right, my lord?"

"Everything is fine. Wonderful. Please bring tea for the next Countess of Wanstead."

The young man grinned. "Right away, my lord. And may I offer you my congratulations?"

Epilogue

THE WARM SUMMER SUN MADE LUCINDA FEEL FAR TOO lazy to do anything about the handkerchief she had brought outside to embroider. The last of the six, it had the H already snuggled up against the L. It just needed its sprig of heart's ease to be finished. And besides, Marmalade had decided her lap made the perfect place to take a nap the moment she cut her first length of silk.

She lay back against the cushions, gazed at the clear blue sky from beneath her parasol and let the throaty call of doves and the scent of new mown lawn carry her on a cloud of contentment.

A snuffle from the direction of the wicker basket at her side propelled her upright. "Belderone, get your nose out of there!"

The lurcher tucked his tail between his legs and stared at her with melting eyes and laidback ears.

"I know, you weren't going to hurt him, but I only just got him to sleep. What with you and his father always poking him to make sure he is real, I'm surprised the child ever sleeps at all."

She pulled back the soft blue blanket and stared at her son's square head and mop of dark hair. Fast asleep, he looked just like Hugo, except for his nose. The poor little fellow definitely had inherited the Armitage proboscis. It suited him. She smiled.

A squeal from the paddock made her look up to see Sophia flying over a log on the back of her pony. Lucinda leaped to her feet scattering Marmalade, her parasol, and the handkerchief, only to realize Hugo had the horse firmly on a leading rein.

Marmalade gave her a stare of disgust and stalked off, tail up, toward the house, no doubt in search of Annie.

Her heart slowly sank from her throat to its rightful place. She dropped to her knees beside Jonathan Geoffrey Hugo Malbury, the new Viscount LeFroy. "I hope you aren't going to frighten me like that when you grow up," she said, tickling his cheek. "You certainly terrified your father enough the day you were born." Thank heaven Mother had arrived to offer support or poor Hugo might have put a bullet in his brain before the end of the night. "Next time it will be so much easier. Do you want a brother or a sister?" She patted her stomach. "We won't tell your father, just yet, if you are a good boy."

The bubble he blew from pursed lips did nothing to reassure her that he would be any less wild than his sister.

"My lady," Jevens called out. Lucinda turned toward the house to find the butler plodding down the terrace steps with three men in his wake, one of them in a blue uniform with flashing gold braid.

"It's Geoffrey," she told the sleeping Jonathan. "Safe and sound."

Hugo must have also seen the visitors, because he had left Sophia with Trent and was striding towards her from the paddock, fastening the buttons of his coat as he went.

"His grace, the Duke of Vale, Captain Armitage and Mr. Arthur Dawson, my lady," Jevens said. He spoiled the solemn announcement with a wink.

"Thank you, Jevens. Please ask Mrs. Dunning to send tea out onto the terrace in a half an hour."

Jevens bowed and shuffled off.

"Lady Wanstead," Vale said. "Please don't get up on our account."

Lucinda held out her hand. "Your grace, how good of you to call. Geoffrey, how wonderful to see you, and congratulations on your promotion. I had no idea you were home."

"Dispatches from Wellington. Pleas for more weapons and recruits. I bumped into Vale at Horse Guards and he offered to drive me down for the afternoon."

Lucinda smiled at the languid nobleman and noted the cool reserve in his grey eyes with a flash of sorrow. "It was kind of you, your grace. I know I speak for Hugo when I say you are always welcome."

"You are very gracious, my lady. You remember Mr. Dawson?" His grace gestured with long elegant fingers.

Lucinda nodded. "Mr. Dawson."

Mr. Dawson winced at her chilly tone. So he should. He had no right to expect a welcome in her home. He had broken his word to Hugo.

Geoffrey hunkered down beside Jonathon's basket and peeked in. "How is my nephew doing?"

"Very well, indeed," Lucinda said.

"Now there is a nose to be proud of, Vale," Geoffrey said. "Look at it."

Vale leaned forward and gave a sage if distant nod. "Very fine, indeed."

Geoffrey chucked the sleeping viscount under the chin and stood as Hugo came up to the group.

"Vale," Hugo said. "Armitage." He shook hands with both men. His eyes narrowed as he turned to greet Arthur. He merely nodded. "Dawson."

"Blast it, Hugo," Arthur said. "Do you have to be so dashed stiff?"

"I think it is time we cleared the air," Vale said.

"The air would be a good bit clearer if Dawson took himself off," Hugo replied.

Arthur glowered at him. "Hear Vale out, and if you are still of a mind to throw me out, so be it."

"I'm of a mind to throw you in the duck pond," Hugo said.

"Hugo," Lucinda said. "Don't be rude. His grace is trying to tell you something."

Vale blessed her with one of his elegant bows. "Thank you, Lady Wanstead. Your kindness overwhelms my humble soul."

"Get on with it, Vale." Hugo's voice held a dangerous edge and a little shiver went down Lucinda's back. Nothing like a little jealousy to send blood tingling through her veins.

Vale chuckled softly as if he had read her mind. "Remember how you thought it was Dawson here who let the cat out of the bag and told Denbigh where to find Lady Wanstead?"

"There wasn't anyone else it could have been," Hugo said with a glare at Arthur.

"There was," Vale said. "I ran into her last week. A Miss Abbott. Apparently, she bumped into Denbigh in Bond Street and quite by chance mentioned the talented and somewhat…buxom archer staying at the vicarage who had beaten her at a contest in Kent. Denbigh gnawed at her like a dog with a bone until he got all the details, then jumped in a post chaise."

"I didn't know Lady Wanstead had gone to the vicarage," Arthur put in.

"No, you didn't," Lucinda said. She stared at Hugo who appeared to be thunderstruck.

He offered his hand. "It seems as if I owe you an apology, Arthur."

The young man let go a long breath. "I don't care about that," he pumped Hugo's hand. "I just want us to be friends like before. I have some wonderful news. My uncle bought me a commission in the army."

"Oh, my word. What did your mother say about that?" Lucinda asked.

"Oh, she's so busy dreaming of weddings for Catherine now that the vicar has finally popped the question, I don't think my news has quite sunk in. Hopefully, by the time it does, I will be on a ship to Lisbon."

"Take care of yourself, young fellow," Hugo said.

Arthur looked down at his shoes and then cast a diffident glance at Hugo. "I was hoping you could give me a few pointers."

"Be glad to. Come to the library. I have some maps there and my diaries. I probably have a spare ground-sheet somewhere, too. Coming Vale?"

"No, I'll stay here and keep Lady Wanstead company."

Geoffrey slung his arm through one of Hugo's. "I'll come, if you promise me one of those fine cigars you had the last time I was here."

"Brothers-in-law," Hugo muttered and clapped Arthur on the back.

"So," Vale said, when the others were out of hearing. "All is well that ends well."

Still smarting at how she had misjudged him, she gave him a shy smile. "And what about you? Are there happy endings on your horizon?"

A shadow darkened the steely gaze, despite the smile. "Given my penchant for traveling, Lady Wanstead, it seems highly unlikely."

"We would not have suited, you know. Your wit is far too acerbic for someone as kind as me. I would have been constantly apologizing for your cutting remarks."

He adjusted his cuffs over his wrists with a small smile. "Oh, dear lady, don't think I am pining away. Quite the contrary. And who knows where a man will find his soul mate. I doubt Hugo expected to find you living on his estate."

"I'm sure he didn't," she said. A soft smile crossed her lips as her glance rested on the straight broad shoulders of her beloved husband as he passed through the formal garden with its yellow roses and purple heart's ease. She watched him mount the steps to the balcony across the back of the house and wondered just how long it would be before their visitors left them to their blue canopied bedroom and the new-fangled bathroom with its tub big enough for two in the chamber next door.

If the duke heard her happy sigh, he gave no sign.

Acknowledgments

I WOULD LIKE TO THANK MY AGENT SCOTT EAGAN FOR his belief in my work and my editor Deb Werksman for her suggestions and effort in making the book the best it could be, as well as all of the other wonderful people at Sourcebooks who have been so helpful. I also want to thank my wonderful critique partners, Molly, Mary, Maureen, Sinead, Susan, and Teresa, for their advice, encouragement, and perseverance.

About the Author

Born and educated in England, Michèle Ann Young loved history growing up, and as a voracious reader of historical novels, she became fascinated with the Regency era. With all the glamour and glitz of high society, the age is modern enough to be familiar some two hundred years later. She loves bringing the time period to life with her stories of women facing the same issues that women face today.

From England she moved to Canada, where she now lives and writes in Richmond Hill, Ontario, with her husband and two beautiful daughters and their adopted Maltese terrier, Teaser. Each summer, Michèle returns to England to visit family and to research her next novel.

Michèle loves to hear from readers. Visit her at her website, www.micheleannyoung.com, or drop by her Regency Ramble blog at www.micheleannyoung. blogspot.com, where, in addition to the odd bit of writing gossip, she shares the sights and sounds of Regency England from her annual travels.